PRAISE FOR THE NOVELS OF KATIE REUS

Mating Instinct

"Katie Reus creates a vivid world filled with sexy shifters, explosive danger, and enough sexual tension to set the pages on fire. A fabulous paranormal romance!"
—Alexandra Ivy, *New York Times* bestselling author of *Fear the Darkness*

"With scorching chemistry between Jayce, an aggressively sexy alpha shifter who won't let anything stand in the way of claiming his mate, and Kat, a newly made shifter who can't deny her feelings for him, *Mating Instinct*'s romance is taut and passionate. Add to that a fast-paced suspense plot and a deftly built paranormal world, and Katie Reus's newest installment in her Moon Shifter series will leave readers breathless!"
—Stephanie Tyler, national bestselling author of *Dire Wants*

Primal Possession

"Reus's world building is incredibly powerful as she seamlessly blends various elements of legend and myth while laying groundwork for future plot points. Her characters manage to both charm and frighten, but the romance between a shifter and human is the real highlight—it's lusty, heartfelt, and shows that love can conquer all." —*Romantic Times* (4 stars)

Alpha Instinct

"Reus shows great promise and you'll look forward to visiting this world again soon!"
—*Romantic Times* (4 stars)

continued ...

"Reus has an instinct for what wows in this perfect blend of shifter, suspense, and sexiness. Sexy alphas, kick-ass heroines, and twisted villains will keep you turning the pages in this new shifter series. *Alpha Instinct* is a winner."
— Caridad Piñeiro, *New York Times* bestselling author of *The Claimed*

"*Alpha Instinct* is a wild, hot ride for readers. The story grabs you and doesn't let go."
— Cynthia Eden, *USA Today* bestselling author of *Angel in Chains*

"Reus crafts a fast-paced action story.... *Alpha Instinct* is awesome, an engrossing page-turner that I enjoyed in one sitting. Reus offers all the ingredients I love in a paranormal romance." — Book Lovers Inc.

"Prepare yourself for the start of a great new series! ... I'm excited about reading more about this great group of characters." — Fresh Fiction

"A well-plotted, excellently delivered emotional and sensual ride that grabs hold and doesn't let go! ... Ms. Reus delivers mystery, suspense, and a romance nothing short of heart pounding!" — Night Owl Reviews

"If you're looking for a new shifter romance to sink your teeth in, then look no further. *Alpha Instinct* is action-packed with a solid romance that will keep the reader on the edge of [her] toes! ... Highly recommended for fans of Rachel Vincent's Werecat series."
— Nocturne Romance Reads

"A strong book full of mystery, intrigue, and a new world to explore.... I thoroughly enjoyed this one as I suspect lovers of the paranormal romance genres will do as well!" — Ramblings from a Chaotic Mind

MATING INSTINCT

A Moon Shifter Novel

KATIE REUS

A SIGNET ECLIPSE BOOK

SIGNET ECLIPSE
Published by New American Library, a division of
Penguin Group (USA) Inc., 375 Hudson Street,
New York, New York 10014, USA
Penguin Group (Canada), 90 Eglinton Avenue East, Suite 700, Toronto,
Ontario M4P 2Y3, Canada (a division of Pearson Penguin Canada Inc.)
Penguin Books Ltd., 80 Strand, London WC2R 0RL, England
Penguin Ireland, 25 St. Stephen's Green, Dublin 2,
Ireland (a division of Penguin Books Ltd).
Penguin Group (Australia), 707 Collins Street, Melbourne, Victoria 3008,
Australia (a division of Pearson Australia Group Pty. Ltd.)
Penguin Books India Pvt. Ltd., 11 Community Centre, Panchsheel Park,
New Delhi - 110 017, India
Penguin Group (NZ), 67 Apollo Drive, Rosedale, Auckland 0632,
New Zealand (a division of Pearson New Zealand Ltd.)
Penguin Books, Rosebank Office Park, 181 Jan Smuts Avenue,
Parktown North 2193, South Africa
Penguin China, B7 Jaiming Center, 27 East Third Ring Road North,
Chaoyang District, Beijing 100020, China

Penguin Books Ltd., Registered Offices:
80 Strand, London WC2R 0RL, England

First published by Signet Eclipse, an imprint of New American Library,
a division of Penguin Group (USA) Inc.

First Printing, March 2013
10 9 8 7 6 5 4 3 2 1

PUBLISHER'S NOTE
This is a work of fiction. Names, characters, places, and incidents either are the
product of the author's imagination or are used fictitiously, and any resemblance
to actual persons, living or dead, business establishments, events, or locales is
entirely coincidental.
    The publisher does not have any control over and does not assume any respon-
sibility for author or third-party Web sites or their content.

ALWAYS LEARNING   PEARSON

For Kari Walker. No matter what, you're always in my corner. Thank you for being my friend, for your input on the Moon Shifter series, and for being my biggest cheerleader. My life is so much richer with you in it and I'm thankful every day we're friends.

Chapter 1

Jayce Kazan parked his Harley in front of December McIntyre's house. The feisty pregnant redhead wouldn't be there because she now lived on the Armstrong ranch with her mate and the rest of the lupine shifter pack who made their home in Fontana, North Carolina.

But Kat would be home.

Or she should be. Even after December moved, Kat had stayed there instead of moving to the ranch. After her brutal attack by the radical Antiparanormal League (APL) group a month ago and subsequent near-death experience, she'd been turned into a lupine shifter out of necessity. Just like him. The only difference between them was he'd been born that way almost five hundred years ago. Well, maybe not the only difference. He was a crass, roughneck enforcer who'd killed more beings than he could ever hope to count and she was . . . fucking perfection.

At least to him.

Right now she wasn't returning his calls. Not that he

blamed her. He hadn't been there for her when she'd needed him most and he wanted to rip his own heart out because of it. At least then maybe he'd be able to assuage some of his guilt. One of the Armstrong pack members had bitten her and turned her into a shifter instead of letting her die. She'd had only a one percent chance of surviving the change, and even though Jayce was grateful that Aiden had saved her, a dark part of him hated that bastard.

He hated the fact that he hadn't been the one to save her. That someone else had had the honor of taking what was his. His human side knew he'd never planned to change Kat—it would have turned her into a walking target overnight if anyone discovered how deep his feelings for her ran—but his animal side didn't give a shit. No one should have ever touched what was his.

Though she really wasn't his, was she? Not anymore anyway. Hadn't been for almost a year. At one time she had been. He'd kissed and teased every inch of her naked body and she'd done the same to his. Things had never been particularly *easy* between them—not with their strong personalities—but with the exception of his MIA brother she was the only person on the planet he'd ever let his guard down around. She brought out the best in him. Hell, she also brought out his worst, protective side. For over a month he'd exercised all his restraint just staying away from her while working for the Council.

After getting only an hour of sleep last night, he was edgy and ready to rip someone's head off. Maybe it hadn't been the smartest idea to roll up to see her the moment he'd gotten back in town, but he didn't care. He needed to see her.

Craved it so bad his canines ached at the thought. She

could slam the door on him for all he cared. He just needed to *see* her face.

As he swung his leg over the bike and straightened, he glanced up and saw Ryan get out of his truck across the street. Though he didn't want to be patient or polite, he waited while the other shifter strode toward him.

Ryan wore a thick down jacket and jeans, and even though Jayce couldn't see an outline, he knew the guy was packing a few weapons. The chilly January weather wouldn't have affected Ryan like it would humans, so he knew the main reason the shifter was wearing a jacket was to hide guns and blades. "Hey, Jayce. What are you doing here?"

Jayce raised an eyebrow at the question. Why the hell wouldn't he be here?

Ryan's lips pulled into a thin line. "I didn't mean it like that. I didn't know you'd be back so early. Thought you were still on Council business or something."

He shrugged. As the enforcer for the North American Council of lupine shifters, Jayce didn't answer to anyone. Not Ryan. Not even Connor Armstrong, leader of the Armstrong pack and also Ryan's Alpha. *No one.* While he might work for the Council, he sure as hell didn't answer to them either. They needed him and he made damn sure they never forgot it. So even if he didn't have to answer the wolf in front of him, or that wolf's boss, he knew that projecting his own bad mood wouldn't win him any friends, and right now he needed all the fucking friends he could get. "Caught an early flight and headed over here. Haven't called Connor to let him know I'm in town, though, so . . ."

Ryan nodded. "I'll let you call him."

He cleared his throat. "Thanks." The word felt foreign on his lips. He should have called Connor the moment he arrived in town out of respect, but he had a lot to discuss with him and some of it needed to be done in person. He'd received information that someone was trafficking vampire blood in the next county. After settling in, he intended to search out some former contacts. Not to mention he still planned to ferret out any possible dangerous APL members still in the area. That problem hadn't gone away and he knew it wasn't likely to anytime soon. More than anything, he just wanted to see Kat. Everything else took a backseat. "When did she get home?" Jayce didn't need to specify who he referred to.

Ryan shrugged. "Few hours ago. She was at the ranch with, uh . . . Aiden, *training*, but she still won't move there to live with the pack. Which is why we're still watching her in shifts."

Jayce already knew that. After the attack from those APL fuckers nearly killed her, she'd been fairly defiant in her demand that she live away from what was now her pack. Connor had jurisdiction over her since she technically lived in his territory, but considering that she'd been turned into a shifter without the proper introduction to pack life and rules, Connor was giving her some leeway. He was a fair Alpha, so Jayce wasn't exactly surprised. Even if he did hate the fact that Connor wouldn't force her to live on the ranch, where she'd be protected at all times.

"You have a key to the house?" Jayce asked, though he was already pretty certain of the answer. Connor wouldn't have left anyone to watch the house without a way to get inside if necessary. Of course they could break in, but cleaning up a mess was a hassle Jayce knew the Alpha wouldn't want to deal with.

Ryan paused. "Yeah. She's gonna be pissed if you just walk in there."

"I know." He held out his hand, not asking for it but silently demanding.

Sighing, the other wolf dug a single key out of his pocket and handed it over. As he headed back to his vehicle, Ryan muttered something under his breath about Jayce taking his life into his own hands.

If he'd had more sleep or was in a better mood, he might have smiled at the statement. A pissed-off Kat was a sight to see. And he'd only seen her truly angry when she'd been human. He could just imagine her attitude as a shifter.

The last time he'd seen her as a lupine shifter had been directly after her transformation. She'd been healed after the change but covered in her own blood. And another wolf had been holding her.

Protecting her.

Comforting her.

Jayce still didn't know the details of what had happened to her during her hours of torture—she refused to tell anyone about it—but according to December she still had nightmares.

And no one was there to ease her pain. Jayce's hands balled into fists as he turned and headed up the stone walkway. Ever since they'd found Kat in that broken-down barn, he'd been living in hell. It was the feeling of helplessness that nearly undid him every time he thought of her. Which was practically every second of every day. The tall, gorgeous woman invaded his dreams when he was sleeping. He should have been there to save her. If he had been, he would have been the one to change her into a shifter.

The second he stepped into the house, he knew Kat wasn't there. Her scent was there, but he couldn't hear a heartbeat. She'd been gone maybe twenty minutes if he had to guess from her fading scent. Had ducked her guard just as he feared she'd do since Connor had let her live apart from the pack.

Jayce knew it wasn't the first time she'd done this either. December had become an unlikely source of information, but she was worried about her friend and often called him with updates on Kat.

This kind of shit was going to stop as far as he was concerned. If she didn't care about her own safety, she needed to at least be concerned about the rest of the pack. And according to December, over the past week Kat had been disappearing for hours at a time. She wouldn't tell anyone what she was doing either. Since Jayce had heard she'd been having difficulty controlling her change from human to wolf, that could be a very dangerous thing for all the local shifters.

Worry and possessiveness rose up inside him. His need to protect Kat was deep-seated, something he still didn't understand completely. He'd felt it the moment he'd met her and it jarred him every time he was near her. Or thought about her.

Inhaling, he followed the trail of her scent out the back door, through December's backyard, and over to the next street. The distinctive scent of roses was so blatantly Kat—every time he smelled the damn flower, he thought of her. But it was slightly different than the actual rose. The classic smell mixed with something sweeter, purer, and all Kat. He would recognize it anywhere.

She hadn't been gone long, so he hurried back to his bike and headed out. He didn't bother telling Ryan that Kat was gone either. No one was going after her except him. Anyone who tried to interfere tonight would probably get hurt. Including any shifters.

On his motorcycle it was easy to trail her in his human form. Hell, as an enforcer he preferred his human form. He was much older than most shifters, and once he let his animal take over, it was always a struggle for control with his inner wolf. Right now he needed to exert as much restraint as possible. Where Kat was concerned, it was important, if not necessary.

A short ride later he pulled into the parking lot of Kelly's Bar and Grill, a local Irish bar in the middle of downtown Fontana. The mountain town in North Carolina saw a lot of tourists in the winter months, and judging from the number of cars in the parking lot, the place was packed tonight.

He rolled his shoulders as he stepped off his bike. Being around too many people—humans or supernatural beings—always put him on edge. All those scents were overwhelming. He'd much rather be outdoors, far from civilization.

As he stepped inside the bar, Kat's scent grew stronger. Even among the stench of perfumes, booze, and other body odors, her sweet rose aroma tickled his nose and wrapped around him. Embracing him like a gentle caress.

"Would you like to be seated in our dining area or would you prefer to find a seat at the bar?" A bubbly blond female wearing black pants and a black T-shirt held a menu in her hand as she looked at him.

"Bar's fine," he said, brushing past her.

A burst of annoyance rolled off the human, but right now all he cared about was tracking Kat down. After a quick lap around the place, he followed her trail out a side exit door.

Once he was outside in the crisp night air, the strong scent of roses enveloped him. She was close. Frowning, he looked around the area behind the restaurant. A Dumpster was to his left, which gave him cover as he scanned the small gravel parking lot, where a few cars were parked. Employee vehicles, he guessed.

And that was when he spotted Kat.

She was leaning against the passenger side of an extended-cab truck with her back to him. Tall, lean, drop-dead gorgeous. Her long dark hair was pulled up into a ponytail that hung halfway down her back. She wore formfitting jeans and a skintight long-sleeved black T-shirt. If she'd still been human, she'd have needed a coat, but thanks to her transformation from human to shifter, she had a higher body temperature now.

Sticking to the shadows, he moved behind the Dumpster and slid along the wall of the restaurant until he was at the edge of the building, twenty yards from where Kat stood talking to a human male.

A growl rose inside him, but he tamped it down and listened to their conversation. As the human talked about heading back to his place to "party," Jayce nearly lost control of his beast. His inner wolf clawed at him with razor-sharp aggression, tearing and stripping away his insides, begging for freedom.

When the human opened the passenger door for Kat and she actually got inside, Jayce's claws extended and dug into his palms. The tearing of his flesh jerked him back to reality. Ducking behind the Dumpster, he somehow managed to keep himself under control as the vehicle pulled out of the parking lot.

Just barely.

As the truck drove past the left side of the restaurant, Jayce raced around the right side and headed for his bike in the front.

Whatever Kat thought she was doing with that guy tonight, she'd better think again.

Kat glanced over at the dark-haired man with the buzz cut next to her. He shot her a quick look and winked as he steered his truck out of the parking lot of Kelly's Bar and Grill. She wasn't sure what she was doing with him and was tempted to tell him to stop, but something held her back.

He was one of the bartenders at Kelly's and had been getting off work just as she'd walked in. The moment she sat down, he'd started flirting with her and buying her drinks. Too bad the alcohol couldn't numb the pain inside her.

Nothing could do that. For the past month it had festered inside her, growing like an out-of-control vine. It twisted and expanded with no regard for anything in its path, least of all her heart or emotions. If she dwelled on the ways she'd been tortured a month ago, she tensed up and her inner wolf wanted out.

Aiden, her friend and the wolf who'd changed her into a shifter, had explained that it was a protective thing. Her inner wolf didn't want her to suffer, so it tried to take over whether she wanted it to or not. Some kind of coping mechanism.

Taking a deep breath, she forced those thoughts from her mind. Tonight she was taking control of her life again. Maybe sleeping with a stranger wasn't the smartest way to go about it, but she needed to be in charge of *something*. It wasn't as if the guy next to her could hurt her. He was human, and sure, he had a sexy edge to him, but she was still a hundred times stronger. He couldn't hurt her physically or sexually.

That was something she kept reminding herself of. *She* was the one in control tonight.

"Surprised I haven't seen you in Kelly's before," the guy, Scott . . . something, said.

She'd been there a few times when she'd been human, but she'd usually been so busy working at the ski lodge — where she'd been an employee until a month ago. Shrugging, she smiled and shifted in her seat, crossing her legs in his direction. She didn't want to make bullshit small talk. That wasn't what tonight was about.

The man's dark gaze drifted down to her covered legs, then back up to her chest. Even though she was clothed, the way he looked at her made her feel practically naked. That should be a good thing, she told herself. She needed to be exposed in front of another person and she hadn't been since that awful night. Maybe this would help with her nightmares. Anything to help her get rid of the nausea-inducing memories she couldn't seem to outrun.

So why did she feel so guilty being out with someone else? She and Jayce had broken up nearly a year ago. He'd made it perfectly clear that she wasn't good enough for him. Oh, sure, he'd loved her in the bedroom, but that was all he'd been willing to give her. He hadn't been willing to make her his bondmate when she'd been human and she sure as hell wasn't going to give him a second chance now that she was like him. Not that he'd actually asked for one. He'd just been calling a lot since her attack.

Acting all concerned.

Well, he could take his concern and shove it. She didn't need him or his help. She would take care of her own problems, the way she always had. By herself. Unfortunately she couldn't seem to keep her head on straight. For a moment back in the parking lot she'd thought she scented Jayce, but she knew it had to be a figment of her imagination.

"So how far from your place are we?" Self-loathing bubbled up inside her as she asked the question.

Scott's dark eyes glanced her way and he grinned before turning his gaze back to the road in front of him. "Not far, baby. Not far."

Baby? She hated that term. Before she could dwell on it she sniffed the air. Something sensual rolled off him and it took her a moment to realize it was lust. She was still getting used to tapping into her extrasensory abilities and deciphering one smell from another. This was like a sweet wine, clean and refreshing.

It reminded her that even though she might not care about this guy or plan to see him again, he wasn't a bad person. It was the reason she'd chosen him tonight. Before she'd been turned into a shifter she'd been a human but also a seer. Just like her mom. Back then she'd only been able to see the true faces of supernatural beings. She'd been able to see the wolves or jaguars or whatever kind of animal lurked beneath the surface of shifters. And with vamps, she'd been able to see their teeth and their hunger for blood. After being turned into a shifter she could also see the truth of humans' nature. It was a weird addition to her psychic abilities. With the ability to see the truth about people, she could see Scott's "real" face. He was just a horny guy looking to get laid. No darker intentions or freaky sexual proclivities.

As they pulled into the driveway of a cottage-style house in a normal-looking middle-class neighborhood, she took another deep breath. She could do this. Couldn't she?

When he put the truck in park, she fought the growing

dread inside her. It moved like molasses, weighing her down and making it hard to breathe. With a numb hand she opened the door and slid out of the vehicle. The second her boots hit the pavement of the driveway she knew she couldn't go through with this. Not if she wanted to look at herself in the mirror the next morning. One-night stands weren't her style, and while she desperately needed control in her life, the thought of this guy's hands on her body made her nauseous. Not because he was bad-looking or gave her bad vibes, but because she didn't want this from a stranger. Not truly. As she started to walk around the truck to Scott's side, she turned at the sound of a motorcycle pulling into the driveway behind them.

Fury popped inside her at the sight of Jayce. Well, fury and something else that she refused to define. It might have been relief, but she wasn't going to go there. Not tonight. Not when anger was so much easier.

Stalking toward Jayce as he slid off the bike, she tried to keep her gaze from trailing down to those incredibly muscular legs. Didn't matter that he was wearing jeans. She'd seen every inch of his naked body and the image was seared into her brain. He moved with such fluidity—it had always amazed her.

Even now, when she wanted to pummel him for having the audacity to follow her, she still had to admire the strength and power he radiated. He would never be called handsome, or even good-looking, but there was something dangerous about Jayce that was incredibly sexy. Without even trying, he exuded a raw sexuality that made women stand up and take notice. With his shaved head and a scar that crisscrossed over his left eye, he had . . . a presence that refused to be ignored. The scar only added to that edginess. And he was directing all of that at her with a *very* heated stare.

"What the hell are you doing here?" she practically shouted.

Before he could answer, Scott was next to her, in front of her actually, partially blocking her from Jayce. "Can I help you, buddy?"

Kat smiled haughtily at Jayce. At least Scott wasn't a total wimp.

But then Jayce trained his gaze on the other man. Jayce was scary when he wanted to be, and as she watched his normally gunmetal gray eyes turn to black, she actually had to force herself to stand her ground. He growled low in his throat. "You can go inside your fucking house and leave us alone."

Scott cleared his throat nervously, then looked at her. "You, uh, know this guy?"

She could smell the fear on him. Bitter and acidic, it stung her nostrils. So much for not being a wimp. Ignoring Scott, she turned back to Jayce and set her hands on her hips. "Did you *follow* me here?"

"What do you think?" he practically purred as he took a step closer.

Now she scented something dark and rich, like chocolate. *Lust.* As a human she'd never had a clue that lust or desire actually had a smell, but now ... this was addicting. She inhaled and for a moment she felt light-headed. But when she saw the knowing look in Jayce's eyes, she snapped. "I think it's pathetic that you're following me around like a little puppy dog." She knew he still wanted her and the knowledge made her feel powerful. Even if she was playing with fire by taunting him, it gave her perverse pleasure to see the anger flare in that newly darkened gaze.

"Puppy dog?" His voice was low, a soft, menacing growl that made the hair on her arms stand straight up.

Next to her Scott actually took a step back, using her body to block his own. Oh, yeah, total wimp. "Should I, uh, call the cops?" His voice was pitched a little higher than it had been earlier.

"No. Just go inside and forget you met me." She didn't look at him and he didn't question her directive. She heard him shuffle away, then fumble for his keys. They hit the pavement once, then seconds later she heard the front door slamming.

Jayce continued to stare at her, his chest falling and rising erratically. Oh, yeah, she'd pissed him off really good.

"Get. On. My. Bike." The words tore from his throat with apparent difficulty.

She really should just give in. Especially when he was in a mood like this. But she wasn't in the mood to be passive or appeasing. She was in the mood to fight. "No." With her gaze still on him, her eyes mocking, she pulled her cell phone out of her pocket. Before she had a chance to call someone for a ride, Jayce plucked it from her hand and shoved it in his front jeans pocket.

Kat stepped toward him until they were inches apart and held out a hand. "Give me my phone."

"If you want it, come get it." He lifted a dark eyebrow in challenge.

Swallowing hard, she looked at the front of his jeans where the bulge of her phone was. Yeah, that so wasn't happening. Glancing past him, she looked at the bike. She could be stubborn and walk home, but that thought wasn't appealing. So she ignored him and strode toward the bike. After sliding onto the back—no helmets for either of them apparently—she sat there and tried to ignore the heated stare he gave her.

A combination of red-hot fury and lust rolled off him,

both of which she could do without. She wasn't scared that Jayce would hurt her, but she didn't want to deal with his anger. Despite her desire to fight with him, when they argued things almost always ended up in the bedroom.

And she definitely couldn't handle that right now.

Too many things had happened since they'd been together, and she had too much resentment toward him. She averted her gaze, purposely ignoring him as he got on the bike in front of her. As he tore out of the driveway she had no choice but to hold on to him.

Sliding her hands around his waist, she tried to ignore the strength beneath her fingertips. His back was incredibly muscular and the feel of it pressing against her breasts was almost enough to take her back to when they'd been together. Back to when they'd actually liked each other, not just physically wanted each other.

Nine months wasn't that long, but it might as well have been a lifetime. She was a different person now even if he wasn't.

When he took another sharp turn she gripped him tighter. Over the sound of the rushing wind, she thought she heard him laugh, but it was impossible to tell.

After what felt like an eternity they pulled up to December's house. Kat immediately jumped off the bike and headed for the front door. She could get her phone later. Before she'd made it up the front steps, Jayce passed her and inserted a key into the lock.

Gritting her teeth, she hung back as he stepped inside without giving her a backward glance. "What do you think you're doing?"

He didn't bother to turn around as he flipped on a light in the foyer. "We're talking. Now."

For the first time since she'd seen him that night she

was beginning to second-guess her decision to bait him earlier. She should have just kept her mouth shut. Sighing, she stepped inside and shut the door behind her. But she didn't bother locking it. Jayce wouldn't be staying long.

Leaning against the closed door, she crossed her arms over her chest as he turned to face her. Under the small decorative chandelier in the entryway his gray eyes almost seemed to glitter. She refused to look away, but she was thankful for the door holding her up. "What do you want to talk about?"

He took a menacing step toward her. "You and your bullshit." Before she could lay into him, he continued. "You might not care about yourself, but every time you go out in public without telling anyone where you are, you put the entire pack in danger. You might be an adult, but you have the skills of a cub. Until you learn to control your urges and your ability to shift, you need to use your fucking head." All his words were gravelly and filled with anger.

"I didn't ask for this life," she snapped.

"No. You didn't. But at least you're alive. It's time to stop feeling sorry for yourself." He covered the distance between them, and before she realized what he intended, he caged her against the door with his body and braced his hands on either side of her head.

Asshole. "I don't feel sorry for myself." Maybe she did, but she wasn't going to admit it to him.

His snort told her he didn't believe a word she said, but he didn't contradict her. "If you have a need to find sexual release, you won't search it out with any other male but *me*." The words rumbled up from his chest in a low growl that sounded more wolf than human.

The statement took her so off guard that she dropped

her arms from their protective embrace around herself. "*Excuse* me?"

He leaned in closer until his entire body was a mere inch from hers and his mouth was next to her ear. His hot breath sent a tingle racing through her, searching out every nerve ending until she practically trembled with the need to feel that mouth all over her. "If you go to another male, I will kill him. That human tonight is lucky he's alive."

"You wouldn't do that," she whispered, even though she knew the truth. Could hear it in his darkly murmured words. She'd known he still physically wanted her, but this . . . was unexpected. And a little insane. Why should he feel all possessive when he was the one who'd decided she wasn't good enough for him by lying to her about the bonding process? It had to be his animal side asserting dominance. That was all. Like a dog peeing on a freaking fire hydrant, he was just acting territorial because he could.

"Do you really want to find out if your *puppy* will bite?" Another low murmur against her skin.

He wasn't quite touching her, but she could feel the heat rolling off him and onto her nonetheless. She didn't answer, partly because she didn't trust her voice but mainly because she knew the question was rhetorical. Jayce was a deadly warrior, not a puppy dog as she'd said earlier. She knew he was reminding her of that.

As she stared at the spot where the curve of his neck met his shoulder, she fought the sensation that shimmied through her. The thought of going to bed with Jayce was tempting. Even thinking about it made her feel light-headed.

He'd said she could find sexual release with him, but that was all it would be to him. Even if he did care about her, he would never give her what she wanted. Not that it mattered anymore. She was so messed up and broken, she had no hope of having anything normal in her life again. And she refused to go to him for any sort of sexual pleasure. Especially since it wouldn't be about control. With him, she'd lose it, not gain it. She could find control of her life in other places. Like revenge.

The word rang loudly in her head. *Revenge*. After what that APL bastard had done to her, she was going to make every single one of them pay. And she didn't need Jayce interfering with those plans.

Ducking out from under his arms, she put a few feet of distance between them in the blink of an eye. Without his spicy, earthy scent overpowering her, she could breathe again. And think clearly. "Get out of here."

Jayce gave her a hard look before fishing her phone out of his pocket. Wordlessly he handed it to her, then opened the front door, but before he closed it, he paused and turned back to her. "Don't test me, *Katarina*. I don't think you could live with the knowledge that you got someone killed."

As the door shut behind him she pushed out a long breath and grabbed the stair railing to brace herself. Somehow, with him gone, the pain and loneliness eating at her were almost impossible to bear.

Which was stupid. She'd left him more than nine months ago. Or almost a year, she reminded herself. It sounded better when she rounded up. Why oh why couldn't she get him out of her system? When she'd first met Jayce she'd been utterly entranced. Not because of his looks—though she loved the dark edge to him—but because of the raw, untamed power that practically rolled off him.

Since she'd grown up with an arms dealer for a father,

she'd never been intimidated by anyone. Until Jayce. Of course she hadn't let him see it. She'd called him a puppy even then, completely taunting him. He'd been so surprised. She would never forget the shocked look on his face as she'd teased him. He deserved the taunt, of course, after saying something rude to her. She couldn't remember the exact phrase, but he'd insinuated that he wanted to do something sexual to her and she'd laughed at him.

From that point on he'd chased her with a single-minded focus. Not that she'd minded. Being on his radar had made her feel empowered and sexy in a way she hadn't imagined possible. Before Jayce men had either been too scared to approach her because of her father's shady dealings—and his violent reputation—or wanted to get close to her *because* of her father. Not Jayce. He'd just wanted *her*. She'd made him wait six months before agreeing to go to lunch with him. At the time she'd thought she could drag out her teasing even longer, but they hadn't even made it to her parked car at that restaurant before he'd kissed her.

And oh what a kiss. He'd told her everything she'd needed to know in that one very long kiss. He was claiming her, making a statement that she was his. Or at least that's how she'd taken it. But it hadn't been a permanent thing. That knowledge made her stomach turn sour. She'd wanted to make a life with him, but when she'd broached the subject of their future, he'd told her that the chance of a human turning into a shifter from a bite was one percent. What he'd failed to mention was the fact that if he'd taken her as his bondmate she would have changed into a shifter without any issues. He'd lied because he hadn't wanted her as his bondmate. He'd never actually admitted it to her, but what other reason could

he have had for lying? Swallowing hard, she ignored the
sudden sting of tears.

Instead of heading directly upstairs to her room, she
made a beeline for the kitchen. Sleep had been elusive
the past month, and even though she hadn't wanted to,
she'd seen a doctor just to get a prescription. After taking two sleeping pills she prayed she would finally get at
least a few hours of uninterrupted sleep. Once in her
room, she didn't bother to take off her clothes; she just
slipped her boots off and slid into bed.

The moment she closed her eyes Jayce's face appeared in her vision, mocking her. It made her want to
scream. Or maybe cry. She turned onto her side and
curled into a ball. She would *not* think about him. She
couldn't afford to give him any power over her when all
she wanted was some control in her life. Well, control
and revenge.

Chapter 2

Crouching low, he kept to the shadows as he crept along the side of the house. A few streetlights illuminated the quiet neighborhood, but he stayed hidden in darkness. His wolf coat was dark, making it easy to blend in, and his victim's house didn't have any working floodlights. He'd busted them earlier.

Dried grass and dead foliage crunched lightly under his paws as he approached the privacy fence surrounding the backyard, though no humans could hear his movements. After a glance around, he saw that he was still alone. The cold January night gave away no other strong scents either. It was the perfect time to hunt.

Giving himself enough room, he ran full speed at the fence. At the last second he used all the strength in his back legs to propel his body over. He landed with a quiet thud on the brittle, icy grass.

His canines ached and his claws extended as he neared the back door. Despite his human side battling him, telling him this was wrong, his beast was winning. It was hungry and this type of hunger couldn't be denied.

The human must die.

For his woman, this male had to die.

His inner wolf roared and clawed and demanded blood. Killing this human was the only outcome tonight, no matter what his weaker human side wanted. His wolf would take blood.

Creeping closer, he peered through the windowpanes of the back door. Wearing pajama pants and no shirt, the male was in his kitchen, looking into his fridge. He pulled out a beer and slammed the door. The stench of annoyance rolled off the human, strong enough that it trailed outside. It mixed with the equally strong stink of booze, which practically saturated him.

Guilt swamped him as he watched the male open a cabinet and pull out a bag of chips. But he pushed it back down and locked it up tight.

There was no room for weakness in him tonight. Channeling all the rage he possessed, he loped across the yard, then turned back toward the house.

He let his power and hatred funnel through him as he launched himself at the door. Glass and wood splintered around him as his large body broke through.

The human let out a startled shout as his beer bottle slipped from his hand and shattered against the tile.

Without giving the male a chance to cry out or run, he lunged, jaws open and claws extended. Despite the slight remorse he felt, his beast craved the spilled blood. The taste of it and the human's fears fueled his rage. The second his jaws clamped around the male's neck, he released a pent-up growl of satisfaction.

It drowned out any and all guilt from his weaker human side.

*   *   *

Parker McIntyre unzipped his tan and brown standard-issue sheriff's jacket as he entered the one-story home. It was much warmer inside—as if someone had turned the heat all the way up—and that only increased the stench of death. Even before seeing the body that was inside, he knew it would be a brutal sight.

The patrolman who'd been sent to check things out after the anonymous call about loud shouting had already retched twice in the front yard. Parker continued down a hallway to where another patrolman stood guard outside what he assumed was the kitchen.

"He in there?" Parker asked.

Tillman, the blond-haired rookie, glanced over his shoulder through the open door, then back at Parker. Tillman's face was pale as he nodded. "Yeah. You, uh, mind if I get some fresh air?"

Shaking his head, Parker stepped past him, but froze in the doorway. What had apparently been a wood table had been smashed to pieces, chunks of wood splintered and scattered across the floor. A stainless-steel refrigerator had been ripped away from the wall and toppled on its side, the door open and the contents spilling across the black-and-white tile floor.

But that wasn't what made Parker's stomach heave. It was the blood and gore covering almost every inch of the oddly bright room. Sunlight spilled in through the open blinds, illuminating a man's decapitated head. It looked like a macabre spotlight shining on it.

The rest of the tile was littered with body parts. Two hands, a torso, one foot mixed in with a ripped-open bag of rotting lettuce.... The coffee Parker had drunk an hour ago swished around sickeningly in his stomach.

Crimson splatters covered almost every surface of the

kitchen. The counters. The fallen fridge. The broken chairs and table.

It was a massacre. As if an animal had torn the victim to pieces . . . *Shit.* Parker scrubbed a hand over his face. The only good thing about this scene, if he could even use that word, was that it had been left undisturbed. Even though his men had been trained not to touch anything until he or Detective Chance Kinsey arrived at a scene, they didn't have many murders in Fontana or the surrounding county in any given year, so he occasionally had to reprimand a rookie for charging into a scene.

Not today. No one wanted to set foot inside the house, which explained why all of his men had been loitering on the front lawn when he arrived.

He felt a presence behind him before a familiar voice spoke. "Holy shit," muttered Chance as he stopped in the entryway next to Parker.

"Exactly."

After a few moments, Chance said what Parker had been thinking. "Any possibility this is a shifter attack?"

"Don't know." But as he stared at the carnage, he *did* know. This attack was too vicious to have been done by humans. Not that humans weren't violent—he'd been shot a little over a month ago by an abusive husband—but this kind of attack was purely animalistic in nature. And Parker didn't know any humans who could rip off someone's head with their teeth. Though they hadn't examined the body . . . *parts* yet, he was pretty sure this guy's head had been snapped off with large teeth. Something Parker had seen before. But he brushed that thought aside. This wasn't the time for a trip down memory lane. Not when he had a job to do.

"I want to check out the backyard, see where the blood trail leads." Parker nodded toward the smashed glass of the windowpanes of the back door. "After we section it off I'll talk to the neighbors. Can you handle this by yourself until Bonnie gets here?" he asked even though he already knew the answer.

Chance took a cautious step inside the room, careful to avoid any blood spatter, though it was difficult. "This isn't the worst thing I've seen, boss."

Sadly Parker knew it wasn't. Chance had served in the U.S. Marines for eight years before joining the department, and he had spent most of those years in various war zones.

In addition to Parker and Chance, there were three other trained crime scene investigators in the department, so it narrowed down who would be working this case. With the current budget and the lack of violent crimes in the county, the department couldn't afford to have full-time civilian employees on the payroll solely for processing crime scenes. The job definitely wasn't like the bullshit on television. The department also didn't have private labs to process fingerprints and DNA. All that was outsourced.

And that was going to make this job that much harder. Sighing, he headed out the front door and motioned to Tillman, the first responder. "Come with me." He walked around toward the back of the house. After putting on gloves, Parker pulled the latch on the gate of the high wooden privacy fence and opened it.

A trail of blood led from the back door, across the yard, then thinned as it tracked over the back of the fence. Which meant that their crime scene had just gotten that much bigger. "Section off this entire backyard and see how far the trail leads. If it leads into the neighbor's yard, explain why you have to section off their yard too."

The officer, now recovered from his earlier nausea, nodded. "Sure, boss."

As Parker headed back toward the front of the house, he clenched his teeth when he saw a local news van pulling up. One of the neighbors had probably called them. Or maybe that bulldog reporter, Julia Martin, had a police scanner she listened to.

It wouldn't surprise him if she slept with the damn thing on her nightstand. Right now the last thing he needed was news of a shifter attack leaking to the media. A couple of months ago he wouldn't have particularly cared, but now things were different. His sister was mated to the brother of the local pack's Alpha. Not only was she mated, she was pregnant, which meant she was as vulnerable as if she was still solely human.

With all the bullshit his department and the Armstrong-Cordona pack had dealt with lately from a radical hate group, the Antiparanormal League, he didn't want the locals getting riled up. For almost two decades they'd lived in peace with the shifter pack, and he wouldn't stand for anything or anyone screwing up the dynamics of his town. Or putting his sister in danger.

Ignoring the presence of the media, he made his way toward a man wearing blue pajama pants with white moose heads on them and a faded black pullover sweater, standing behind the cordoned-off section of the front yard. The college-aged guy waved Parker over, then rubbed a hand over his face. By the time Parker reached him, the stench of booze surrounded him. The guy had a couple of days' growth of stubble and smelled like a brewery.

"Do you need something?" Parker asked, getting right to the point.

The guy nodded and yawned, then said, "My name's Blake. I live down the street."

"And?"

"And I know Scott, Scott Ford, the guy who lives here. What the hell's going on?" he demanded, though it was hard to take him seriously when he wore frog slippers.

"I can't discuss an ongoing investigation. Please stay behind this tape." There was no way he could tell anyone what had happened until the victim's family was notified, least of all a nosy neighbor.

"Listen, Sheriff, I *just* saw him last night. What's the deal with the ambulance and all these uniforms? Is he all right?"

Parker's eyebrows rose. "You saw him last night?"

"Yeah, he's a bartender down at Kelly's Bar and Grill. I was hanging out with some buddies and saw him chatting up some hot chick."

"A hot chick?"

"Yeah, tall, sex on legs, man. I've seen her around before, but I can't remember where. I do know he left the bar with her."

That could describe too many women. "Around what time was this?"

"I dunno, midnight maybe. I was pretty messed up last night."

Parker took a step back and motioned for the guy to walk with him so he could take an official statement. He hadn't been to Kelly's in a while, but he was pretty sure the bar had video surveillance. If he could find out whom Scott Ford had left with, they might have their first lead.

Jayce made his way toward the main house of the Armstrong-Cordona ranch. After last night he was edgy and still pissed off about his confrontation with Kat. Telling her to stop feeling sorry for herself made him feel guilty, but she had to snap out of what he knew was a downward spiral before she got hurt. Or someone else did.

And if she decided that sleeping with random males was a way to purge whatever issues she was having, then someone was definitely going to get hurt. If anyone touched Kat, that person would die. It was as simple as that. The territorial animal inside him wouldn't allow it. But more than anything, his feelings for her had never died. Just because she'd left him didn't mean he'd been able to cut those ties to her. He wished to hell he could. Every damn day he wished it, but it just wouldn't happen.

His wolf and his human side were in agreement. Man's laws could shove it. So could pack laws as far as Kat was concerned. His inner beast would draw blood before his human side even had time to *think* if he smelled a male on Kat.

But he shouldn't have told her to stop feeling sorry for herself. Maybe he should have used kid gloves, but it hadn't seemed like she needed that. She would probably have thought he pitied her. Which he didn't. He hated what had happened to her—even though he didn't know all the details, he could guess—and he just wanted to *fix* it. But he didn't pity her. She was tough, and if she allowed herself time to heal, she could survive anything. But he wanted her to let him help.

Shoving those thoughts aside, he opened the door to Connor and Ana's home. Once inside, he veered toward the living room and found he was the last one to arrive. Something that shouldn't have happened, but he'd been distracted this morning. Cursing his lateness, he nodded at Connor, Liam, who was the Alpha's brother, and Brianna, the fae warrior who'd infiltrated the APL and helped save Kat a month ago. Brianna had gone to Ireland for a few weeks to talk with her leaders and had just returned to Fontana.

Sitting on the edge of a love seat, the petite blonde nodded politely at him. Liam, who sat on the long leather couch across from her, grunted a hello. Connor pushed off from his position where he leaned against the fireplace mantel and gave him a look that told him he understood exactly what he was going through with Kat. That just pissed him off. He wasn't used to anyone knowing his business, but it seemed that everyone in this pack knew he'd gone to see Kat last night.

Though all he wanted to do was pace, he kept his body loose and dropped onto the couch next to Liam. "So what did I miss?" He was in Fontana for a multitude of reasons and this meeting should cover the APL business. Afterward he needed to talk to Connor about the possible vampire-blood-trafficking bullshit.

Connor shot an annoyed look at Brianna, who shrugged. "I'm going to infiltrate the APL again and your wolf friends don't like it."

Wolf friends? Despite the tension humming through him, Jayce had to resist smiling. Brianna was part of the Fianna, legendary fae warriors from Ireland that most people thought were complete myth, and as far as he knew, they usually stayed with their own kind. Her presence here was abnormal, but they could use her, even if she didn't understand pack laws. "So what's the problem?" He directed his question to Connor.

"I'm not sending anyone in to work undercover with those assholes, especially a female." Connor's deep voice was resolute as he looked at Brianna.

The blonde simply gave Connor what Jayce considered a patronizing smile. "My brethren disagree. I appreciate you giving me shelter for the time being, but I don't *need* it. In fact, if this is representative of your pack's attitude toward *teamwork*, I am not interested." She rose slowly, the action almost regal, as if she were addressing peasants.

Connor growled low in his throat. "Sit."

The fae female might not have agreed with Connor, but there was a lot of power behind that one word. She did as he told her.

Before anyone else could speak, Jayce stood. Even if Connor had issues with her involvement, it was going to happen. Most supernatural beings minded their own business and didn't interact much with other supernaturals. Hell, a hundred years ago it wasn't uncommon for vicious battles to occur between shifters and the fae. Or the fae and vampires. Or any number of combinations. When supernatural beings wanted something like land, they usually took it or died trying. Strength mattered to all of them and civility was a fairly new concept. Over the past forty years there had been a substantial decrease in supernatural warfare, though, partially because shifters formed official councils all over the world and were better at communicating now. Then, as of twenty years ago, they'd had to start worrying about humans watching them too. And right now they had a common goal: destroy the APL. So while Connor was hesitant, it wasn't his decision. "The Council wants us working with the Fianna. We both want the same thing, and if she's comfortable going undercover again, we have no reason to stop her. If it's because she's female—"

"That is not the reason." Connor's voice had a deadly edge to it as he straightened, moving into an offensive stance.

Jayce's eyes narrowed. "We all saw what she did to Adler." Using her supernatural gift of harnessing pure energy, Brianna had taken off the head of the human scum who'd ordered the kidnappings of both Liam's mate, December, and Kat. As far as Jayce knew, Adler hadn't been the one to torture Kat, but he'd been complicit. And he'd been working on someone's orders. Right now Jayce *needed* to find out who'd given those orders. Because whoever it was a dead man walking. "She can hold her own against any of them."

Something they all knew. Jayce just felt Connor needed a little reminder. Brianna had been working undercover with the APL for months, controlling Adler's sick mind with a lot of psychic energy, even though it had kept her in a constant weak state. She'd been willing to sacrifice herself to save Kat. Killing Adler had expended so much of Brianna's energy that she'd passed out and could have been killed by other APL members if not for the intervention of Connor's pack. For that, Jayce would stand by the woman for pretty much anything.

"We don't know that she hasn't been compromised and we need to keep a low profile. For the good of the pack," Connor said.

"Everyone who knew of her involvement with us is dead," Liam interjected, earning him an annoyed glance from his older brother.

"All I want is the chance to utilize the list of names and addresses your pack found. If I can befriend a few APL members it will help both our causes." Brianna crossed her legs and settled in the love seat as she watched Connor.

A month ago they'd hacked into a flash drive that Jayce and Liam had found at the house of a dead APL member. And Connor was sitting on the contents at the moment, refusing to let anyone use it again. The information on it gave names and addresses of all known APL members in the area. He'd agreed with the Council and the fae to work with Brianna so they could help each other bring down the APL before it grew too big. Jayce didn't understand why Connor was stonewalling the fae warrior.

Rubbing a hand over his face, Connor sighed. "We can't afford to stand out among the humans. Not now. And I don't give a shit what the Council says," he said to Jayce, his voice heated. "I have to protect *my* pack. After everything that's happened to us in the past few months, I won't let them be targeted again."

Liam stood now, his body as tense as Connor's. "I understand wanting to protect the pack and my *pregnant* mate, but we can't bury our heads in the sand. We have to go after them and strike hard."

Jayce was silent as he watched the interaction between the two brothers. No matter what any of them said, Connor was Alpha. In the end he would make the decision he thought was best for his pack. He had to protect not only his mate but his own warriors and all the Cordona females he'd taken on when he mated with Ana. Their lives and welfare were his responsibility. And Jayce sure as hell didn't envy Connor's position.

The room was silent as they all waited. Finally, Connor gave Brianna a hard look. "We work together in targeting the APL and I know where you are at *all* times. No lone ranger bullshit." He cut Jayce a sharp look too, but Jayce ignored it and focused on the female.

Her expression was unreadable. As far as he knew, the fae hadn't been targeted by the APL yet. But the APL was growing and the possibility that it might expand overseas was real. The fae wanted to figuratively—or maybe literally—cut off APL heads before they reached fae shores. Which Jayce respected.

Brianna's lips pulled into a thin line. "For once, both of our species want the same thing. I will share any information I come across and I expect backup if I require it."

Connor gave a short nod. "Agreed."

Jayce waited until Liam and Brianna left, then sat down again. He and Connor had a few things to discuss, including the vamp blood situation, but mainly Jayce wanted to know what the hell the Alpha planned to do about Kat's blatant disregard of pack rules.

Kat steered down the long driveway to the Armstrong-Cordona ranch and fought the raw energy humming through her. Normally she experienced the same intense excitement when she came to train with Aiden, but today was different. She knew there was a chance she might see Jayce there.

Doesn't mean I have to talk to him, she reminded herself. She was here for one reason and one reason only: to hone her fighting skills. She might be able to turn into a wolf, but in her human form she still had limited skills. She'd taken kickboxing for years and was in good shape from skiing, but she needed to be better. She needed to be a walking weapon.

If she wanted to take down APL members, she couldn't afford to be weak in either human or animal form. All the strength in the world wouldn't make up for a lack of skills. If someone shot her or injected her with enough silver, she'd be screwed.

After leaving her Jeep in the covered barnlike parking structure, she headed across the expansive area of land. The houses and cabins on the ranch created a circle around the main house, where Connor, her Alpha—she

was still getting used to that concept—and his mate
lived. All the homes were far enough apart from one another that the pack members had some privacy, but over-
all, the ranch reminded her of a small village.

As she entered the barn, where she and Aiden usually
met before training, she looked around in confusion.
Most of the horses were gone, which made sense since
she guessed most of the males were out patrolling, but
she didn't detect the scent of her trainer. Even with the
other scents of hay, manure, and animals, she could usually pick his out.

Walking the length of the building, she froze once she
reached the other end. Jayce was nearby. Something
earthy and all primitive male tickled her nose. Before
she could turn to search him out, two muscular arms
grasped her and tackled her to the ground. All the air
rushed from her lungs, but oddly the fall didn't hurt. Her
attacker had rolled their bodies so that he took the brunt
of the fall before moving back on top of her.

For a moment all she could do was stare up at Jayce,
wondering what the hell he was doing. Just as quickly,
annoyance surged through her. She shoved at his chest,
and to her surprise, he nimbly jumped up. When he offered his hand she ignored it and picked herself up off
the ground.

"What the hell is wrong with you?" she asked as she
wiped dirt and pieces of hay from her hands.

"Lesson one. Always be aware of your surroundings,"
he said, as if what he'd just done was perfectly normal.

"Lesson *one*?"

He gave a short nod. "You're training with me today,
not Aiden."

She narrowed her eyes. "Does Aiden know about
this?"

A slight smirk touched Jayce's lips as he nodded. "He doesn't have much of a say in the matter." Before she could respond, he continued. "If you want to continue training with him, go ahead, but you and I both know who the better warrior is. So, do you want to be trained by the best or not?"

Kat gritted her teeth at his arrogant tone. Some prideful part of her wanted to tell him to shove it, but she held off. The arrogant wolf was right. He *was* the best. He wouldn't be the enforcer for North America if he weren't. Even though he might drive her insane and would probably distract her, she could learn a lot from him.

Keeping her anger toward Jayce contained would help her learn the type of skills that he could give her. And she desperately wanted that. The need to be able to protect herself in any situation ate away at her. She couldn't sleep without having torturous nightmares. Maybe Jayce could give her back some of the normalcy she so badly needed. "What's lesson two?" she asked in a muted tone.

His eyes widened for a split second, as if he was surprised that she wasn't arguing. Just as quickly, a calm mask fell into place. For the first time since she'd met him, she felt like she was getting a peek at his more militaristic side. "First we'll go over my rules. Then your lessons."

Despite her desire to remain calm around him, annoyance bubbled up inside her at his egotistical tone. *"Rules?"*

"During training sessions, you listen to me. If you have a question about something, fine, but this isn't time we're going to spend arguing. Your training is about you honing your skills so you can defend yourself in *any* situation."

Defend? She didn't want to simply be able to defend

herself; she wanted to be able to hold her own, to attack any threat that came her way. She shrugged. "Fine."

He paused again, sizing her up, as if he didn't quite believe her agreeable attitude. Then he continued. "Rule number two. The saying that all's fair in love and war is true. When you're fighting for your life, fair fighting is bullshit. *Anything* can be a weapon. Today I'm going to show you how to use your bare hands to defend yourself against humans."

The way he said "humans" made her pause. "Who else would I need to defend myself against?"

"Fighting with humans is different from fighting with vampires or the fae or even other shifters."

"How so? And why would other supernatural beings want to hurt me?" She'd thought that since supernatural beings came out to the world, they were all okay with each other—that humans were the ones that had the problem with different species.

Jayce's smile was wry, his gray eyes flashing an eerie, almost iridescent shade for a split second before returning to normal. "You really have a lot to learn, little wolf," he murmured, almost absently.

For a split second he showed her a softer side of himself. His almost gentle expression reminded her of the time when they'd been together. When she hadn't had to keep her guard up at all times. When she'd known that being in his arms was the safest, warmest place she could be. But all that was over now. Straightening, she pushed her shoulders back and kept her limbs loose. Now wasn't the time to reminisce. She needed to keep her focus. "So teach me already."

Just like that, Jayce slipped back into battle mode, his face hardening. Without warning, his hand struck out at her, lightning fast. He made contact with her temple, but it was only a glance, not a strike intended to harm her. His touch was whisper soft as he grazed her temple. "This can be a killing blow if you hit hard enough. Or you might knock someone out instead. *Then* you can kill them. Try it on me. Don't hold back."

Kat eyed him warily, but did as he said—and only because she knew that if and when she struck him, she wouldn't hurt him. Balling her hand into a fist as he'd done, she lashed out.

Jayce dodged to the side, easily avoiding her would-be strike. So she tried again, and again. And he continued to evade her with a fluid grace that fascinated and annoyed her.

Her heart rate increased as adrenaline pumped through her. He'd said all was fair in fighting. As she struck out with her right hand, she simultaneously struck out with her left foot. Her foot connected with his stomach even as she missed her punch.

The moment her foot made contact with him, he grabbed her ankle and flipped her onto her back. The hard earth was unforgiving as she slammed into it.

For some reason, Jayce looked pleased with her. "Good. Use your entire body to come at me. If you can strike *me* in the temple like I showed you, you can strike *anyone*. Don't hold back."

This kind of training was different from what she'd been doing with Aiden. He'd basically showed her how to punch and kick and they'd done a lot of running. To stay in shape, he'd said. Jayce's training seemed less structured and she found she liked it. Pushing to her feet, she didn't pause as she advanced on him.

For the next couple of hours, she went at Jayce like a missile. More often than not she was able to strike him with her feet—and half the time landed on her ass afterward—but it was damn near impossible to hit his face or head.

He dodged like a freaking butterfly, flitting with a supernatural grace that was maddening. She'd never seen anyone move so fast. What he wanted her to do was so simple.

As she struck out again, Jayce ducked, then snatched her wrist in a tight grip. Before she could react, he'd spun her around and pulled her tight against his front. His muscled chest at her back was impossibly firm. "All you have to do is hit me *once*. You're not trying hard enough," he growled.

Not trying hard enough? The sports bra she wore under her long-sleeved top was damp with perspiration. More than a little sweat poured down the sides of her face, and her legs and arms strained under the constant movement. Just one solid strike. That was all she needed.

Wrenching out of his embrace, she yanked her long-sleeved black T-shirt off and tossed it to the ground. Cool air rushed over her bare stomach, but she hardly noticed it. Her focus was on Jayce and his changing eyes, which had now turned a much darker shade. They were almost black.

His hands hung loose at his sides and his breathing was slightly erratic as he stared at her.

Fighting fair is bullshit. That's what he'd told her.

And she intended to follow that advice, which was why she'd taken her top off. If she could distract him with her body, she would do it. Without warning, she struck out again.

This time she connected with his temple in a sharp, satisfying blow. His head jerked back a bit, almost as if she'd barely touched him, but she felt the hard sting on her hand and knew the blow had made serious contact.

"If I was human, I'd be on my ass right now. Not dead, but definitely unconscious." There was a slight note of pride in his voice as he looked at her.

Taking a chance, she struck out again, but he grabbed her hand in his own fist and twisted until he had her pinned on the ground, flat on her back.

Without even thinking about the move, she kneed him once in the groin. His hold loosened as he groaned, but just as quickly his hand tightened on hers again.

"Does that not hurt as much to shifters?" she growled between gritted teeth.

"It hurts," he rasped. "We just know how to channel the pain better than humans."

"That doesn't seem fair," she muttered, trying to wriggle out from his hold. Maybe she should feel bad about kneeing him, but after hours of his form of training, she was beyond guilt. The feel of his hard body on top of hers did things to her she'd rather ignore. Her entire body heated and the juncture between her thighs was embarrassingly damp. Feeling all that muscle and strength against her made her remember the many, *many* times they'd been in this very position before. With a lot fewer clothes involved.

"Fair . . ." Jayce's gaze trailed to her mouth and instinctively she licked her lips.

The instant she did, she felt his erection, hard and unmistakable, pressing against her lower abdomen.

Before she could tell him to stop—or even mentally protest to herself—Jayce's lips covered hers. His tongue delved into her mouth, searching, hungry and needy. As his grip on her hand loosened and moved to cup her cheek, she could feel herself falling.

Falling under the weight of his desire and his kisses. The scent of his lust combined with her own was damn near suffocating. She felt as if she were drowning in sensations as his tongue probed her mouth, not gently but expertly and wickedly. He knew exactly what he was doing. Exactly what she needed because he'd kissed her a thousand times.

And she'd let him.

But not now. No matter how much she enjoyed it. No matter how much she'd fantasized about being with him again, this would never, ever work between them. He hadn't wanted her enough to turn her into a shifter when she'd been human. She couldn't give in to what were purely physical desires now. Even if her new animalistic side wanted only that. She was still in control of her actions. Panic bubbled inside her as she shoved against his chest.

Thankfully he didn't fight her, but he also didn't move fully off her. Just kept his muscular body over hers, pinning her to the ground until finally she pushed him again.

"I thought training was supposed to be professional," she said as she got to her feet. Without glancing at him, she grabbed her top from the ground and stalked out of the barn. Jayce didn't follow and she was glad. Getting away from him was the most important thing for her sanity right now.

He might have kissed her, but she'd definitely kissed him back. She couldn't afford to make that mistake again. She needed Jayce for his skills and training. Getting tangled up with him again . . . She shuddered. No, thank you. She might need him, but she wasn't enough of a masochist to invite the kind of agony he would bring her in the end.

Chapter 3

How could I be so stupid? Kat hurried across the open yard toward December and Liam's house. She shouldn't have allowed herself to be vulnerable to Jayce like that.

Taking off her top probably hadn't been the best idea, but damn it, she'd needed to get a punch in before her arm fell off. Being pinned underneath him with no shirt on . . . She shivered, and it had nothing to do with the icy chill in the air. The feel of all his muscle and strength and raw power was way too familiar. It would have been so easy to give in to that kiss, to wrap her legs around him and . . . Nope. Not going there. She gave her head a sharp shake as if that could somehow force away memories of their hot, sweaty bodies tangled up together.

When she reached December's doorstep, she knocked once. Moments later the door opened and her redheaded best friend stood there with a slightly swelling belly. Petite and much shorter than Kat, December practically glowed. Pregnancy definitely agreed with her. Her blue eyes widened slightly. "Kat! Come in."

Kat pushed down the guilt. Her friend shouldn't be surprised to see her, but Kat had been keeping her distance since December and Liam moved back to the ranch recently. After the torture Kat had endured, both of her friends had lived with her for a little over a month, and for that she was grateful. She should have visited here more. "If you're sure you're not busy and I'm not interrupting anything—"

December rolled her eyes, grabbed Kat's hand, and tugged her inside. "You can join me in the kitchen. I can't seem to stop baking. Though of course I can't eat any of it without puking it back up. But I like the smell. I think I'm driving Liam a little crazy."

Kat snorted softly at she followed her friend into the country-style kitchen. "I don't think that's possible." Her eyes widened when she saw the racks of cupcakes, cookies, and a couple of cakes. "Holy crap, you weren't kidding."

"I *know*." A timer went off and December opened the oven, pulling out what looked like lemon squares, and Kat's mouth watered.

"Is that what I think it is?"

"Yes, and you can take the whole thing once I'm finished." December didn't look up as she grabbed a metal tin from the pantry, so Kat took a seat in one of the chairs at the center island.

"I'm sorry I haven't been around lately."

December shook her head as she started to dust the contents of the pan with powdered sugar. "You don't have anything to apologize for."

But she did. December was just too forgiving. And an incredibly good friend. She'd never once pressured her to talk about what had happened to her in that barn. Well, December had tried to talk Kat into seeing a therapist, but she hadn't been pushy. Considering that December had been turned into a shifter too—though she'd undergone the change because of her pregnancy and wouldn't be able to shift forms until after the birth—she had her own issues to deal with, but she'd been the best friend Kat could ask for. "I just stopped by to see what you and Liam were up to. I'm surprised you're not working today." Especially since it was Saturday. One of the busiest days at her friend's bookstore.

"Right now Erin's watching the store, but I'm going in around lunchtime. I'm going to try selling some of these baked goods, see if there's a market for them."

Kat inhaled deeply, dying to dive into the lemon squares, especially after the workout she'd just had. "I can't imagine any of this stuff lasts very long in your store."

A small smile touched her face. "Or in this house. Liam's like a garbage disposal."

Kat grinned. "So, what's your man up to today?" In addition to avoiding December she'd also been steering clear of the entire pack and Liam. She felt like a jerk for avoiding the two people who'd been so good to her when she'd needed it most. But she hadn't wanted to bring them down with her issues. Not when they were newly mated and soaking up the bliss of their new relationship. Plus Kat had begun to feel like a third wheel around them.

"He's with his brother." December shrugged, but Kat didn't miss the tart, almost bitter scent that emanated from her friend. It was subtle, but Kat was learning to read scents better.

"And?"

December glanced up as she set her hand sifter down a little harder than necessary. Powdered sugar scattered across the counter. "Liam and Brianna seem to think it's all fine and dandy for Brianna to infiltrate . . ." She cleared her throat as she trailed off, her eyes widening.

Kat brushed past the awkward pause. "The APL?"

December nodded. "Yeah."

"And you don't agree with your mate?"

"No. And neither does Connor. With all the stupid newscasts lately trying to paint a poor picture of shifters I think it's smarter if we keep a low profile. We're not doing anything wrong, and going after them will only invite trouble." December growled low in her throat as she yanked another cookie sheet out from a cabinet, and Kat guessed she wasn't even aware of it.

She also knew that the reason December was getting worked up was because of her brother, Parker. The local sheriff had recently taken some flak from the town news, insinuating that he was covering up shifter wrongdoing. Kat had to bite back a snort at that thought. *As if.* The sheriff was too good a man. Even though Kat didn't agree with December, she didn't voice her opinion. "So he and Connor are out hunting down APL members?"

December shook her head. "Not exactly. Liam, Connor, and Brianna are out scouting some of the addresses from that damn *list*."

"List?"

"Yeah. About six weeks ago Liam and Jayce found a flash drive at the house of that asshole who tried to kidnap me. It's got names and addresses of a lot of local APL members or supporters and now Connor's given Jayce, Liam, and Brianna a copy. I don't know exactly what they're doing today, but I think Brianna wants to see who will be her easiest target. Or at least that's what Liam insinuated."

They had a list of APL members who lived in the vi-

cinity? Kat's fingers ached to get hold of it. Her hands clenched in her lap. Even knowing it was out there made her palms damp and her heart rate increase. But she didn't let her excitement show. It would only worry December if she knew Kat wanted the list. And if she knew Kat was interested, it would make it that much harder for Kat to get a copy for herself.

Hating herself at that moment, Kat stood. "Mind if I use your bathroom?"

"Of course not." December didn't glance up as she scooped out a cup of flour and poured it into a mixing bowl.

Kat fought the surge of guilt that forked through her, jagged and twisted, reaching all her nerve endings with a sharp warning note, telling her how wrong her plan was. But she ignored it as she bypassed the bathroom and hurried to Liam's office. She needed this. Had to do something to find closure. Connor had made copies for his brother, Jayce, and Brianna, but of course he hadn't given her one or even told her about it. She didn't know much about pack dynamics, and it made sense that he hadn't involved her, but she didn't plan to ignore this bit of knowledge. She wasn't even sure if Liam would have the list lying around, but before she checked Connor's house, she had to eliminate the possibility that it was here. Searching her Alpha's office wasn't an idea she relished. Granted, searching her best friend's house made her feel like shit too, but it had to be done.

Jayce slowed his bike and steered down the nearly hidden turnoff from the two-lane highway. After talking to Connor about the importance of working with the fae in regard to the APL—and giving the Alpha some vague information about possible vamp blood issues—he'd made his way to one of the last places he wanted to be.

Ned Hartwig's house. Well, "house" was a bit of a stretch. The guy lived in a run-down trailer half the time, and the other half he lived in a hollowed-out school bus. Ned was a bit of a freak and had worked with the APL on occasion. However, he wasn't a white supremacist. Nope, first and foremost Ned was a drug dealer. Mainly weed, but Jayce had received a tip that Hartwig had expanded into vampire blood. The guy wasn't in Connor's territory, though. Unfortunately this wasn't the only tip Jayce had received about vamp blood trafficking in the state. There was another supposed dealer closer to Winston-Salem, but that was in the opposite direction and Jayce would rather talk to someone he knew first.

Seemed the shit was popping up everywhere lately. And no one had any idea who the source was. Or if it was multiple sources. If it was voluntary or if some dumbass humans had captured a vampire that they were now using as a blood source. God help anyone who was stupid enough to do that.

Vampires might be more individualistic and scoff at the type of pack mentality shifters embraced, but if someone fucked with one of their own, they got pissed and retaliated. There was nothing subtle about the way vamps reacted either. If they thought someone had wronged them, they more or less killed first and asked questions later. So in addition to that concern, Jayce was definitely worried about what would happen if the wrong person got hopped up on vamp blood. He could just see the headlines, and it made him cringe.

Moss and low-hanging branches from an abundance of thick, old trees nearly blocked the crumbling paved path. The fact that it wasn't completely dirt was a miracle. Part of the reason was because the property Ned lived on had once held an antebellum mansion. That structure was now just ruins, lying about a mile from Ned's trailer.

After hiding his bike in the underbrush, Jayce ducked into the woods and jogged parallel to the path. He knew for a fact that Ned had booby traps rigged, and even though he could survive damn near anything, he didn't feel like getting his ass blown up and he didn't want to announce his presence sooner than he had to.

About thirty yards farther along he noticed a trip wire stretched between two trees. He avoided it and slowed his pace until he came to the clearing where the rusty school bus and trailer were. Listening, he heard a steady heartbeat from the direction of the trailer. So he made his way to the bus.

He checked for traps, then hoisted himself up and through one of the open windows. Once inside, he froze for a moment. The seats had all been removed and what looked like one long, haphazardly built bench lined the left side. Odd.

Jayce tapped on it, then ran his hand along the rough-hewn material until he realized that it wasn't nailed down. It was like someone had just nailed some wood together to create a giant L shape and then shoved it over . . . a bunch of mini-refrigerators.

Anger burst inside him as he removed the wood covering. Before he'd even opened one of the fridges, he knew what he would find inside. He opened one after another, fury building in him with each display of long, cylindrical tubes containing blood. Just to make sure it was what he thought it was, he opened one and smelled its contents.

Vampire blood had a sweeter, more distinctive odor than human blood. This was definitely vamp blood. He replaced the wood cover on the refrigerators, then slipped out the way he'd come in. Once on the ground, he realized that the electrical cord he'd seen draped from a hole in the bus must lead to a power source. Following it, he was silent as he crept up to the trailer. The windows were boarded up and he could see a couple of mounted video cameras, so he avoided them.

As he neared the trailer he changed his mind and backtracked to the bus. He would bring Ned to him. Grabbing the cord with both hands, he wrenched it apart. The soft hum of the refrigerators died instantly.

Jayce grinned to himself. Ned was a survivalist conspiracy-theorist type who didn't believe in banks and hid all the cash he made from drugs only God-knew-where, so Jayce had no doubt that the guy had an alarm rigged to his refrigerators.

It would be silent, of course, but the amount of blood in those things was worth at least half a million. Maybe more. Jayce wasn't sure what the current street price for the shit was. If more had flooded the market recently—and it seemed as if it had—then the price might have dropped a fraction.

Pressing his body against the side of the bus and making sure one of the wheels blocked any view of his legs, he was silent as he heard a curse from the direction of the trailer, then the trailer door opening. Jayce tugged down the zipper on his jacket, but didn't draw either of his blades—or either of the two guns he had on his person. He waited only thirty seconds before revealing himself.

As he stepped out from behind the bus, he found Ned with his hand on the back door of it, his eyes wide with surprise. "Hey . . . man. Jayce, what the fuck are you doing here?"

"What the fuck are you doing selling vamp blood?"

The fear that rolled off Ned was pungent. Some of the

stench was probably because the guy hadn't showered in a few days.

At six feet tall, with thickly muscled and tattooed arms, slicked-back hair, and a full beard and mustache, Ned didn't look like a man easily intimidated. To any other observer he would even have looked calm and collected. But the human couldn't hide the smell of his terror from Jayce.

"What are you talking about?" There was a waver in Ned's voice, so slight that Jayce might not have heard it if not for his extremely sensitive hearing.

"I've been in your bus." His voice was monotone.

Now anger punched off the human. Anger and that roll of fear again. Ned swallowed hard. "Why the hell do you care? You're not a vamp."

"Thanks for stating the obvious." Jayce kept his gaze on Ned steady as he allowed his wolf to show in his eyes. He knew he could look like a scary bastard when he wanted to.

To Ned's credit, he didn't step away. Probably because he was frozen to the spot. Finally the human shrugged. "It's none of your fucking business what I do. There's money in vamp blood, and I'm not hurting anyone."

"Who's your dealer?"

Okay, now that fear turned to something acidic and . . . dark. Interesting. "None of your business."

"How many clients are you selling to a week?"

Ned held up a hand and reached into his jacket pocket slowly. "Just grabbing a cig." As he lit up, he said, "If I didn't know better I'd think you were trying to move in on my territory."

Jayce snorted; that thought was ludicrous for a multitude of reasons. "Who. Is. Your. Dealer." He injected his animal side into his voice.

Ned shook his head, the acidic stench back. "I tell you, I'm dead," he whispered.

"I'll kill you if you don't tell me." Jayce wouldn't, but he wanted to see Ned's reaction.

Ned shook his head as he took a drag from his cigarette. "What he'll do to me is worse." He spoke so low Jayce almost didn't hear him. It was as if Ned was afraid someone could actually overhear them.

There were no other humans nearby. Jayce couldn't scent or hear anyone, but something told him Ned wouldn't believe him if he told him. "Damn it, Ned. I don't want to hurt you but I will." Jayce quickly removed one of his blades, hoping the show of force would loosen the human's lips. It's not that he had any particular feelings for this guy, but he wasn't eager to cause him pain either.

Moving lightning fast—fast enough to let Jayce know the human was taking his own product—Ned pulled something round from his pocket and tossed it into one of the bus windows.

A click and a soft hissing sound moved Jayce into action. Using all the strength in his legs he launched himself away from the bus. Out of his peripheral vision he watched as Ned sprinted in the opposite direction.

Before he had time to think of a plan of action, a loud explosion ripped through the air. Heat licked at his back, the impact of the bomb pulsing into his eardrums and lifting him off his feet. Jayce flew through the air and slammed into a tree, his stomach taking the brunt of the impact.

As he fell back onto the dirt, grass, and patches of ice, he rolled over and pushed to his feet in a few fluid movements. Blade still in hand, he started after Ned. The school bus burned incredibly fast, telling Jayce that Ned must have had other explosives already inside.

He'd been prepared for this possibility.

It could be something as simple as that the guy had been fearful of the cops and this was his backup plan to dispose of evidence, but something told Jayce otherwise. Ned had been shitting-his-pants afraid of someone. Someone apparently scarier than Jayce.

One of his eardrums had ruptured, and for a dizzying moment, nausea roiled in his stomach. Just as quickly, his body started mending itself. As he headed toward the trailer, his ear had already healed. His age had a lot to do with his abilities to regenerate. The older shifters were, the quicker, stronger, and more powerful they became.

Instead of following Ned, Jayce hurried into the trailer. After scanning it for possible traps, he zeroed in on the guy's makeshift "office." Meaning the desk and laptop he had set up in the only clean corner. Careful not to touch anything else, Jayce snagged the laptop and raced back to his bike. He could have followed Ned but decided against it at the moment. He already had a decent head start, and knowing his tendencies, Jayce would expect that Ned had probably set up a ton of traps.

With the giant fireball that had ripped through the sky, he didn't want to be anywhere close to Ned's place when the cops finally showed up. For all the bullshit and strange conspiracy theories that Jayce had heard Ned spout more than once in the past, something told Jayce that if he could crack the encryption on the laptop—and he knew it would be protected—he'd find a gold mine of information. At least he hoped so.

As he sped away, his cell phone buzzed in his pocket. Keeping an eye on the road, he fished it out. A text from Erin. *Kat stopped by ranch, but headed home. Think she's going out tonight. Thought you'd want 2 know.*

Pressing down on the accelerator, Jayce gunned it

back to Fontana. Wherever Kat was going tonight, he planned to be there too.

You are a giant asshole, Kat thought to herself hours later. She was still suffering under the oppressive weight of guilt. She couldn't believe she'd found that list of names and addresses. It hadn't been in Liam's office; it had been in December and Liam's bedroom—not exactly hidden, but not in plain sight either. And she knew why. Because Liam would never expect anyone on the ranch to steal from him. Shifters all left their doors unlocked. It was just the pack way. Which made Kat feel even scummier for invading their privacy. She hadn't been able to take it or even make a copy, but she'd taken pictures of the five pages with her cell phone. She wondered why he didn't have it with him today, but December had said he was out with Brianna, so if the female fae had a copy too, it made sense that he didn't need his. Whatever the reason, Kat was just grateful she'd gotten access to it. Well, grateful but filled with guilt.

She'd been too nervous to stay in their room more than a minute for fear her friend would catch her. *How awful was that?* Her face burned with shame. The only thing that managed to keep her from calling December and confessing was the knowledge that she might be able to find some APL bastards soon.

Even though she was now a shifter, she still had her seer abilities and that extended to humans now as well. Being able to see a person's true face was a gift she'd never balked at and now she was more thankful for it than ever.

One of the addresses she'd found was the name of a bar about an hour from Fontana. She was glad it wasn't closer to town; right now she just wanted to see what some of these people looked like. Get some names and faces and possibly follow someone back to where he or she lived. She didn't think she could actually kill someone if she wasn't provoked, but given her past, she wasn't even sure about that anymore. The rage inside her was growing every day. It came from a dark place—her inner animal, Aiden had told her—and it wanted out. It wanted blood and that scared the crap out of her human side. But the more she got used to the wolf living inside her, the less and less she wanted to listen to reason.

Like a homing beacon, she felt herself being drawn to this location. According to Liam's list, APL members congregated at Billy's, a fairly wild biker bar that she'd heard of but had never known to be a haven for monsters. Since it was Saturday night Kat hoped she'd be able to blend in easily. If it was teeming with people, she figured it wouldn't be that hard.

As she steered into the parking lot, relief slid through her when she saw it was packed even though it was only nine o'clock. After some searching she found a parking spot. The place wasn't exactly in the middle of nowhere, but it was about ten minutes from the last gas station she'd passed right off the highway. From the outside it looked like a typical place to party and get rowdy. Country music blasted loud enough to be audible out in the parking lot. A giant neon sign hung outside the two-story building announcing this as BILLY'S PLACE, though the E of the sign flickered on and off.

Looking down at herself, Kat hoped she'd picked the right outfit. Dark jeans and a skintight black leather corset that laced up the back—and gave her a decent amount of cleavage. Over it she wore a fitted leather jacket. With all the leather she figured she'd fit in.

Not bothering with a purse, she'd tucked her cell

phone into her jacket pocket and put her money and ID
into her back pocket. With a glance in the rearview mirror, she knew she was as ready as she'd ever be.

A surge of adrenaline raced through her as she
stepped onto the pavement of the parking lot. Which
was stupid. She'd been to bars before—though not by
herself and never with the intention of acting like a private investigator.

Shaking off her insecurities, she wove between the
cars, the heels of her boots making rhythmic clicks
against the pavement. As she neared the front of the bar
where a line of motorcycles sat, she froze.

Then gritted her teeth. Jayce leaned against his bike,
his muscular arms crossed over his chest as he stared at
her. His face was an unreadable mask but she could
scent the annoyance from him. Even with all the other
smells, the sharp spike in the air hit her nostrils . . . and
so did something else.

Something undeniable. It was that dark chocolate smell.
Damn it. *Lust.* Normally she liked her new extrasensory
abilities but this was getting to be annoying. She shoved
her hands in her jacket pockets as she came to stand in
front of him. "You know, you smell."

He arched an eyebrow and she felt her face flame. "I
didn't mean it like that. I just meant . . . Never mind.
What are you doing here?"

He shrugged and stood. Even though she was five feet
eight and was wearing heels, he seemed to tower over
her. "Grabbing a beer."

"Why not find a bar closer to the ranch?"

"I could ask you the same question," he murmured
and took a step closer, bringing him within inches of her.

Crap. This was definitely dangerous territory. Instead
of calling him out on following her—because it would

only invite questions she didn't want to answer—she swiveled toward the doors. "Why don't you grab one with me, then?" Without waiting for a response, she started walking.

Before she'd taken two steps Jayce fell in next to her and put his hand at the small of her back in a proprietary manner. Her first instinct was to shrug it off, but the second they stepped inside, she thought better of it. From the looks of this place, it was more than just "fairly wild." Using her gift of sight, she could tell there were some hard-core criminals on the left side of the bar by the pool tables. Whether or not they'd actually done jail time she had no clue, but they were bad men. Murderers, thieves, a couple of rapists. She still didn't understand how she knew what she did about them, but it was as clear in her mind as if they had their crimes tattooed across their foreheads. She sucked in a deep breath as she stared at the dark auras surrounding the four men wearing black jackets, all with matching insignias.

"What is it?" Jayce murmured, his mouth close to her ear.

She hadn't felt him move until he was right up on her, and even though he knew about her gift, she wasn't about to tell him what she saw. "Nothing." Continuing her visual scan, she realized the rest of the place was a bit tamer than she had originally thought. There was a dance floor and what looked like a lot of college-aged kids dancing, drinking, and having a good time. The majority of their auras were very faint oranges and purples. Lusty people with a lot of energy and vitality. Yeah, that made sense. A lot of them probably came from the Beech, Fontana, or Sugar Mountain ski resorts. She was still getting used to the fact that she could read humans now instead of just seeing the "faces" of supernatural beings.

Rather than heading toward the main bar by the dance floor, she made a beeline for the smaller bar next to the pool tables. Behind her she heard Jayce curse, but he didn't miss a beat before falling in line with her. "What are you doing?" he asked.

"This bar is less crowded and I'm thirsty," she said sweetly as she took a seat at one of the swivel stools.

Instead of sitting, Jayce leaned against the bar next to her so he faced the pool tables. "What made you want to come here anyway?" he asked without looking at her.

"I've heard it's a lot of fun."

"You know I can smell when you're lying." His voice was whisper quiet, but she had no problem hearing him above the din of the packed bar.

"And I can smell when you're turned on," she shot back.

His mouth actually quirked up as he turned back to face her. "That seems to be a permanent problem around you."

She nearly jerked back at the honesty of his statement. Well, damn. For a moment she was speechless until a female bartender wearing tight black leather pants and a shirt that pretty much looked like a bra sauntered up to them. She eyed Jayce with blatant interest, and in addition to scenting the woman's lust, Kat could actually *see* the faint purple aura—which made Kat want to growl and let her claws loose—so she turned away and checked out the area by the pool tables again while Jayce ordered them drinks. That was when she realized the insignia on the backs of the four humans' jackets was lettering. An *A* was in the middle and it almost looked like an anarchy symbol, but then she realized the slashes were a *P* and an *L*. For *APL*. Her eyes narrowed for an instant before she caught herself. This was definitely the place she'd been looking for.

"Something you find interesting over there?" Once again Jayce's mouth was so close to her ear he could practically lick it.

And that thought made her want to squirm in her seat. Instead of answering, she crossed her legs and swiveled so that she faced the bar. Just in time for the bartender to set their beers in front of them. Kat paused, digesting the fact that Jayce remembered what she liked. Not that she was really surprised. Nothing got by him.

"Tell me why you're really here," Jayce finally said.

"I told you—"

He cut her off by grabbing her seat and swiveling her to face him. His face was inches from hers, his eyes a mercurial storm. Now he wasn't trying to hide anything from her.

And she realized she didn't have to hide anything from him. He couldn't stop her from doing what she wanted. "I heard APL members hung out here," she said quietly, though the chance of humans' overhearing them was practically zero.

His gaze hardened. "And just what were you planning on doing to them?"

She shrugged and leaned back in an effort to put some distance between them. "I don't see how that's any of your concern."

A rumbling sound came from deep within his chest. Almost a territorial growl. "Everything you do is my concern." The look he gave her confused and angered her. He had no right to look at her as if she mattered to him. As if he cared about her. Not when it was obvious he wanted her only as a bed partner, nothing more.

"Not anymore it's not." She took a sip of her beer, savoring the refreshing coolness as it slid down her dry throat.

"Did you plan to fight them? Kill them? Follow some of them home?"

When she didn't respond, he let out an annoyed sigh. "Leave through the front of the bar, but meet me around back in a couple minutes."

Surprised, she looked at him. "What?"

"It's time for your second lesson. Never underestimate your opponent."

"What are you going to do?" She eyed him suspiciously. He was being far too relaxed.

"Start a fight," said.

Before she could respond, he was striding toward the pool tables with that arrogant swagger she recognized all too well.

Shit. If he was starting a fight, she had no doubt he'd be the victor. She'd seen him in action a couple of times and the man had a liquid grace and raw strength that scared the holy hell out of her.

Chapter 4

Jayce was almost positive Kat had come here looking for trouble. Or APL members, to be more specific.

After that hot kiss they'd shared earlier he hadn't been able to get her out of his mind—though when was she ever far from his thoughts? He was always wondering what she was doing, where she was and whether she was okay or not. Hell, even when that explosion had tossed him through the air barely hours ago, she'd still been in the recesses of his brain. The feel of her underneath him in that barn, arching up against him, all sexy and pliant, made him ache. He hadn't wanted to stop at kissing. No, he'd been so caught up in the feel of her long, lithe body that he'd broken his own damn rules. They'd been training. He should have had more control.

He'd followed her to apologize but she'd gone to December's house, so he'd waited for her. When he'd seen her leaving, he'd sensed guilt from her. It hadn't been overt—for someone so newly turned she was surprisingly adept at controlling her emotions—but it had struck him as odd. He'd wondered if she felt guilty for kissing him, but quickly dismissed the idea, as it didn't make sense.

Now that he'd followed her here, he wondered if that guilt had anything to do with her appearance at this bar. He'd just barely made it back to Fontana in time to track her. He'd left the laptop with one of Connor's packmates who'd followed Kat back to December's. While he wanted to know what was on it, he wanted to talk to Kat a lot more.

Without outright accusing her, he wouldn't know if she'd taken the list of APL members from Liam's house. Connor had printed out a handful of copies and one had definitely gone to his brother. Unless Kat had been doing some undercover work of her own recently, Jayce couldn't figure how she'd *known* APL members hung out here. And he didn't believe in coincidences.

Jayce had known about this hangout thanks to intel that one of the Council leaders had given him a few weeks ago. The kind of APL members that frequented the bar weren't the kind of guys Kat needed to tangle with. Shifter or not, she was about to learn that things aren't always what they seem. Unless his intel was wrong—and he hoped the hell it was—these guys were likely hopped up on vampire blood, which would give them enhanced strength. It wasn't permanent for humans, but as long as they were drinking it, they could take on vamps and shifters and be on fairly even footing.

Now he was about to find out if the rumors that a certain violent sect of the APL was indeed drinking vamp blood were true. He'd already confirmed that there was at least one dealer in the vicinity selling the shit, so it was likely. And Ned sold to anyone. Not to mention that he'd clearly been taking his own product. Which made sense. He couldn't sell stuff that made his clients super strong without being able to protect his product and himself.

Jayce didn't usually go around starting fights, but right now he had no choice. Kat needed to see what she would have been up against if she'd come in here with guns blazing. The thought of her going off by herself and something else happening to her made him shudder. Nothing would happen to her again. Not as long as he was around to protect her.

Jayce scanned the bar for other possible threats and found none. At least these guys would have a slim chance against him if they were taking vamp blood. Not that he cared one way or another. This was about teaching Kat. He glanced over his shoulder and saw her ducking out the front door.

Perfect.

He quickly reached the pool table where two men, probably in their forties, were playing. Two others, in their mid-twenties, lounged against the wall, both smoking cigarettes.

The two younger guys looked at him curiously, but the two playing pool didn't glance his way.

Time to change that.

Jayce grabbed one of the almost full beers on the edge of the pool table and took a big swig. Then he slammed it down on the table, sloshing the amber liquid everywhere.

One of the men glared at him. "Motherfuc—"

Jayce bared his canines, letting them elongate, then drew them back in. There was a moment of shocked silence; then someone sucked in a quick breath.

Four sets of eyes narrowed at him with pure hatred.

Grinning just to piss them off, Jayce picked up the beer again and took another swig. "I'll be out back if you pussies want to join me." Without waiting for a response, he headed for the exit.

Once outside he spotted Kat leaning against the wall, her arms crossed over her chest, looking sexy as sin. No time to admire her sleek figure, though. "Get behind the Dumpster. *Now*." As he said it, he glanced around. Directly behind the bar was a thick cluster of woods. No cars or people back here thankfully. And more important, no video surveillance.

For a moment he thought Kat might argue, but she muttered something under her breath about him being bossy and then ducked behind the giant green box. Just in time too.

The metal door opened, slamming against the outside wall with a sickening bang. Out burst the four men, cocky and ready for a fight. One already had a gun with a silencer drawn and another held a knife.

Jayce's inner wolf smiled. This was going to be fun. Stripping off his leather jacket, he blindly tossed it toward the building. Before it had hit the concrete wall, Jayce had drawn the two blades he always kept strapped to his chest. The razor-sharp titanium-like weapons gleamed wickedly under the moonlight.

As the enforcer, he preferred fighting with blades and in human form. He didn't trust himself enough to let his beast out. Not for these guys. The situation would have to be a hell of a lot more dangerous for him to do that. He wasn't fully in control of his wolf form, and when he let it out, things tended to get bad and bloody. Of course, they were probably going to get bloody in a few seconds anyway.

One of the younger guys, who had a spiked Mohawk, spoke up. "Where's that slut you walked in with? When we're done with you we'll show her a good time." Lust and something evil oozed out of him.

Jayce didn't think. The blade was out of his hand and embedded in the guy's chest before he could stop himself. The thought of any of these men touching Kat made him want to spill their blood and savage their bodies. He almost never lost self-control. Not over a simple comment. But where Kat was concerned . . . sense didn't enter the equation.

Time seemed to freeze as the man's eyes widened and his mouth opened. But nothing came out. A trickle of blood dripped from the wound and onto his T-shirt. Before anyone could react, the man's body began to disintegrate rapidly, turning to dust and leaving only his clothes behind.

That was when Jayce knew that these men—or at least that one—were taking vamp blood. Likely a lot of it, considering what had just happened. Drinking vampire blood wouldn't turn humans into vamps—it just gave them a lot of strength. Unfortunately for these humans, his two blades, passed to him by his father, had been blessed by the fae about a thousand years ago with a very specific purpose. While against humans they were as deadly as any regular blade, against vampires they were positively lethal. Since the guy was ingesting the supernatural elixir, the magical blades had done what they were made to do: literally suck the life out of those with vamp blood in their system.

In the expanding silence, Jayce wanted to curse himself for his reaction. He hadn't wanted to kill any of them. He'd just wanted to rough them up and show Kat she couldn't afford to underestimate her opponents. If she'd gone up against these guys by herself, she wouldn't have been able to hold her own. Not until she had more training.

No time to dwell on what had happened. The man

with the thick graying beard reacted first. He lifted his pistol and fired at Jayce.

The puffs of air emitted when the bullets passed through the suppressor echoed in Jayce's ears as he used his supernatural speed to dodge out of the way. He rolled to the dirt and gravel surface with lightning speed, striking out with his foot at the closest male.

As Jayce's foot connected with the guy's ankle, the male tumbled back, slamming against the hard earth with a grunt.

Jayce jumped up, extended his arm, and slammed his blade into the guy's chest. The man didn't even get out a cry of surprise before his body also began to deteriorate at sickening speed.

Pain shredded through Jayce's shoulder before he could turn toward the other two men. He'd been shot before, so he knew the sensation, but at least it wasn't a silver bullet. If it had been, the pain would have been more acute.

As adrenaline pumped through him, he dove for his first fallen blade. Picking it up, he threw it again. The sound of flesh tearing and a man's cry greeted his ears, but he ignored it as he hurled himself at the man with the gun.

With his other blade Jayce sliced the man's gun-toting arm, knocking the weapon from the guy's hand and onto the ground. The wound sizzled from the impact of the blade. Groaning, the man lashed out with a balled fist that connected with Jayce's jaw.

The strength behind the punch made it clear that this guy had a hell of a lot more than human strength flowing through him. Jayce exaggerated the effect of the blow, letting his head jerk back as he stumbled.

The man pounced, coming at him with fists flying.

Taking the hits, Jayce twisted under him and shoved up hard with his blade, piercing the guy's heart and penetrating straight through him. Blood began to pour out, but just as quickly it stopped as the man crumbled into nothingness.

The leftover dusty remains spread over Jayce and the ground. There were two heartbeats nearby and one was Kat's. He knew she was safe and that was all that mattered. While he wanted to worry what the effect of her seeing this kind of violence might be, he couldn't allow himself to do that. She needed to be aware of her weaknesses so she could hone her skills and become stronger. The other heartbeat belonged to the fourth man, who was trying to run away. Jayce's eyes narrowed on the back of the man limping toward the corner of the building and carrying Jayce's blade.

"Stop and I'll let you live," he called out.

The older man turned and stumbled forward, clutching the weapon tightly. "Screw you." Blood dripped down his arm, staining the gravel beneath his feet.

Covering the distance in seconds, Jayce stood in front of him. He tapped his blade in his free hand. "Where are you getting the vamp blood? Is Ned Hartwig selling to you?"

The man snorted as if the thought was ridiculous. "We don't go through a middleman." His face paled as soon as he'd spoken.

Yeah, he definitely hadn't meant to let that slip. Jayce's eyes narrowed. "Who is your provider?"

Despite the influence of the vamp blood, the man had still been struck with a fae-blessed weapon. His wound sizzled, light trails of smoke rolling off him as if he'd been burned with acid. He would eventually heal, unless Jayce delivered a fatal blow.

"Why should I tell you?" the man rasped out, a level of fear similar to what Jayce had sensed from Ned rolling off the guy.

"I won't kill you if you do."

The man glanced past Jayce, no doubt to look at Kat, whom he heard walking up behind him. Jayce gritted his teeth. She wasn't supposed to come out yet.

"Doesn't mean you won't let that bitch kill me," he said as his gaze trailed behind Jayce. "Besides, he'll do worse to me than kill me." Before Jayce could stop the guy, he lifted the blade and shoved it through his own heart.

Just like the others, he fragmented into dust instantly. Jayce cursed under his breath. *Damn it.* Who the hell was this guy that he instilled more fear than Jayce did? Even though the Council had learned of the use of vamp blood by humans, they still didn't know who was supplying it. They knew only that popular dealers now had it available. Capturing a vampire wasn't easy. And keeping one captive definitely wasn't. It was entirely possible that a vampire was actually supplying humans with the stuff of his own free will, but Jayce didn't favor that theory. After the way Ned and now this loser had reacted, Jayce figured that whoever was behind this was powerful and scary as fuck. Yeah, there had to be one central provider. The way the APL member had said "he" was too specific. Hell, maybe a shifter was selling it—though that didn't sit right with him either.

"Holy *shit*. I didn't know your blades did *that* to people." Kat glanced around at the piles of clothes before her gaze snapped back to his. "Where can I get one?"

Surprised by her lack of revulsion, he shook his head and motioned to the clothes. "You *can't*, but I'll explain what just happened later. Pick up those clothes and make sure their wallets don't fall out. We can't leave any trace of them behind." Unfortunately the bartender had seen the men head outside after Jayce and he didn't exactly have an unforgettable face. But he knew a vamp who owed him a few favors and he figured it wouldn't be hard to talk his contact into coming down here and scrubbing the bartender's memories.

If humans had known that some vamps had *that* ability, things would have been a lot different when supernatural beings had come out to the world twenty years ago. As it was, each species that came out had kept more than a few secrets from humans. They'd wanted to integrate and have semi-normal existences so they wouldn't have to keep relocating every few decades. That didn't mean they had lost their sense of survival. If anything, it was even sharper now.

Instead of doing as he'd instructed, Kat stared at his shoulder, where blood was dripping down his arm onto his shirt. "Were you shot?" The question came out as a harsh whisper.

The bullet had gone straight through him and the wound was already healing. Ignoring pain like that was easy. It wasn't as if the guy had been packing silver bullets. Jayce had dealt with a hell of a lot worse in the last five hundred years. "This is just a scratch, I promise." But he couldn't risk any humans seeing the blood since he didn't want to draw attention to himself.

After sliding his blades back into their leather sheaths, he grabbed his jacket from the ground, put it on, and zipped it up. Then he palmed the fallen gun and tucked it into the back of his pants. Definitely couldn't afford to leave that behind.

"What are we going to do?" Kat picked up the closest pile of clothes and rolled everything into a tight ball.

"Give me the keys to your Jeep."

"Apparently I'm talking to myself." Kat shook her head as she pulled her keys from her jacket pocket and tossed them to him.

Ignoring her, he retrieved her vehicle and drove it to the side of the bar, as close to the back as he could get without exposing it to anyone who might stumble outside. He didn't like leaving Kat, but it was quicker for him to get the Jeep than to explain anything to her. Right now, time was critical. He'd been damn lucky that none of the drunk patrons had stumbled outside. Or worse, one of the staff. The fight had taken only a couple of minutes—as he'd known it would—but they needed to get the hell out of there. Hanging around a crime scene was not in anyone's best interest.

Leaving the vehicle running, he hurried around the back of the building and grabbed the clothes from Kat. "Come on," he ordered, not waiting to see if she listened.

She mumbled something under her breath but at least she followed. After he dumped everything in the backseat, he practically shoved her into the driver's seat.

"What the hell are you doing?" she finally demanded.

"I'm going to do another sweep and make sure we didn't miss anything. Head to December's house. I'm leaving as soon as I'm finished here. Do *not* detour anywhere else."

A pause. "Okay."

"I'm serious, Kat."

She held up her hands in mock surrender before grasping the wheel. "I won't go anywhere else. And . . . be careful," she snapped before yanking the door shut.

Once she was gone he found bullet casings and a knife that one of the men had dropped. After nothing else turned up, he quickly kicked over the bits of gravel tainted by blood. The men had turned to dust before they'd lost too much blood, so he didn't think that anyone would notice. Especially since no one knew people had been killed back here. Over the years he'd learned that people didn't pay attention to anything unless it directly involved their own lives.

Once he was sure there wasn't anything left behind, he headed back inside. The bar was getting even more packed and the bartender wasn't paying him the least bit of attention. Two sets of couples had taken over the pool table abandoned by the APL bikers.

Jayce continued scanning the bar and did a complete sweep through the entire place. He didn't spot any video surveillance—but that didn't mean there wasn't any. When he asked his vamp contact to attend to the bartender, he would make sure to inquire about surveillance at the bar.

The drive to get to Kat seemed to take forever, but in reality he got there in twenty minutes. Instead of heading straight inside, he made the call to Nikolai.

"What's up, wolf?" Niko's voice was exceptionally gravelly. Before he'd been turned into a vamp he'd almost died as a result of having his throat slit. After he'd been turned, that voice hadn't changed.

He didn't bother with small talk. "Need a favor."

"Lay it on me." After Jayce told Niko what he needed, there was a short pause. Then, "You're sure that's all you need?"

"Yeah. When can you be there?"

"Couple hours, max. I'm a state over, but it won't take me long. I'll be there before they close."

"Thanks. I'll owe you." Since his friend was an ancient vamp, he could fly, a gift that not many vamps had. In fact, Jayce could count on one hand how many he'd heard of with that ability.

Niko grunted. "Right. I still owe *you*. Next time you call, make sure it's for something that'll even the score between us. You know I hate owing a shifter *anything*." Despite the joking tone, Jayce didn't miss the roughness of his voice. Jayce didn't take it personally. Niko didn't like owing anyone, not him specifically.

"I'll see what I can come up with."

After he disconnected, he headed for the front door. There was no one watching the house tonight. When he'd given the laptop to the shifter watching Kat, he'd asked him to pass on the message to Connor that he himself would be guarding Kat for a while. The pack didn't have the resources to keep an eye on her—something she didn't seem to understand, but that he planned on explaining soon—and he didn't want her out of his sight anyway.

Especially not after tonight.

Before he had a chance to knock, the door flew open. Kat stepped back to let him in, and as soon as the door shut behind her, she started in with the questions. "Did you have any trouble?"

"No."

"What about that bartender? Even if the bodies of those guys disappeared—you still have to explain how you did that, by the way—she probably saw them follow you outside."

"She's been taken care of."

Her blue eyes widened. "What do you mean, 'taken care of'? Oh my God, did you ... do something to her too?" A trace of fear laced her voice.

"Damn, woman. No. I ... I'm grabbing a beer." He scrubbed a hand over his face and headed toward the kitchen. Did she actually think he'd killed an innocent woman? Maybe that shouldn't hurt him so much, but if she truly thought so little of him it pierced a part of himself he didn't want to admit existed. He swallowed hard, shoving back the foreign emotion that pushed up inside him. He didn't give a shit what anyone thought about him. Something he needed to remind himself. Most shifters had an opinion of him simply because of his reputation. That opinion being that he killed first and asked questions later. Maybe it shouldn't surprise him that Kat would jump to that conclusion too. Unfortunately it did. He'd showed her a side of himself that he'd never showed anyone else. She should know better.

"Grab me one too," she called out.

With two domestic beers in hand, he found her in the living room sitting on the couch. She had her feet tucked under her and her arms wrapped tightly around herself. "I didn't mean to imply you'd killed that woman. Well, maybe I did, but I didn't mean it as an insult. I just wondered what you meant when you said you'd taken care of her."

Jayce took a long swig of his beer before collapsing on the other end of the couch. There was enough distance between them that he couldn't reach out and cup her cheek or run his hands through her hair even though that was exactly what he wanted to do. "I called in a favor. A vamp friend of mine is going to scrub her memories."

Kat blinked in astonishment and the sweet scent of shock rolled off her. *"What?"*

Now that she wasn't simply human anymore, there were certain things he could tell her. "There's a lot you don't know—and it's going to take more than one conversation to cover all this—but when vampires and the shifter Councils from around the world decided to reveal their existence, we didn't tell humans everything."

"Like the fact that vampires can apparently scrub people's minds?" She arched a dark eyebrow at him.

"How do you think *that* would have gone over? First we reveal that we can turn into animals and that vamps drink blood to survive, then let the humans know that some vamps *also* have the ability to make humans forget things if necessary. Probably would have made our 'acceptance' a little different."

Things were still tense in certain parts of the world even twenty years later and not everyone had accepted their existence—the APL was proof enough of that. Giving humans more ammunition would have been a poor tactical move.

"Good point." She shook her head before downing half the beer. "Holy crap. I can't believe that." She bit her bottom lip for a moment and all he could think about was how he'd like to tug it between his own teeth. But then she continued. "I guess no one knows your blades can turn people to dust either?" There wasn't fear in her voice or her scent, just a certain amount of wariness as she eyed him.

"They don't turn *people* to dust. My blades were blessed by the fae about a thousand years ago. Without going into the hows or whys, my blades were designed specifically to kill vampires." Long ago their species had been at war. Hell, all supernatural species had battled each other at one time or another.

"Really? I thought all the supernatural beings got along. There's a she-cat and a fae living at the ranch."

"That's not normal. Neither is you living away from your own pack," he added.

Kat scowled at that, but didn't comment. "You said

your vampire friend was doing you a favor. Why would you want something that can kill them?"

"It kills feral shifters too." He kept his voice devoid of emotion.

"You didn't answer my question."

"No. I didn't. I'd much rather talk about why you were at that bar tonight."

She swallowed hard and glanced down at the beer in her hand. "I already told you."

Even if he couldn't scent the lie, he could tell just by looking at her that she wasn't being truthful. Instead of calling her out, he decided to try a different tactic. "I know there's a lot you don't understand about pack life, but stealing something from anyone in your pack is grounds for punishment." In some packs, the Alpha would have the right to whip a transgressor. Humans might view the practice as archaic or brutal, but shifters weren't human and animals lived by a different code. In Connor's pack, Jayce figured the Alpha would probably put Kat under lockdown for a couple of weeks.

Her jaw clenched, but she didn't respond. Damn, he'd forgotten how she used to stonewall him. If she didn't want to talk about something, it'd be hell getting it out of her. Tonight he didn't want to argue or interrogate her to find out if she'd stolen information from Liam or December. He just wanted to be with her. So far she hadn't kicked him out, and as late as it was, he wasn't going back to the ranch. Something he wasn't sure she realized. "You saw what happened to those APL members tonight?"

Kat's head snapped up at the question. "Yeah."

"The reason they disintegrated like that is because they were drinking vampire blood. They weren't actually vampires, but they had enough vamp blood in their systems that my blades destroyed them." Jayce had mentioned this intel to Connor, who oddly enough hadn't seemed surprised. Now that he'd located actual people taking the stuff—and unfortunately killed all of them—the Alpha needed to know that humans in his area were getting hopped up on it.

"They were stronger than normal humans, weren't they?"

He nodded. "Yeah. If you'd decided to go after them by yourself, you'd have lost. They'd have likely killed you. Probably worse."

Her face paled and he hated himself for the pain and haunted memories he saw there, but she needed to understand that she wasn't indestructible just because she was stronger now, and if she put herself in certain situations, the outcome would be bad.

"You're not invincible just because you're a shifter," he said softly.

"I know," she whispered, her voice wobbly.

Now he really felt like shit. Staring into her blue eyes, he opened his mouth but couldn't find any words. Not when she looked at him like that. Not when he saw pain and agony there and knew he couldn't do a damn thing about it.

His hands balled into fists almost subconsciously. He had to force himself to open them again and relax. Seeing Kat in any sort of pain made his animal side come roaring to the surface. It didn't matter that the man who'd hurt her—in what ways Jayce still didn't know—was dead. His beast wanted blood from someone. Anything to assuage Kat's grief.

She was the first to look away. As she did, she set her beer on the coffee table and he knew she was planning to leave the room. Probably heading to bed. But he couldn't let her go. Not just yet. He wanted to spend more time with her.

"What did you do with those clothes?" he asked.

"Left them in my Jeep." She leaned forward slightly, as if she were about to get up.

His heart pounded mercilessly and he hated himself for the weakness. Around her, he always felt like a randy cub. So out of his element it was fucking embarrassing. "I'll dispose of them later. You feel like watching a movie?"

She faltered and scooted back a couple of inches. "Uh, yeah?"

"Is that a question?"

"Yes. I mean, no. I do want to watch a movie." Her cheeks tinged pink as she reached for the remote and turned on the television. She scrolled to the movie listings. When she hovered over the latest action release, she arched an eyebrow. "This okay?"

"Sure." He didn't care what the hell they watched as long as he was with her. It didn't matter that he'd spend the next two hours fantasizing about holding her, kissing her, licking her everywhere until she moaned; he could deal with the discomfort if he could just be near her. "So how's your father?" he asked as she leaned back against the couch and grabbed an afghan to wrap around her shoulders.

His fingers itched as he stared at the afghan and found himself jealous of an inanimate fucking object.

"Good, I guess, but I haven't told him about what happened."

Jayce's eyebrows shot up. "Why not?"

She gave him a tart look that said he should already know the answer. "Because I don't need him to bust in here and ruin the life I've started. If he found out someone hurt me he'd go after anyone he thought might be a member of the APL. It would get too messy. Hell, he'd probably want to hurt Aiden for turning me even though he saved my life."

A low growl built up in Jayce's throat. He had fantasies of hurting Aiden too, but for different reasons. "Maybe that wouldn't be such a bad thing," he said under his breath.

Kat narrowed her eyes. "What's the matter with you? Aiden is a good wolf. If it wasn't for him, I wouldn't be here," she snapped.

Even though she was right, the obvious protectiveness she felt for Aiden ratcheted up Jayce's anger. Aiden had had the same protective scent when Jayce had told him he'd be the one training Kat from now on. Yeah, that hadn't gone over well at all with the other wolf. But Jayce couldn't think about him or even talk about him without getting pissed. Right now, he just wanted to spend a couple of hours with Kat without arguing. Well, he wanted more than that.

Sure, he missed sex with her. What sane male wouldn't? Being celibate since she'd left him was damn near torture. But just sex wasn't what he wanted right now. She needed to know he'd be there to support her no matter what came her way. That she wasn't alone anymore. Yes, she had her pack, but more importantly she had him. Whether she liked it, or accepted him, didn't matter. He might not have been able to protect her before, but that wasn't ever happening again. By training her he was trying to give her the means to look out for herself in any situation. Even if they didn't have a future together as mates, she was his to protect and he would do that at all costs. Instead of answering her, he turned toward the television and propped his boots up on the coffee table.

Next to him Kat sank deeper against the seat, letting her head fall slightly back against the couch. She wasn't entirely at ease—the discomfort he'd sensed from the moment he'd seen her strutting toward him at that bar looking like pure sex and sin remained—but at least she wasn't running away from him.

It wasn't much, but it was a start.

Chapter 5

Kat opened her eyes at the insistent ringing sound. Blinking, she shook her head and looked around the living room. The muted earth tones were bathed in streams of bright sunshine coming through the partially open wooden-slat blinds behind her.

Why am I sleeping in the living room? And fully dressed? Looking down at the leather top and jeans she still had on, she felt the night come crashing back. Jayce had killed those men—she still wasn't sure how she felt about that—then they'd come back here and started to watch a movie. She didn't remember any of it, though. Must have dozed off almost immediately. She hadn't had any nightmares either. That gave her pause. Being around Jayce had always grounded her, but that couldn't have been why she'd slept so peacefully. Could it?

Ding-dong.

It wasn't a ringing sound. Someone was pressing the doorbell. Clearing her throat, she softly called out, "Jayce?" With his incredible senses she had no doubt he'd hear her.

No response.

Throwing off the warm afghan, she hurried to the front door. When she looked through the peephole and saw Parker and another police officer standing on the front porch, her heart jumped in her throat. Parker was in uniform, so she knew this wasn't a social call. Instead of answering the door dressed as she was, she raced up the stairs, threw on a pair of long-sleeved pajamas, then dashed back down.

As the bell rang again, she pulled the door open. "Parker? Is everything okay?"

His nod was curt. "We need to talk to you about something."

Warning bells went off in her head. Had someone seen them last night? Where was Jayce? Now that she was fully awake she scented traces of him in the house, but they were weak. He must have left a while ago. She kept her features bland. She'd lied to the cops before when she'd been kidnapped. She could do it again.

"Okay. What is it?"

"This would be better if we talked about it down at the station."

Those warning bells now turned into full-fledged alarms. "Am I under arrest?"

"No. I'd just like to know where you were the night before last."

"Two nights ago?" Relief flooded her. Parker didn't want to know about last night. She shrugged. "I was up at Kelly's Bar and Grill. Why?"

"Did you leave with anyone?"

She could feel her face flame at the question. "How is that any of your business?"

"Kat, I really don't want to do this here." He looked

at the uniformed officer, who wore a stony stare as he assessed her.

The fine hairs on Kat's arms rose but she shook the feeling off. She tried to use her seer abilities to get a read on him, but it was like he had a stone wall in front of him. He was just blank. Maybe he was one of those people who had a natural psychic shield. Parker actually did too, for the most part, but she could at least see a muddy, dark blue aura very faintly around him before it faded. It wasn't a science, but she'd been slowly figuring out what colors coincided with obvious emotions and Parker was definitely worried about something. Her, maybe? God, she hoped not.

"Fine. You can wait outside while I get changed. I'm not going down to the station wearing my pajamas."

The officer made a sound like he wanted to protest, but Parker simply nodded. "We'll be waiting."

After shutting the door, Kat fought the panic rising inside her. If this had been any other day she'd have told the sheriff she wasn't going down to the station unless they were arresting her—even if he was December's brother, she knew her rights. But she'd noticed that her Jeep was missing from the driveway and Jayce's motorcycle was still there. Maybe he'd gone to dispose of the evidence from last night. Whatever he was doing, she didn't want to have to deal with him and questions from the cops if he got back soon. Especially if he hadn't gotten rid of those clothes. The jackets they'd taken were easily identifiable. Not to mention that she had no clue what Jayce had done with the weapons he'd picked up from the dead APL members last night. If they were lying around December's house, she wouldn't be able to explain them away if Parker decided he wanted to come inside. December was the one who owned the house, and Kat wasn't sure what the laws were.

It was definitely better to be safe than sorry. She quickly changed into jeans and a sweater. After running a comb through her tangled hair, she brushed her teeth and grabbed a small purse.

She wiped her palms on her jeans as she descended the stairs. As long as Parker wasn't questioning her about last night, she figured she was okay. She hadn't committed or witnessed a crime two nights ago, so she had nothing to feel guilty about—something she needed to remind herself of if she wanted to convince the sheriff that she was above reproach.

A couple of hours later Kat resisted the urge to punch the detective sitting across the table from her. Detective Chance Kinsey had rough, calloused hands. A workingman's hands. He was also incredibly good-looking, and he'd been trying to use that against her from the moment he'd taken a seat. As if Mr. Tall, Dark, and Sexy with the gorgeous toothpaste-commercial smile was going to sway her. *Please.* First, he definitely wasn't her type. Second, her father was an arms dealer. Not something she was proud of, but she knew her rights and she knew these guys were fishing for information. About what, she still hadn't figured out. As soon as she got an idea of what they wanted from her, she was leaving.

"So you're saying you just left Scott Ford's house because you changed your mind about sleeping with him?"

"Yep." She kept her expression cool.

"You don't think that's a little odd?"

"Last time I checked, no means no and I don't owe some guy sex because he bought me a few drinks. I changed my mind about hooking up with him, so I left."

His dark eyes narrowed. "Without a car?"

"For the third time, yes."

"It's January." He said the word slowly, as if she were stupid.

She knew what the detective was getting at. Walking home in the middle of the winter was crazy. But she was a shifter, so it wasn't that crazy. Plus December's house wasn't all that far from Scott's place. There was no way in hell she was telling this guy Jayce had followed her to some human's house and she'd left with him. Especially since she was beginning to think Scott Ford was dead. After the way Jayce had acted around that human, she was a little fearful that he'd gone back and done something. Even if he had, she wasn't going to narc him out. Instead of responding to the detective—since he hadn't asked a question—she sat still and waited for him to make the next move.

Finally he spoke again. "Did you ever go inside Scott's house?"

"No." At least she could answer that honestly.

"Are you sure?"

"I'm sure." *Don't offer up any information and keep your answers short if you're ever questioned by the cops.* How many times had her father drilled that into her head when she was growing up? That was one of the first lessons he'd taught her and she'd only been eight. At the time she'd hated it. And hated him a little if she was honest. She'd always wanted a normal family. One that didn't think cops were the enemy. Now she thought maybe normal was overrated.

"What about his truck? Will your fingerprints be in there?"

Her eyes narrowed as her annoyance increased. Even though she wanted to keep her cool, this was getting ridiculous. "What do you think? I rode with him from the bar to his house. Now why don't you tell me what all this is about or I'm going to walk right out the door. You're not arresting me, and if you do, I'll call my lawyer." To prove her point, she stood up.

The moment she did, Kinsey's face darkened, all charm disappearing. The handsome detective took on a dangerous edge she hadn't noticed before. The man was almost a closed book as far as her seer abilities went. He definitely had natural psychic walls, sort of like Parker. She got only brief glimpses of his aura. A sharp flash of red almost seemed to pop off him for a moment, but then it dissipated like mist. Red meant a lot of things, including anger. And she had no doubt the man was angry. She didn't need any of her seer abilities to figure that out, though. Right now she could actually *scent* his fury. Something raw and sharp burst into the air, jarring her. He opened the manila envelope that had been sitting in front of him and dumped out a handful of glossy eight-by-ten photos.

Kat felt the color drain from her face as she stared at the pictures of blood and gore in front of her. It took a moment for her brain to compute what she was seeing. Body parts. Everywhere. All over what looked like a kitchen. Bile rose in her throat, forcing her to turn around. She slapped a hand over her mouth, trying not to throw up on the dingy tile floor. She clutched her stomach while gagging until she felt the detective's presence behind her.

He held the small trash can she'd seen in the corner of the room in his hand. "Do you need this?"

Shaking her head, she swallowed a few times until she was sure she wouldn't be sick, then sat back down. Thankfully, he'd put the pictures away.

The detective leaned against the table next to her seat, looking down at her. She knew what he was doing, trying to use his size and position to intimidate her. At the moment she didn't care. Breaking her own rule of not talking more than necessary, she asked, "What was that? Or who . . . was that?"

"Scott Ford." His face betrayed nothing.

She blinked once, still trying to grasp what she'd seen. "And you think *I* did that?" She couldn't keep the incredulity out of her voice.

"Did you?"

"No." She gritted her teeth.

"We know you were turned into a shifter not long ago."

Her brow furrowed. She hadn't publicly announced it, but it wasn't a secret. If this guy actually thought she was capable of what those photos showed, she decided to prove she hadn't done it. She could hear her father's voice in her head telling her to get a lawyer, but she squashed it. She'd done nothing wrong. Well, two nights ago she hadn't. "You want my DNA to prove I didn't do that?"

The detective leaned back slightly, gauging her. "You're not required to do that."

"I know, but if it'll help eliminate me as a suspect to find whoever did"—she motioned to the now closed envelope—"that, I'm willing to cooperate." The second the words were out of her mouth, the door opened and Parker walked in.

"Come on, Kat." Parker motioned with his hand.

Detective Kinsey shook his head and stood. "I can take her—"

"I've got her." Parker's voice didn't leave room for argument.

As soon as she was out in the hall with Parker, his face softened. Luckily that muddy blue aura had completely disappeared so maybe he wasn't worried about her anymore. "I'm sorry I wasn't in there. Since you're friends with December, there couldn't be any appearance of impropriety. As soon as we get your DNA, you can leave. I'm sorry we dragged you down here, but you were on the video surveillance with him at the bar and your prints were in his truck."

Kat swallowed at the words "video surveillance." If she was on it, that meant Jayce was likely on it too. Something heavy settled in her stomach. She hoped Jayce hadn't been behind that awful attack, but if he had been she really hoped the cops didn't link him to it. Even though she knew he should be punished if he killed that guy, she hated the thought of him being caged. Or worse. She knew a man like Jayce wouldn't go to jail and the humans wouldn't let a crime like this go unpunished. And since when had she stopped thinking of herself as human? Her animal side was taking over faster than she'd expected and it scared the crap out of her. Giving herself a mental shake, she smiled politely at Parker as he held a door open for her. "I understand, Parker. You should have just told me what you wanted instead of wasting all this time, though."

She needed to keep it together while she was here. As soon as they let her go, she had to find Jayce.

Kat pulled her sunglasses down over her eyes as she exited the police station. She'd called December to ask her for a ride since Parker had driven her to the station. She would have asked him to take her home, but he'd been called away and she wasn't going to get into a vehicle with that detective even though he'd offered. Not that he put off a bad vibe; she just didn't like him after that long, tedious interrogation.

As she looked around the parking lot, her stomach clenched when she spotted two very pissed-off-looking shifters headed her way. Connor and Jayce were practically stalking toward her, their boots thumping on the pavement. *What was their problem?* It wasn't as if she'd said anything to the cops.

She opened her mouth to ask what was going on, but Connor grasped her elbow firmly. "Come on," he growled.

Jayce caged her in on the other side as they directed her back to Connor's truck. She swallowed hard at her Alpha's tone. Ever since she'd joined his pack he'd been nothing but nice. And he'd saved her life back when she'd been human and two lunatics had kidnapped her with devious purposes. Of course that was before she'd been taken the second time. She owed Connor and she trusted him. Now there was a deadly edge to him that reminded her of Jayce.

"Why are you guys here?" Why did her voice have to shake? She'd done *nothing* wrong.

Neither responded until they were in the vehicle. She sat in the front seat, Connor in the driver's seat, and Jayce in the back.

Connor let out a low, annoyed breath. "Why the *hell* didn't you call me when you got brought in for questioning?"

She frowned and looked back at Jayce, then Connor. "Why would I have done that?"

"Because I'm your Alpha." There he went with that growl again.

Oh, crap. Maybe she'd broken a pack law or something. "I didn't know I was supposed to."

"It's not her fault," Jayce said quietly. "She hasn't had much education about our ways."

"And that's my fault." Connor's gaze narrowed on her once again. "You're moving back to the ranch tonight. I can't have something like this happening again. You are mine to protect. I know you don't understand everything about pack laws, but there's a hierarchy and you're going to learn it, starting now."

Fear spiked inside her, sharp and jagged. Its cloying scent nearly suffocated her, but she couldn't smother it or hide it from them. Her throat closed up impossibly tight as she fought to breathe. She'd had her freedom taken from her a month ago. Living on the ranch wouldn't exactly be a hardship, but she couldn't be forced into anything. Especially not when she was still suffering from nightmares. With everyone's extrasensory abilities, there was no telling who would hear her if she cried at night. There was no way that was happening. It was one thing to wake up crying and sweating and terrified from memories that wouldn't leave her alone and it was another for others to be aware of her weakness. No, thank you.

Before she could respond, Jayce cut in. "I'll stay at December's house with her. I'll be her shadow and teach her about pack laws. She won't ever be out of my sight."

"Like this morning?" Connor diverted his attention to Jayce.

"You know why I was gone this morning," Jayce snapped.

The testosterone in the air was worse than it had been during her earlier spike of fear. The scent helped her to get herself under control. She cleared her throat. "I don't need anyone watching over me."

Connor stared at her hard. "I don't care what you want or what you think you need. You have two choices. Live at the ranch or have Jayce live with you temporarily.

Then once he's gone, you'll move to the ranch permanently unless you wish to find another pack."

Gone? For some reason Kat hadn't even thought about Jayce leaving. He wasn't part of Connor's pack. Kat knew that, but it just hadn't registered with her that he would be leaving again—probably once they'd gotten rid of the APL faction here. Or at least that was her guess. She still wasn't completely sure why he was back in Fontana. He was so private about what he did for the Council. And she knew that she wasn't the sole reason. Or even the reason at all. So why did she feel like he'd be betraying her—*abandoning her*—when he left? She shouldn't even care about him after the way he'd lied to her, but deep down she liked his presence in her life. She also hated it. It was a weird dichotomy. Despite their history and Jayce's tendency to put her on edge while simultaneously pissing her off, she knew he had her back. The thought of him leaving tore a hole inside her gut. "I'm not—"

"Choose." There was so much raw power in that one word—an order—she understood why Connor was Alpha.

Something bone-deep inside her wanted to hide as she felt his strength ripple over her. "Jayce can stay with me." The words were out of her mouth before she could stop herself.

Sleeping under the same roof as Jayce would be torturous, but it was better than being cooped up on the ranch and feeling like a prisoner. At least with Jayce she would have some semblance of control over herself and her comings and goings. On the ranch everyone would know her business. That thought made her shudder. With the exception of December, Liam, and Aiden, she hardly knew anyone else. But the pack knew how she'd been found and that she'd been turned because she'd been at death's door. She didn't want to be the subject of gossip. What happened to her hadn't been her fault. She knew that on an intellectual level. But that didn't make the nightmares any easier and she refused to be around a bunch of strangers who would pity her or look at her differently.

"Fine. What did the cops want with you?" Connor switched topics so smoothly, his demeanor toning down, it surprised her.

She shot Jayce a quick glance before looking at Connor. "They wanted to know my whereabouts two nights ago. I left a bar with this guy, a human, but I never went inside his house." Feeling almost guilty at the thought of betraying his presence there, she didn't mention Jayce.

Her Alpha nodded. "I know. Jayce told me."

Okay, so she had no reason to feel guilty. "Oh. Well, the guy is dead. Ripped apart, actually." Even remembering what those pictures looked like made her stomach heave. "After hours of going around in circles with their questioning I finally told them I was leaving if they didn't tell me what they wanted. They thought I was involved with Scott's—that was his name—murder. So I offered to give them my DNA."

Both men swore at the same time. Surprised, she looked back and forth between them. "What's wrong with that? I didn't do anything to that guy."

"We don't ever give our DNA to cops unless they have a court order." There was no room for argument in Connor's voice.

"But why not if I'm innocent?"

"Pack law and Council law." Connor's jaw clenched tightly. "If you're ever questioned by the police again, call me or him. He's the lawyer for the entire pack." He handed her a white business card with simple black lettering listing a pricey attorney's name that she recognized. Even her father couldn't get this guy on retainer.

She didn't understand Connor's reasoning, but she didn't press him further.

"What else did they want to know?" Jayce asked.

Kat filled them in on everything, including her lie about walking home by herself. Jayce and Connor were both pissed that she'd lied because someone might have seen Jayce, but she hadn't been thinking about that. She'd only been thinking about protecting Jayce. She wanted to ask him if he'd been involved with Scott's death, but she decided to wait until Connor was gone. She might be angry with Jayce for a lot of things, but she wouldn't throw him under the bus. Since there was so much she still didn't understand about shifter rules and regulations, she figured keeping her mouth shut was the best thing at the moment.

After Connor dropped them off at December's house, Kat couldn't wait until they were inside to start questioning Jayce. "Did you get rid of all those clothes?"

He nodded as he shut the front door behind them. "And the weapons. Why did you go with the cops this morning?"

Starving after being cooped up all day, she shrugged and headed for the kitchen. "They had questions for me."

As she started to open the refrigerator door, his big hand landed right by her head, keeping it shut. With her back to him, she couldn't see his expression, but there was an odd scent coming from him. It wasn't lust, but she couldn't put her finger on it. It was dark and rich but she'd never smelled it before. And it put her on edge in a way she couldn't explain, making her tense.

"I know your father taught you better than that. You didn't have to go with them. Or answer the door, for that matter." His voice was a low purr next to her ear.

She tried to fight the shiver that twined through her, but it was useless. And considering that Jayce's chest was pressed up against her back, she knew he had to feel it too. "My Jeep wasn't here and you were gone. I didn't know when you were coming back and I didn't want them to see you."

"You also lied to them about my presence at that guy's house. If I didn't know any better I'd think you were trying to protect me," he murmured so close to her ear that she wouldn't have been surprised if he'd sucked her earlobe between his teeth.

Even thinking about him doing that made her knees turn to jelly. But she couldn't let him know. If he sensed any weakness, he'd pounce. After that kiss yesterday she couldn't afford to let her guard down around him. She might not want him in trouble with the police, but that didn't mean she planned to let him back into her life. Steeling herself, she snorted, dismissing his statement. "Don't flatter yourself. I was looking out for myself."

That rich scent intensified and wrapped around her, flooding all her senses as if he were actually embracing her. Her eyes drifted shut as he pushed closer for an instant. The feel of all that strength behind her made her want to turn around and wrap her arms around his neck. Press her lips to his. Feel his chest pressing against her own. Give in to her cravings. It would be so easy. He'd already made it clear she could come to him anytime she wanted sexual release. Her lower abdomen tightened as she envisioned them tangled together, sweaty and out of breath while he gave her the kind of pleasure she'd only ever known with him.

Then he pulled away and she jerked back to reality. Jayce left the kitchen. She wasn't sure how much time passed, but she eventually opened the fridge door. She stared at the contents without really seeing anything. She'd almost given in to him. What was the matter with her? She needed Jayce to help her train. Nothing more. As long as she remembered that, she'd be able to hold on to her self-control.

Chapter 6

Brianna steered her car into the parking lot of Gwen's Bakery. According to December, they had the best pastries in town. Not that Brianna cared one way or another. She was here for one purpose: to make contact with the wife of an APL member.

As a member of the Fianna, or fae warriors, Brianna had certain mental capabilities. Her strongest skill was influencing some humans' thoughts for brief periods of time, but nothing on the scale that vampires could. She certainly couldn't erase memories and replace them with new ones, though she wished she could. Still, she could hold her own in battle.

But that wasn't why she'd been sent undercover by her leaders. She'd been chosen because of her gender and appearance. Unlike other fae warriors, who were unusually tall and graceful, she was petite and nonthreatening in appearance. She might hate that she stood out so blatantly among her own people, but it was much easier for her to blend in among the humans.

Her two older brothers were angry that she'd decided

to come back to Fontana, but luckily their rulers dismissed their concerns. Only one hundred years old, she was centuries younger than her brothers, but tired of being coddled. She'd gone undercover on her own and even though that monster Adler had been a constant drain on her mental capabilities, she had her strength back now. More importantly, she'd learned how humans thought. Unlike the black-and-white world of the fae, the world of humans was colored in shades of gray. So many were easily fueled by hatred, ignorance, love, passion, and a million other emotions. It made them unpredictable at times, but to her they were absolutely fascinating.

As she opened the glass door, a little bell jingled above her, but Brianna ignored it. Her focus was solely on the brunette in the frumpy clothes pouring creamer into her medium-sized cup of coffee. The same as she'd done yesterday.

As soon as Connor had given her that list of names and addresses, she'd gone hunting, and what she'd found was a possible way in again. Most of the male APL members she'd checked out weren't married, so her pool of targets was very limited. Of the few who were married, she'd found only one easy target. But first she had to befriend this woman. Jackie Anderson.

Brianna headed for the counter where extra napkins, creamers, straws, and sugars were. Then she stumbled in her boots and collided with the woman, effectively knocking her coffee over.

"I'm so sorry," the woman said.

The fact that she apologized when the fault had been completely Brianna's reinforced her decision to target this woman. After watching her yesterday Brianna had noticed an inherent loneliness about her. She'd come to the bakery in the morning, gotten coffee and a bagel and stared out the window, simply watching people pass for hours. The loose jeans and oversized sweater did nothing for the woman's small frame and almost seemed to be a shield from the outside world.

"The fault is completely mine. Let me get you another drink." When Brianna smiled, the other woman gave her a tentative smile in return and Brianna found herself experiencing a totally human emotion. Guilt.

She didn't like using people, especially someone who seemed almost broken, but she had no choice. This group had to be stopped before their influence spread. So far Ireland was untouched, but the fae hadn't remained strong for centuries by ignoring problems. Eliminating the APL was a priority. If she had to pretend to be friends with someone, well, she'd certainly done a lot worse in the past.

Kat stepped out of December's house, battling the continuous guilt that flowed through her. She and Jayce had come to the ranch well over an hour ago. She'd assumed he'd be having dinner with her, December, and Liam, but he'd walked her to the door of their home and then left after telling her that he had something to do. Of course he hadn't given her any details, so she'd stayed and had dinner with her friends. Neither of them knew she'd taken photos of that list of APL members with her phone and e-mailed them to herself. And she hated that sick feeling in the pit of her stomach—the one that told her she was a liar. But the animal inside her ruthlessly shoved her feelings aside. She was going to bring down the APL any way she knew how. There was no room for guilt right now.

As she trekked toward the barn she waved at a few of the pack members out walking. Some of the males were

coming in from the fields and woods, no doubt from patrolling, and a few females were sitting on their porches
talking with each other. Deep inside, Kat craved fitting
in with this group of shifters, but she was too afraid to
put herself out there. Growing up she'd never had a lot
of friends—who in their right mind wanted to let their
kids be friends with an arms dealer's daughter? Forget
about having relationships. Most men had been afraid to
approach her and the ones who hadn't been afraid had
just wanted an in to her father's business.

Until Jayce.

He hadn't been afraid of her father in the least and he
hadn't needed her as a contact to get to know her father.
Jayce had simply approached him on his own. And then
he'd approached her. It had taken months, but she'd finally agreed to go out with him.

He'd been so arrogant and infuriating, but he'd in-
trigued her like no other man ever had. She'd only
agreed to go out with him in an effort to prove to herself
that she could handle it, that she wouldn't get tangled up
with him. How wrong she had been. Some days it felt
like going out with him had been the biggest mistake of
her life. If she hadn't done that, she would never have
known the pain of leaving him. That had been worse
than the torture she'd endured, because it just wouldn't
heal. Even though it had been her decision to break up,
she felt as if someone had ripped her heart out of her
chest with their bare hands. Unfortunately the damn
thing had just kept on beating. Moving to Fontana and
starting fresh hadn't made a difference either. She
couldn't outrun her feelings.

Gritting her teeth, she shook her head. Thinking
about the past served no purpose. She just wanted to go
home, take a hot bath, and sleep. Even though part of

her hated the thought of sharing a roof with Jayce, another part of her reveled in it. Last night she'd actually slept soundly. She couldn't help but wonder if her animal side had felt safe for the first time since her attack. She didn't want to give him that much credit, but she wasn't stupid. It couldn't be a coincidence that she hadn't had any nightmares last night when she'd suffered them every night for a month before that.

As she entered the barn, she froze. Jayce was on top of Erin, straddling the she-wolf's petite body. Something sharp pierced Kat's heart. The burning sensation spread through her chest like acid. She fought to breathe. When he turned those gray eyes on her, she was locked in position. Even though she ordered her feet to move, they wouldn't. Trapped by that penetrating stare, it was like she wore concrete boots that forced her to stay in place, to endure the torture of seeing him with another woman. Her inner wolf screamed at her to attack the other female. The impact of the emotion slammed through her body. She needed to get away before she lost control. But she couldn't move.

Jayce's head tilted slightly to the side, as if he was confused by her arrival. Guess he hadn't expected her so soon. And she hadn't expected him to be fooling around with someone else. She might not have any claim on him, but after he'd told her to come to him for sex, she'd just assumed he wasn't seeing anyone else. How utterly stupid she'd been. Bile rose in her throat. She needed to get out of there.

Before she could take a step back, Erin twisted underneath him and slammed her elbow across his face. At that moment Kat realized that Jayce hadn't been getting intimate with Erin—they were *training*. He'd had a wooden sparring baton pressed against Erin's neck. Kat just hadn't noticed it. All she'd seen was Jayce on top of another woman. She hated that she couldn't un-see it either. Something raw and primitive festered inside her as that vision played over and over in her head. She had no right to care what he did with other women. So why did an annoying voice in the recesses of her subconscious scream *mine*?

Now he was flat on his back and Erin had a giant grin on her face as she pressed a similar-looking baton to his throat. "Way to lose your concentration, *teacher*."

Seeing the two of them so relaxed together made the dagger already embedded in Kat's heart twist. It also gave her the much-needed ability to step back. Turning away from them, she left the barn and headed for one of the fields to go for a run in wolf form. She thought she heard Jayce curse behind her, but she ignored the sound.

Being near him right now wasn't good for her sanity. She couldn't believe she'd let the sight of him with Erin affect her. Obviously nothing had been going on between them, but for all she knew Jayce had someone else waiting for him. Or had been with a dozen women since they'd broken up. He was a very sexual male, and even though he'd been absolutely faithful when they'd been together, she didn't doubt that he'd found someone else to warm his bed since they broke up.

The thought of that made the dagger not only twist but shred her insides. The blood drained from her face as unwanted visions swamped her. Jayce wasn't hers anymore and it was something she needed to remind herself of. He'd said she could come to him for sex.

Sex.

Nothing more. Considering that she didn't want anything else from him either, why did she care so much if he was screwing other women?

Picking up her pace, she sprinted until she reached the tree line. Then she stripped and left her clothes in a neat pile by a giant oak tree. If she didn't expend this raging energy inside her, she was likely to snap and do something stupid. Like start a fight with Erin for no reason. Thanks to her higher body temperature now that she was a shifter, the cold didn't affect her as much as it had when she'd still been human.

Aiden had told her that those who had been turned into shifters as opposed to being born shifters had to really concentrate to undergo the change from human to animal, but Kat had never had that problem. The moment she let go of her constant efforts at mental control, her inner beast took over. The change flowed over her with a violent intensity, forking through her like jagged lightning, hitting all her nerve endings.

Just like the other times she'd shifted, the pain was short-lived, soon replaced by a pleasurable, soothing sensation erupting inside her. She was suddenly sharply aware of her surroundings. Because it was winter there weren't many forest animals in plain sight, but she thought she scented a deer nearby. Even though the instinctive part of her wanted to hunt the other animal down, her human side actually laughed. She couldn't kill Bambi if she wanted to live with herself. The other rich, earthy smells of the forest soothed her most primal side. Patches of snow covered the ground, but she barely felt the cold beneath her paws as she began running over dried grass and foliage.

Jumping over fallen branches, she felt the wind roll over her with abandon. She'd never understood it before she'd been turned, but running provided one of the few times she felt utterly free. Nothing mattered as she ran. She could even pretend it hadn't bothered her to see

Jayce on top of another woman. Too bad that was a lie. Her stomach still ached in a way she hated and could barely understand. She shouldn't want Jayce as much as she did.

Despite everything that had happened, she couldn't get him out of her system. Not with the memories she held on to. They suffocated her to the point where she wanted to throw caution to the wind and go to bed with him again. Just to have a taste. Maybe it would help her exorcise him from her mind. He couldn't be as good as she remembered. Yeah, that was a lie too. He might have been her first lover, but she wasn't stupid. The way he'd played her body, the things he'd made her feel . . . it had been amazing. Since she'd also been dumb enough to fall in love with him, the sex had been that much better.

As she came upon a fallen oak tree she jerked to a halt. It looked as if it had been ripped from the ground. But by what? Deep striations—claw marks, she realized—encircled the giant trunk. Nothing human could have done this, and she didn't think any normal animal could have either.

Moving closer, she realized she scented someone familiar. She'd recognize his spicy, earthy smell anywhere. There was a slight underlying whiff of cedar that made the scent unmistakable.

Jayce.

All over the area and all around the fallen tree. Had he done this? If she'd been in her human form, she would have frowned at the thought. As she circled the tree she felt another presence nearby. Then she heard what sounded like footsteps—of a horse.

It was Jayce. Despite the fading scent around the tree, the all-natural aroma of him teased her senses.

She waited by the stump until he rode through the

thicket of trees. Looking like an incredibly sexy cowboy, he galloped right for her but abruptly stopped and looped the horse's reins around a low-hanging branch of a sycamore tree. Wearing faded jeans, now dirty from his recent sparring session, and a beat-up leather jacket he'd had as long as she'd known him, he walked toward her. Heart in her throat, she stood silently while he crouched in front of her.

The look he gave her was indescribable. Some foreign emotion she'd never seen played across his face. She couldn't define it even in her animal form when everything was so much clearer. It almost looked like yearning, but . . . that couldn't be right.

He reached his hand out, slowly, waiting for her acquiescence before softly petting her head. His raw strength was undeniable, but the feel of him touching her so gently put her at ease. Which was crazy. She wanted to keep running, to expend all her anger and energy until her legs ached and she could barely breathe. But with him stroking her head, she felt oddly calm.

"When you were taken, I tried to find you." His words were rough, uneven, and she wondered if he would be saying them if she had been in her human form. Moving from his crouch, he sat on the ground and continued to pet her.

She savored the feel of his strong fingers running through her fur. They sat there so long she wondered if he'd continue. She wanted him to. Oh God, did she. When she'd been held captive she'd called out for him to save her so many times her throat had turned raw. After she'd been found naked in that barn, she'd been too ashamed to see or speak to him. She'd been humiliated enough and she hadn't wanted to see pity in his eyes, so she'd avoided him as long as she could. It wasn't as if he was the only one she'd been keeping at arm's length though. She hadn't told a soul what she'd gone through at the hands of that monster. Greg something. Odd that she couldn't remember his last name. He'd been working for that bastard Adler, who was also dead now. But Adler had a boss, and if it was the last thing she did, she was going to find out who'd given the orders to kidnap her.

Finally Jayce continued, his words slicing through her thoughts. "I looked anywhere and everywhere I thought you might be. A couple times I found your scent but . . . it was no use." His face was drawn so tight, so controlled, she knew he was using all of his enforcer strength to keep his emotions in check. "I've never felt so helpless in my life. After I let my wolf out, I was afraid I'd kill someone innocent, so this tree bore the brunt of my aggression." His voice was strained, as if getting those few sentences out was difficult.

Her gut twisted as she sat there, listening to the erratic beat of his heart and trying to digest his words. Jayce didn't talk much and never that much at once and never before with such emotion. What he'd just admitted to her . . . she didn't know what to think of it or how to take it. He'd *searched* for her. She'd known it because December had told her, but to hear him admit it, to put so much raw emotion into those few words . . . it made her ache inside. When she'd called out for him he hadn't been there, but he'd been looking. If he'd been able, he would have saved her. She hadn't realized how much she'd needed to hear that from him until now.

She wanted to stay in her wolf form so she wouldn't have to respond. But doing so made her feel too much like a coward.

Pulling back from his touch, she underwent the change. A rush of adrenaline overtook her as her bones broke and shifted back to her human form. Even though she'd been shifting for a little over a month, she didn't think she'd ever get used to the sensation. Every time she came back out of it, it was like she'd been on another planet or something. The disorientation was short-lived, but it always jarred her.

Blinking, she tried to shake off the instant chill that came upon her. After the change she was more aware of the elements, even with her higher body temperature. Especially since she was naked. Kneeling on the ground, she tried to adjust to her surroundings. Before she could move, Jayce was wrapping his leather jacket around her.

Without thinking, she slipped her arms into the long sleeves and pulled it tight around her body. Then he snagged one arm around her waist and pulled her into his lap. Maybe she should have felt exposed, considering she wore no underwear or bra under his jacket, but in his arms she'd always felt safe. Now was no different.

She desperately wanted to say something, to respond to what he'd just told her. But she couldn't find the words. When she'd been dying not so long ago, she'd held on to a mental picture of him. Of them, actually. They'd been in the ocean, entangled in each other's arms and legs, and the outside world hadn't existed. He'd told her he wasn't a beach person, but she'd changed his mind when she showed him just how much fun the ocean could be. Her life had been so different then. Complicated, yes, but still so much easier. As much as she wanted to dwell on what Jayce had just said to her, she couldn't allow herself to. His admission made her think about being tortured and dying and right now she couldn't go down that road.

Her gaze drifted over his face in a lazy assessment. The deep scars crossing over his left eye were like a warning to anyone who thought they could mess with him. It took a lot to scar shifters—or so Kat had been told. Even though she and Jayce had shared so much with each other, he'd never told her about his scars.

Reaching up, she traced her index finger over one of the long-healed gashes. He shuddered under her touch. Not overtly, but since she was in his lap it was hard to miss. She also didn't miss his very insistent erection pressing against her hip, but she chose to ignore it. For the moment.

"You never told me how you got these scars."

One of his hands slid up her leg and rested lightly, mere inches from the hem of his jacket, which barely covered her upper thigh. His fingers tensed slightly as he spoke. "My brother gave them to me."

She knew a little about his family history but not much. Just that his parents had died centuries ago and his younger brother had been missing for so long that Jayce wasn't sure whether he was dead or not. "I thought you guys were close before he ran off."

"We were, but he was angry and I let him take it out on me." His voice was almost devoid of emotion.

"You *let* him?" Scarring someone to that extent—someone you loved, no less—seemed excessive even for a male shifter.

Jayce paused so long that Kat wondered if he would even answer, but he finally spoke. "Aldric's mate had just been killed by a rogue coyote turned feral. She'd been pregnant and weak as a human, unable to defend herself. It was a massacre." The last word was barely above a whisper.

Kat's throat tightened with emotion at the pain she heard in his voice. His brother had been suffering, so Jayce had let Aldric hurt him. To the point where he'd allowed him to actually mutilate him, probably almost blind him. If it wasn't for their ability to heal so quickly, Kat guessed that Jayce would have lost his eye.

She didn't understand why he was opening up to her or even why he'd followed her out here. Maybe he sensed her vulnerability. Whatever the reason, too many emotions were swirling inside her. It was hard for her to remember the need to keep their relationship on a professional, even footing when he was letting his guard down in a way he never had before. And when his hand was inching up her thigh.

As she looked into gray eyes that made her feel things she didn't want to feel, that dark scent she'd smelled earlier wrapped around her, stronger than before. She didn't know what it was but her own lust spiked sharp and fast. Warmth spread through her lower abdomen to the aching between her legs.

Kat told herself to stop him. But God help her, she didn't want to.

Chapter 7

Jayce growled low in his throat at the rich scent Kat was throwing off. She always smelled like roses, but when she was turned on it was even more potent. He'd only come out here to talk to her. After the hurt look she'd given him in the barn, he hadn't been able to stay away. Her expression tore at his heart. He didn't like thinking he'd hurt her, even inadvertently.

Now she wasn't feeling anything other than desire. He could scent it clearly on her. No pain, no anger, just want. His hand continued inching up her bare, creamy leg. Even if he wanted to stop—and he didn't—he didn't think he could get his body to obey him. Kat's tantalizing scent was like a sweet siren's song.

Luring him in. Taunting, teasing him. Reminding him of everything he'd once had and couldn't have again. Maybe temporarily, but not permanently. He couldn't have a place in her life forever, but for now ... His hand stopped when her thighs clenched together, caging his hand between them and effectively stopping him inches from his destination.

Her breathing was ragged as she stared at him. There was a silent question in her eyes, one he couldn't read and didn't understand. Doing the only thing he hoped would relax her, he covered her mouth with his.

He intended to keep his kisses soft and tame, but the moment their lips touched it was impossible. In a frenzy he hungrily tangled his tongue with hers. The need to take her on the forest floor was damn near overwhelming, but Kat wasn't ready for that. Hell, he didn't think he was either. Just the thought of being inside her again after so long pushed at the threads of his control.

Before that happened, he had to taste her. He'd been fantasizing about it for too damn long not to indulge. When she'd left him she'd taken a piece of him with her.

Covering the short distance up her thigh, he cupped her mound with his hand. Soft and wet, she tensed under his touch, so he kept his hand immobile. Just savored the feel of the most delicate part of her body. A place he'd kissed and stroked too many times to count. He still had no clue what had happened to her in that barn or if she'd been raped—something he couldn't and *wouldn't* think about right now—but he knew he needed to go slow.

"You're so fucking beautiful," he murmured against her mouth.

As they continued kissing, she gradually relaxed. Her body became pliant and her thighs loosened around his hand, spreading wider and giving him what he wanted. The pressure on his chest eased as she let her guard down with him. Slowly, he rubbed one finger along her wet folds.

Even though he could scent her arousal, to feel the slick proof of it made something primal inside him growl in satisfaction. She was turned on because of *him*. Not some random male.

She became bolder in her kisses, almost needier as her tongue invaded his mouth. The already strong rose scent she emanated completely surrounded him. When she started to shift positions, he froze and pulled his hand back. He couldn't risk moving too fast and scaring her.

But she swiveled and straddled him in a fluid movement, making her intentions clear. "Touch me," she murmured before pressing her lips to his once again.

Gladly. Her wearing only his jacket and nothing else was probably the sexiest thing he'd ever seen. Instead of resuming his stroking of her wet heat, he brought his hands up to her face. Threading his fingers through the mass of her long, dark hair, he cupped the back of her head with one hand. He slid his other hand under the jacket until he grasped her behind.

Her muscles clenched for a moment, but then she thrust forward until her pelvis ground against his. His entire body tensed at the feel of her long, lean body on top of him. His cock pressed painfully against his zipper, begging to be unleashed. He might have jeans on but she had no such barrier and every part of him was aware that all he had to do was free himself and he would be inside her tight sheath in seconds.

Moaning into their kisses, she began slowly riding him. More than anything, he wanted to tear away the barriers of their clothing, but he didn't want to risk separating from her. For all he knew, she was lost in the moment, and he couldn't bear to tear her out of it. All her body language said that she trusted herself with him and he had to show her that she could trust him. Implicitly. Some primal part of him craved it with frightening intensity.

Despite his clothing, the heat from between her legs

was enough to scorch him. Unable to stop himself, he reached for the front of his jacket and drew it apart. The instant he palmed one of her breasts she arched into him. And that sweet scent of hers grew even stronger.

He'd been with her enough times to know it wouldn't take much for her to climax. She was stimulating her clit each time she moved over his cock. That was something she used to do back when they'd first been together. Back before they'd actually had sex. In the beginning of their relationship when he hadn't trusted himself with her.

As a human she'd been physically weaker, and her mere presence had gotten him hotter than any naked woman ever had. So they'd fooled around *a lot*. She'd been so sexual yet oddly innocent as they'd explored each other's bodies. By the time he'd finally gotten inside her, it had been fucking heaven. When he eventually died, he was pretty sure heaven wasn't somewhere he was headed—if heaven even existed at all. But with Kat, it was like he'd gotten a taste of it.

It was like . . . coming home.

That thought had struck him then, and it hit him even harder now. But he ignored it. Some primal part of him desperately needed her to climax. He hadn't been able to save her before, but he could give her pleasure. Hopefully enough to make her forget her pain.

Tweaking her nipple between his thumb and forefinger, he pulled, but not too gently. The instant he did, she tore her mouth away from his and moaned. Still writhing over him, she blazed a trail of hot kisses down his jaw and neck until she nipped his shoulder through his shirt.

His cock jerked at the hungry action and he continued teasing her breast. With his extrasensory abilities he could hear her heart rate increasing. Each time she moved over him and each time he teased and rubbed one of her nipples, her heart rate ratcheted up in tune with her erratic breathing.

The sounds were like an erotic symphony, pounding out until finally she threw her head back and moaned his name. He grabbed her hips as she rode against him through her climax. Though he wanted to stroke her with his hands, to push his fingers deep inside her as her orgasm pulsed through her, he held back. If she'd been sexually assaulted, he was afraid he might trigger a memory. He couldn't handle seeing pain on her face.

The sweet scent of her pleasure intoxicated him as much as the sounds she made. His hands itched to tug his zipper down, free himself, and plunge deep into her. Feel her tight walls clenching around him, milking him. His beast clawed to the surface, the most primitive part of him wanting out. He wanted to take her hard and fast and make up for months of celibacy. His body practically demanded it.

As if she read his thoughts—or more likely the way his body tensed—she froze. Still basking in her postcoital bliss, she blinked a couple times as she stared at him, as if trying to clear her head. But he could see the wariness creep into her eyes.

It grew each second that passed. Her hands loosened their death grip on his shoulders and she rocked back. Still straddling him, she put a few inches between them and yanked the jacket closed, covering herself. Though the distance was small, it might as well have been the Grand Canyon.

A slight tremor shook her and she looked almost like the proverbial deer caught in headlights as their gazes clashed. He saw regret in an instant.

His throat clenched at the thought that she felt any sort of remorse for what had just happened. He wanted to say something to soothe her, but was afraid that whatever words he chose would be the wrong ones. Some sort of battle was raging in her head right now and he couldn't get a read on her emotions.

Too many scents swirled off her. Pleasure, wariness, and fear all vied to overtake each other.

"Kat," he murmured, not sure what he planned to follow it up with. Whatever it was, he would never know.

Wordlessly she shoved off him and stripped off his jacket. He had only a moment to appreciate her smooth, toned skin before she shifted to her animal form and ran deep into the woods.

Away from the ranch and away from him.

He wasn't sure what had just happened and he didn't know how to make it right. If he went after her now, he'd be taking away what little control she had over this situation. That would only increase the chasm between them.

His inner wolf clawed and ripped at his insides, begging to be freed to run after his woman. But despite the loud voice in his head demanding that he follow her, he ignored it. For now he would leave the next move up to her.

Erin grasped the takeout bag she'd just brought from Big Earl's Diner and quickened her pace. Not long after Jayce had run off during their training, she'd gotten a call asking if she could pick December up from her store. Liam had needed to meet with someone—more real estate stuff. Considering how much Liam had been running around lately, she had a feeling that Connor was buying up all sorts of interesting property.

She could have asked someone else to head to town, but she knew that the reason Liam had asked her was because December felt more comfortable around her. Hell, she hadn't even had time to shower since her work-out with Jayce, so she was more than ready to get home and clean up. But December had been craving a Greek salad, and since that was one of the few things the preg-nant shifter could keep down, Erin had had no problem getting it for her. Well, she hadn't wanted to leave the store, but it would have taken forty-five minutes for them to deliver, which was silly when she could just jog the few blocks and get it.

Plus December had been running her end-of-the-day reports and had promised to keep her door locked. Twin-kle lights adorned a lot of the streetlamps, giving down-town Fontana a winter-wonderland kind of feel. As Erin hurried down the sidewalk she blinked when she real-ized that December was standing *outside* the store, her purse held defensively against her chest as a taller woman with dark brown, unkempt frizzy hair stood in front of her.

What the hell?

Setting the takeout bag next to a lamppost, Erin stepped off the sidewalk and ducked behind one of the few cars. Quickly, she crept behind the next couple of cars until she came up behind the woman. She could hear the conversation clearly and wanted to strangle the stranger for upsetting December. Before she could make a move, December shot her an almost imperceptible look that told her to back the hell off.

Okay then. Erin unzipped her jacket—she'd had to strap her blades to her chest instead of leaving them hooked to her belt—and slowly removed one blade. She would hold off for now, but if this woman made one wrong move, it was on.

"You need to get out of this relationship while you

can. What were you thinking, marrying one of those animals?" the stranger hissed.

A low growl emanated from December, taking Erin by surprise as she held her position barely a few feet behind the unaware woman. "That *animal* is not only my husband but my mate and I'm carrying our child. Also what you would consider an *animal*. You need to back the hell off right now." Her voice was deadly calm. Another surprise.

Erin was livid just hearing the stranger's hateful words.

The woman held out a hand, but December immediately took a step back. "Don't touch me."

"I just hate what you're doing to yourself. To your brother. You used to be such a respectable girl. Always volunteering at the literacy center. Always going to church."

"I still do those things," December said.

"If you'd just listen to me." She reached into her purse and Erin tensed, ready to spring, but the stranger pulled out what looked like a flyer and shoved it in December's direction. "This is a place for people like you to meet and talk about what's been done to you."

December flicked a glance at the paper, then back at the woman. "*Done* to me?"

"You know, the brainwashing."

Erin couldn't help it. A bark of laughter escaped and she had to force herself not to double over clutching her stomach. Liam might have *done* a lot of things to December—none of which Erin wanted to know about— but brainwashing wasn't one of them.

The stranger whirled around and gasped as the paper fell from her hand, silently fluttering to the icy sidewalk.

Erin took a menacing step forward and grinned when the woman noticed her blade. "Get the fuck out of here and don't come back. If I see you anywhere near this store or December again, I'll do a lot more than *brainwash* you."

The stench of fear that spiked off the woman was so potent it almost made Erin gag. Without another word the stranger sprinted down the sidewalk, throwing a few fearful glances over her shoulder until she disappeared around a corner.

December groaned once they were alone. "You probably made things worse."

Erin shrugged as she sheathed her blade and zipped her jacket. "Whatever. I wasn't actually going to hurt her, but if that fucking lunatic actually believes you've been brainwashed, then nothing I say will make a difference. Who was she?"

December's lips pulled into a thin line, but she didn't answer.

Realizing why, Erin rolled her eyes. "What, you think I'll go after her?"

A grin tugged at December's lips as she let out a sigh. "You're hard to read and you get the same angry look Liam does when he's being unpredictable. . . . Her name is Mary Katze and she's definitely harmless. A little nutty, yes, but I'm not worried about her. She lives with a bunch of cats and doesn't seem to have a solid grasp on reality."

"Why were you standing *outside* with her? You promised—"

December threw her hands up and Erin felt a little bad about harassing her; she was pregnant, after all. "I know! I hadn't planned to open the door, but she kept knocking insistently and it felt rude when she could clearly see me inside. Up until recently she's been a very loyal customer."

Erin rubbed a hand over her face. December had an innate need to be polite to people because of societal norms and the way she'd been raised. Something Erin didn't suffer from, but it was also something she was trying to understand. Instead of arguing, she asked, "You ready to get out of here?"

December nodded and held up her keys. "Yes."

"Let me grab your food." Erin hurried down the street to grab the bag she'd discarded. As she turned back, the sound of squealing tires made her jerk around. A truck had screeched to a halt in the middle of the road right in front of December's store.

"Shifter-loving whore!" a male voice called out as he threw something.

Everything funneled out around her as Erin sprang into action. She could see two people in the truck. Both likely male—at least the one hanging out the passenger-side door was. Diving in front of December, Erin realized the guy had thrown a rock. The arc was high and obviously intended to shatter the store window.

Using all the strength in her legs and lightning-quick reflexes, Erin jumped in the air and caught it. The rock slammed into her open palm with a smack. She barely felt the sting since she was so pumped up on adrenaline.

She heard a low, angry curse from one of the males as her boots thudded back onto the sidewalk. As the truck took off she ran after it, hauled her arm back and threw the rock right at the back window. It shot through the air like an arrow until it struck its target.

As the back window exploded, she grinned. After waiting a few moments to make sure the truck didn't come back, she turned toward December and froze. The pregnant shifter's face was pale and she looked exhausted. "Are you okay?" God, the question sounded so lame. Of course she wasn't okay.

Swallowing hard, December shook her head. "No. Yes. I don't know. It's been a long day and I'm tired of dealing with so much hostility. After that shifter attack last night people have been weird today. I just want to go home."

Erin wasn't good at the comforting thing, but she nodded in sympathy. "I'll call one of the guys to hang out in front of your store tonight. Make sure those little punks don't come back."

"Were they teenagers?" December's voice actually sounded hopeful. As if the fact that they weren't adults made the situation better.

"I think so. Let's not worry about it, though. There's been no damage to your store and you're tired and hungry." She once again picked up the fallen takeout bag. "It's only salad, so I'm sure it'll still taste great," she said as she handed it to December. "Come on. I'll follow you back to the ranch."

"Thanks." Some of the tension eased out of December's shoulders as she took the bag.

Once she was back in her car, Erin immediately called Connor and told him about the incident, then called Liam. Liam was livid, but he would be in a better frame of mind by the time he got back to the ranch, and that was the most important thing. December needed a calm mate right now.

Less than an hour later, Erin twisted her damp hair up into a clip before pulling on a pair of cargo pants and a long-sleeved sweater. Out of habit she strapped her two blades onto her belt. Even though the ranch was fairly well protected at the moment, she would never allow herself to be vulnerable again.

As a member of the warrior class, shifters born to protect others in their race, she didn't care that she was simply going to go play a game of poker with some of her packmates. Her weapons went where she went.

Stepping out into the hallway, she was nearly bowled over by Vivian, the ten-year-old jaguar cub Connor and Ana had adopted, and Lucas, the only other cub on the ranch, though he was a lupine shifter. Dodging to the side, she was careful to keep her weapons away from them. Hurting these little cubs, even inadvertently, would slay her.

"Hey, Erin." The dark-haired she-cat jerked to a halt in front of her. "I think Ana and Noel are making popcorn and watching a movie tonight. Are you staying in too?"

"No." Lucas answered before Erin could, the blond ten-year-old boy's voice full of authority. "It's game night at the guys' cabin."

Vivian looked back at her, eyebrows raised. "Why would you want to hang out with all those males?"

"Because she's not a girly-girl like you." Lucas tugged on one of Vivian's pigtails, then raced away.

"Hey!" Vivian whipped around, her two long braids flying as she chased after him.

Their footsteps thumped loudly down the stairs and were soon followed by the front door slamming shut. Erin cringed at the sound. She knew Ana hated it when they did that. Almost like clockwork, Ana walked into the foyer carrying a bottle of wine as Erin was descending the stairs.

Her dark eyes turned Erin's way. "Was that the cubs?"

Erin shrugged, unwilling to give them up. "I'm just heading out."

Those eyes narrowed slightly, but the corners of Ana's

mouth curved up. "Nice evasive way of answering, just like my mate."

Erin shrugged again, but didn't bother hiding her smile. Ana was the perfect mate for an Alpha. Sharp and deadly if she needed to be, but protective and motherly at the same time. Connor had done well by mating with her. Considering that he'd saved Erin's life over a year ago, she was glad the Alpha had found happiness.

"You know you're always more than welcome to join us." Ana motioned with her hand toward the living room, where Erin scented Noel, Ana's sister, already waiting.

"I know and I appreciate it." She genuinely liked the other females, but she preferred hanging out with the males. Carmen, Ana's younger sister, had been killed a couple of months ago, and her death had been a stinging reminder that Erin couldn't afford to develop female relationships. Dark-haired Carmen had been so full of life and energy, exactly the kind of friend Erin had needed when they'd moved to the ranch. She'd told Carmen things she hadn't told another soul. Like what had happened to her before Connor's pack had saved her from that disgusting alley she'd been dumped in and left for dead. Then Carmen had been taken from this world. Erin's throat squeezed tight as the emotion bubbled up inside her. "I just need to blow off some steam with the guys."

"See ya later then." Ana shrugged and continued toward the living room. Female laughter drifted out, but Erin ignored it as she opened the front door.

The moment she stepped off the front porch into the cool night air, she scented *him* before she felt his presence or even saw him. The annoying male was like a freaking ghost. With that inky black hair and his equally dark eyes, Noah Campbell practically blended in with the shadows when he wanted to, even in human form.

Ignoring his presence—wherever *that* was—she strode across the yard toward the cabin where most of the males lived together. And just like that, the tall, intimidating shifter fell in line with her.

"Playing poker tonight?" Noah's voice was like pure liquid sin. That soft Southern drawl belied the deadliness she'd seen him display more than once.

"Yep." She kept her eyes straight ahead, unwilling to give in to her desire to look at him. He was her one weakness and she'd sworn never to allow a male to get past her defenses again.

"Why don't you come to dinner with me instead?" It felt as if he purred the question directly in her ear even though he wasn't remotely close enough.

A shiver feathered over her body like a thousand kisses, making her skin tingle and her heart beat just a little bit faster. Somehow she said, "No."

Now he growled at her, grabbed one of her arms, and pinned her against the closest tree with his body. The hold wasn't hard and she knew he didn't intend to physically harm her, but her inner wolf reacted nonetheless. Before she could stop herself she'd drawn one of her blades and had it pressed against his inner thigh, right over his femoral artery. She could slice through it in one swipe, incapacitating him. Shifter blood clotted at incredible speed, so it wouldn't kill him, but if he'd been a true enemy, it would slow him down enough that she could try to mete out a killing blow or run from him.

Right now that second option looked pretty good. The coward in her wanted to run from the sensual feelings he stirred inside her. Reining in her frustration at her instinctive action against a friend, she quickly withdrew and sheathed her weapon.

He still didn't move. Just narrowed his dark eyes at

her, as if he wanted to see her innermost thoughts. "You *afraid* to have dinner with me?"

She knew he was baiting her, but she didn't care. Hell, yeah, she was afraid. Afraid to be alone with him because she couldn't think straight around him. Afraid that once he got her alone he would see how truly fucked up she was and realize he could do so much better than her. Why he hadn't figured that out by now was beyond her. Falling for a shifter like Noah was the absolute dumbest thing she could ever do. Once he realized she wasn't what he needed, he would move on to a sweet little beta.

Being the good guy that he was, he would try to let her down easy. God, in her head she could actually *hear* how the damn conversation would play out. Since he was nearly a foot taller than she was, she was forced to look up to meet his steely gaze. "I'm not afraid, just not interested. Why can't you get that through your thick skull?"

"Not interested?" His voice was incredulous and she knew why.

It was a constant struggle to hide her scent of need and desire when she was around him. Not to mention that they'd kissed a few times in the past couple of weeks. Tasting what she could never have was just plain stupid, but that hadn't stopped her. The only reason she *had* stopped was the knowledge that he would eventually want to take things to the next level. And that meant having sex. Something she didn't think she could ever do again. The last man she'd trusted with her body— abruptly she cut off that line of thought and shook her head. "Fine. I'm attracted to you. Big deal, Noah. That doesn't mean I want a relationship, and the last time I checked, no still means no."

At her words, he stepped back as if she'd slapped him.

Immediately guilt suffused her. She ruthlessly shoved it away.

"I know what no means. I'd never hurt you, Erin," he said softly.

The guilt she'd just pushed down popped right back up, threatening to suffocate her. She swallowed hard. "Not intentionally you wouldn't."

He opened his mouth, but she cut him off. "Look, Noah, the only thing I can offer you is friendship. I know we've gotten ... *friendlier* than usual the past couple weeks, but that has to stop. I don't want anything else, and if you can't accept my friendship, then we can't even hang out one-on-one anymore." When he didn't respond, she continued. "Take it or leave it."

"Friends," he muttered, slight disgust lacing his voice.

Even though it was exactly what she wanted to hear, something sharp twisted in her chest. The pain was unfamiliar and uncomfortable. She'd been so used to feeling nothing for so long that this took her off guard. If she didn't know better she'd think she was actually disappointed that he'd acquiesced so easily.

Anthony Mayfield pulled out one of his many disposable cell phones from the top drawer of his desk. He quickly dialed the number of his contact in the Fontana Sheriff's Office. He'd been waiting all day on news about Katarina Saburova. She'd been taken in for questioning regarding a shifter attack two nights ago. Just like he'd known she would be.

Though most of Anthony's Fontana subordinates in the APL were dead—including Edward Adler, his main contact in the region—he still had a few members he could count on. Right now he needed everyone he could get for the APL's media campaign against supernatural beings. Losing Adler had been an unexpected blow, but the man had been unable to kidnap humans. Since Adler couldn't even do that, it was probably a good thing Anthony was rid of him.

His contact answered on the second ring. "Yeah?"

Anthony could hear a steady din of voices in the background. Which meant he was at the police station. "So?" He didn't elaborate. The only time he called was for something specific.

"Give me a sec." A pause, the sound of a door shutting, then the background noise faded. "She gave up her DNA."

Tapping a finger against the hard surface of his desk, Anthony frowned. "What?"

"I was as surprised as you are," he said, his voice barely above a whisper.

Shifters didn't do anything human governments asked of them unless they were presented with a warrant. They might have come out to the world, but they weren't pushovers. Their resistance to man's laws was another example of their animal nature. They wanted to be able to live freely and by their own rules. As if they were better than everyone else. They held their immortality so close to the vest—as if they were gods—keeping it from more deserving humans like himself. "Do you know why?"

"No, but her Alpha was here to pick her up when she was released and he looked pissed."

That was interesting. Maybe she wasn't following her new pack's rules. Shifters were brutal in the enforcement of their laws. "Why didn't you call me earlier?"

"Because I've been fucking busy." Though he didn't raise his voice, the sharp edge was hard to miss.

Anthony chose to ignore it. "It doesn't matter that

she's given her DNA. They still know a shifter killed that bartender. We can leak it to the media—Julia Martin. She's fair." He was met with silence. "What?"

"Not yet. She just got burned with that story about those dog attacks. Besides, it's not like the recent attack is exactly a secret in town. People are talking about it even if the news isn't."

The local reporter who covered most of the news in Fontana and the immediate surrounding region had gone on the air with concerns about shifter attacks before. Of course she'd also gone right back on record when it had turned out a rabid dog and not shifters had killed a couple of humans a little over a month ago. Some asshole had gotten a dog and hadn't trained it right. At least people knew about the attack last night. Sometimes gossip and speculation were better than hearing things from a respectable source. People would let their imaginations run wild. "Yes, she'll be hesitant to report anything dealing with shifters so soon," he said almost absently. Quickly he turned the topic in another direction. "Use our secret weapon tonight. Don't pick someone with a record. Find someone clean."

"No." The answer was immediate and made Anthony's anger spike.

"Why not?"

"We can incite the people here without going after innocents. I'm not going to kill someone who doesn't deserve it." His voice was so damn calm that Anthony wanted to strike out at him.

The bartender they'd killed had had a record, but he hadn't been violent. That didn't seem to matter to his contact as long as their victims were criminals. The guy had a weird fucking moral code. And Anthony knew when to pick his battles. He needed this guy. Pausing a moment, he chose his next words carefully. "Two of our members with records—armed robbery and assault with a deadly weapon—will be at Tango's tomorrow for midnight bowling." Then he gave their names, aware that his contact would know exactly who they were. Though he didn't live in Fontana at present, Anthony knew that Tango's was a bowling alley that saw a lot of business late at night. The five-dollar pitchers pulled in a young crowd, usually including the two punks he had named. He wouldn't lose any sleep over it if they were eliminated.

But Anthony didn't push things any further. He just let that statement hang in the air. If he ordered the other man to kill them, he would naturally resist.

"They're APL—our people." The statement was almost muted, as if he was trying to convince himself they didn't deserve to die since they belonged to the same organization as Anthony and his contact.

"Their deaths would serve two purposes." It would rid the world of two scumbags—at least in his contact's eyes—and it would hopefully incite the town against shifters once it came out that two more people had died at their hands. But he didn't spell all that out. He didn't need to.

A long pause. Then, "They'll be taken care of. . . . I'm also taking care of someone else tomorrow. During the daytime will work best for this victim."

That piqued his curiosity. "Who?"

"Someone with a long record, recently let out on parole." There was so much disgust in his contact's voice Anthony knew the victim would likely deserve to die. And he didn't care how many murders their secret weapon had to carry out.

"Good." He smiled to himself as they hung up, not

bothering to question his contact further on the other intended victim. Three kills in one day was genius. It was only a matter of time until the APL brought down Jayce Kazan, enforcer and representative of the North American Council of lupine shifters. After that it wouldn't be hard to target the Council themselves. Step by step he would rip them apart, and if he had to sacrifice some humans along the way, so be it.

These immortals had turned their noses up at him once and they were all going to pay. Back when he'd been in the prime of life, barely thirty, they'd come out to the world, flaunting their longer life spans and supernatural abilities. And he'd desperately wanted what they had.

Already incredibly financially successful at such a young age—all of it earned on his own, with no help from his father—he had been a perfect candidate for immortality. He'd approached the vampires first, though not overtly. Female vamps were known for their hedonistic lifestyles as much as the males and he'd reveled in the open sexuality of their kind. But they'd refused to turn him. After a while he'd realized that the women he fucked were never going to change him into a vampire. He was just a plaything for them. Something to pass the time. In truth that was all they'd been to him too. But he wanted what they had so badly that he sold his pride for one vamp female. He let her dominate him, do whatever she wanted to him. Of course that was before he realized she never intended to turn him. In the end she discarded him for someone else. And *him*, she turned into one of them. He'd been a nobody. A fucking bartender with no direction or money, but she'd apparently thought her next lover was more worthy. Scorching-hot fury burned inside Anthony as long buried memories assaulted him.

After that, he'd turned to shifters in an attempt to gain immortality, but they hadn't even been willing to talk to him. They'd all brushed him off, as if he were a nuisance, a bug to be squashed. So in the past twenty years, since their emergence to the world, he'd spent his time learning everything he could about them. Shifters closed ranks to any outsiders they perceived as a threat, but their strength of pack was also their weakness.

Unlike vampires, who existed mostly in vacuums, shifters lived and breathed family. It made it easier to use and threaten them for his own purposes. Just like he was doing now. Soon they would all regret ever having thought they were better than him.

Chapter 8

Kat scented him before she opened her eyes. That spicy, earthy, subtle cedar scent twined around her. Before she could move, she felt her thick, warm comforter being dragged off her. Immediately she jerked up in bed to find Jayce at the foot of it with a slight grin breaking up the harsh lines of his face. "What are you doing?" she asked as she pulled her knees up to her chest and wrapped her arms around them. Thankfully she'd worn clothes to bed last night. A quick glance at the digital clock on her nightstand told her it was five in the morning.

"Time to get up, sweetheart." His voice was a smooth purr.

But it wasn't full of fun promises of sinful sex—not that she should be thinking about that with him anyway. After he'd brought her to climax yesterday, they hadn't said much to each other. She'd gone straight to her room and proceeded *not* to sleep. Instead she'd tossed and turned for hours until falling into a fitful slumber. Not because of nightmares of her torture, but because she'd been tormented with memories of what it had felt like to have Jayce stroking her to orgasm. His touch had been so gentle, so perfect, it made her crazy with need. She couldn't believe she'd let him touch her so intimately yesterday, but she'd felt damn near powerless to stop herself from straddling him, kissing him . . . wanting him so bad she ached for his touch. And the tender look in his eyes as he'd made her climax—no, no, no. She couldn't go there. Instead she forced herself to focus on the man in front of her.

Kat glared at him. "I'm not working today, so if you don't mind . . ." She might have quit her job at the ski lodge, but she still helped out at December's bookstore. She leaned forward, ready to grab the comforter back, but he stepped out of her way, dragging the cover with him.

"I know. You're training with me. Get up now and I might let you get some coffee before we leave."

She flicked her gaze over his muscular form. He was wearing black jogging pants, a black sweater, and a black knitted skullcap. The only color on it was the small white skull and crossbones on the front. "You look like a cat burglar." When he didn't respond, she continued. "It's still dark out."

"And?"

She flopped back on the pillow and curled onto her side, but kept her eyes on him. "It's not normal to be up at this hour if you don't have to be." Especially after the night she'd had.

"Do you want me to coddle you, *princess*?" The mischievous gleam in his gray eyes wrenched her out of bed and onto her feet in seconds.

"You don't get to call me that anymore." That had been his nickname for her back before they'd started dating. She knew he didn't think she was spoiled. Back then he'd just liked to get under her skin. It certainly did the trick now.

"Whatever you say, princess. Whenever you're ready, I'll be downstairs." Then he disappeared out the door without a sound. *Like a freaking ghost*, she thought. If she hadn't been watching him, she wouldn't have heard him. That was the kind of stealth she wanted to learn.

After washing her face and brushing her teeth she changed into a pair of jogging pants and a loose sweatshirt. As she arrived downstairs, Jayce was opening the front door.

"What about coffee?" she asked as she pulled her hair into a ponytail.

He shrugged and pushed the door all the way open. "Next time you'll get up earlier."

"That's not fair. I didn't even know we were training so early."

"Not my problem." His lips pulled up slightly at the corners, as if he was trying not to laugh.

Which only infuriated her more. "You were a lot nicer when we were together."

He stepped closer until he was mere inches from her, that spicy scent drowning her in its sensuality. "If we were still together we'd be in bed right now and I'd be buried deep inside you."

Heat flooded her cheeks, the warmth spreading all the way down her neck and to her breasts. Even though she couldn't see it, she could feel the flush along her skin. She opened her mouth, then snapped it shut before hurrying past him and out to the stone steps. His comment woke her up faster than coffee ever could have. After the way he'd played her body yesterday afternoon, she'd been starkly reminded of the intimate way they'd once known each other and the way he, and only he, had ever made her feel. If he kept saying stuff like that, it was going to make it that much harder for her to keep a level head around him. "So, what do you have planned so freaking early that we couldn't wait a couple hours to start?" she asked as he shut and locked the door behind them.

Coming to stand next to her, she could feel his energy wrapping around her, potent and strong. "You'll find out when we get to the ranch."

When he started jogging, she let out a little yelp and jerked into action. "Hey." Her legs were long, so she didn't have any trouble keeping stride, but . . . he couldn't mean they were running all the way to the ranch, could he? "What are you doing?"

"What does it look like?" The thumping of his sneakers hitting the pavement of December's street sounded in tune with Kat's own stride.

"But it's over ten miles." She knew she sounded a little whiny at the moment, but she hadn't even had a cup of coffee. This just wasn't right.

Jayce didn't respond, so she didn't say anything else. Just gritted her teeth and kept pace. She'd been in good shape before she'd been turned into a shifter, and since her transformation she found she was a lot faster, even in her human form, and she had a heck of a lot more endurance. Running ten miles wouldn't take her as long or drain as much energy as when she'd been human, but still, at five in the morning, it was so wrong.

Half an hour into their run—not jog—she stole a peek at Jayce. The man hadn't broken a sweat. Even if it was so cold out she could see her breath curling in front of her like white smoke, she still had a sheen of sweat dotting her forehead and her lower back was damp with perspiration. Yet Jayce looked as if he was out taking a Sunday stroll.

She growled low in her throat, which earned her a surprised glance from him. "What?"

"I know you're getting some kind of perverse pleasure by dragging me out here, making me sweat."

The piercing look in his gray eyes nearly made her stumble. "Making you sweat has always brought me pleasure."

Now she did trip over her feet. Not because of what he said, but the way he said it. Like he was remembering the way she tasted. She caught herself and kept her mouth shut the rest of the run.

When they arrived at the ranch, a few people were milling about, most of them headed toward Ana and Connor's house, where the pack would hang out just to socialize. She started to head that way after they jumped the main gate, but Jayce cocked his head toward the barn. "This way."

What? "I want coffee."

"Too bad."

"You're a cruel, cruel man," she said quietly, but couldn't resist nudging him with her hip as she spoke. It was stupid to let her guard down around him, but sometimes it was so hard not to. They'd been more than lovers once; they'd been friends. When she'd left him, losing that easy friendship had been devastating.

"I'd forgotten how much you hated mornings." There was a quiet note of laughter in his voice.

When they entered the barn, she froze for a split second. Erin was already there, a wooden sparring stick the size of a long dagger in her hand. A pop of unwarranted jealousy detonated inside Kat, but she thrust it into that mental box where she kept all her nightmares. The image

of Jayce on top of the petite redhead was something Kat
wouldn't be erasing anytime soon. Even though it hadn't
been a sexual thing, it still made her claws ache to be
unleashed. To slice and strike in violent slashes. Even
now her canines throbbed to the point that she had to
take a couple of deep breaths and physically restrain
herself from lashing out.

"I can't believe you let him drag you out here so
early," Erin said to her. Her expression was friendly and
her voice light.

Kat had worked with Erin before at December's
bookstore and she genuinely liked her. Mentally shaking
herself, she shoved away her petty jealousy and forced
herself to smile. "He refused me any sustenance too."

"Yeah, that sounds about right." Shaking her head,
Erin bent down and grabbed a bottle of water from a
cooler and tossed one to her. As Kat started to open it,
she watched in surprise as the redhead rushed at Jayce.

Without missing a beat he dodged what would have
been a vicious blow to his chest and rolled to the dusty
ground, picking up a matching sparring rod. The sleeves
of his sweater were pushed up to his forearms and she
couldn't help but watch the way his muscles flexed.

She wanted to rake her teeth over those hard lines
and tendons, then follow up with soft, wet kisses, teasing
and licking his skin. Heat rushed between her legs at the
thought and she wanted to curse herself. Erin and Jayce
were so focused on their mock fight they didn't seem to
notice.

Trying to keep her erratic emotions under control, she
finished the bottle of water, then leaned against one of
the empty stable doors to watch the workout. Erin was
smaller and leaner than Jayce, but she was quick. Impres-
sively so.

Kat knew he suspected the other woman was an enforcer so he was going to be training her also, but Kat had assumed that she and Jayce would have more time alone together. She should be grateful for the third party keeping them apart. As she started to retie her ponytail so it would be tighter, Jayce turned and threw his sparring rod in her direction.

Instinctively she ducked. It hit the stable door behind her with a loud clatter. As she narrowed her gaze at him, he took a few steps toward her. "Lesson three. Always be ready for an attack."

Jayce and all his rules and lessons. So far he'd given her two rules and now three lessons. She doubted he'd actually quiz her, but she was memorizing them all just in case.

Before she could respond, he continued. "You should have caught it."

She started to argue but then remembered his stupid first rule that she had to listen to him during training. It might annoy her, but she wanted to learn to defend herself in any situation. Without comment she picked up the rod, finding it heavier than she'd imagined. She held it in her hand, lifted her eyebrows, and waited for him to tell her what he wanted next.

His eyes narrowed slightly, exactly like they had yesterday. It was as if he expected her to argue with him. For that reason alone, she found herself wanting to do just that.

He tipped his head in Erin's direction. "We're going to come at you from both sides," he said as he bent to pick up another rod that he threw to her. This time she caught it. He continued. "You're going to try to block our blows."

Kat glanced at Erin. Her expression was no longer

friendly, but completely in battle mode. From the few moments she'd seen Jayce and Erin sparring, it was obvious the woman had trained with a blade. Even if Kat hadn't seen them strapped to the woman's thighs before, she would have known from today alone that she was skilled.

Swallowing back her nervousness at having to fight two attackers at once—even in a training situation—she braced herself as Erin launched herself at her.

As the nimble female flew through the air, rod in hand, Kat brought one of hers up to meet it. The force of the blow almost knocked her off her feet, but she dodged out of the way—only to be faced with an attack from Jayce.

She managed to block her thighs with one of her rods, but his slammed across her knuckles. Biting back the jarring pain, she managed to hold on to her weapon. No matter what happened today, she planned to keep the two defenses she had in her grasp. Jayce hadn't actually said it out loud, but she knew that was part of her lesson too. Holding on to her weapons.

Two hours later she was tired and sweaty, her knuckles were bruised, bloodied, and very raw, but she felt good about herself. She hadn't been able to block all of the blows—only about seventy percent—but in the course of the session her confidence had shot up a hundred percent. The hits had hurt, but she found she could now compartmentalize pain in a way she hadn't been able to when she'd been human. Her wolf took her pain and made it something sharp and deadly inside her. It felt like all the pain she'd experienced today was being honed into a weapon she could use against her opponents.

"Grab some water," Jayce finally said as he pulled his phone from his pocket.

Because of her ultrasensitive hearing she'd heard it buzzing earlier. Kat waited until Erin put her own sparring rods down to set hers aside, then headed for the cooler of water. Her stomach rumbled loud enough for even humans to hear if they'd been around.

Erin shot her a concerned look. "Have you eaten this morning?"

Before she could answer, Jayce strode up. "I've got to check on something. I'll be back in a few hours," he said to Kat. Then he focused on Erin. "Take her for a five-mile run and then you're finished for this morning."

Not for the *day*, but the *morning*. Kat inwardly winced, guessing he had more in store for her later, but five more miles wasn't too bad. Her adrenaline was pumping overtime.

"She needs to eat," Erin said.

"Soldiers don't always get to eat." There was no compromise in his voice.

Erin's gray eyes seemed to almost darken. "She's not a fucking soldier and this isn't—"

Kat appreciated the other woman's concern but she didn't need her help. "I'm fine. If I'm about to pass out I'll let you know. Now can we go so I can get some food afterward?"

Jayce gave her a look she couldn't describe, but it was gone so quick she couldn't begin to guess what it had been. Erin mumbled something under her breath about Jayce being a jerk, but nodded at Kat and headed out of the barn. Without looking at Jayce, she fell in line with Erin as they took off across one of the fields. They started running along a horse trail. The terrain was rougher than a paved road but good for her reflexes. Her stomach might be screaming at her for food, but she didn't care. She was going to train as hard as it took to get to where she wanted to be. A little hunger never killed anyone. If anything, her hunger for Jayce was a whole lot worse than some physical discomfort.

Unable to tear his gaze from Kat's long, lean form as she ran with Erin, Jayce watched the two women head off together. She had an unequivocal grace when she ran, even when she'd been human, and it had always stunned him. Her moves today hadn't been graceful, though. They'd been determined and vicious and she'd completely tapped into the part of her wolf that wanted to survive. He'd known because he'd seen the cold focus in her eyes. Watching her had impressed him. She had a ways to go, but it had almost seemed that she'd let her wolf take over as she took the hits to her hands and body. He hadn't held back his speed today, just his strength. Substantially. As had Erin.

The sparring lesson had been about teaching Kat to dodge and deflect blows, not about hurting her. Though if he was honest with himself, if it had been anyone else, he would have likely struck harder in a session. With Kat, he found he simply couldn't. Even seeing her wince at the blows she'd taken had sliced into a part of him that he tried to keep locked down. As he was around her more and more, he realized she was burrowing her way past his defenses. Worse, he knew she wasn't even trying.

Only once Kat was out of sight did he turn and head back toward the main house. Somehow he pushed back the simmering guilt inside him. He'd felt like a dick after Erin had said Kat needed to eat, but he wanted to push her as much as he thought she could take. If she was so focused on learning to fight and defend herself, she wouldn't be able to think about anything else. Most of the time when he looked at her, he saw a haunted expression that carved a knife into his heart. But when she was training, she just looked motivated and hungry to learn. She was tough and he trusted her to let someone know if she was being pushed too hard.

As he reached the front door, he started to open it—shifters weren't all that concerned with privacy, especially on a ranch like this, separated from humans—but paused, reminding himself that he wasn't part of this pack. He was an outsider. Before he could raise his hand to knock, the door opened and Vivian, the ten-year-old jaguar cub living with Ana and Connor, looked up at him in surprise. Carrying two large books and a pink and brown backpack, she was obviously going to school. "You need any help with those?" he asked.

Smiling broadly, she shook her head, sending her two long braids swishing around her face. "No, thank you. They're not heavy."

"And if they were, I'd carry them for her anyway." Lucas, the wolf cub who lived with Ryan, stomped up the steps behind Jayce and placed himself in front of Vivian in a protective stance that surprised and impressed Jayce. The boy scowled at Jayce momentarily before turning to Vivian, with a much softer expression on his young face.

"What are you doing here, Lucas?" Vivian asked.

Despite what she'd said moments ago, the blond cub took her books and shrugged. "Thought I'd walk you to Esperanze's."

Jayce knew from Connor that the two cubs didn't attend human schools, but were taught by one of the beta females at the ranch. From what their Alpha had said, they were both far ahead of their human counterparts in school. And from the dossier he had on beta shifter Esperanze—he had a file on every shifter in this pack—she was highly intelligent, with a master's *and* a doctorate in education. He had no doubt the cubs were in capable hands.

Vivian looked up at him again. "We've got to go if we don't want to be late, but Ana and Connor are in the kitchen."

The two cubs hurried off, with Vivian telling Lucas she was sure she did better than he had on their last science test.

Jayce's lips twitched with the urge to smile. It had been a long time since he'd interacted with cubs and it was surprisingly nice to be around them. A sudden sharp pain cut through him as he remembered how happy his brother had been the day he'd learned his mate was pregnant. It was one of the last times he'd seen his brother smile. One of the last times he'd seen him at all.

Shutting that thought down with the iciness of another darker memory, he called out, "Connor, Vivian let me in." Remaining in the foyer, he waited. From the direction of the kitchen he heard what sounded like two shifters kissing, then a very definite feminine sigh.

"In the kitchen." Connor's voice was a low growl of male sexual frustration.

If Vivian had just left for school, no doubt Ana and Connor had planned on some alone time. Considering how busy their house had to be, he doubted they'd get any time together until much later tonight. As he moved through the expansive dining room with its long table big enough to fit twenty people comfortably, Ana walked out of the kitchen looking flushed.

She smiled. "Off to do my rounds."

He nodded, then pushed open the swinging door and found Connor pouring himself a cup of coffee. The Alpha nodded at a couple of mugs Ana had likely put out for visiting pack members. "Coffee's fresh."

He shook his head. "I'm good, but thanks. Just got a call from a contact of mine—I might have a lead on a dealer selling vamp blood in the next county. Not in Winston-Salem, but it's on the way there."

"Who's your contact?"

Jayce shrugged. He'd followed up with Niko and asked him to keep an ear to the ground for news of someone selling the stuff. Part of Jayce had wanted to keep the business of vampire blood trafficking to himself, but he was glad he'd informed Niko about it. Since it was likely someone who had targeted his own kind, Niko hadn't had any problem helping him out. When he'd spoken to him, the vamp had been unable to get away. He'd sounded like otherwise he would have followed up with the dealer himself. "Not important—and he doesn't live in your territory."

Connor appeared to slightly relax at that, but his eyes narrowed slightly. "Where did you get that laptop you asked Ryan to hack?"

Jayce had been waiting for this question; he'd just been hoping to hold off a little longer. Connor had allowed him to use Ryan as his own personal go-to guy for all things computer-related without much of a fuss. Sure made Jayce's life a hell of a lot easier, since it meant he didn't have to courier stuff up to the Council. Unfortunately it also meant he needed to keep Connor in the loop more. Sharing information just didn't come naturally to him. He liked to hold things close to the vest. "It might be related to the blood trafficking."

"*Might* be?"

Jayce shrugged. "We'll find out when Ryan cracks the encryption."

Connor just stared him, his expression dark. "I know that's part of the reason you're here, so if there's something I need to know as Alpha—"

Jayce held up his hands in a placating gesture. "Right now I'm just checking up on leads. Saturday I followed up with a dealer I've done business with before. It was *not* in your direct territory. He's someone I've used for information gathering—though after our run-in he won't willingly work with me again."

Connor sighed, eyeing him warily. "That have anything to do with the explosion of an abandoned school bus in Lenoir?"

Jayce raised his eyebrows. "How'd you know about that?"

"I watch the news. . . . And I'll take that as a yes. If that shit rolls into my territory, I want to know. I'm talking one fucking drop sold in Fontana, I better not find out you knew about it and didn't tell me." Connor's voice was low and deadly.

"You have my word."

Connor relaxed, then asked, "When are you heading out?"

"Now. I just wanted to let you know." He didn't have to, but considering that the Alpha was letting him live on his ranch and train one of his packmates, and wasn't giving him too much grief about using Ryan as a resource, Jayce had no problem showing Connor the respect he deserved.

The Alpha set his mug down. "I'll go with you."

Jayce worked alone, and he was about to tell Connor it wasn't necessary when there was a light knock at the front door. If they hadn't been shifters they probably wouldn't have heard it. Then the door opened.

Before she called out a soft "hello," Jayce knew who

it was. Brianna, the fae warrior who looked anything but, had a distinctive fresh spring scent.

"In here," Connor said as he placed his mug in the sink.

The blonde pushed open the door and nodded at both of them, a polite smile on her face. "Do you have time to talk?" she asked Connor.

The Alpha nodded.

Instead of taking the opportunity to leave, Jayce leaned against the counter as the female took a tentative seat on one of the chairs at the kitchen table. "The apartment Liam found and furnished for me is nice. Thank you and please tell your brother the same."

"You're not here to thank me." Connor's voice was soft but it was obvious he didn't want to waste time making small talk.

She shook her head, the movement so slight it was almost imperceptible. "I wanted to let you know in person that I've made contact with an APL member's wife. She's . . . weak where it comes to her husband and it allowed me to glean information from her."

Connor and Jayce both straightened. "And?" Jayce asked before Connor could.

Brianna shrugged. "She has given me nothing of interest—yet—but I wanted to let you know I will not be coming back out to the ranch for a while."

Connor growled low in his throat. "Why not?"

The blonde's eyebrows drew together. "Do not growl at me. I won't be coming back here because I don't want there to be any risk of my being connected to your pack."

It was smart, but Jayce understood how Connor thought. Sure enough, Connor said, "You are in my territory and therefore under my protection. You will accept one of my warriors as your shadow. He will stay at the apartment with you."

The lines around her mouth and eyes deepened. "I am not a child."

"Then don't insult me by acting like one. You will take this protection. Angelo will go with you when you leave here."

Brianna's face tilted slightly to the side. "Angelo, he is . . . the pretty shifter?"

Jayce couldn't help the laughter that escaped. Connor shot him a look that told him he was biting back the same response.

The Alpha cleared his throat. "Uh, pretty?"

She nodded. "The one you are referring to is of Spanish descent, I believe. He has dark skin, dark hair, and bright, exotic green eyes. He reminds me of a pretty feline."

Jayce forced himself not to laugh again. She was so blunt when she spoke, it was as if she hadn't spent much time around humans, despite the fact that she'd infiltrated the APL before. "Whatever you do, do *not* let him hear you compare him to a fucking *cat*."

"Or call him pretty," Connor said before continuing. "Exactly what has the woman you befriended told you?"

"She's lonely, in need of a friend, and I didn't have to use much influence to get her to open up except when it came to her husband. He is part of the APL, something she doesn't agree with. When I used my gift of persuasion, she admitted she heard a phone conversation he had with someone mentioning an attack, but she didn't hear more than that. Like I said, nothing of importance yet, but I have faith she will be very useful."

"How are you feeling, physically?" Connor asked.

"I'm fine. Adler," she said, referring to the radical APL member who had kidnapped Kat and was now dead by Brianna's own hand, "was a constant drain on my emotional energy. He was a true psychopath in every sense of the word. An anomaly. Keeping a tight rein on his mind was not something I have ever experienced before and is highly unlikely to happen again, if that's what you are worried about."

Connor nodded silently.

She continued. "If you're worried about my ability to protect myself, then please don't be. My powers are at full capacity and without that steady depletion of my power reserves I will not go into a comalike state again if I have to defend myself. I do not need someone to watch over me."

Jayce knew the fae warrior could harness energy when she needed to. It came out in the form of an electrical current, like vivid blue lightning, from what he'd heard secondhand. He also knew Connor didn't give a shit about any of that.

He was proved right by the Alpha's next words. "Humor me, then. Angelo will be here within the hour. He's on patrol right now." Without waiting for a response, he slid his cell phone from the front pocket of his jeans and called Angelo.

Brianna looked at Jayce, as if for support. "This is a waste of resources."

Jayce shrugged. "Not my territory."

"But you work for the Council. Can't you make him—"

He cut her off before she could finish. "I'm here on official business, but this isn't my land and I have no authority over his decisions." Technically he could push the subject if Connor was in any way putting shifter and human relations in harm's way. But he wasn't. He was simply protecting what he viewed as someone under his purview.

And Jayce respected the hell out of him for it.

Brianna's lips pulled into a thin line as she stared at him. Her attention diverted to Connor the moment he ended his call. It appeared as if she might say something, but the Alpha cut her off. "You're free to wait here until Angelo arrives. He'll be following you, but won't be interacting with you in public." Then he turned to Jayce. "I'm ready if you are."

Jayce nodded. Just because he didn't need the backup didn't mean he couldn't appreciate the company. He'd been living and working by himself for so long it was oddly . . . nice to have someone go with him on a hunt. Someone who didn't wreak havoc with his hormones every second he spent with her.

There was no doubt in his mind that this was a hunt. Some asshole was providing vamp blood to dealers, APL radicals, and God only knew who else. That shit wasn't going to last long in this area. Not if he had anything to do about it.

Fletcher glanced over at the human who was forcing him to do these things. Forcing him to kill for his psychotic cause. The APL was a bunch of bigoted fools who thought shifters and vampires were intent on taking over the world. As if they hadn't been around long before humans even knew about them.

Why couldn't they understand that his kind just wanted to live in peace? Just wanted to be left alone. Hell, as a rule shifters and vamps didn't even care about politics. At least not in the human world. They had their own problems.

But these monsters had found his weakness. Every mated shifter had one, whether they were alpha, beta, or

Alpha leader. One simple word explained Fletcher's weakness.

Mate.

But there was nothing simple about his need to protect, to defend his sweet, pregnant mate. It didn't matter that he was one of the weakest of the pack, physically speaking. In his wolf form he was still stronger than most humans. And most humans couldn't defend themselves against him when he was in his animal form. Right now he had rage burning through him, a need to kill for his mate and their unborn young.

Shifters would give up anything for their mates, even defy their Alpha. As he'd had to do. His leader didn't know he was currently in Connor Armstrong's territory, being forced to carry out deeds that made him ill every second of every day.

And he hated it. As a beta his actions went against everything inside him. But he had no choice. These APL monsters held his mate captive somewhere and he had no way of tracking her. Didn't even know where to start. If he escaped—which wouldn't be hard—they would kill her instantly and he would never even find her body. Of that he had no doubt.

The blond-haired man next to him—the one wearing a badge and gun against his hip—was restless today. More than that, his captor seemed almost edgy as he slid another cigarette out of his half-empty pack.

The man's wariness was rubbing off on Fletcher. "What are we doing here?" His captor had told him nothing. He'd just dragged him from his prison in the middle of the day and told him he had work to do. Like this was some fucking job.

Now they sat in his captor's personal car on the side

of a dirt road that led to five ramshackle trailers. The man had pulled into some weeds at least six feet tall, giving them decent enough cover from whatever it was they were hiding from.

"Waiting." Typical clipped answer.

"For what?" He should probably keep his mouth shut, but it was the middle of the day and he was more than a little curious. Something big had to be going on, though he couldn't imagine what in this nearly deserted place. The trailers all looked like throwaways. Not to mention the abandoned cars, washing machines, and other crap littering the giant field next to them.

No answer from his captor. He just took a drag on his cigarette and blew out the smoke, filling the interior of the vehicle.

Gritting his teeth, Fletcher rolled down his window. He didn't like to show this guy any sort of weakness, but the smoke was disgusting.

"What are you doing?" the man snapped.

"Breathing."

The man's jaw clenched, but he didn't make a move to roll the window back up.

After a few more minutes had crept by, Fletcher was starting to get antsy. He swiveled when he heard a vehicle behind them. He turned and saw nothing, but he could hear it in the distance. Dust rose in the air, leaving a trail as the vehicle drew closer.

The man next to him tensed, causing Fletcher to do the same. Just who were they waiting for?

Another minute later a rusted blue truck drove by, though the driver didn't even glance in their direction on the west side of the road. The driver moved slowly enough that Fletcher got a decent look at him. Flannel shirt, dirty ball cap, and dirty blond hair that reached his shoulders.

"You're going to kill him," the man next to Fletcher said quietly, the edginess rolling off him in pungent waves.

The way his captor was acting today was different than he had acted with the last kill. The last one he'd been calm, sure of himself, and Fletcher knew he'd gotten orders from someone else to do it.

"Why?" He would do it, a fact they both knew, but Fletcher wanted to know why.

"We'll kill your mate if you don't," he said absently as he put his vehicle in gear and pulled back onto the road.

Grinding his teeth at the reminder, Fletcher kept his gaze straight ahead as they steered down the trail where the truck had gone. The dust had settled as his captor pulled up next to the rusted truck. When the man made a move to get out, Fletcher couldn't hide his surprise. The last time he'd gone into his victim's house alone, but he didn't bother with questioning the guy now. Instead he followed suit and slid from the vehicle.

His captor spoke in low tones as they headed for the front door. "This man's a pedophile. Fucker's out on parole and he's just going to keep hurting kids until someone stops him."

Fletcher let out a growl before he realized it, earning himself a sharp look from the man next to him, as if he was surprised by his reaction. Yes, he hated what he was being forced to do, but he also hated anyone who could hurt a child. His inner beast clawed at the surface as thoughts of protecting his mate and unborn young assaulted him.

When they reached the door, Fletcher was surprised when his captor slammed his booted heel against the door, smashing it open. He withdrew his gun but didn't make a move to go inside.

There was a shout of alarm from somewhere in the trailer.

"Do it," the other man ordered, his voice a mixture of anger and possibly relief.

Relief that this guy was going to die? Probably. Fletcher didn't have the luxury of questioning the other man's emotions or reasoning behind anything. His inner wolf took over in seconds, the rage flowing through him as he shifted.

When he bounded inside on all fours, his shredded clothes trailing behind him, he was bombarded with a variety of scents, but the pungent stench of fear rose above the mold and days-old food.

The man he'd seen driving the truck earlier stood next to a blue couch with a pink-flowered pattern. He hovered, as if he'd just jumped up and wasn't sure what to do.

Running would be the most obvious move. Too bad the guy wouldn't be fast enough to outrun Fletcher. With a loud growl, he shoved all human thoughts aside and gave in completely to his beast as he lunged for the human's throat.

Chapter 9

"You don't have to come with me into town—not that I don't appreciate the company," Kat said to Erin as they pulled down the long dirt driveway leaving the ranch, heading for the highway. After their five-mile run they'd showered, and Kat had had to borrow clothes from the petite woman. Knee-high boots covered the fact that the jeans she had on were just a little too short, but they were like a second skin.

"I want to see December too, especially after what happened last night. Plus I don't trust anyone to drive my car." The redhead shot her a sharp glance.

Kat resisted the urge to smile. The latter was probably the real reason she was going to town. Well, that and Jayce had likely said something to Erin about shadowing her. But Kat didn't push it because she didn't care. She liked Erin enough that it wasn't annoying. "When did you get this baby?" she asked, referring to the new cherry red Challenger they were riding in.

"Couple weeks ago." She smoothed a hand over the

dash, and for the first time since Kat had met her, a true sense of happiness rolled off the other woman.

"It's nice."

Erin snorted. "Nice? It's fucking awesome."

Kat allowed herself to relax against the seat. "Okay, it's awesome."

"So why aren't you and Jayce together anymore?"

The unexpected question caught her completely off guard. "Uh ... I don't know. Why aren't you and Noah together?" Kat had seen the way the wolf with the jet-black hair looked at Erin. And vice versa.

"It's complicated." From Erin's tone it was obvious she wasn't going to divulge any more.

"Same here." That was an understatement. Even if it wasn't, she didn't know the redhead well enough to open up to her anyway. Hell, December was her best friend and it had taken Kat a while to tell her everything.

"Okay, fair enough. That was a bad choice of topic. I was just curious what kind of woman made the only *enforcer* in North America so crazy."

She made him crazy? Good. "From what I hear, there's going to be two soon."

"I guess." Erin shrugged and Kat didn't have to be a shifter to sense the other woman's insecurity. It was a sharp, pungent sting to her nostrils.

Kat shot her a surprised look. "I've seen your moves and I know you guys were holding back on me today. You're really fast and accurate from what I can tell."

Another shrug, this one a little jerkier. "I still have a lot to learn, but Jayce is a good instructor. Something new every day."

Kat nodded but didn't respond. Nothing about his methods were particularly structured. Which made sense to her. Fighting for your life wasn't structured and by forcing her to simply defend herself today he'd made sure she had to dig deep and use her instincts. Of course he'd stopped her a few times and shown her different techniques, which had helped a lot. But she'd still relied on her inner wolf today to guide her.

"We've never slept together, in case you were wondering." Erin's frank statement jerked Kat out of her thoughts.

"Who?"

"Me and Jayce. He's just training me."

"Okay." She hadn't thought they had, but there'd been a small part of her that had wondered. Seeing the easy camaraderie between the two had dug talons into her chest on occasion. Sharp, painful jabs that she could now dismiss.

At lunch Kat was almost embarrassed by how much she'd ordered until Erin ordered the same amount. December had been waiting for them at the restaurant and her meal was on the light side—because of her ever-present morning sickness.

"Think we should order something to go for Nikan?" Erin asked as the server brought them their meals.

Kat glanced out the window of the small diner. It was only a few blocks from December's bookstore, but that didn't matter. Nikan, a tall shifter with obvious Native American roots, was December's shadow for the day. He was in his truck across the street. Thanks to the tinted windows she couldn't see him clearly but his outline was visible enough. Kat had talked to him only a couple of times but he seemed nice. Quiet but kind. And there was a dangerous gleam in those eyes that didn't surprise her. Each of the male warriors in the pack had a deadly edge that said he was no stranger to violence.

"Good idea," December said. "I made Nikan a batch

of cookies he was supposed to share with the guys tonight, but they're almost all gone except for *two*."

Kat couldn't help the grin that spread across her face. "If you want to be really mean you should tell him they were meant for Esperanze and her sisters." Kat might spend practically zero time at the ranch except to train, but even she'd seen the way the tall, intimidating shifter looked at the sweet beta female he'd recently mated with. The man was head over heels for her.

Erin laughed, the sound sharp and loud and completely unexpected. "You *have* to do it while I'm around. I want to see his face. Big, bad alpha is so smitten, and he does anything she or her sisters ask."

December shook her head, her bright red hair swishing softly around her face as she chuckled. "You two are mean. . . . I swear I don't know where either of you put the amount of food you eat. You all have such high metabolisms it's disgusting."

Kat had always had a high metabolism, but since being turned she'd found she ate more and burned it off much easier. One very good thing about her transformation. "I don't know what you mean by 'you all' when you're a shifter now too."

December rolled her eyes and carefully stabbed a forkful of her Greek salad—one of the few things she could keep down without getting sick. "You know what I mean."

The rest of the meal passed by too quickly, but once they were done they walked December back to her store and waited until Nikan had parked and joined her inside.

As they started to get into Erin's car, Kat motioned toward a young girl, maybe sixteen years old, who was loitering in front of the empty store next to December's place. She wore black thigh-high combat-style boots with purple laces and a short black-and-purple-checkered skirt—too short for her age as far as Kat was concerned. Only a small area of leg was visible between the bottom of her skirt and the top of her boots but she also had on black tights. At least she wasn't showing a bunch of skin. The rest of her ensemble was black too. Long-sleeved top with a tank top layered over it, fingerless gloves with purple stitching. Her hair was black, with slashes of purple. That hair was thick, long, and straight, thanks to her Asian ancestry. She looked like a typical teenager, full of angst and anger at the world. Her eyes were a striking gray that stood out against her pale skin, but that wasn't what drew Kat's attention. It was the wolf underneath her skin that did.

Kat's seer abilities had always allowed her to see the true nature of paranormal beings. And this girl was a lupine shifter. Her wolf was right at the surface, clawing and angry. The closeness of the girl's inner animal reminded Kat of Jayce's and Erin's wolves. It was different from those of the other lupine shifters Kat saw on a daily basis. This girl's animal was more prominent. Kat didn't know if it was because she was young and hadn't learned to control it yet or if there was another reason.

Without saying anything to Erin, Kat shut the car door and headed back toward the sidewalk. She knew without looking that Erin would follow.

The young girl straightened and crossed her arms over her chest in a clearly defensive gesture when she saw them. Even if she hadn't been a seer Kat would have been able to scent that the girl was a shifter. She smelled of earth and animal. It was very distinctive.

"Hi," Kat said. "What are you doing in Fontana? Are you with one of your pack members?" As far as Kat understood, shifters didn't just traipse into another Alpha's territory without calling and asking permission first. Pack rules.

She shook her head. For a moment Kat saw through the clothing the girl obviously wore as armor and found a scared young girl. Just as quickly, the fear bled from her eyes and she put her hands on her hips. "I want to be taken to see Jayce and I know he's at the Armstrong-Cordona ranch."

Kat's eyebrows shot up.

"Why do you want to see Jayce?" Erin demanded.

She paused before answering and Kat guessed it was because she was gathering her courage. "Because I'm going to be an enforcer like him."

Kat's eyebrows rose higher. She looked at Erin, curious as to her reaction. The redhead was contemplative. Finally her gray eyes—similar to the young girl's—narrowed. "What's your name?"

"Leila Jeung."

"Where are your parents?" Kat asked.

"Dead." There was a wealth of sadness and anger in that one word.

Kat had the urge to hug the girl. Instead she took a tentative step closer. There were a lot of questions she wanted to ask her, but mainly she just wanted to get her off the sidewalk and back to the safety of the ranch. "How did you get here?"

Her eyes shifted behind Kat and Erin to an older-model sedan. It looked like the kind of car a mom would drive. Kat turned back to face the girl. "How long"—she tried to think of a way to phrase her question without stating anything about Leila's deceased parents—"have you been on your own?"

A shrug and Leila wrapped her arms tighter around herself. "Couple months . . . well, a little longer."

Something heavy settled on Kat's chest. The thought of any young girl by herself in this world made Kat angry. "Why didn't your pack take care of you?"

"We were packless."

Packless? Kat looked at Erin, who just gave a quick shake of her head. Kat took that to mean she would explain later. Instead of asking all the questions she had, she held out a hand. "Give me your car keys. I'm driving you back to the ranch. We'll follow Erin."

For a moment it looked as if the young girl might argue, but instead she dug into the black satchel she had slung across her chest and slapped the keys in Kat's hand as she strode past her to the car. "You can drive but I'm not listening to old people music."

Old people? Kat shook her head as she slid into the front seat. Before she got in, Erin cursed under her breath.

Kat followed her line of sight to see two teenagers sauntering down the sidewalk. They were about a block away, but the sidewalk wasn't crowded and their cocky demeanor was obvious even from where she stood.

"What is it?" Kat asked.

"I think those are the two shitheads who tried to throw a rock through December's store window."

"How can you tell?" December had told Kat what happened, but she hadn't thought they'd been close enough to see who'd done it.

"Gut instinct . . . Plus I can scent them." Without waiting for a response, Erin took off at a brisk pace in their direction.

The two boys, probably the same age as Leila, froze for a moment as they stared at Erin. They looked at each other, then ducked into the nearest store. A high-end art gallery. Erin didn't even break stride. She continued walking and then stormed through the front door of the place.

"What's she going to do?" Leila asked quietly.

"I have no idea." That scared Kat a little. Erin was very contained and seemed to be in control of herself, but she'd been pretty pissed about what happened. This was a public place, and even if the guys were punks, they were still teenagers.

Less than a minute later the two boys practically ran from the store, with Erin a second behind them. As they sprinted in the other direction, she didn't even glance over her shoulder at them; she just headed toward Kat and Leila.

Erin nodded at Kat and palmed her car keys. "See you at the ranch."

Kat guessed she wasn't going to find out what had happened anytime soon. She wanted to push the subject, but Erin was already getting in her own car, so Kat slid into the driver's seat of Leila's car. The new hostile tone from many of the locals had happened practically overnight.

It stunned Kat a little. Today at lunch she'd tried to ignore some of the heavy stares she'd felt at her back—and some outright angry ones. She'd thought about saying something, but December had seemed almost relaxed and Kat hadn't wanted to upset her.

After she'd been questioned by the police she'd known that there would be some people who figured the cops weren't doing their job or were trying to cover up shifter wrongdoing or something else equally ludicrous. Still, she hadn't been prepared for downright hostility.

After an hour of driving, Jayce and Connor had finally reached their destination. They were sitting in front of a run-down two-story building with peeling, indecipherable red lettering on the outside wall. It wasn't completely dilapidated, but there were some random spray paint tags and some of the windows had been knocked out. It was in the middle of nowhere, surrounded by overgrown grass and trees behind it. About a mile before they'd reached the place, they'd passed a couple of middle-class suburban neighborhoods, so it wasn't that far from civilization.

They hadn't quite reached the town that was the midpoint between Fontana and Winston-Salem, where they suspected someone was running vampire blood. This had probably been a factory of some type at one point that provided work for the neighboring town.

"I hear heartbeats," Connor said quietly.

"Me too." At least six. Before he could decide what their first move would be, a man wearing a down jacket, jeans, and boots walked out.

The man's dark hair spiked with frosted blond tips and his swagger was cocky enough that it annoyed Jayce. Without hesitation, the man headed straight for Connor's truck. Connor rolled down the window, and even though he looked relaxed, Jayce knew he was ready to strike if necessary.

"Who the hell are you?" the guy asked.

"We're here to see Donny." Jayce gave the name his friend Niko had given him.

The man—who looked more like a boy of eighteen or nineteen the closer Jayce inspected—stared at them for a long moment. "You two cops?"

"Do we look like fucking cops?" Jayce kept his voice bored but put some bite behind it.

He pointed at Jayce. "You can come in, but your friend stays."

Jayce glanced at Connor and it looked like the Alpha was holding back a smile. As if keeping him outside would make him any less of a threat. Connor nodded once and Jayce got out.

"You have to leave your weapons," Spiky Hair said before Jayce had shut the door.

Jayce glanced at him as he pulled his guns from their respective sheaths. "I'll leave my guns but I'm bringing my blades."

The guy snorted. "Blades against our guns? Suit yourself."

Jayce shot Connor a covert look. The Alpha's expression revealed the same thing he was feeling. This wasn't an organized operation. Whoever these guys were, they weren't high on the totem pole—probably low-level dealers. But they might be able to offer some information. Like a name. And that could lead to more names. Jayce planned to soon find out who the hell Ned Hartwig and that APL member had been so afraid of.

The moment they stepped through a rusty metal door with an EXIT sign above it, someone shoved a gun against Jayce's head. Something he'd more or less expected.

The guy who'd entered with him made a move for his open jacket. "Did you really think we were going to let you walk in here with—"

With the speed of a shifter, Jayce kicked out at him, breaking his kneecap at the same time he swiveled and brought one of his blades up, slicing at the arm of the man wielding the gun. It dropped to the floor with a clatter. The guy he'd cut open cried out but tried to dive for his weapon.

Jayce slammed a fist across his jaw, then kicked him in the chest. He flew backward and crashed against a wall before collapsing in a motionless heap on the floor. Next to Jayce, Spiky Hair moaned in agony on the floor, clutching his leg. He hadn't even tried to make a move for the gun that Jayce could see sheathed in a holster under his pant leg.

After divesting the guy of all his weapons and his wallet, Jayce pulled out the ID and looked at the name and address, then back at him. "That was just rude, *Luis*." He injected a lot of power into the guy's name.

"We didn't . . . want to . . . kill you. Just make sure . . . you weren't armed." He struggled to speak through gasping breaths, his face contorted with pain.

"Whatever. Where's your boss located in this building?" Since more people hadn't stormed into the small front room Jayce had stepped into with Luis, he guessed they didn't have video surveillance inside.

Luis pointed at the other door on the north side of the room. "Through there, up . . . stairs, make . . . left. Second door . . . on right."

"Any video cameras on my way up?"

Clutching his leg, Luis shook his head in a jerky motion. His face was ashen and Jayce had no doubt he'd be passing out in the next couple of minutes. "Where are the cameras?" He'd seen two outside, so he wanted to gauge if this guy was being truthful. Lies had a disgusting metallic scent but fear and agony were pouring off this guy in waves, so it was almost impossible to sort anything else out.

"Two in front . . . two in back . . . connected to laptop . . . upstairs."

The guy was being surprisingly helpful, so Jayce asked him why.

"Didn't recognize you . . . at first. Don't want to die." The human's head fell back and his entire body went limp as he passed out.

Great. Not wanting to risk being seen on the video cameras outside, Jayce texted Connor to let him know what had happened. Then he checked the pulse of the guy he'd kicked and discovered he was dead. From the kick to the chest or the impact against the wall, Jayce didn't know. Even if it made him a monster, he didn't care. The guy had put a gun to Jayce's head. End of story.

Following the directives from Luis, Jayce eased the door open after listening for heartbeats. He could hear four distinct beats far enough away that he could tell the men weren't waiting for him on the other side of the door. Once outside the second door upstairs Jayce weighed his options. Taking them by surprise seemed the best way to go. If he politely knocked, he had no doubt about the type of reception he'd get.

Kicking the door in, he quickly surveyed his surroundings to determine the biggest threat. One guy lounged on a cot by a window, watching a laptop with four separate screen shots of the outside. Two more sat at a table with vials of what looked like blood. Likely vampire blood. The fourth stood by another window with a cell phone up to his ear. Jayce had no doubt he was Donny. His entire demeanor screamed that he was the boss of the small group. Not to mention that the others were doing tasks a lead guy wouldn't.

Jayce heaved one of his blades back and tossed it at Donny. It flew through the air with sickening speed, pinning the arm that had pulled a pistol to the wall. The weapon crashed to the floor.

The other three leapt into action. The one on the couch was the quickest, jumping up with SIG in hand. Before he'd pulled it level to shoot, Jayce had crossed the room and lifted the guy off his feet. He tossed him at the other two men like they were bowling pins and the man flying through the air a bowling ball. Shouts erupted from all of them and in a whirlwind of motion he knocked the three of them out but didn't kill them. For human thugs they weren't very skilled in combat moves.

Then he focused on Donny, who was trying to pull the blade free from his arm. Blood poured from his wound in a crimson stream. He groaned in pain with each struggling attempt. Jayce jerked it free and savored the howl of agony the man let out.

A slight shuffle by the door had him swiveling and ready to throw the blood-soaked blade, but he stopped at the sight of Connor. Jayce knew the Alpha was powerful but the fact that he'd masked his scent said a lot.

Connor's eyes narrowed at the struggling, practically crying man Jayce held up by the front of his shirt, before glaring at the few vials of blood that hadn't been shattered in the struggle. "I'll collect these while you question that garbage."

Out of the corner of his eye, Jayce watched while Connor packed the remaining vials of blood into a small case. Then he shut down the computer and put it into a duffel bag—loaded with money—that he'd pulled out from under the cot.

"We're taking everything you've got here today, Donny."

The man's blue eyes widened in fear.

"Are you really surprised I know your name?"

Swallowing hard, he shook his head. "What do you want, man?" he rasped.

"Names and information. If you give it to me, I won't kill you."

The stench of fear rolling off him was putrid and pathetic. "How do I know you won't anyway?"

"You don't. But if you make me torture you to get what

I want"—Jayce trailed his blade along the guy's throat and settled on his pulse point—"I guarantee you'll wish you were dead." He kept his voice light because it was a simple fact, and if he went into detail about exactly what he'd do, the guy would be too scared to talk. When he didn't respond, Jayce pressed the blade against his throat a fraction harder. "Any of your guys taking vamp blood?"

Those blue eyes flicked to the right, where one of the guys had fallen, then back to Jayce. He shook his head and the stench of his lie pushed through the other smells.

Without warning Jayce dropped him and strode to the blond-haired man Donny had looked at. In a quick move, he slammed his blade into the guy's chest, puncturing his heart. Seconds later, the guy disintegrated, leaving behind clothes, shoes, a wallet, and nothing more.

Jayce scented the acrid stench of urine. Donny would definitely talk now.

And he did. After ten minutes Jayce and Connor had everything they needed. Not much and definitely not what Jayce had been hoping for. Just the name of a dealer in Winston-Salem where Donny bought his supply and the names of a few other dealers that guy also sold to. Donny's competition. When it got to that part, Donny had no problem giving up information.

While Jayce had been questioning Donny, Connor had cleaned out the entire room—with the exception of the cocaine and weed stash—restrained the other men with ties, and done a sweep of the rest of the warehouse. Having backup wasn't such a bad thing after all.

"So, what happens now?" Donny asked as he pressed his hand to his other arm, trying to stop the bleeding.

"You call the cops and turn yourself in for dealing drugs. And if you bring up that you saw either of us here today, you're dead."

"No fucking way! I'm not—"

"Do it or I burn this warehouse down with you and your buddies still in it. If you somehow manage to escape I'll be waiting outside to finish you off. Do your time like a fucking man or die. You choose."

Nodding, Donny sniffled and pulled a cell from his pocket. Once he'd made the call, Jayce and Connor headed out, but Jayce paused at the door. "You try to run out before the cops get here . . ." He bared his canines and took pleasure when the other man paled. He might not have known what Jayce was before then, but he had an idea now.

Once they were in the truck Connor finally spoke. "I'll have Ryan check tonight to make sure they've all been arrested. Though I wonder how they're going to explain the dead guy in the entryway."

Jayce shrugged. "Who cares as long as they leave us out of it? What are you going to do with that money?"

Connor's answer was immediate. "Give it to the literacy center Kat and December volunteer at."

"Good." Jayce nodded as his thoughts centered on everything Donny had just told them. He wouldn't head to Winston-Salem tonight or probably even this week, but now he had a place to start. Once he gained enough intel on whom he was hunting, he'd go after them hard and fast. He might even involve his friend Niko. Just depended on who the main provider was.

As they pulled onto the highway Connor shot him a sharp look. "Ana just contacted me—telepathically. We've got company at the ranch."

His whole body tensed as thoughts of Kat being unprotected assaulted his mind. He'd left her in capable hands, but maybe he shouldn't have left her at all. "Who?"

"Erin and Kat ran into a teenage girl in town. A lupine shifter who wants to be an enforcer."

Jayce's eyebrows rose at that. "What?"

Connor just tapped his head. "That's all I know. Guess we'll find out more when we get back."

Jayce allowed a small measure of relief to slide through him. As long as Kat wasn't hurt, he could allow himself to relax for the rest of the ride.

Chapter 10

Kat sat on the edge of the love seat in Connor and Ana's living room. Well, Noel, Erin, and Vivian lived in the house too, but she still thought of it as the Alpha couple's place. It amazed her that the Alpha of this pack—her pack, she reminded herself—lived with so many females. For some reason it struck her as funny.

Next to her Leila had her legs crossed, her arms folded over her chest, and a scowl on her face. But the subtle trace of nervousness trickled off her every so often.

Kat might have had a father with an awful profession but at least she hadn't been alone. To be sixteen—or Kat guessed that's how young Leila was—and alone was a scary prospect.

Erin sat on the longer couch across from them, next to Ana. Both were silent. Ana had tried asking Leila a few questions but the girl had clammed up. Kat had a feeling it was because of all the shifters in the room. She was probably more scared than she was letting on. It wasn't exactly a tense atmosphere, just incredibly awkward. Since Kat hadn't spent much time at the ranch and barely knew anyone herself, she totally felt Leila's pain.

At the sound of the door slamming, Kat cringed and turned toward the entryway. Vivian and Lucas and their teacher, Esperanze, walked in.

Vivian's eyes widened as she looked at Leila. "Cool hair! Ana, can I do my hair like that?" Her little head swiveled in Ana's direction, but before Ana could answer Vivian bounded up to the young girl, oblivious to the defensive vibes Leila was putting out. "Is that dye? How'd you get the purple to stay so bright?"

"They're clip-in pieces," Leila murmured, the tight grip she had around herself loosening.

"Well, I really like them." Vivian beamed in that absolutely adorable way she always did and it was apparent she'd put the girl at ease.

"I have more, so . . . if you want to try these out, you can." She unfastened a couple of the pieces and handed them to Vivian.

"Thank you!" The she-cat snapped them up, but then looked at Ana questioningly.

With pursed lips Ana nodded. "Why don't you go upstairs and try them out?"

After thanking Leila again, Vivian ran out and Lucas trailed after her, both of them stomping up the stairs. But Esperanze still stood there, looking slightly uncomfortable. Ana motioned for her cousin to sit, but the petite woman shook her head. So Ana stood and covered the distance between them.

Esperanze's voice was soft as they walked out of the room together. The conversation drifted off and silence once again reigned in the small room. As Kat tried to think of another question that might put Leila at ease, the door opened and Jayce's distinctive scent teased her. Instantly her lower abdomen tightened with unwanted need.

Next to her Leila straightened and scooted a couple inches closer as Jayce and Connor entered the room.

Connor walked in ahead of Jayce and headed directly to them. "I take it you're Leila?"

The young girl nodded and stood, smoothing her skirt nervously. "I know I should have contacted you before entering your territory and I'm sorry I didn't."

"Why didn't you?" He motioned for her to sit back down as he took a seat next to Erin.

Kat noticed that Jayce didn't move from the doorway; he just stood there, staring right at her and making every nerve ending she had flare to life. When Leila spoke again, she managed to tune out his presence. Sort of.

The girl shrugged. "I was scared you wouldn't let me enter and when I found out the enforcer"—she shot a nervous glance at Jayce—"was here, I just drove."

"What happened to your parents?" Connor's voice was so soft, so soothing that Kat was surprised it had come from the big shifter.

Leila scooted another inch closer to Kat, who had to refrain from putting an arm around her. She didn't want to scare the girl more.

"Killed by vampires," Leila answered, her voice a broken whisper.

Connor sucked in a breath and his gaze darkened. "You're sure?"

A jerky nod from Leila.

"Did you tell the Council?"

Another nod.

Connor looked sharply at Jayce, who held up his hands. "I never heard anything about this."

Leila jumped in. "They said to contact the local police, but they'd already closed the investigation, saying it was a home robbery gone wrong."

"Why would they do that?" Connor asked.

"My family was packless, so we had no one to turn to when a couple vamps tried to extort money from my parents. They called it protection money but my parents refused to pay. They owned a deli and I worked there with them after school and—"

Leila's voice cracked and a tear slipped down her cheek. *Screw it*, Kat thought. She wrapped an arm around Leila's shoulders and was surprised when the girl turned her head into Kat's neck and quietly sobbed. Her thin shoulders shook violently until she finally dragged in a ragged breath and turned back to face the room, just about the time Ana walked back in. The Alpha's mate took a seat next to Connor as Leila continued.

"Someone broke into our home when I was out with friends and shot my parents with silver bullets. Their bodies were completely riddled through. . . . Then they . . . took their hearts out." She sniffed once but continued. "I might be young but I'm not stupid. Someone robbing us wouldn't have done that—and nothing was taken anyway. It was a warning to others in the neighborhood. I just know it."

"You're too young to be on your own. Didn't the Council offer to place you with a pack?" The lines around Connor's mouth deepened.

"When they wouldn't help me find out who killed my parents, I told them to fuck off."

Kat gently squeezed her shoulders. "Don't curse." She didn't mean to reprimand the girl—it just slipped out.

Leila's cheeks tinged pink as she turned back to Connor. "I didn't know what else to do, so I lived with human friends for a while, and then when I heard about Jayce Kazan I decided to come here."

"Why do you think you're an enforcer?" Jayce asked.

Leila tensed and Kat didn't blame her. If she didn't know Jayce, she'd be intimidated by the vicious scars running across his eye and his generally dark disposition. Not that he was doing anything overt; his entire demeanor just screamed danger.

"I . . . sort of hacked into that forum you and the other enforcers from around the world use to communicate."

"You *what*?" His voice rose, just a notch, but it was enough to suck all the air out of the room.

"I was bored one day and stumbled across the forum. I didn't realize what it was at first but after I'd hacked into it—you guys have some wicked firewalls by the way . . ." She cleared her throat when Jayce's eyes narrowed. "Anyway, I, uh, did some poking around. Some of the things you guys had listed as enforcer traits—"

"That's enough," he snapped, straightening to his full height.

Kat glanced at Connor and saw the speculation in his gaze. If she'd had to guess, she no idea about the forum or what enforcer traits were. That didn't surprise her, considering what little she knew about pack rules and shifter life in general. The enforcers seemed to operate with a completely different set of rules than everyone else. She knew there were a few enforcers placed around the globe, but she didn't really know much about them. She did, however, notice that Leila had gray eyes just like Jayce and Erin. And that trait didn't seem to be common at all among shifters.

Before anyone else could speak, Ana stood and motioned toward Leila. "Come on. I want to get you settled.

You guys can talk about all this later. You'll be staying here until we figure things out."

Leila stood, then surprised Kat by turning back to her. "Will you be here . . . later?"

She nodded. "I don't live at the ranch but I'll be here in the morning. I'll join you for breakfast. And don't worry about Jayce. He's more bark than bite," she whispered even though Jayce could hear. Definitely not true, but it had the intended effect and Leila's shoulders relaxed a fraction.

As soon as the girl had gone upstairs, Jayce let out a string of curses. Then he glanced upward before looking at Connor. "We need to have this conversation outside."

Kat cleared her throat. "If you guys don't need me for this, I have dinner plans." She'd called Aiden earlier and asked him to dinner. Since he was her maker she would always have a special bond with him and tonight she needed advice from him that had nothing to do with pack life.

"With who?" Jayce growled.

Bristling at his proprietary tone, she glared at him. "Not that it's any of your business, but Aiden. He'll be taking me home afterward so don't worry. I won't need you to babysit me."

"Jayce is training me anyway. At least you won't be bored here," Erin interjected smoothly, which earned her a dark look from Jayce.

Connor cut them both off with a sharp glance around the room, before settling his gaze on Jayce. "She'll be fine. Outside. Now."

Without waiting for the response that she knew would be forthcoming from Jayce, Kat strode out ahead of them. As she crossed the expanse of land she passed a few houses before she reached the cabin where the single males lived.

Aiden was waiting on the front porch, his dirty-blond hair tied back at his neck. Compared to most of the male shifters at the ranch, his hair was longer than almost everyone else's except Nikan's. His dark eyes lit up and he grinned as he took in her appearance, no doubt because of the skintight jeans. She might have dressed up to go to the last two bars, but around him she'd worn nothing but sweats or yoga pants. "Shut up," she growled, even though he hadn't said a word.

"Lookin' good, Kat. But I should warn you that you're not getting lucky tonight even if you do look smoking hot." His boots thudded on the short set of steps off the porch. She rolled her eyes as he fell in step with her and dropped a casual arm around her shoulders. "Jayce is gonna be pissed when he scents me on you."

"And you *want* to piss him off?" She didn't exactly worry about Aiden being able to take care of himself, but since Jayce had threatened to kill anyone she slept with, a little bit of angst niggled its way inside her even though she and Aiden never had and never would venture into that territory.

As if he read her mind, Aiden just chuckled. "I can take care of myself. It's fun to mess with males fighting their mating instinct."

She nearly jerked to a halt but caught herself. "What?"

Aiden shrugged. "I could be wrong—though I doubt it—but Jayce thinks you're his intended mate."

She snorted. Jayce might want her physically and act all dominating and proprietary, but she knew the score. He hadn't wanted her as his mate when she was human, so even if he did now—which she doubted—he wasn't getting a second chance. But that didn't mean she couldn't have sex with him.

As stupid as it was, that's all she'd been able to think about all day. It was why she'd asked Aiden to dinner. She wanted to talk to him without anyone else around. And she trusted his opinion.

"I know you're apparently the pack gossip, but I want to talk to you about some stuff and I want it to stay private." She threw in that last part even though she knew he wouldn't betray her trust.

He pressed his free hand to his chest mockingly. "I'm hurt."

"Yeah, right. I don't want to talk about it until we're off the ranch, though, so why don't you fill me in on more of your *gossip*." Even if she liked to pretend she didn't care about pack business, the more Aiden told her about everyone, the more she wanted to get to know them. Part of her was afraid they wouldn't accept her. They didn't really have a choice though, since she'd been turned without any introduction into pack life.

Aiden cut off her train of thought with his next statement. "First off, Ryan and Teresa are barely talking to each other even though I know he wants her and she wants him."

Kat had seen the way the computer genius looked at Teresa and she believed Aiden. "What's his deal anyway?"

He shrugged. "No one knows, but when Jacob mentioned he was thinking about asking her to dinner, Ryan threatened to cut off his balls."

She laughed as they passed the main house, where Connor and Jayce were outside talking. Somehow Kat kept her face straight ahead and only watched them out of the corner of her eye. Once she and Aiden were at the parking structure and out of sight, she let out a sigh of relief.

"You hold more power over him than you realize. You must know that," Aiden said, suddenly serious.

Kat swallowed hard but didn't say anything. Aiden was wrong on that front. She had no power over Jayce other than his apparent sexual hunger for her. But she wanted to wait until they were away from the ranch before she opened that can of worms.

Two hours later she still hadn't found the courage to open up to Aiden. They'd talked all through dinner about the pack and everything else under the sun except the one thing Kat wanted to discuss. Jayce.

As they strolled through downtown she felt as if her stomach was twisted into a jumble of confusing knots. The scenery was so pretty, but it was hard to concentrate on anything other than thoughts of Jayce. His scent, the way he made her laugh, the way he made her feel, the occasional smile he gave her but no one else.

Sighing, she glanced in one of the closed shops. Even though Christmas and New Year's Eve had passed, downtown Fontana had sparkly lights and a few holiday decorations still up.

"For the love of God, Kat. I think I've been patient. What do you want to talk about?" Aiden didn't break stride as they reached the final store on the edge of downtown. They'd left his truck by a park earlier since she'd wanted to walk off all her pent-up energy. Unfortunately walking wasn't helping.

But she was glad for the longer distance from the restaurant to his vehicle. "Jayce and I sort of, uh, fooled around yesterday."

Aiden let out a low whistle but didn't respond.

"Well?"

"Well, what? You're a big girl and you two obviously want each other."

"You're not going to give me a lecture about how it was stupid?"

Grinning, he shook his head. "Nope. Sometimes doing what's bad for you has positive consequences."

"That doesn't even make sense."

He paused so long she wasn't sure he'd continue, but thankfully he did. "I was involved with a vampire once. A long time ago. We were best friends, but thanks to . . . circumstances, it didn't work out." There was a strangely painful note in Aiden's voice, one she'd never heard before. It was completely at odds with his normally relaxed demeanor.

She crossed her arms across her chest. "What are you trying to say?"

Aiden nodded a polite hello at a young couple passing them in the park before answering. "I fucked up and it's too late to go back and change things, but you and Jayce . . . hell, he's right in front of you and what he feels for you isn't casual, and I *know* you have feelings for him."

"He didn't want me when I was human—"

"Are you sure about that? Has he ever come out and actually said it?" Before she could answer, he continued. "Even if it is true, sometimes people deserve a second chance, especially dumbass males. The night we found you—"

She sucked in a quick breath but didn't make a move to stop him from continuing. Just motioned to a nearby bench and collapsed on it. Aiden followed suit, but Kat didn't look at him. Instead she stared at the jungle gym in front of them. Its primary colors were vivid against the dark night, thanks to the bright glow of a nearby light.

"The night we found you, Jayce came close to killing me for a chance to hold you."

She swiveled toward him. "What? I might have been crying and in pain but I remember that night clearly. He did no such thing."

Aiden snorted softly. "The look on his face was full of so much raw emotion when he looked at you but when he looked at me . . ." He shook his head. "Pure death. He wanted to protect you, to hold you, and he thought about killing me to do it. I saw it in his eyes."

She bit her bottom lip as she digested his words. That night she'd been too emotional to look at Jayce. Hadn't even wanted to talk to him. She'd been so embarrassed that he'd seen her at her absolute worst. After suffering through the torture and near death at the hands of that APL member, she'd been bloody and naked for everyone to see. By the time Jayce had arrived she'd been covered, but she still hadn't been able to face him. And she'd refused all his calls. The first time she'd seen him had been a couple nights ago and it had brought out a firestorm of emotions inside her.

Even knowing they had no future, she wanted nothing more than to welcome him into her bed. Sighing, she turned to Aiden but stopped at the sound of a distant shout for help.

It was from the direction they'd just come from. Before she could say anything Aiden jumped up. "Come on."

They sprinted down the sidewalk, then ducked through a part of the park that was thicker with trees.

The couple they'd passed earlier were struggling with three teenage thugs who appeared to be mugging them. One had a knife pressed to the man's throat, one was rifling through the woman's purse, and the last one had his arms around her in a bear hug from behind.

"Just take our money and leave," the guy said as he attempted to struggle, but when he did, the teenager dug the knife in deeper, drawing blood.

"Shut the hell up," the guy holding the woman said.

The coppery scent hit Kat's nose. She glanced at Aiden, who motioned toward his left. "I'm going to confront them. You loop around that way, then take out the guy with the knife. I can handle the others but I don't want that guy slipping and accidentally killing the man."

Without pause, she did as he said, falling back into the cluster of trees and using them as cover.

"Nice night for a stroll!" Aiden's loud voice boomed through the air.

Kat shook her head as she sprinted through the park. He was going to have no problem distracting—and likely agitating—the three muggers. Breaching the opposite end of the opening where the others stood, she glanced around a giant oak tree.

Sure enough, they all watched Aiden as he rambled on about the weather and what a dangerous place this was for young people at night.

Creeping up on the guy with the knife, she didn't make a sound or order him to drop it. With lightning-quick moves, she reached around his lean body, grabbed his arm, and yanked it back until it broke. His cry shattered through Aiden's ramblings.

In the next instant the two others looked toward Kat, but in the short time it took them to move, Aiden had yanked the teenager off the woman, knocked him out with a swift punch to the jaw, and had the third guy on the ground with his hands behind his back.

"Make a move and I'll make you regret it," Aiden growled in his ear.

His words were low enough that the other humans

couldn't hear, but Kat had no problem hearing him, thanks to her extrasensory abilities.

The woman was crying as she ran to her male companion and wrapped her arms around him. Both of them were obviously shaken, but at least the man was holding it together as he pulled the woman away from the teenager crying on the ground over his broken arm.

Before Kat could say anything, Aiden strode over to the couple. "Do you want me to call the cops, or deal with these punks on my own?" He bared his teeth slightly to let them know what he was.

The couple looked from Aiden to Kat, then back again. A dark red aura surrounded both of them for an instant before it faded. It indicated they were both in survival mode. Despite the situation, Kat found it fascinating that they'd both shown the exact same reaction at the same time. They were very much in sync. The woman spoke first. "I just want to go home," she said through sniffles to the man holding her.

The man's arms tightened around her. "Take care of it yourself. . . . And thank you, we won't forget this or tell anyone."

Aiden nodded slightly and waited until the couple was out of sight before he turned back to the teenagers. The dark look on his face was so out of character it almost made Kat take a step back.

Before he could move, she placed a hand on his forearm. "I don't think they meant to do anything other than rob them," she murmured. She'd seen the darker aura surrounding the teenagers as they'd come up on them, but they weren't evil. Just punks. Unlike the APL members whose crimes she'd seen practically tattooed on their foreheads, these young men were different. Currently a muddy brown color lingered around them. It was faint but wasn't fading. Yeah, these kids were all scared shitless.

"You're sure?" His question was a soft growl.

"Yeah."

He paused for a moment, then nodded. "Okay."

She wasn't sure what "okay" meant, but she watched as he went to each male, pulled out his wallet, and searched for other weapons. He didn't find anything besides the original knife.

As he pulled out their IDs, the guy he'd knocked out was waking up from his stupor. Aiden shook his head at them, disgust in every line of his face. "You're all eighteen, and from what I can see, you live in middle-class neighborhoods so you don't even have the excuse of stealing because you need the money—not that I would have given a shit if you did. What the hell is wrong with you three?"

The one lying facedown twisted his head so he was looking at Aiden. "Can I sit up?" he squeaked.

Aiden nodded and waited until the kid had rolled over. "I'm still waiting for an answer."

"We were just fucking around," the one with the broken arm rasped.

"Fucking around by terrorizing a young couple not bothering anyone? Fucking around by wielding a knife so close to that guy's throat you actually drew blood? Fucking around with people in your *own* community?"

The three of them swallowed hard, the sound audible even above their rapid heartbeats and heavy breathing. Kat held no pity for them. Even if their intentions weren't murderous, things could have escalated out of control in seconds. All it would have taken was for the one kid to slip up and nick an artery.

Aiden turned to her. "I think those two"—he motioned toward the two fairly unscathed teenagers—"deserve to get an arm broken too. What do you think?"

Kat eyed the three of them. Growing up with her father, she'd had some of his brutal lifestyle bleed into her own life. Enough that she understood if you didn't punish transgressors, they'd take advantage. If they didn't make these kids regret what they'd done, they would do it again. And they might kill someone next time. She also understood that the way Aiden wanted to handle this was part of pack life. Something she'd better get used to. Still . . . these were young kids and their fear was nauseatingly potent. "Maybe we give them a break. *Once.*"

Another, purer scent filled the air at her statement. It smelled a lot like hope. Like a soft spring rain. Almost as if the three boys were linked like that couple had been, a sharp burst of emerald green and canary yellow flowed off them for an instant. It was so bright it took Kat off guard for a moment.

Aiden turned and glared at the two boys. "What do you think? Think I should give you a break?"

"We won't do anything like this ever again, we swear." Sincerity was strong in his voice.

Kat also knew he might be sincere now but that could change in the future. Only time would tell.

Aiden nodded at the kid who'd wielded the knife. "Help your friend up. We'll drop you off near the hospital."

The wounded guy moaned in pain and another of the three was actually crying. Guilt flowed through her and she wanted to curse at herself. She shouldn't feel guilty. These kids were lucky they weren't being arrested.

Other than their cries of pain, the drive to Fontana's hospital was quiet. After giving them a warning and a promise that sounded more like a threat to check up on them in the next couple of days—and after making a show of keeping their IDs—Aiden let them out about two blocks from the hospital.

"You don't think we should have called the police?" Kat asked as soon as they were alone.

"No." His answer was immediate. "At least not now. If any of them got thrown in prison they'd be eaten alive— which they might well deserve—but they might still have a chance at being decent human beings. I'm going to have Ryan run their names and see if they have records, check up on them, and make them do a hell of a lot of community service."

"You're going to continue their punishment?"

"Hell, yeah. And community service isn't harsh punishment."

"You think they'll tell the cops I broke that guy's arm?"

He shrugged, his broad shoulders lifting casually. "Maybe, but I doubt it. The fear rolling off them was real and they knew we could have done a lot worse to them. Instead, we showed mercy."

She waited a moment before asking another question. "You don't think it'll come back to hurt the pack?"

Aiden gave her an unreadable look. "Do you care?"

Surprise punched through her. "Of course I care!"

A small smile tugged at the corners of his mouth and she realized he'd been baiting her. "It wouldn't hurt you to spend more time at the ranch, get to know everyone more."

She narrowed her eyes at him. "I'll be there tomorrow for breakfast."

"Good. And to answer your question, I don't think it will hurt the pack. Connor wants to stay here and he wants to make good with the locals. We just saved two people tonight and we'll hopefully save three wannabe thugs from a dangerous path. Only time will tell on that front. And I know what that guy said, but he's going to tell his friends what we did to save him and his female and that will only spread goodwill for us. Not a bad thing, considering the bad will we've been feeling the past couple days."

Kat leaned back against the passenger seat and stared out the window. Getting used to pack rules and life was going to take time, but right now, despite what had just happened, she still couldn't get Jayce out of her head. Especially after what Aiden had said about him the night they'd found her. An unexpected shiver rolled over her. Considering they'd be sharing a roof for another night, she didn't know if she'd be able to control herself much longer. Giving in to what her body wanted sounded so much more enticing.

Chapter 11

Jayce scrubbed a hand over his face as he skimmed the printout Ryan had given him on Leila Jeung. Korean father, American mother. Sixteen years old, but she'd already graduated high school and had enough college credits to cover her first year. She'd been accepted into a dozen schools but hadn't picked one yet. Even though her family had been packless, with no Alpha to protect them, they'd been doing very well for themselves financially. Both parents were born in the last century, and from his notes, it looked like they were more in tune with the human world than the shifter world. They'd just wanted to live their lives the way they saw fit. And someone had killed them. Jayce's fist started to clench on the paper as he thought about Leila being on her own for so long. He wasn't exactly surprised that the Council hadn't told him about her family, but he was pissed. They were sure as hell going to hear about it soon.

"They didn't deserve what happened to them." Ryan motioned toward Jayce's printout about the Jeungs as he handed Jayce another one.

Jayce nodded tightly. A quick glance at the second printout showed him all the information he'd wanted on the drug dealers he and Connor had rounded up earlier. More ammunition for him to use in finding the source of the vamp blood. "Thanks. So . . . any progress on that laptop?" Cracking the encryption was a priority. There might not be anything good on it, but Jayce would find out one way or another.

Ryan's jaw clenched as he cursed under his breath. "No. I can't believe it's taking me this long. Whoever encrypted it is damn good."

"Thanks for working on it. I'll let you know if I need anything else, but keep me updated if you crack anything."

Just as Ryan started to respond, the door to the cabin opened and Teresa walked in. The petite she-wolf stopped short at the sight of them and for a moment it looked like she might bolt. Jayce was surprised because she was an alpha in nature and had never seemed fearful of him in the past.

When Ryan didn't say anything, but just stared at her hungrily, Jayce realized that the source of her hesitancy was Ryan. Jayce shook his head. "Hey, Teresa."

Her gaze jerked toward him and she shoved her hands into her jeans pockets. "Hey. Is Aiden around? I didn't think he was patrolling tonight."

Before Jayce could answer, Ryan took a step toward her, annoyance pulsing off him in waves. "Why the hell do you need to see Aiden?" His question came out demanding and full of fury.

Teresa's eyebrows shot up in surprise; then fire sparked in her dark eyes. "Don't you dare speak to me like that, Ryan O'Callaghan."

Jayce stepped forward, papers in hand. "He's out to

dinner with Kat, but he should be back soon if he's not already." At least he'd better be back. It didn't take that long to have dinner. At that, Jayce said another thanks to Ryan and then hurried out. Whatever was going on with those two, he didn't want any part of it. He had his own damn problems to worry about.

He made it to December's house in record time—and broke more than one traffic law—but Kat wasn't there. The moment he stepped inside, he knew it. Her scent was there but it was too subtle. Not subtle enough for him to ignore, however. That classic rose scent wrapped around him and he instantly got hard thinking about her.

"Just fucking great," he muttered, hating his body's reaction to her. Losing control because of someone wasn't something he was accustomed to.

As he headed for the kitchen, he heard a vehicle pull into the driveway, then two doors shut almost simultaneously. He waited a few beats, then jerked the front door open.

Only to find Kat's arms wrapped around Aiden in a tight hug. Much too tight and much too close for his inner wolf's sanity. Without thinking he lunged for Aiden, but Kat stepped out of the other wolf's embrace and jumped in front of him with a liquid grace.

"What's the matter with you?" She shoved against his chest, urging him back to the house. Over her shoulder she glanced at Aiden, who had a smirk on his face directed at Jayce.

"Thanks for tonight," she said quietly to the other wolf.

That only brought Jayce's beast closer to the surface, but the feel of Kat's palms against his chest soothed him. Moments later they were inside, but he wasn't as calm as he wanted to be. Placing his hands over hers and keeping them in place, he took a few steps forward, forcing Kat's back against the wall by the staircase. "I don't like seeing you with another male," he growled, not surprised by his honesty. He'd been bottling this up for too long.

She rolled her eyes—actually rolled them—as she shook her head. "Yeah, I kinda got that, Jayce. You *know* nothing is going on with Aiden and me. He turned me into a shifter and I trust him. I need to have someone in the pack I can go to when I need to talk."

"You have December." *And me*, he wanted to say. At one time they'd talked to each other about almost everything.

Her lips pulled into a thin line. "She's just as new to pack life as I am. But it doesn't matter either way. Aiden's my friend and you can't act like a lunatic just because I went out to dinner with him."

"You were hugging him." And had her breasts pressed tight against the bastard.

"Yeah, but I wasn't kissing him and I sure wasn't sleeping with him," she said as if the thought was ludicrous.

Which helped a little, but not much. He growled low in his throat. Even thinking about her with another male made his canines ache for release. He became territorial, possessive, and yes, irrational. Admitting it didn't bother him at all.

Kat was his.

"You're mine," he snarled.

A burst of annoyance popped off her and she shoved him. He let her, but he kept his hands in place and forced her to move with him. Slightly twisting to the side, he sat down on the stairs and tugged her right along with him until she straddled him.

"You're such an arrogant jerk sometimes." She pulled against his hands, so he let go but just as quickly grabbed her waist, holding her in place. Feeling the juncture between her thighs over his cock was fucking perfection. Well, it would be if they didn't have any clothes on. To his surprise, she didn't move. Just folded her arms over her chest and glared at him.

"I might be an arrogant jerk, but I fucking love you. You're all I ever think about and you're driving me fucking crazy. I haven't even been able to fu—sleep with other women since you left me. And believe me, I've tried."

Her arms dropped from her chest as she stared at him, those pale blue eyes wide with confusion and some other emotion he couldn't even attempt to define. "You tried to sleep with other women?" Damn it, she sounded hurt, which pierced him far too deep.

He scowled. "I tell you I love you and that's what you ask?" And why wasn't she saying anything back to him?

Her cheeks turned pink but she didn't answer him. "Well?"

"Yes. I tried. More than once. I couldn't even *kiss* anyone else. Finally I gave up because my cock only wants you." The thought of other women repelled him in a way he didn't fully understand. He only knew that thoughts of Kat kept him up at night. While he might not have much experience with love, he knew what he felt for her.

"So romantic." She pushed at him again, but he didn't give her a chance to move.

Instead he came at her fast until his mouth covered hers. It was obvious she wasn't going to audibly respond to his declaration and he wasn't a masochist. Wasting time waiting for something she might never say wasn't going to happen. Not when he could be buried inside her.

She didn't even pause, just met him with a feverish

hunger as her tongue danced with his. Shock punched through him, but he didn't have time to contemplate it. All he cared about was that she was in his arms and willing.

Kat licked and bit and teased him, and when she tugged his bottom lip between her teeth, he groaned.

They needed their clothes off, *now*. Leaning forward until he was almost sitting up, he grappled with the bottom of her sweater, hungry to tear it off. He was fearful that if he broke contact with her mouth, she'd change her mind or come to her senses and realize she was way too good for him.

Luckily, she grabbed his sweater and did the same thing. She tugged at it with a surprising urgency. Lust danced in her pale eyes in a way he'd never seen before. Grasping her butt, he lifted her, leaving both their tops on the floor, and hurried up the stairs.

Wrapping her arms around him, she gently nipped his earlobe before moving lower and licking his neck. When she scraped her teeth over his pulse point, he tripped on the top step and nearly crushed her. Somehow he managed to turn so that he took the brunt of the fall and she wound up splayed against his chest.

Pushing up and straddling him, she let out what he could only describe as a giggle as she stared down at him. Kat did not giggle. But that was what it was. "I forgot what it was like with you," she breathed out, her voice light as her palms played over his chest.

She actually sounded relaxed. Something he hadn't heard from her in too damn long. Not bothering to move from their position on the floor, he reached behind her back and unclasped her bra. As the straps slid down her arms, he hissed out a breath once she was bared to him.

Unable to stop himself—not that he wanted to—he cupped her breasts, needing to feel and stroke them.

When he flicked his thumbs over her nipples, the pink nubs turned a darker shade to a candy apple red as they hardened.

He glanced up to find her looking at him through heavy-lidded eyes. Those normally pale blue eyes darkened to almost midnight and he knew it wasn't the light playing tricks on him. Now that she was a shifter, her eyes literally changed with her emotions. And right now, she was turned on beyond belief.

Which was a damn good thing, because he was too. His entire body felt primed. It had been a long time since he'd had sex, and even though he wanted to let all of his pent-up energy and lust out, he knew he couldn't. Not this time. Not their first time together again.

Though it sliced deep that she hadn't responded when he'd told her he loved her, he shoved that thought deep inside him. So what if she didn't return his feelings? She was here with him now. That's what mattered.

Before he could lean forward and take what he wanted, Kat grabbed him by the back of his neck and brought his mouth to one of her breasts.

"Kiss me like you used to," she said in a rush.

He growled softly against her breast while he brought her nipple between his teeth. Her back arched into him, giving him more of herself. Palming her back, his fingers dug into her satiny skin as he ran his tongue around her areola.

With each stroke and lick, she shuddered over him, her legs squeezing his hips. He could hardly take it anymore. The need to fill her, to feel her clenching him was about to short-circuit his brain.

Still holding her close, he used his reflexes and agility to switch their positions. She gasped as her back hit the floor. Once she was under him, her dark hair pillowing out on the runner beneath her, her eyes widened a fraction.

For a moment he worried that she was going to change her mind. When she grasped his belt and deftly unhooked it, then started on his button, he reached between them and stilled her.

"Changed your mind?" she murmured, a trace of uncertainty in her voice. She pulled her hands away from him and propped herself up on her elbows. The action pushed her breasts out farther and he almost forgot how to speak as he focused on them.

"No fucking way," he rasped out, reaching down for one of her legs. He found the zipper to her boot and tugged on it. After quickly discarding her footwear, he found the button of her jeans and barely refrained from just ripping off her clothes. He almost asked her if she was sure, but held the question back.

If she wasn't ready, she would tell him, but he was a selfish bastard. Right now, he needed her so bad his entire body ached and trembled. His cock strained painfully against his zipper and the only reason he hadn't let her fully undress him was because he didn't trust himself not to come in her hands.

He refused to fucking embarrass himself like that. He had no problem with stamina, but being denied Kat's sweet body for so long had taken a toll. As he pulled her jeans down her legs, he bent down, kissing her inner thighs—and earned a wave of lust so potent it nearly knocked him on his ass. He continued a hot path down her knees, her inner calves, and finally he nipped at her instep.

Her feet had always been sensitive and thankfully that hadn't changed. She let out a low groan as he followed up by raking his teeth over the delicate arch.

"Are you planning to torture me?" she demanded, her voice husky and slightly teasing.

He couldn't even respond. He just slowly made his way back up her legs, kissing and raking his teeth over her soft skin until he settled between her open thighs. A perfectly trimmed strip of dark hair covered her mound. He wanted to bury his cock between her folds, but first he needed to taste her. Had been fantasizing about it for too long to deny himself now. The instant his tongue touched her sweetness, she jerked against him and grabbed his head.

In bed she'd always been ready to do anything, so damn giving it floored him. Right now he wanted her to feel all the pleasure she'd ever given him. The need to make her come, to make her shout his name as she did, pulsed through him with a vengeance.

Dragging his tongue along her most sensitive area, he inhaled her sweet scent and barely held back his growl of satisfaction when she whimpered his name. He looked up at her for a moment and his breath caught in his throat.

With her legs bent, her thighs spread, and her body so deliciously naked, she looked like an offering. And she was all his. At least for this moment.

Continuing his teasing, he focused his tongue directly on her clit. He'd been with her enough times that he knew exactly the pressure and teasing she needed to find release. He could tease her for as long as he wanted, but right now he didn't want to drag it out. Not when the urge to feel her clenching around him was so great.

As he continued stroking her with his tongue, he inserted one finger, then two, inside her in quick succession. The abrupt action had her hips lifting off the floor and he could just barely hear the sound of her heartbeat increasing above the pounding in his own ears.

Drawing his fingers along her inner walls, he shuddered in satisfaction as she clenched tighter and tighter around him. It wouldn't take her long. He just had to find that perfect rhythm.

"You're killing me, Jayce," she hissed.

The sound of his name on her lips brought his inner wolf right to the surface. It made him want to claim her and dominate her. It scared the hell out of him.

Increasing the pressure with his tongue and his stroking fingers, he tensed as he waited for her to climax. Moments later, her body pulled bowstring tight right before her orgasm.

Her hips jerked and her inner walls clenched around his fingers as the first wave hit. Light moans filled the air as the pleasure surged through her. After her back arched one final time before she collapsed against the floor, he stripped off his boots and pants with supernatural speed. The need to feel her tight body around him was the only thing that mattered.

As he positioned himself between her legs, she stared up at him with dazed, pleasure-filled eyes. Instead of kissing her, he kept his gaze on hers as he thrust into her.

Her mouth parted but she didn't break the gaze either as he buried himself deep inside her.

"Fuck." The word tore from him as she tightened around him, and then he immediately cringed at his crassness.

A small smile pulled at the corners of her lips as she cupped his face with her long, elegant fingers. Stretching up, she pressed her lips to his and invaded his mouth with her tongue in erotic, toe-numbing strokes.

He pulled his hips back and slid into her tight sheath over and over. When he felt her heels dig into his ass, urging him on, he let himself go. He couldn't stand it any longer, feeling her silken sheath wrapped around his cock.

Afraid of holding on to her and bruising her soft skin, he slammed his palms down on either side of her head as he found release. It felt like an eternity passed as his orgasm rocked through him until finally he propped himself up above her. Staring down into the pale blue eyes of the woman who owned him, an ache settled in his chest. She hadn't returned the words he'd spoken to her. Words he'd never said to another woman. And never would.

She blinked once and it was as if a haze cleared from her vision as she watched him. A fist tightened around his heart as he waited for her to speak. To say anything.

When she did, the tenseness in his shoulders loosened. "That was just as good as I remember."

"Better," he rasped out immediately. It was fucking better.

She smiled and wiggled slightly underneath him, then froze, her eyes widening in horror. "I'm not on the pill anymore. I went off—"

"You're fine. If you'd been in heat I would have sensed it—and you'll know when you're in heat." She would be consumed with the need to mate, to have sex, and he'd be damned if she'd go to anyone else but him when that time came. He couldn't admit what he wanted from her out loud, not yet, but in his gut he knew things had irrevocably changed between them tonight.

Her pretty lips pulled into a thin line. "Heat?"

"Twice a year you'll ... uh, your body will prepare to mate in every sense of the word. In human terms, it means you'll be ovulating, but it's a hundred times more potent than ovulation in human females. It's the only time you can get pregnant."

"Oh ... Aiden only told me about the no-diseases thing."

He knew what she meant. Shifters and vampires couldn't get or transmit sexual diseases. Since it was also difficult for both species to procreate, condoms weren't commonly used. But he didn't care about any of that now. Instead of responding, he slowly pulled out of her, then scooped her up from the floor. She instantly curled her body into his and wrapped her arm around his neck as her face nestled against his shoulder. The feel of her against him like this warmed him from the inside out.

Their first time since their breakup shouldn't have been on the floor at the top of the stairs, but he couldn't pretend to be sorry. Not when Kat had finally let him back into her life. It might be a small start, but it was a start nonetheless.

After laying her on her bed, he grabbed a washcloth from the bathroom and wet it. When he began gently wiping between her legs and saw tears pooling in her eyes, surprise slammed into him.

Shit.

His heart rate increased. Seeing Kat cry had always done something primal to him. It wreaked havoc on all his senses. His inner wolf ravaged his insides, telling him to make her stop. To make it better. But damned if he knew how. He didn't know why she was crying and the thought that he'd put those tears there cut him impossibly deep.

He quickly finished, then slipped into bed beside her, pulling her back close to his chest. She sniffled a few times but didn't say anything, so he didn't either. Hell, he'd already laid himself bare to her. He didn't know what else to say, and if she didn't want to talk, he would respect her privacy. Not to mention that his fear of pushing her away was too great. So he did the only thing he could. He held her.

Chapter 12

Fletcher tried to breathe through his mouth as the blond, blue-eyed man next to him slowly dragged on his cigarette before blowing out a puff of the nauseating smoke. "So what did these two humans do?" Fletcher asked, the first words he'd spoken since they pulled up to the biker bar on the outskirts of town. Apparently his killing spree for the day wasn't done.

After the morning he'd had, he was curious what fucked-up logic this human would use in forcing him to kill these men tonight. The bartender he'd had to kill first had a criminal record—one count of fraud and another of criminal negligence—though nothing murderous. Hadn't mattered to the man in uniform next to him. As long as his victims had records the guy didn't seem to have any compunction about snuffing out their lives.

Who's the monster now?

The guilt that rode inside him about killing the bartender seemed to be a never-ending wave eating away at him. Of course Fletcher didn't feel guilty about the pedophile he'd killed that morning. The man next to him might be a psycho, but he hadn't lied about his last victim's crimes. If he had, Fletcher would have been able to scent the lie.

Wordlessly, the man who supposedly upheld the law pulled a thin manila folder out from under the armrest of the truck's center console and handed it to him.

Flipping through the few pages, Fletcher read over the list of crimes, none of them pretty. Assault, armed robbery, assault with a deadly weapon, sexual assault . . . The list just went on. Killing these two would actually be doing the world a favor. Still, he didn't like being anyone's slave. And he just wanted to be back with his mate so bad it was hard to control the rage inside him.

Each time he let it out he worried that he wouldn't be able to rein it back in and would eventually turn into a feral wolf. The thing all shifters feared. "So you're a vigilante?"

The man flicked a glance at him, his ice blue eyes narrowing. "You're the monster. Why do you care?" Before Fletcher could respond—not that it would do any good—the man continued. "These two are hopped up on vampire blood. Will that be a problem?"

His eyes widened, surprise sliding through him like a fast-moving river. This human male didn't seem to know much about paranormal creatures. Fletcher might be stronger than most humans, but he wasn't invincible, and since he wasn't an alpha in nature, going up against two humans on vamp blood . . . "We should target them one at a time."

"Why?"

"I'm a beta."

"And?"

He bit back a growl of frustration. This stupid human hated his kind enough to join the APL but didn't understand what the term "beta" meant. "I'm strong, but vampire blood gives humans super strength. If they're taking enough of it or if the blood source is particularly strong, it's likely they'll kill me."

The human flicked his cigarette butt out the partially open window. "Guess you better think about that mate of yours. If you kill these two, I'll let you talk to her tonight."

His breath caught in his throat. It had been three days since he'd spoken to her. Three long days. At least they weren't torturing or abusing her. From what it sounded like, they were holding her in a home of some sort. Just like him. She was at least being fed and well cared for even if she was a prisoner.

"I want to see her," he demanded.

The man laughed, and the low, evil sound grated on Fletcher's nerves. "You think I'm fucking stupid? She's the only reason you're on a leash right now."

"She'll be giving birth soon. How long do you expect me to keep up this ... work for you?" Fletcher knew they never planned to let him go, but he played along like they did. If he could just figure out where they were keeping her or convince them to let him see her, he'd break free.

"Just another week or two," the human said absently, staring at the front door of the bar as if he could will it to open. Almost as if by magic, it did, and the two humans they'd been waiting for stumbled out.

Fletcher's body tensed and primed as they watched them walk around the side of the bar. To where their motorcycles were parked. They had punctured the tires of the two bikes earlier, so those two guys wouldn't be going anywhere.

"We'll do it here," the human said.

We? There was no *we*. Just him doing what he had to do. He wanted to argue that it was too public, but that would be useless. How could he argue when they had his woman? His bargaining power was almost nonexistent.

"I'll bring them to you. Head for the line of woods behind the bar," the human said.

The biker bar was on the outskirts of town, where there was very little lighting and no other civilian population. The cold January air surrounded him, seeping into his veins. He might have a higher body temperature than humans, but as a beta he didn't fight the chill as well as his alpha counterparts. Not that it mattered. The chill he felt now went bone-deep and had nothing to do with the cold.

It was guilt. "Why these two humans? Just because they're criminals?" he asked as he stripped off his shoes and sweater and tossed them to the floor of the truck. He'd keep his pants on until he got to the woods.

"They're APL members, if you need another reason." The human gave him an unreadable look, then stepped out of the vehicle.

He couldn't stop the surge of surprise that shot through him. So that's how the human was going to convince the two men to enter the woods. But why was he targeting members of his own group? Whatever the answer, it wouldn't change the outcome of tonight or his choice to kill them.

Using his supernatural speed he sprinted for the woods. Once he breached the forest line he let the change come over him.

In this form, his weak human guilt washed away. *Protect my mate. Protect my young.* Those were the important things in life. Nothing more.

Through a crystal-clear gaze he watched the human

who held him captive speak to the two human males cursing by their bikes. Though they were about fifty yards away, he could hear most of the conversation. The human was telling the other two humans that he'd been tracking a shifter and had him subdued in the woods.

The rage and anger rolling off the two humans on vamp blood was powerful. Good. At least he wouldn't be attacking defenseless humans tonight. These two would fight back. It was the only thing that assuaged his ever-growing human guilt.

Guilt that he worried he'd never be able to erase. Would he stay in wolf form this time? Would he give in to his urges and become feral?

Growling low in his throat, he thought only of blood and rage as he crept back into the shadows. Tonight his prey was coming to him.

Kat opened her eyes with a start, then immediately relaxed. Jayce's strong arms were wrapped around her, holding her close. No matter what, she knew he would always keep her safe if he could. By his steady breathing and equally steady heartbeat she guessed he was asleep.

She breathed out a slow sigh of relief. After last night—and a quick glance at the digital clock on her nightstand that said five a.m. told her the next day was officially here—she didn't want to think about facing him.

First of all, he'd told her he loved her. Holy shit, she didn't know where to go with that. At all. He'd said the words so casually, but the admission had pummeled through her with the intensity of a tornado. Then when he'd admitted he'd tried to sleep with other women but couldn't because of her . . . she didn't know where to go with that either. It hurt her with a vicious intensity that he'd even tried to go to another woman, but at the same time it warmed her that he hadn't been able to.

Then she'd started crying last night. The horror of it made her cringe even now. Thankfully he hadn't mentioned it. If he had, the floodgates would have opened and she'd never have been able to stop. She'd have probably told him she still loved him and would have hated herself in the morning for the admission.

She loosely grasped his wrist and slid it back and over her body. When he didn't stir she eased out of bed and quietly made her way to the bathroom. It surprised her that he hadn't moved, but she didn't question it. After shutting the door she nearly sagged against it, but didn't waste time. She brushed her teeth, then got into the shower.

Kat needed the strong jets pummeling down on her to ease some of her aches and stress. Usually a bath helped, but she didn't have time for that now. If she was going to face Jayce with a clear head once he woke, she needed some time to herself.

As the water rushed over her, soaking her, her shoulders relaxed until she heard the quiet snick of the bathroom door opening. She should have known Jayce wouldn't stay asleep for long.

Without turning around, she felt more than heard the shower curtain slide back. She stayed facing the tiled wall, staring at the luminescent glass backsplash that made the large enclosure seem to sparkle.

Big, calloused hands settled gently on her hips and Jayce pulled her close to him. The feel of his erection at her back was unmistakable and it sent a spiral of heat right between her clenched thighs.

"Why didn't you wake me up?" he murmured, that deep voice rolling over her skin like silk.

She shivered at the sound but didn't respond. Just
leaned forward, placing her hands on the cool tile and
pushed her backside into him. They'd made love enough
times in the shower that he knew exactly what she
wanted.

Talking was beyond her at the moment. She didn't
trust herself around him. Not now. She was likely to say
something asinine, like she loved him too. That so wasn't
happening. Not if she wanted to live with any semblance
of her pride still intact. When she'd been only human he
hadn't wanted to bond with her, linking them so she
would stay young just like him. Instead he'd lied. She had
to remember that even though he'd said he loved her.

She shook herself, shoving those thoughts far away.
She didn't want to focus on that. Pleasure was the only
thing that could drown her emotions. When she arched
into him, he growled deep and low as he slid one of his
big hands around to her stomach. He moved lower until
he was cupping her mound, then gently began stroking
her clit with his middle finger.

Her nipples tingled and her fingers splayed against
the hard surface of the wall. "I want more," she whispered. The sound seemed overly loud in the small enclosure.

"Tell me exactly what you want." His voice was just as
quiet as his stroking slowed over her sensitive bundle of
nerves.

Her inner walls clenched, needing to be filled by him.
"You."

Jayce lightly nipped her shoulder with his teeth. "Give
me details."

She let out a frustrated sound. This was a game they'd
played back when they'd been together. He'd loved
pushing her to her limits and out of her comfort zone.

And talking during sex had always made her blush. While he might not need or even care about talking, she knew he loved to get her worked up. And this was sure to do it. "Don't do this," she murmured.

He slowed even more, his finger barely working her. Moving her hips, she tried to force him, but he just chuckled against her skin and nipped her shoulder again. This time it felt like an actual bite. The sting was oddly pleasurable and made her nipples ache with a pent-up need to be teased.

"Then tell me what you want or I'll do this all day." He followed up with the satisfied laugh of a male who knew he held all the cards. In this instance he did. But payback would be fun.

So she gave in. "I want to feel your cock inside me, filling me, making me come until I can't think straight," she said on a breathless whisper, unwilling to say the words as loud as he no doubt wanted.

It didn't seem to matter. His body jerked behind her and the scent of that dark male lust intensified, wrapping around her so tightly it was nearly smothering.

Before she realized what he intended, he drew his hand back, grasped both her hips, then plunged into her in one solid stroke.

Despite the fact that they'd made love last night, it had still been a while before that—almost a year—since she'd been with him. Her body needed a moment to adjust. Something he thankfully seemed to understand, because he remained where he was, buried deep inside her, panting hard behind her yet not moving.

The energy vibrating off him was almost palpable. That heavy scent of dark chocolate—of course his lust had to smell that good—was back in full force, threatening to push her under.

When he began moving inside her, her lower abdomen clenched and her nipples tingled with each steady stroke. Sex with him had always been amazing, but now that she was a shifter it seemed even more intense. Each time he thrust, he hit that perfect spot deep inside her that made her moan his name and forget the outside world and all the reasons she and Jayce would never work.

Because when he was inside her, it was impossible to care about anything other than pleasure. Anything other than him. In the quiet morning in this sparkly, luminescent shower all she cared about was finding release with the man who had such a tight hold on her heart it was terrifying.

"Say you want me, Kat," Jayce said behind her, a soft almost imperceptible whisper.

"I want you."

"Only me." A low growl.

"Only you." *Always you,* she thought but couldn't bring herself to say. Her back arched as the orgasm began to build and then intensify.

All her nerve endings tingled with an awareness that left her feeling raw and exposed. Letting Jayce dominate her like this made her vulnerable in a way she would never allow anyone else to witness. Because it was him. Because she trusted him on a level no one else could ever come close to.

When he reached around and cupped her breasts exactly as she'd been craving he would, strumming her nipples with expert fingers, she let go and the climax rippled through her.

His name fell from her lips as she bucked against him, unable to control herself. Those strong hands squeezed her breasts before they found her hips and held on tight enough to leave marks. Not that she cared. Part of her liked the thought of him marking her. His own shout of her name intermingled with her cry as he released himself inside her.

The feel of his heat in her made her toes curl along with the remnants of the orgasm still spinning through her. And when she felt his teeth dig into the soft area where her neck and shoulder met, she let out another cry of pleasure until she was panting and barely able to move.

As he pulled out, he wrapped an arm around her waist. Holding her tight against him, he softly nuzzled her neck. For an instant she wondered what it would be like to bond with him. For him to take her from behind under the full moon and sink his canines into her flesh, linking them forever. Linking them so that nothing would ever separate them except death. Just as quickly she banished the thought. Thinking about something that would never happen would only bring her a bitter agony she wasn't prepared to deal with. Not now, not ever.

When her knees threatened to give way, he held her tighter for a moment, then moved toward the built-in bench. Despite the heated water rushing over them, the tile was cool beneath her as she sat.

Before she could ask him what he was doing, he grabbed her bottle of shampoo. As he started to wash her hair with hands so gentle that her insides twisted, she could feel those traitorous tears begin to fill her eyes again. She turned back toward the tile and let him get the back of her hair. She absolutely refused to cry in front of him. Not again.

It would be so easy to lean into him and let the tears fall. To let him hold her and ask him why he'd told her that he loved her. Ask him why he hadn't been willing to bond with her before. But the words stuck in her throat. She wasn't ready for the answers, so she wasn't going to ask those questions. If he told her she hadn't been good enough as a human, it would crush her soul. And if he told her that he might love her but they still had no future—and she really couldn't see Jayce settling down—living with that knowledge would slice her right open.

Right now she would just take the time she'd been offered with Jayce. It was enough for her. It had to be. She knew him—he would be leaving soon enough.

Chapter 13

Jayce stared at Kat's back as she pulled a long-sleeved black T-shirt over her head. As all that expanse of smooth skin disappeared from sight, he resisted sighing. She wasn't wearing a bra.

"You not wearing a bra on purpose?" The question slipped out before he could stop himself. It didn't matter why she wasn't wearing one, just that she wasn't. Fewer clothes for him to take off of her later.

She looked over her shoulder as she pulled her hair free from her shirt, her hair a dark, silky waterfall that he wanted to run his fingers through. It was still damp from their recent shower. Her cheeks tinged pink and she shrugged as she bent to tug her jeans on. "What do you think?"

"I think it's an interesting choice."

She rolled her eyes but her cheeks flushed an even darker shade. "Losing it later seems like a foregone conclusion." He started to say she should just go naked, but she shook her head. "Don't even think about suggesting I start running around here without any clothes on."

"It would save us a lot of time," he murmured. He'd planned to go to the ranch to train Erin and Kat hours ago, but after last night he had known it wasn't going to happen. He was taking the day off. Well, a couple of hours off this morning. He craved spending more time alone with Kat. Just the two of them. He needed it on a level he wasn't yet willing to admit.

If he could he'd take off all day—hell, all week. He would, but after this morning he needed to check in with Brianna to see how her infiltration was going and then he wanted to sit down with Leila and figure out what he was going to do with her. By her cedar scent and eye color—which was so rare among their kind—he had a feeling she was like him, was perhaps an enforcer. But it was too soon to tell. Those were just a couple of signs she might be one of them. He needed to see how she fought. How she moved, how quickly she learned.

After that, if he had time he might take a trip into Winston-Salem to check out one of the names that dealer had given him. Jayce had wanted to wait to see if that laptop gave him anything useful, but mainly he knew that once he went he'd probably be staying there for a few days while he got familiar with the territory. Leaving Kat right now wasn't something he was willing to do, not even for his job. He simply couldn't.

When Kat pulled a pair of socks out of one of the drawers of an antique-looking dresser, he paused. "What are you doing?"

"Uh, what does it look like?" she asked without turning around.

"Like you're putting on far too many clothes." His inner wolf snapped at him, telling him to strip her and take her again.

"I promised Leila I'd be there for breakfast this morning. She looked so lost yesterday I don't want to disappoint her."

"Oh." Kat's big heart was one of the reasons he loved her, but his own heart ached at the lack of her reciprocation from his stupid admission last night. What had he been thinking? The more time that elapsed after what he'd said, the bigger the ache inside him grew. He'd thought he would be okay with simply her body and her affection, but damn. That would never be enough. But how could he ask her for more when he wasn't sure they even had a chance together? How could he ask her to be his when she would then become an instant target for the hundreds of enemies he'd made over the centuries? She'd been through more than enough already. He wouldn't place her in danger ever again.

Unfortunately he'd already made a mistake this morning by marking her in the shower with his teeth. His inner wolf liked it, and even though he didn't want to admit it, so did he. He hadn't planned to do it, but it had happened and he wasn't sorry. It wasn't permanent—only bonding would be—but he'd marked her so that any paranormal creature would know that she was taken. That she belonged to him. Was it selfish? Hell, yeah. He just couldn't work up any remorse. If she found out what he'd done ... He swallowed hard. For some reason he couldn't think straight around her. Not that it was anyone's fault but his. He should have asked her first. Better yet, he shouldn't have done it at all. But he'd let his primal side take over and his most primal side wanted Kat forever.

Her husky voice cut into his thoughts. "Don't give me that sad-sounding 'oh.' I'm sure we'll have plenty of time later to ... you know."

"No, I don't know. Why don't you tell me?" He wanted

her to spell it out for him. She always blushed when she talked dirty and it turned him on like nothing else could. The way she turned red always reminded him of their first time together. He'd spent hours working her up until she was panting and ready for him, so he'd gone down on her for quite a while. At first she'd been embarrassed that he wanted to kiss her between her legs. Her entire face had flushed crimson, but after that first climax, embarrassment had been the last thing on her mind.

"Whatever." She shook her head as she zipped up her boots. "I'll let you grope me during training . . . Oh, maybe I will wear a bra," she said absently and opened the top dresser drawer.

"No training today." He would just switch his intended schedule around, handle everything this morning and take part of the afternoon off.

She whipped around, sports bra in hand. "Why not?"

He shrugged and had to resist walking over to her, pulling her into his arms, and heading right back to bed. "I've got some stuff to do, and most of it involves you naked."

"You can't just cancel everything. . . . Well, I guess you can," she murmured and he noticed the way her nipples tightened under her sweater. When that classic rose scent of her lust intensified, rolling off her in a deep wave, he grinned and didn't bother restraining himself. It was her natural scent, but when she was turned on it was much stronger. His legs quickly ate up the distance between them until he was grabbing her hips and pulling her tight against him.

It soothed him that she didn't argue about taking the day off and that she hadn't been acting different around him this morning. She'd gotten into the shower without him—when she'd thought he was sleeping—and he hadn't been sure what kind of reception he'd get when he joined her. She'd been more than willing, though, so he couldn't ask for more. Well, he could and he would, but in time.

He still wasn't sure what the hell he could do with his feelings for her. Shoving them away again wasn't an option. He'd walked away from her once and he didn't know how he could do it again. Especially since he'd marked her. Fuck, what had he been thinking? He hadn't. That was the problem. Around her, coherent thought took a vacation. His feelings were all fucked up. He'd never had trouble focusing on his job before, but now . . . Kat changed everything.

He hadn't bothered with a shirt because he'd known it was unlikely they'd make it out of the bedroom before making love at least once more, and as she ran her hands up his bare chest, he covered her mouth with his.

Hungrily he teased her lips open, invading her mouth with his tongue. His hips jerked almost involuntarily against her, pressing his erection against her lower abdomen.

She made a low moaning sound that cut straight through him. Grasping the bottom of her T-shirt, he paused only when he heard the insistent buzz of his phone dancing across the nightstand. He wanted to ignore it. Should ignore it.

Kat pulled back first. "Go on. You don't know who it could be and we need to head to the ranch." There was something in her eyes that he didn't want to acknowledge.

Not relief exactly, but damn close. His phone buzzed again. "Yeah," he answered on a snarl.

"Don't come to the ranch today." Connor's voice was quiet.

A burst alarm of jumped inside him. "Why?"

"Cops are here. There were three murders yesterday. First at a trailer park, a lone man in the middle of the day was ripped apart *inside* his home. Guess he didn't check in with his parole officer or he wouldn't have been found so quickly. The second attack happened last night—two males. APL members."

"All of them killed by a shifter?" Out of the corner of his eye, he noticed Kat straighten, but he didn't turn toward her. She would be able to hear the entire conversation since her senses were more sharpened now.

"Yeah. Bodies were definitely ripped apart by a shifter, according to Parker. Same teeth imprints as the first attack." Connor's voice was grim.

Shifters had larger jaws and teeth than their regular animal counterparts. Not to mention that the first human had been attacked inside his house. And now it seemed as if yet another human had been attacked the same way. The likelihood of those attacks being from an animal was slim, so if the imprints were the same for the second attack, it seemed like a good assumption it was a shifter. "What're the cops doing?"

"DNA tests. They've got a court order for everyone who lives here. I know you're not a member of the pack and don't live here, but . . ."

"I got it." If he was there they might attempt to test him and that sure as hell wasn't happening. Not without a fight and that would just get messy. "Did you learn anything?"

"Humans must forget we can overhear everything. They only said the first attack took place inside a trailer, but they didn't mention a location or other specifics. The attack on the bikers took place behind that biker bar you and Erin busted up a month and a half ago."

"I'm on it."

"Call me the second you figure out anything. I know they're going to be watching the ranch after this, so I'm keeping everyone under lockdown for the time being, but if need be we can get away for backup."

"Good idea. I'll be in contact." He disconnected and turned to meet Kat's worried gaze.

"Do you think anyone at the ranch was responsible for this?" There was uncertainty in her voice.

He shook his head. It didn't make sense, though at this point he couldn't rule anything out. "No, but at least we've got a lead." For a moment his gaze dipped to the outline of her breasts. Some days he wondered what it would be like if he had a normal job—then he quickly dismissed that thought. He'd be bored out of his mind. "Get dressed. You're coming with me."

Her pale blue eyes lit up. "I am?"

There was no way Jayce was leaving her behind. She was his to protect. "I know you heard that conversation, so pack a gun. If you don't have one, I've got extra. Or you can use one of my blades." He'd never made that offer to anyone and never would again. Showing Kat how he felt about her by offering up something so important to him was the only way he knew how to communicate. Telling her what she meant to him wouldn't do a damn thing anyway. Clearly. He'd told her he loved her and she hadn't responded. Maybe she needed to *see* how serious he was.

Now her eyes widened. "You serious?"

He shrugged as he turned on his heel, heading for the door. "Be ready in two minutes. I want to get out of here in case the cops decide to come sniffing around December's house."

By the time Jayce made it downstairs Kat was already

waiting for him, wearing a thick black jacket belted over her dark jeans along with knee-high boots. He saw the faint outline of a gun at her back before she turned to him. A very small gun, likely a .380. Or that's what she'd had back when they'd been together—a gift from her father. The lightweight weapon had an easy grip and was made to be concealable. He'd seen her at the range and knew she had no problem wielding it. Her accuracy was beyond impressive.

"Ready?"

Kat nodded, her arms crossed over her chest. It wasn't overt, but he could almost sense her pulling away from him. In the subtle way she stood by the front door, there was almost an invisible wall between them. It was thin, but if he didn't do something about it now she'd keep building layers.

He knew her too well. And he refused to let her do that to him. To them. Grabbing her hips, he tugged her close.

She let out a yelp of surprise, her fingers splaying against his chest to balance herself. She opened her mouth, but he didn't let her speak. Just crushed his mouth over hers in a move that was purely meant to dominate.

Eventually he pulled back and she stared up at him, breathless and looking more than a little dazed. "What was that for?"

"You don't get to walk away from me. Not after you let me back in your life. Don't think that's an option," he growled.

She blinked once. "I wasn't—"

"No walls between us. And no lies."

Kat was silent for a long beat, and he could hear her racing heart. Her eyes narrowed slightly. "No lies?"

He nodded.

"So you won't be telling me any more giant lies like the one about shifters and bonding?"

He shook his head. Of course she'd bring that up. She had every right, but he didn't want to fight with her this morning and he didn't want to explain why he'd lied to her. She would just argue with him, convinced that she was right. Maybe, deep down in a place he couldn't even acknowledge, he knew he should have given her a choice and told her the truth. But letting her knowingly make herself a target? He shuddered at the thought. "No more lies," he ground out.

"Good to know." Jayce waited for her to continue, but she stepped out of his embrace and grasped the door handle. "We should get out of here."

Growling under his breath, he stepped in front of her. Male shifters always went out first. It was a matter of checking for danger. Back when they'd been dating it had driven her crazy, until he'd explained what he was doing. Sending a female into an unknown situation made no sense and he didn't understand the human tradition of males letting females walk into buildings first.

As he glanced around the quiet neighborhood with a newly fallen layer of frosty snow on the ground, Kat brushed past him, pure attitude rolling off her.

He wasn't sure what was going on in that head of hers, but he liked watching the sway of her ass as she headed for his bike.

Wordlessly she put on the helmet he handed to her and snapped the tinted visor in place, blocking his view of her eyes. Sighing, he slid in front of her and savored the feel of her arms wrapped around him as he pulled out of the driveway. When she pressed her breasts tight against his back he figured he could deal with her anger as long as she was in his life.

"So what exactly are we doing here?" Kat whispered to Jayce as she peered around a giant oak tree. They'd parked about a mile off the highway, then trekked through the woods to come up behind a biker bar where two APL members had been killed. She certainly wouldn't be losing any sleep over their deaths. She could just barely see the outline of the one-story building through the cluster of trees. Crime scene tape looped around a few trees and the scent of death tickled her nose. It was fading but there nonetheless.

"Trying to get a scent," he murmured without looking at her.

"Of who?" They hadn't been able to talk on the ride over and she hadn't wanted to talk to him as they'd run through the woods. Too many conflicting thoughts raced through her head.

"Whoever killed those men. The cops seem pretty sure it's a shifter because of the bite imprints, and if it's the same one who killed that bartender Friday night, he's escalating. Three new kills in a twenty-four-hour period is extreme."

"Could it be a feral shifter?" She'd heard the term a few times, though she wasn't exactly sure what it meant other than a shifter gone crazy.

Jayce shook his head. "A feral shifter doesn't think about stealth hunting or hiding from its prey. It goes mad, its eyes turn bloodred, and when it goes on a killing spree, it's usually put down almost immediately."

"Why?"

"Because feral shifters have no survival instinct. They attack anything that smells like food, but they don't worry about protecting themselves. Whoever did this planned the killings. They're too far apart for it to be a feral wolf—but too close together for this to be anything other than shitty. Not to mention that two of the killings were indoors. Ferals go for easy, accessible prey."

"Oh." The bartender she'd gone home with had been killed on Friday and it was now Tuesday morning. Not even a full week had passed. And this time three men had been killed. That was a definite escalation. She might not know much about shifter life, but she knew the locals would start to get angry if things got any worse. They'd already started to show signs of hostility—the crazy lady harassing December and then those teenagers trying to vandalize her store. If they'd been more evil-minded they could have thrown something worse than a rock. And it could have hit December. Not to mention the antagonistic vibe Kat had gotten at the restaurant from other diners. Angry locals would be bad for the pack ... her pack. The sudden, territorial urge to protect her own surprised her. It surged through her violently. The thought of anyone doing this and causing her pack harm made her see red. "Do you scent what you came for?"

He shook his head. "Stay here." Without waiting for a response, he moved with a speed that stunned her.

She blinked and he was twenty yards in front of her by another giant tree. He'd definitely been holding back during their jog here. It always amazed her to see him in action. Jayce looked like a roughneck but he had amazing grace and skill.

Moments later he was back. "Come on."

Without questioning him, she fell in line as they began their trek back to his waiting motorcycle.

Once they reached it, she leaned against the bike, perching on the edge of the seat. They were far enough off the road that they'd be hidden if anyone drove by. "So what did you find?"

A curious frown marred his face. "I scented a beta wolf who's been missing from the Menuci pack."

"Menuci pack?" That sounded vaguely familiar.

He nodded. "They live near the coast. Four or five hours from here. I stopped there on the way back to Fontana at the Council's request, but they didn't have any new leads and I couldn't help them with a missing-person case gone cold."

"I thought betas were supposed to be weaker or at least less aggressive."

"They're both of those things. In wolf form a beta could kill humans, but he would have to have a damn good reason to do so. It goes against their nature."

"So what would make a beta wolf kill four humans unprovoked?"

She could practically see the wheels turning in Jayce's head. "He and his pregnant mate are missing."

The bottom dropped out of Kat's stomach. She wouldn't put it past the APL to use a pregnant woman as leverage to control someone. There might be no connection, but . . . "You think the APL has his mate?"

Jayce's face was grim. "I don't know. It would make a good incentive for him to become a killing machine. And I've seen it happen before. Alphas who want to use betas will sometimes threaten their mates."

"Alphas *do* that?"

"They don't stay in power long, but it has happened." His voice was razor-sharp and she had no doubt that he had eliminated Alphas like that.

That made her smile internally. She'd heard that shifters were afraid of Jayce, but he wasn't some mercenary.

He meted out justice and helped those who were weaker. It made her proud.

"So what are we going to do?"

"Track him. The scent is faint, but I can smell it near the road from here. He headed south, back toward town. If we're lucky, he's staying nearby."

"You're taking me with you?" She couldn't hide her surprise.

"I'm not letting you out of my sight." His words were a soft growl.

She wasn't sure if that was a good thing or a bad thing. His confession of last night still rang loudly in her head. *I fucking love you.* Even the way he'd said it was all Jayce. If he'd gotten all mushy she probably would have scoffed at him, but he'd been blunt, honest, and exactly himself. Why did she like that so much? Instead of responding she slid the helmet on her head, thankful that it covered her eyes from his penetrating gaze.

Riding around with Jayce might wreak havoc on her hormones and her heart, but it was damn interesting learning more about pack life. For the first time in over a month she felt useful again. Not like a shadow of her former self just trying to train enough to defend against potential attackers. She actually felt good about what they were doing. If they could figure out who was behind these killings, it could exonerate her pack from any wrongdoing. The more she adjusted to her new body and life, the more she realized she wanted to embrace them as her own.

Erin stood around Connor and Ana's kitchen drinking coffee with Noah and Ryan. The cops had left—judgmental jerks that they were—so Connor and Ana were getting everyone else settled down again. Erin wasn't worked up, though; she was just annoyed.

She hated anyone taking her DNA. The swab was painless, but it just felt invasive. On one level she understood why the cops were doing it. The recent killings had apparently been vicious and there was no doubt they had been perpetrated by a shifter. Especially since the first man killed had been massacred in his home, his head completely torn off. Regular animals just didn't do that. But law enforcement didn't treat humans this way. If someone was killed by "normal" standards, the authorities didn't round up all the humans in town and test their DNA. On an intellectual level she understood that it wasn't the same thing at all, but it still irked her inner wolf. Made her testy and ready for a fight.

Unfortunately they were on lockdown until Connor said otherwise. Of course Jayce was out there—not that he was a member of the pack—with Kat, having all the fun of tracking down whoever had been doing these killings. Erin's fists clenched. Someone was making their pack look bad and they were going to pay. If Jayce didn't find them first, she was itching for a go at whoever was responsible.

Jayce had said he'd tell her when she was ready to act on her own as an enforcer, but she felt ready. Maybe not to be completely on her own—not that she'd admit that to anyone, especially him—but a small investigation on her own was something she knew she could handle. But Jayce hadn't given her the go-ahead.

"I hate being on lockdown," she growled.

Noah shrugged, his dark eyes unreadable. Ever since she'd told him they could only be friends—all of a day and a half ago—he'd been different. Not weird, but she felt like he was plotting something. Being all acquiescent and okay with what she'd said, when he'd been her shadow for a year. It was infuriating.

Bored and feeling edgy, she shot Noah a look she hoped he understood as Ryan murmured his agreement into his cup of coffee.

Noah's eyebrows raised a teeny tiny fraction—just enough that no one else would have noticed it. But of course she did. She noticed everything about him whether she wanted to or not. "I wonder how long Connor will keep us on lockdown," she said.

Ryan's shoulders lifted. "Who cares?"

She knew why he didn't care. It meant no duty assignments away from the ranch, which meant no time away from Teresa. He might not be willing to admit it, but he was pining for her something fierce. So when Erin turned to Noah she barely held the grin back. "I bet Teresa's bummed. Didn't you tell me she had plans with some human male in town? Matt, right? The man who owns that Native American store with his mother?"

Noah didn't miss a beat; that was one of the reasons she adored him. For all his seriousness, he loved to play with her. "I think it's more than plans. He's got a big date in the works—"

Noah was cut off as a low, menacing growl worked its way deep from Ryan's throat. Erin had just wanted to mess with him, but the dark look on his face stopped her cold. "Shit, Ryan, we were just messing with you."

Ryan glared at both of them. "Fuck! That's messed up. I expect it from you"—his eyes narrowed on Erin—"but not you, man." He shook his head and for a moment Erin thought he was really and truly pissed, but then he laughed under his breath. "Payback's going to be a bitch, short stuff."

She rolled her eyes at the nickname, though inside it

warmed her. Her relationship with the warriors of this pack was more comfortable than with her last pack. Not that she'd truly let her guard down around them. She'd seen firsthand what happened when you trusted someone and they betrayed you—she had the scars to prove it too. Scars that went far deeper than the faint ones that marred her back and sides. Shaking off the dark memory, she pasted on a smile. "Whatever—"

Erin stopped abruptly as Vivian raced inside with Esperanze, Lucas, and Leila in tow. Lucas and Vivian were in shifted form and the little cubs were absolutely adorable.

Esperanze, the pretty shifter with hair longer than anyone else in the pack—the kind of gorgeous locks Erin wasn't afraid to admit she envied—looked completely frazzled. "Erin and Noah, you two are in charge of these little hellions," Esperanze said as she motioned to Vivian and Lucas.

"No problem." Erin wrangled Vivian out from under the table. "Come on, you little she-cat. It's time for a run." As Erin pulled her out, she saw Noah trying to wrestle Lucas out from the pantry, where he was hiding behind some canned food. For one completely insane moment she could actually picture what it would be like to have cubs with Noah. The thought alone sent a brutal, knifelike sensation jamming through her chest. As her breath caught, Noah looked over and frowned.

The concern in his gaze nearly undid her, but she ignored him and focused on Vivian, who was trying to scramble out of her grip.

Once she got the she-cat under control, she turned back to face Esperanze and stilled.

Almost as if he'd appeared out of nowhere, Nikan was suddenly in the room. The tall Native American shifter who'd recently mated with Esperanze was standing next to her, his stance completely protective and proprietary. "Do you need help with anything?" Nikan asked.

Esperanze shook her head, fine lines bracketing her mouth. "No. Leila already has some college credits, but we're going to go over what classes she might be able to opt out of through testing and I can't do that with the cubs—"

"I don't need to finish school," the young she-wolf muttered, earning her another exasperated look from Esperanze.

Erin eyed the girl, curious as to whether she was like her, and wondering what Jayce was going to do about it. Leila had gray eyes and that unique yet familiar cedar scent that Jayce had told her was common among enforcers—few though there were. And if Erin had to guess, she'd say Leila preferred fighting in her human form. She really wanted to know if the young shifter had any fighting skills, namely if she had a preference for blades, but at the same time she didn't think one so young should be fighting anyway. Thankfully, Jayce was the one who would figure out if Leila was like them.

"You're going to listen to what Esperanze has to say anyway," Erin said quietly.

Leila crossed her arms over her chest, a sulking expression covering her face. "Fine."

Before anybody else could say anything, the front door banged open. "Everyone in the living room. Now." Connor's voice carried to whoever might be in the house.

Even Vivian settled against Erin at Connor's command. There was something about an Alpha's voice that just made you listen.

As they all hustled into the room, Erin wasn't surprised to find almost a dozen more pack members filing in. Absolute quiet descended as Connor flipped on the giant flat screen he'd recently installed. Erin stood next to one of the couches, conscious of the fact that Noah was directly behind her. All that male heat could burn her if she let it.

Suddenly her thoughts of the sexy man at her back disappeared as the reporter's words on television registered.

The pretty brunette wearing a sharp black pantsuit with a black-and-white-checkered scarf stood outside the police station, holding a microphone in front of a woman who was probably in her early forties. At the bottom of the screen the word LIVE appeared in red all caps.

"In light of these recent killings allegedly committed by shifters, how do you feel about the safety of your family?" the reporter asked.

The woman brushed her hand over her curly hair, obviously nervous. "Any killings in our town make me scared."

"Do you fear members of the Armstrong-Cordona pack who live on the outskirts of Fontana?"

The woman shrugged and tugged on her hair almost absently. "I . . . Well, yes, especially with what's been happening. I don't understand why the cops haven't made an arrest yet."

"Do you feel that Sheriff McIntyre's relationship with this pack has compromised his ability to do his job where these shifters are concerned?"

"She's spoon-feeding her leading questions." There was raw fury in Ana's voice.

On the screen, the woman took a small step back from the reporter, her eyes wide. "Well, his sister is married to one of those shifters, so I guess anything's possible, but—"

"We're about out of time, but thank you so much for talking to me this morning." The reporter turned back to the camera and began a diatribe of borderline slander, not quite saying that the sheriff was dirty, but implying it. She also implied that their pack was behind these recent killings, but at least she mentioned the criminal records of the victims—damn, that reporter worked fast.

The entire situation made Erin's blood boil. Whatever happened to responsible journalism?

Connor turned the television off. "This is why we're all going to be sticking close to the ranch until this mess is settled. We don't need to be in town and possibly inciting any humans. And if for some reason a human tries to physically or verbally spar with you, walk away. By now I'm sure you all know what happened at December's store Sunday night. Thanks to Erin there was no damage, but that's not even important. Those actions are reflective of how the locals are starting to look at us and we all need to be prepared for any situation at this point."

As a few pack members asked questions, Erin raked her free hand through her hair. The woman who had been interviewed was clearly afraid of their pack. If the local news team kept reporting slanderous stories, the view of shifters among Fontana's citizens could turn even worse. It would take only a handful of really angry people to turn the tide. And that could create a volatile situation that none of them wanted to face.

Chapter 14

Brianna tucked her blond hair behind her ear, a very human gesture that she never would have made before her first attempt to infiltrate the APL. Now she tried to mimic humans as much as she could. It helped her blend in. And her mannerisms seemed to put the woman across the booth from her at ease.

Jackie Anderson. Stick-straight shoulder-length brown hair, brown eyes, and frumpy clothing that hid her shape. It was what Brianna saw when she looked at Jackie's outward appearance. But the woman was also kind. And scared. She hadn't come out and said the words, but Brianna could sense it whenever she talked about her husband.

Even when Brianna used her gifts of persuasion to get Jackie somewhat relaxed around her, she still sensed a lingering fear. Unlike shifters, Brianna couldn't scent things, but Jackie wore her emotions like a thick winter coat. Right on the outside for Brianna to see.

"I should probably get going," Jackie murmured as she played with the handle on her plain white coffee mug.

It was empty and they'd already shared two cups. Brianna looked directly into Jackie's sad eyes and concentrated as she dropped her voice an octave. "But you were just telling me about the conversation you heard last night between your husband and someone."

Those brown eyes dilated slightly as Jackie stared at her. "Uh, yes, it was a cop, I think. Or at least it sounded like it. Ralph has some friends on the force. He also said something about their secret weapon and a man named Mayfield not being on the ground, whatever that means. My husband told his friend he'd made the right choice in targeting criminals. And—"

A loud crash sliced through the air as one of the waitresses dropped a tray containing two large breakfast plates only two booths away. The sound jerked Jackie out of her slight trance. "I should probably get going," she said again and this time she stood. "Ralph has today off and he doesn't like it if I'm gone too long."

Brianna's eyes narrowed for an instant as she allowed anger to well up inside her, but she quickly pushed the emotion back down. "Of course. I'll call you later this week. Maybe we can go see a movie or something?"

Jackie fiddled with the zipper on her coat. "Maybe. Thanks for meeting me today. It's nice having someone to talk to."

Brianna smiled. "Same here."

Once the human left the diner, Brianna looked around for Angelo, her new shadow, though she'd already guessed she wouldn't see him anywhere. The attractive shifter caused heads to turn wherever he went—and something foreign twisted inside her every time a female looked at him, something she would never acknowledge—but today she hadn't seen him following her from her new apartment.

Still, she knew he was nearby. The man was like a ghost. Her innate senses as a member of the Fianna told her someone was watching her and had been all day. Those same senses told her it wasn't a dangerous watcher either. That's how she knew it was Angelo. After leaving money on the table, she made her way out of the restaurant, pausing only to open the door for an older woman.

It was chilly outside, and shivering slightly, she burrowed deeper into her heavy, ankle-length coat as she hurried down the block. She'd parked her car in front of a Christmas shop that wasn't open yet. As she shut the driver's-side door, a deep voice from the backseat made her nearly jump out of her skin.

"How did your meeting go?" Angelo asked from his supine position. She could see him clearly in the rearview mirror, which had been slightly turned, no doubt for that very reason. One of his arms was propped under his head and those astute green eyes were trained right on her.

Instead of turning around and giving away that someone was with her—even if the windows were tinted—she adjusted the mirror and started the vehicle. "It was fine."

"Just fine?" His incredibly deep voice always sent a thrill through her.

Even as it annoyed her, Brianna found herself looking forward to the times Angelo spoke. "That's what I said." She didn't have orders to report to him, so she didn't offer up any information. She would call Connor as soon as she was in the safety of her apartment, where she had a cell phone with scrambling software on it. After that she would call Jayce. Angelo would certainly hear everything she said then and she didn't like to repeat herself. Plus, something about Angelo's attitude annoyed her.

She couldn't tell what he was thinking. Ever. He stared at her with those penetrating eyes that seemed to see straight through her. It was infuriating, an emotion she wasn't used to feeling. She was always in control, but this shifter made her want to lose her temper.

"So what's on the agenda now?" he asked.

"We are going back to the apartment." The apartment Connor had insisted that Angelo share with her. She didn't know everything about shifters, but she knew they liked their space. Living in such a small place must be agitating him. "Would you like me to drop you off somewhere so you can expend some energy?"

A low, dark chuckle filled the car. "I can think of plenty of ways to expend energy inside our apartment."

Brianna could feel her cheeks flame as the meaning of his words set in. Among her people, she was revered for her rank and because her family was considered royalty. No one had ever spoken to her like that. "It is not *our* apartment. You are there as a courtesy."

"Whatever you say, princess," he murmured, his voice making her imagine things she had no business thinking.

Dark, erotic thoughts of seeing what lay underneath his clothes. He had broad shoulders, but he was lean and tall, like the majority of her people. Except for his bronzed skin he would fit in better than she did in the height department. Instead of responding, because she knew that was exactly what he expected, she kept her gaze straight ahead.

As soon as she finished this job she would return to Ireland and forget all about this tall, dark shifter who made her belly tighten and her mind spin off into fantasies.

Damn it. Jayce idled at a stop sign in a middle-class neighborhood on the outskirts of downtown Fontana. It wasn't inside the city limits, but just outside by a few blocks, if he remembered the map he'd studied. He'd lost the scent of Fletcher Monroe, which was completely distinctive, as it was for all shifters. His was a blend of fir and spruce, and right now that scent mushroomed off in too many directions. As if he'd driven around or run around trying to confuse his scent. If that was the case, he had done a fine job of losing anyone who might be tailing him.

"What is it?" Kat asked quietly, her helmet still on and her arms wrapped tightly around him.

Thanks to his extrasensory abilities, he could hear her perfectly despite the helmet. "The scent is too diluted."

"So what are we going to do?"

Glancing around, he established that they were relatively alone. He pulled out his phone and brought up the list of APL names and addresses he'd saved. "We're going on a fishing expedition."

Kat flipped her visor up and leaned around him to see what he was doing. "What do you mean?"

He held up his phone. Connor had originally given him a physical printout, but Jayce had asked for a digital version. He might be older than most shifters, but he loved certain aspects of technology. "This has names and addresses of APL members in the area. We're going to drive by each place to see if I can get a handle on Fletcher's scent. If it's stronger at one place that's a good indication that he's staying there or was there in the past."

Kat nodded but didn't say anything, so Jayce continued. "You already have this list, don't you?"

She bit her bottom lip and the faint thread of guilt he'd scented from her days ago was back in full force. "Well, yeah. Part of it, not the whole thing. I sort of, uh . . . God, I feel like such a jerk. I found the list in Liam and December's house and took pictures with my cell of a few pages."

He'd figured it had to be something like that. "You're going to eventually need to tell them what you did."

She sighed, the sound heavy and tired. "I know. I just feel so bad. December's been such a great friend."

"Then she'll forgive you." Of that he had no doubt. He was glad Kat had admitted her small indiscretion to him. Stealing from a packmate wasn't necessarily small, but he knew Liam and December would let it go, especially after everything Kat had been through. Her intentions hadn't been malicious. The fact that she'd told him meant she was beginning to trust him again. That had to count for something.

"I hope so," she said quietly.

"Hold on tight. I'm going to start with the farthest address and work my way back." He'd visited a handful of the homes before and hadn't scented Fletcher—though he hadn't been looking for him then—but he was still going to stop by those places too.

After a few hours they still hadn't found what they were looking for even though they'd driven past almost every residential listing. Jayce didn't let frustration take over, though. He'd been doing investigations for the Council long enough to understand that things just took time. If he allowed himself to get worked up, he'd have gone crazy a long time ago.

Behind him, however, he could feel Kat getting antsy. She kept shifting against the seat, and he could practically feel the anxiety rolling off her. Not that he blamed her. She wanted action. Something told him that would happen soon enough.

As he steered through Fontana's historic downtown

and toward Avalon Street, he felt her tense behind him. Her fingers dug into his sides questioningly.

"I'm hungry and I know you must be by now too," he said, knowing she'd hear him despite the wind and her helmet. The truth was, he could go for long periods without sustenance, but he wanted to sit down, have a meal with Kat, and talk. They were getting nowhere as it was, and a break wouldn't kill them.

It wasn't as if he'd be leaving Fontana anytime soon. With the recent killings and now the possibility of a missing shifter being involved, Jayce had to stay. His investigation into the blood trafficking, while important, wasn't as important as keeping strong shifter-human relations in this region. And of course there was the matter of Kat. Leaving her . . . Nope. He couldn't even think of that.

When he felt his phone buzz in his pocket, he thought it might be Brianna again, so he pulled in front of Sala's, a high-end art gallery, and parked. She'd called earlier and relayed her conversation with the wife of an APL member. He'd been by that house before and hadn't scented a shifter there, but he planned to head back tonight or in the morning and do a little reconnaissance, see what else he could dig up. Especially since Brianna seemed to think the woman's husband had friends in law enforcement. He'd contemplated going by today, but when the police presence at the ranch materialized, he'd decided to hold off. Connor's pack didn't need any extra attention right now, and he wasn't going to take the chance of accidentally starting something.

As he glanced at the caller ID he was surprised to see Liam's number. "Hey, man."

"Hey. I need a favor. Pretty much everyone's on lockdown at the ranch and Connor wants to keep it that way.

I've got a meeting soon about half an hour away. Real estate stuff. Don't want to miss it and don't want to take anyone away from the ranch, but I'm not leaving December either—"

"Kat and I are a block over from her bookstore. We'll stop by and keep her company until you get back."

Liam pushed out a big sigh of relief. "Thanks. This isn't life or death, but it's been brutal trying to nail down a time to meet with this guy."

Jayce understood that for all the problems the pack was facing, life and business needed to go on. They couldn't operate in a vacuum. "See you in a few."

As he parked his bike in front of December's Book Nook, Kat quickly took her helmet off. She raked a hand through her dark hair, giving her that bed-head look he couldn't get enough of. What he wouldn't give to take her to bed right now. She looked so fucking sexy straddling the back of his bike . . . he couldn't hide his groan.

Kat's head jerked up to look at him, eyes slightly widened as she slid off the bike. "You have got to learn to tone down your lust."

"Why?" he murmured, reaching out and cupping her cheek. The need to touch her was overwhelming sometimes—a living thing inside him. He knew exactly what it meant too. He just wanted to deny it because it meant he couldn't run away from what he wanted anymore.

"Because it smells like chocolate and it makes me hungry," she said tartly as she swung her leg over the bike, letting both booted feet hit the pavement.

A laugh burst from him and he dropped his hand. "Sorry, sweetheart. I can't stop my reaction to you. It just is. Come on, I'm sure you heard my conversation with Liam."

She nodded, her eyes lighting up. "December's been

on a baking craze lately, so I hope she brought some good stuff to the store."

Unable to help himself, he leaned down and nipped her earlobe. "You hungry for chocolate?"

Swallowing hard, she gave his chest a small shove. "Don't even start. If you get me worked up with no release, I'll make you pay for it tonight."

"What if I promise to drizzle chocolate all over myself and let you lick it off?" And after, he wanted to lick every inch of her.

She blinked once at his question. They'd never played with food before—he'd always been too eager to get inside her to even think about indulging in any games—but the thought was wildly erotic.

Even though her cheeks flushed pink, she nodded, a grin playing across her full lips. "That sounds like a plan."

"Please just leave that," Kat said as she took December's empty dinner plate from her. After spending the afternoon at her store, Kat had invited her and Liam over for dinner. It was still December's home after all, though December had transferred most of her pictures and personal items to the ranch.

December reluctantly let it go and started to sit back down at the kitchen table, but Liam snagged a hand around her waist and pulled her into his lap. She instantly curled into his embrace, wrapping her arm around his neck in a familiar hold. Seeing them so happy with each other warmed Kat's heart.

"At least she listens to you," Liam grumbled and Kat guessed he was only half joking.

"He wants me to work less," December said, her focus on Kat as she started to clear the table.

"Sit," Jayce murmured as he took over clearing away

the dirty dishes. He'd also cooked—something that immensely shocked her.

Too surprised to do anything else, she did as he directed, crossing one leg over the other as she sat back down and looked at the happy couple. "Work less or not at all?"

"What do you think?" December raised an eyebrow.

Kat just shook her head. "It's good for her to be on her feet and stay active while she's pregnant," she said to Liam.

His dark eyes narrowed. "Is taking her side a female thing?"

"No, it's a best-friend thing. But it's also true. She'd go crazy if you kept her cooped up at the ranch all the time."

"See? I told you." December dropped a quick kiss on her mate's lips, earning a ghost of a smile from him.

Wanting to change the subject for December's sake— Liam had that look in his eye that said this conversation was not over—Kat veered toward something much safer. "So I take it your baked goods have been a success?" At the store today they'd been practically sold out by the time Kat and Jayce had arrived.

December's blue eyes brightened. "Yes. I think it's a combination of them being good and people interested in seeing me now that I'm different." She used air quotes as she said the word "different."

What people might not realize was that December didn't have many shifter abilities and wouldn't until after the baby was born. She healed faster than a normal human, but she was still incredibly vulnerable. It wasn't like the change had affected her personality either.

"Have you noticed a difference in attitudes toward you?" Jayce asked quietly from the sink even though Kat figured he already knew the answer.

He'd been at the store today and *nothing* got by that man. Maybe he just wanted December to vocalize it for clarification.

Moving against her mate, December nodded. "Yeah. People I thought were friends are distant, some almost hostile, but on the plus side my business has almost tripled."

Kat idly ran her finger along the stem of her wineglass. She'd noticed some angry glares from a few customers at the store today but prayed it wouldn't turn into a large-scale thing. The locals were angry about the recent killings and Kat couldn't really blame them. Right now that wasn't the most important thing on her mind though. Taking a deep breath, she decided to bite the bullet and confess to her friends what she'd done a few days ago. She'd thought about waiting, but having Jayce here gave her strength. He hadn't judged her when she'd told him she'd taken pictures of that list from Liam. No, he'd just told her to own up to it.

"Listen, guys, I need to tell you something." Out of the corner of her eye, Kat saw Jayce straighten and lean against the counter in front of the sink. Right about now she wished he was holding her hand, but she needed to face this on her own. Not act like a coward. She'd done a crappy thing and it was time to come clean.

December's eyebrows drew together. "What is it?"

"The other day when I stopped by your house, I, uh . . ." She just needed to get it out. "When I asked to use your bathroom, I was lying. You had mentioned something about that list of APL members, so I went searching for it. I totally took advantage of your trust, and when I found it, I took pictures of some of the pages with my cell phone. Not all of it, but it doesn't matter. I shouldn't have violated our friendship or your home that way and I'm so ashamed. And I'm so incredibly sorry." She looked back and forth between Liam and December. "I just hope both of you can forgive me."

Surprise registered on both their faces, making her feel even crappier. Clasping her hands in her lap, she looked down at her white knuckles and quickly blinked away tears. As she did, she felt strong hands settle on her shoulders. She hadn't even heard Jayce move, but there he was, supporting her. Savoring his strength, she risked looking up to find December half smiling at her.

"It's okay, sweetie. I'm not gonna lie—it surprises me, but it's not like this is a big unforgivable thing." December reached out and squeezed her hand.

Kat wasn't so sure about that.

"I'm going to have to tell Connor, Kat," Liam said quietly. "We leave our doors unlocked and our homes open to all pack members because there's a built-in level of trust. I know you don't understand that now, but it's something that's important to the very core of what makes pack life strong, unbreakable."

Her throat tight, she nodded, afraid that the hot tears burning her eyes were going to spill over at any moment. What Liam did next surprised her. He kissed his mate's neck, then slid December off his lap and pulled Kat into a tight hug. "You're part of our pack now, Kat. If you want something, all you have to do is ask," he murmured against the top of her head. "And if you need me to spell it out, of course we forgive you."

That did it. The tears fell freely then, but she also felt a sense of freedom. They both forgave her, and even if they trusted her, she still planned to make it up to them. With a lighter heart, she pulled back and accepted December's embrace, then finally Jayce's as he wrapped his arms around her from behind.

After serving dessert and talking for another couple of hours, December and Liam left and Kat found herself alone with Jayce. Something she'd been looking forward to all day. Especially since he'd made such wicked promises of mixing chocolate and sex: two of her favorite things.

But something heavy weighed on her heart and she needed time to adjust to the emotions raging through her. Things between her and Jayce were happening so fast. Being around him had turned her world upside down once again and she still didn't know what the future between them was. He was here because of his job and training Erin. But would he be here otherwise? She didn't think so. And she didn't want to ask.

Kat slid the lock on the front door into place and leaned her forehead against it. Thanks to the winter air outside, it was cool against her skin. All she wanted to do was curl up under the covers, close her eyes to the outside world, and sleep. Alone. Telling Jayce that, however, wasn't going to be fun.

Especially since he'd been so supportive tonight. She felt Jayce's presence before strong arms slid around her, pulling her back tight against his chest. He lightly nuzzled the spot on her neck right below her ear. Right where she was ultrasensitive.

A shiver curled through her, but she fought it. "Jayce . . ."

He stiffened behind her, maybe because of her tone. Slightly lifting his head, he didn't loosen his embrace. "Why do I think I'm not going to want to hear this?"

"I need some space tonight. Not because of you." Well, that wasn't entirely true. She needed to think clearly and that was impossible if she had a naked Jayce in her bed.

"Space? As in you want to sleep alone." Not a question. A stark statement that left her feeling cold.

"Yeah." While she might want his strong arms around her, she needed time to think. As she'd watched Liam and December's interaction tonight, she'd felt a scratching pain deep inside her. Their communication was so easy, so natural, and they looked so damn happy together that it made her ache. Kat was so happy for her friend, but at the same time, seeing them together was a reminder that she and Jayce would never have that.

He'd said he loved her and she believed him. But his version of love and her version were two different things. He was the enforcer for the Council. And while she might not exactly want the whole white-picket-fence thing—that was a little too boring for her—she did want to settle down and have a family eventually. Not now, but she knew herself well enough to realize that she'd end up wanting more than Jayce could give her emotionally. He'd proven it before and she didn't know if she had the strength to deal with another heartbreak from him. After what he'd told her about his brother—and what she knew about his father—she couldn't see him *ever* giving her everything she wanted. He'd never had any examples of lasting relationships. Hell, his father and brother had both had their mates torn from them. Jayce wasn't motivated to give all of himself to her, and part of her understood why. The longer she was with him, the harder it would be to pull away later—at this point she didn't think she could. Damn him for making her open up her heart again.

She clenched her fingers into fists, her nails digging into her palms, making her focus on her physical discomfort and not the lancing pain in her chest as Jayce took a step back from her.

"You know where I'll be if you need me," he said quietly, his voice so distant it broke her heart.

Turning around, she blinked to see him already gone. He'd moved so quickly, so quietly, she wasn't sure if he'd returned to the kitchen or gone upstairs.

For a moment she wanted to go after him, find him, and drag him to bed with her. But she held herself back. If she ran after him, she'd have no one else to blame when he eventually broke her heart again.

Chapter 15

*P*ain splintered throughout her body.... Her ribs were broken, maybe a leg too ... pain, so much fucking pain. She tried to cry out but her mouth was taped shut.

Apparently the bastard had gotten tired of her screams, though he'd seemed to like them enough in the beginning. Her throat was too raw to scream anymore, so it didn't matter.

"Jayce," she said in her mind. Why wasn't he there? Why wasn't he saving her? When she'd been taken from the hospital parking lot, she'd held on to hope even as this monster strung her up with rope so that her toes barely touched the ground.

Even when he'd stripped off her clothes, she'd held on to pathetic shreds of hope that Jayce would magically appear.

Now, all she wanted to do was die. Anything to stop this pain. She'd fought as best she could, but her arms were bound, her mouth was taped, and her insides hurt so damn bad she knew she had internal bleeding.

Knew it with a certainty that didn't scare her anymore.

Death was close. So close she could practically taste it. See it surrounding her. And she was so tempted to give in to it.

But why wasn't Jayce here? Why wasn't he helping her? He'd promised to always be there for her, no matter what. Even when she'd broken up with him. He'd told her that he would never let her down. All she had to do was call . . .

The monster with a human face walked to her again, rage mottling his features, turning his face a bright red. Rage because he was an impotent fuck. It was the only thing that gave her any sort of satisfaction. When he raised the whip again, she closed her eyes and tried to scream—

Kat's eyes flew open to the feel of someone stroking her head. Fear jumped in her gut, a raw, clawing animal. It took a few long moments of terror for her to realize that there was no danger. Only calm, and quiet.

She wasn't in her human form anymore. Looking up, she saw Jayce sitting on the edge of her bed, softly petting her head. As she glanced around the bed she realized her pajamas were shredded and the comforter was a tangled mess at the foot of it.

Had she been crying in her sleep? She must have been. It was the only explanation for why she'd turned into her animal form without consciously thinking about it. Her inner wolf wanted to protect her from all her pain. Too bad nothing could do that.

But something else could drown out her sorrow, even if it would be fleeting. Taking a deep breath, she let herself relax as she underwent the change back to her human form.

Jayce didn't move, just sat there staring at her. She lightly shook her head, clearing the haziness from her vision and trying to adjust to her body once again.

"You screamed," he said, explaining his presence.

Something she'd already guessed. "What happened?" Jayce's voice was quiet and soothing and she knew his question was about the past. About what had happened to her in that barn.

She yanked the covers up to shield her nakedness. Something dark inside her hated that he'd put himself out there for her. Telling her he loved her with no expectations. And he was being so fucking nice it broke her heart. He hadn't been there for her when she needed him most. He hadn't saved her!

Yet he was all concerned and damn near perfect now. She wanted to throttle him. Wanted to throttle anything at the moment if it would make the pain inside her disappear. The rage grew, twisting inside her like a living thing. Her heart hammered; her breathing turned shallow. Even though she knew it was irrational, she dropped the covers and launched herself at him. She pounded his chest with her fists.

He didn't deserve this, but she couldn't stop herself. It was as if she was possessed. "You weren't there for me!" The words tore from her throat even as she hated herself for saying them, let alone thinking them. Jayce wasn't omniscient. He might be a skilled warrior, but he couldn't be everywhere, couldn't fight every battle.

He swallowed hard, his face twisting into a pained expression that she'd never witnessed before. "I know, and I'm so fucking sorry. I'd have traded places with you in a second." His deep, ragged voice rolled over her, soothing her as it simultaneously made a burning shame surge through her. Like lava, it scorched her insides and hurt worse than any torture she'd endured. The pain in his voice was an almost tangible thing, making her ache worse with each second that passed.

His complete submission to her blows stunned and

stilled her. He thought he deserved to be punished. That was why he hadn't stopped her.

She should pull away and leave him alone, but she couldn't let him suffer like she was suffering. He didn't deserve it, no matter the anger-injected words she'd just flung at him like sharp daggers. She wrapped her arms around his neck tightly and buried her face against his chest, unable to control the sobs wracking her body. She'd cried so much directly after what had happened, but she'd never allowed anyone to hold her or comfort her. Not like this. And not while she was naked and vulnerable. She'd also never told anyone what happened to her.

"He . . . didn't rape me, but he tried. More than once."

His body stiffened and his grip around her waist grew tighter. With one hand he stroked the length of her spine, letting her continue.

"He couldn't get it up. It was the only thing that made his beatings bearable." The more she spoke, the easier it was to get things out. Even if uncontrollable tears still tracked down her face, she almost felt a sense of freedom. "I don't know how much Aiden or one of the others told you?" She formed it as a question, pausing to let him answer.

"Just that you were near death and covered in blood. He also mentioned that you likely had internal bleeding." The hand on her waist flexed once before he returned to his preternaturally still state.

She knew the animal part of him was enraged right now. Though he didn't make any overt moves, the air seemed to be pulsing with a scary sort of energy. Not directed at her, though; its object was her dead attacker, whom neither of them could do anything about now. Something she hated every single day.

"He beat me with a whip and touched me any way he wanted and I couldn't do a damn thing." Her voice broke on the last word and she realized she was trembling when Jayce started rubbing her back in circles and murmuring soothing sounds.

"I'm so fucking sorry, Kat." His voice was just as broken as she felt inside.

Stretching out on the bed, she covered him with her body, not caring that she was naked and he was nearly so. The feel of his muscular body underneath her was an anchor she desperately needed. "You don't have anything to be sorry for," she said through her tears and sniffles. *The attack wasn't his fault.* She knew it on an intellectual level, but her head and heart couldn't seem to sync up. Why was she so angry that he hadn't saved her? "I don't know what's wrong with me."

If she'd been doing this to anyone else she would have been embarrassed for blubbering all over him, but this was Jayce. The man who'd seen her at her worst and never judged her. The man she loved but couldn't tell. Couldn't say three little words to him because she was too afraid.

As his hands gently stroked down her back and then directly back up, she realized he was pulling the bedding over them. He was covering her, taking care of her, and it made her want to kiss him and soothe the pain she could feel emanating off him in pulsing waves.

Lifting her head, she looked into gray eyes swirling with a sorrow she never wanted to see again. She'd put it there, which made it even worse. Biting back more tears, she cupped his cheek with one hand. "I . . . I'm sorry I blamed you. When I was abducted, I . . . I called out your name. I waited for you to come for me." When he jerked back as if she'd physically struck him, her stomach roiled.

This wasn't coming out the way she intended. She'd never had a problem with words before, but seeing Jayce vulnerable messed with her head and she needed to make this right. "No, I'm not telling you this to hurt you. I'm telling you because you're the one person I knew— know—I can always count on. If you could have been there, I *know* you would have. I know it with every fiber of my being. I'm sorry for what I just said. I was fighting remnants of a nightmare, but I don't blame you. Maybe I did on a subconscious level, but I don't now. Not truly. My attacker is dead and I have nowhere to place my anger. The monster who hurt me and the APL are the only ones responsible. No matter what happens between us, please know that."

The pain she'd witnessed in his eyes partially subsided. "I would have done anything to save you. Given up a limb, my life, *anything*. I only wish that fucker hadn't died. I would have made him regret his very existence." The darkness in his words sent a shudder snaking through her.

Before she could respond, he claimed her mouth in a gentle, sensual kiss completely at odds with the tough-looking man he was. He threaded strong, calloused fingers through her tangled hair, gripping her head in a move that could only be called possessive. When he rolled his hips beneath her, his erection pressing against her abdomen, she reached between them and wrapped her fingers around his cock over his boxers. He generally slept naked, so he must have thrown those on when she screamed.

Shoving the boxers down his legs took only a moment. Before he'd even shimmied fully free, she'd opened up to him, sliding herself onto his hard length. With a gasp, she settled on his cock, taking a moment to let him fill and stretch her completely.

As she did, he cupped her breasts and began strumming her nipples in rhythmic tweaks, making her inner walls clench around him. The way he worked her body was perfect, sending delicious shivers throughout her.

"You set the pace tonight, sweetheart," he murmured.

The words made her abdomen clench. He always set the pace and it was usually hard and frantic. He wasn't trying to take over, to dominate, something that was so ingrained in his character that it was simply who he was. She was so used to him taking the lead between the sheets. Even if she initiated things, Jayce was so damn dominant that he usually ended up on top. Not that she'd ever minded. But he wasn't making a move to change positions.

He knew how fragile she was and he was letting her take control. He was truly letting her set the pace. Oh, this would be fun. She wanted him to feel nothing but pleasure. For the pain she'd put in his eyes only moments before and because she loved him. And because she wanted to forget her nightmare—and Jayce was the only one who could make that happen.

Lifting herself to her knees, she sucked in a breath of pure pleasure as he moved within her. She rolled her hips, repositioning herself high enough that just his head was inside her. Her inner walls clenched. She wanted him to fill her, and by the growl that emanated from him, he wanted that too.

But torturing him just a little, drawing out the pleasure for both of them, would be worth it. She had no doubt.

When Jayce's hands found her hips and grasped them tightly, trying to force her to increase her speed, she encircled his wrists and held them above his head. Of course if he'd wanted to be free, he could have easily broken her grip, but he let her guide him.

"If you don't keep your hands here, I'll tie you up," she promised.

His eyebrows rose. "Try it." Another soft growl, this one not quite as gentle as before.

But something told her that he would let her if she wanted. "Hold on to the headboard," she ordered in a soft whisper.

He did as she said, wrapping his fingers around the iron posts as his gray eyes darkened with need.

She ran her hands up her ribs until she cupped her own breasts, holding them just as Jayce had done too many times to count as he took her from behind. Lightly, oh so lightly, she pulled one of her nipples between her thumb and forefinger, gently rolling it.

Jayce let out a groan as his hips jerked, his cock pumping into her in a hard, uncontrolled thrust. "You're enjoying torturing me."

"Maybe a little." She was also torturing herself. It would totally be worth the payoff. Still cupping one breast, she leaned back, but kept herself impaled on him, only rolling her hips in small, measured movements.

With her free hand, she trailed a slow path down her stomach, enjoying watching Jayce's hungry eyes track her every move. Using her finger, she began stroking her clit. She tightened around him with each caress and he groaned in unison with her clenches.

The headboard shook dangerously. "Fuck, you're trying to kill me," he ground out, the muscles in his forearms and neck pulled tight. So powerful, yet letting her have the control.

"If I wanted to kill you . . ." She slowly lifted off him until she was completely free. Her entire body tensed, mourning the loss of him filling her, but . . . "I'd do this," she murmured as she shimmied down his body, bringing her mouth over his hardness.

He jerked again, then seemed to get control of himself as she took his length past her lips, as deep as she could go. Instead of continuing to stroke him with the wet heat of her mouth, she licked the underside of his shaft, enjoying the tension rolling off him. He practically vibrated and she knew he was trying to keep himself from taking over.

Something that was difficult for a man like him. Continuing her teasing assault, she moved up a little higher and lightly swirled her tongue around the tip of his cock, never fully letting him past her lips.

"Do something. Please." Jayce's voice was a guttural growl.

It was the "please" that undid her. Pushing up, she caged his hips with her hands. "You'd really let me keep doing this all night, wouldn't you?"

"I'll let you do whatever you want—just do it faster."

The man had no patience sometimes. Crawling up his body, she kissed him with a hunger she couldn't deny as she once again opened herself to him and let him slide inside her. To her surprise he was still grasping the headboard with white knuckles and she had a feeling his fingers were going to leave permanent indentations on it.

She couldn't tease anymore. Too many emotions and too much need hummed through her for that. Gripping his shoulders she began riding him. Her fingers dug into his hard flesh but he didn't seem to notice.

All his attention was on her face. Being under such a scrutinizing gaze made her want to look away, but she couldn't. As if mesmerized, she stared into the gray eyes she knew so well. With each thrust inside her, his eyes seemed to darken with intensity until finally her head fell back and she let herself be swept away with her own hunger.

She'd wanted to hold out longer, but when she felt his hands clasp her hips, her orgasm shattered her, sending bursts of pleasure to every single nerve ending. She felt it with her entire body. Her toes curled as waves of sweet release swept through her.

Jayce's grip on her hips tightened, his fingers marking her flesh in a way she knew he meant to do. "Look at me," he rasped.

Her head snapped back up. Looking at him through a haze of bliss, she stared into his eyes as he came. There was nothing graceful about his climax; it was raw and loud, his shout filling the room and taking her with a triumphant possessiveness. His reaction was all because of her. Her nipples tingled with the aftershock of hearing such a guttural cry from him.

Before she realized what he was doing, he'd switched their positions and had her underneath him. She wrapped her legs around his waist, holding him tight. Staying nestled between her legs, he kissed her jaw in gentle little nips that made her clench around his still-hard length. "Don't you ever get tired?" she whispered.

He paused only long enough to answer before gently biting her ear. "Of you, never."

Jayce was fucked. Truly and utterly. He'd known it last night—well, technically this morning—after making love with Kat.

He could finally admit out loud what he'd been trying to deny to himself from the moment he'd met her. He'd known it all along, but he'd been living in a state of denial. She was his mate and after last night he knew he wasn't walking away from her.

Ever.

His enemies could be damned. When she'd left him before, it had taken all his strength not to run after her. Hell, when he'd received his orders to come to Fontana he'd practically run here like a randy little cub. The first place he'd gone to hadn't been to the Armstrong ranch like he was supposed to. No, he'd gone directly to Kat's. He couldn't and wouldn't stay away from her.

Unfortunately he didn't know if he'd lost his chance for permanent bonding. After last night he wasn't sure about anything. She could just be using him for sex, as a way to get through her pain. Hell, she still hadn't said she loved him, and last night would have been the time to do it. For all he knew, this was temporary for her.

Scrubbing a hand down his face, he hurried down the stairs. The scent of freshly brewed coffee had trailed into the bathroom while he was showering, so he knew exactly where Kat was. Not that he couldn't follow her sweet scent anyway.

She was leaning against the counter, coffee cup in hand, when he walked in. Wearing formfitting jeans, knee-high boots, a black bustier, and a fitted leather jacket, she was a wet dream come to life.

Her pale blue eyes narrowed at him. "We're not leaving until I finish my coffee. Now that we're sleeping together again, you will *so* afford me this." Her voice was light and playful, making relief burst inside him like fireworks.

"I wasn't thinking about leaving," he murmured as he crossed the distance in the blink of an eye.

Taking her cup from her, he set it on the counter and claimed her mouth. The taste of coffee and chocolate teased his tongue. Smiling, he pulled back and nipped her bottom lip. "Chocolate for breakfast?"

She grinned and shrugged. "I can't help it. You put off that lust scent and I'm hungry for it all the time, so it's kind of your fault."

Kissing her forehead, he chuckled and gave her some space. "When you're done, we're leaving." While she'd been in the shower this morning he'd spoken to Connor about his plans for the day and the Alpha was on board with them. He'd run everything by Kat and she was on board too, eager to visit the house of the APL members Brianna had been trying to infiltrate. Since they suspected that the husband had a friend in law enforcement, Jayce would focus on picking up any scents at the house that would support that idea.

Then he was going to stop by the police station and see if he could match those scents with a cop. Most scents were residual, at least to him. He wouldn't be able to follow an old scent anywhere, but if he could match it, he might be able to figure out who this guy's cop friend was. From there, maybe he'd find another lead.

Investigation was tedious, but he was patient. Unfortunately he might have to start using stronger methods if these shifter-perpetrated killings didn't stop. Mingling with any APL members right now when Connor's pack was under scrutiny wasn't his first choice, but if the killings continued, he would be forced to question APL members. Sometimes his questioning methods got messy. Something he didn't relish. But if it came down to doing that to stop more carnage in Fontana, so be it.

"Did you talk to Erin this morning?" Kat asked as she set her mug in the sink.

He nodded. "Texted her. She's pissed that we're getting to have all the fun, as she put it, but she's under Connor's control and he wants her on lockdown at the ranch with everyone else."

"And he doesn't care about me being out with you?"

He and Connor had exchanged a few choice words over that very thing earlier this morning, but Jayce had won. Once he'd explained how things were between him and Kat, Connor had backed off immediately. Connor might be Kat's Alpha, but Jayce was making a claim on Kat. Even if she didn't realize it yet, she would soon enough. Connor was mated, so he understood Jayce's need to keep Kat close.

He needed time with her to reestablish their former trust with each other. Not to mention that she could be helpful to him. Of course he'd like for her to be under lockdown at the ranch, but he knew her well enough to realize that she would hate him if he tried to force that on her. By letting her help him, he was letting her get her revenge on the APL in a nonviolent way. And she would never be out of his sight. If he could see her, he could damn well protect her. Of that he had no doubt. "Connor and I have an agreement."

A frown tugged at her pretty lips. "What does that mean?"

"It means you're coming with me today," he said instead of telling her how he felt about her. How she wasn't leaving his sight because as his mate, she was his to protect.

"Good," she growled, her voice low and determined. "I want to bring these assholes down."

He palmed his keys as they headed for the front door. "Remember, never underestimate your opponent."

"Lesson number two. I remember." He shot her a surprised look, at which she shrugged. "I remember all of them. I thought you might give me a freaking quiz or something," she muttered.

Smiling—something he seemed to be doing a lot

more of lately—he stepped outside and headed for his bike.

He'd checked the location earlier using an online mapping system. From the aerial view he knew the house was across the street from a park. A thickly wooded one at that. That was how they were going to make their entrance.

As he drove toward the house, he tried to keep his thoughts professional, but it was hard to do that when Kat's arms were around him and her lush breasts were pressed up against him. He'd woken her again early this morning and taken her from behind. The memory of her cries was still fresh in his mind and all he wanted at the moment was a replay.

He forced himself to think of violent memories instead. God knew he had enough of them. It sucked, but it was the only way to keep his body under control. Steering into the park, he was thankful to see it deserted. Not that he'd expected anything different.

In a poorer section of town, this park was a far cry from the well-kept one near downtown. Most of the equipment was rusted, a few swings broken, and it was apparent that probably no one had cleared the layers of snow from the merry-go-round all winter. Hence the rust coating everything. The new park used plastic equipment—more proof that this was an older place. Continuing past the play area, he slowed his speed along the winding paved road until they were deep into a thick cluster of trees.

Waiting a beat, he listened for the sounds of human hearts in the direct vicinity and didn't hear any. Good. They wouldn't have to worry about any homeless people seeing them.

"Should I leave my helmet here?" Kat asked as she slipped it off.

"Yeah. But keep your gloves on." He wasn't sure if anyone would be home, but if the house was empty, he was planning a little B&E.

She nodded, tugging on them as if to make sure they were still there. He flexed his own fingers, the leather of his custom-made gloves soundless with his movements.

"This way." He nodded east, deeper into the woods. If the map was correct, one of the overgrown trails would eventually deposit them on the street where Ralph and Jackie Anderson lived.

"How do you know they'll be gone?" Kat whispered.

"I don't, but Brianna was able to glean that the husband works a three-two shift." Three days on, two days off, then two days on and three days off. "He should be at work today."

"What if the wife is home?" No one was visible except a few animals in the trees, but she nevertheless spoke quietly.

"Let's just hope she's not." Brianna had said she was supposed to meet the wife for coffee today, so hopefully they wouldn't have to wait long for her to leave.

As the woods started to thin slightly, he realized they were close to their destination. He stepped in front of Kat without missing a beat. "Stay behind me."

Her measured movements were almost as silent as his. If he'd been human he doubted he would have heard her walking. She was honing her abilities very quickly. Even as a human she'd been almost preternaturally graceful. Her fighting skills, raw though they still were, were impressive.

Stopping about ten yards from where the woods opened onto the street, he motioned toward the small yellow house with white shutters. It was across the street, about four houses down from their position. "That's the one." His heightened sight allowed him to see the numbers on the mailbox, but he also recognized the house from the street view of the online address locator. Technology was a scary thing sometimes and only reminded him why supernatural creatures had decided to come out to the world twenty years ago. They wouldn't have been able to hide their existence much longer.

Walking parallel to the street, they veered off the overgrown paved path and cut through the brush. Except for a few small animal tracks, most of the snow here was untouched. They would need to cover their tracks when they came back.

As Jayce stopped in front of the house, he felt Kat sidle up next to him. "Can you tell if anyone's home?"

"Be still and listen. What do you hear?"

She was silent for several long beats. "Lots of things. How do you decipher it all? I hear a few televisions, a couple arguing, someone probably taking a shower, and what sounds like two people having sex."

He grinned because he'd heard that too. "You'll learn to focus and hone your senses the older you get. It's just a matter of time. The yellow and white house and that one"—he pointed three doors down to a one-story blue ranch-style house in need of a paint job—"are empty. I promise you'll eventually be able to sense those things." Maybe not as clearly as he was able to, but she would get much better.

She let out a frustrated sound and he didn't blame her. He'd been doing this for five centuries. Sifting out sounds and scents was second nature to him. Hell, most shifters didn't have the exceptional gift he did. But to him, separating what was important and what wasn't was like breathing. That innate sense was why he was a good investigator.

"I'm going to cross the street, jump the fence, and go in through the back door if they don't have a security system. Once I'm in I'll open the front door for you. When I give you the signal, run to me." Jayce knew she wasn't as fast as he was, but if she concentrated she should be able to move fast enough so that unless someone was looking directly at her, she would be able to get inside almost completely undetected. And if not undetected, at least there'd be no way anyone could give a description of her. She would just look like a blur of movement. Most people saw what they wanted to see and would write off seeing her as their imagination.

"Sounds good." Her nod was curt.

He'd known Kat long enough to know that she'd have no problem with this, especially if it would give them a lead on finding the shifter who was killing people.

After a quick visual scan, he sprinted across the street in a burst of speed, barely touching the ground before launching himself over the fence. Unfortunately they had a chain-link fence rather than a privacy fence. He might be fast, but he'd still have to pick the lock on the back door. But he stopped when he spotted a sensor in the corner of the kitchen through a back window. So they did have a security system.

Crouching low, he crept around the side of the house, conscious of the windows in the house next door. The drapes were pulled shut and they were a dark color, none of that sheer stuff that allowed people to see outside. He wasn't too worried about anyone seeing him from that house, though; he could still hear the moans of two people having sex inside. Something he wished he was doing with Kat that very instant.

After pulling the breaker to shut the power down, he hurried to the back door once again and made quick work of the lock. If the system was wireless, he might be screwed, but he was betting it wasn't. As the door creaked open, he waited for an alarm, but no sound came. Quickly he checked the house to make sure there weren't any surprises—and picked up all the scents he needed—then opened the front door a bit and waved Kat over.

She sprinted across the street, not quite as fast as he had. He'd already have taken care of what he needed to without her, but she needed to be part of this. "First we're going to the main bedroom so you can get the owners' scents. It's unlikely that they invite anyone else into their bedroom, so it's an easy way to distinguish which scents belong to them and which don't once we scan the rest of the house."

"That makes sense," Kat whispered.

Once in the bedroom, he quickly picked up both their scents, but he wanted to see what she got. "What do you smell?"

She slowly looked around the neat room—queen-sized bed, two dressers, elongated oval mirror in the corner, and open closet door. "A light vanilla scent, but not the kind from a lotion or food. It's really subtle."

"Good. That's the wife."

"How do you know?"

He shrugged. "I just do." Males and females had distinctive differences in their scents, but this wasn't the time to explain it. He wanted to see what she picked up; then he wanted to get her the hell out of there. "What else?"

"I smell cologne—the cheap kind—and cigarettes, but I don't think anyone smokes in here. It's just"—she glanced toward a wicker hamper visible in the closet— "subtle, like it's coming from someone's clothing. I also smell something oily. I can't put my finger on it, but it smells almost . . . rotten. It's so faint I can barely pick up on it."

"Damn." Jayce knew what that smell was. It was hatred. It poured off some people in such pungent waves that it left behind a trail. Jayce knew it was the husband. It blended with his natural scent. Humans couldn't smell it, but they could see it in people in other ways. They picked up on visual cues or they listened to that intangible thing called their gut instinct. Not enough humans listened to it. "That's very good, Kat."

At the sound of a vehicle door slamming, they both froze. Before she could move, he hurried to the front of the house and carefully peeked out one of the windows. His heart rate ratcheted up a fraction.

The wife's car was in the driveway and she was striding up the front walk.

He still had to flip the breaker back on to make it seem like there had been a power surge, and thereby mask the fact that someone had intentionally turned the system off. He hadn't done it before because he wasn't sure if the alarm system was the type that would reset automatically.

Hurrying back to the bedroom, he found Kat still standing there. As he heard the sound of a key sliding into a lock, he motioned toward the window.

With wide eyes, Kat nodded and went to it. She unlocked it, opened it, then slid out soundlessly, though he could hear her heart rate increase. Quickly following, he pulled it back in place just as he saw the wife entering the room.

Ducking down, he pointed toward the other side of the street. "Jump the fence and meet me back in the woods."

She paused, looking unsure. "What are you going to do?"

He didn't want to be having this conversation now. "Flip the breaker back on. Now go." Without waiting to see if she would do as he said, he crept back to the edge of the house, then crossed the backyard toward the other side, where the breaker was.

If the husband had been the one coming home, he'd have likely checked this out as soon as he realized the power was off. Jayce was just hoping it would take the wife a little longer. As he flipped the metal switch back into place and shut the box, he heard the sound of the back door opening and the woman talking to herself under her breath.

The survival need that was so embedded into his kind kicked in, giving him an extra jolt of speed as he jumped the fence and practically flew across the street.

"She didn't see you," Kat murmured as he came to a stop in front of her. Continuing, she said, "I wonder how long she'll be there."

"Doesn't matter. I got what I needed."

Her pale blue eyes widened. "You did?" Before he could answer, her lips pulled into a thin line. "You didn't even need me with you, did you?"

Jayce shook his head. "I got the scents as I swept the house. It's second nature." So why did he feel guilty about that? He hadn't planned to tell her that, but she'd realized it and he wouldn't lie to her.

Surprising him, she cupped his cheeks and kissed him so thoroughly he felt it everywhere. Her tongue swept past his lips, completely invading him. When she finally pulled back, he didn't bother hiding his surprise. "What was that for?"

"For taking me with you when you didn't need me.

For taking the time to teach me about my new skills when you should be focusing solely on your investigation. For letting me do this because I need to strike back at the APL in any way. Mainly, just for being you." She dropped another kiss on his lips, then turned on her heel and started heading back through the woods.

You're wrong about one thing. I do need you, he thought. He needed her more and more each second that passed. Unfortunately he wasn't sure she needed him as much.

Chapter 16

Kat glanced around Jayce at the building they should so not be headed into. "You're sure about this?"

"You just helped me break into someone's house. Of course I'm sure." His response was slightly playful, but there was an edge underlying his words. Not directed at her—she was a hundred percent sure of that. He just wanted this mess settled.

She did too. The more time she spent with Jayce, the more vengeance and revenge took a backseat. Well, not completely. She wanted justice for the people who had participated in her torture. Technically only one man—if he could even be called that—had tortured her, but someone had given him the orders. Maybe not orders to torture her, but it didn't matter to her. From what they'd discovered, Adler—the direct boss of the monster who'd hurt her—had a boss too. Someone high up within the APL. He needed to be brought down. They needed to strike at this organization hard, before they got too powerful.

Still, no matter how much she craved bringing down the

APL, she found she was coming to crave Jayce so much more. Back when they'd been dating, he'd been sweet with her, but the way he'd been acting lately was different. Good different, but it was like he was claiming her in some way. It freaked her out more than she would admit. Last night she'd tried so hard to convince herself that he could never completely give himself to her emotionally. How could he? The more she was around him, however, the more she wondered if that wasn't her own fear rearing its ugly head. She hadn't even been able to admit to herself that there was now a difference in their lovemaking. In the shower yesterday he'd rocked her to her core with his passion and the way he'd actually bitten her.

"Where'd you just go?" Jayce asked quietly.

She blinked, brushing away the haze of her thoughts, and shook her head. "Sorry, zoned out. I'm ready if you are."

He eyed her curiously, but didn't question her further. He just placed his hand on the small of her back as they strode toward the police station. Parker would be in today, so she was dropping by to say hello. Or at least that was the excuse. She knew Jayce hated police stations, but this was his plan and she trusted him. Hell, he'd been able to pick up five different human scents in the house they'd broken into. She was still trying to figure out the difference between the scents of people standing right in front of her. Figuring out leftover scents was a little beyond her at the moment.

Jayce was hoping one of the scents from the house would match someone here. Brianna had said the wife was sure that one of her husband's APL friends was in law enforcement, so this was the best place to start.

As they entered the building, Kat and Jayce ran right into Detective Chance Kinsey. Tall, dark, and handsome, he gave her the once-over, apparently with far too much appreciation in his gaze for Jayce's taste, considering the way his fingers tightened against her back. Obviously now that she wasn't in the interrogation room anymore, the detective felt free to check her out and he wasn't being subtle about it. His aura was still fairly unreadable except for a faint purple haze that sizzled around him before fading. She almost snorted. The man had pretty damn good psychic shields, but his lust was shining through.

If it hadn't been bothering Jayce so much she might have laughed. She would have sensed Jayce's reaction even without the physical response against her back. He was territorial and he didn't hide it well.

"I've only got one type, pretty boy, and you're not it." The words were out before she could stop herself, but her inner wolf didn't like the fact that his look was upsetting Jayce. Before she had time to dwell on her response, the detective's head snapped up from appraising her assets.

Maybe it was the bluntness of her words or maybe he was embarrassed that she'd caught him staring—or maybe it was because she'd called him "pretty boy"—but the tips of his ears tinged crimson in embarrassment.

Kat bit back a satisfied smile. This guy had almost made her throw up by showing her those horrific crime scene photos. If she'd had breakfast that morning, she probably would have puked. It was petty, but she was glad she'd been able to get under his skin.

The detective cleared his throat. "Uh, everything okay? Why are you here?"

"We're here to see the sheriff," Jayce answered, taking a step forward and not quite subtly placing himself between Kat and the detective.

The man looked back and forth between the two of them, nodding as if understanding, then held up a hand. "Hold on a sec." After radioing Parker, he nodded at them again. "Come on. I'll walk you back."

Kat was surprised by how nice he was being, but she figured the detective felt a little guilty about being such a dick to her during the interrogation. After swiping a security card, he led them out of the main lobby and back to a desk-filled space where men and women in uniform were milling around.

Parker gave them a curious look when the three of them filed into his office. An officer named Derrick Bird—according to his gold-plated ID—the same man who'd been with Parker when he'd picked Kat up the other morning, was in the office, but Parker murmured that he could go. Kat watched the officer as he left, trying to pick up on his aura, but she got absolutely nothing. The guy was like a blank slate. Detective Kinsey mumbled a polite good-bye, then left, shutting the door behind him.

Parker rounded his desk and gave Kat a quick hug. Jayce might not have liked it, but at least he didn't growl at the man. "Is everything okay?" he asked as he stepped back and leaned against his desk.

Kat nodded. "Yeah."

"We want to know if you like having dirty cops on your force." Jayce's words dropped into the quiet room with the subtlety of a live grenade.

Kat grimaced. As enforcer for the North American Council, he'd worked with human law enforcement before—not that he liked it. Kat knew Parker was aware of Jayce's presence in Fontana, but as far as she knew they hadn't crossed paths in such a direct manner before. Jayce certainly knew how to break the ice.

Parker straightened to his full height, which made him a couple of inches taller than Jayce, and the blue eyes that were so similar to his sister's flashed in annoyance. "What the hell does that mean?"

Jayce lifted his broad shoulders casually. "Just a question."

"You saying there's someone dirty on my force?"

Another shrug from Jayce. "It's a possibility. How do you feel about someone on your force being part of the APL?"

Kat already knew the answer to that. The APL had gone after Parker's sister more than once because of December's relationship with the Armstrong-Cordona pack. As far as Kat knew, Parker would go to hell and back for that woman.

"You got proof?" he asked quietly, his voice razor-sharp.

Jayce shook his head. "Not yet. I just wanted to gauge your reaction. I'll be in contact soon." Without waiting for a response, he jerked the door open.

To Kat's surprise, Parker didn't try to stop them or question them further. Probably because he knew it wouldn't do any good. Jayce wasn't someone who answered questions unless he was good and ready to. As they stepped back into the main room of the station, the hum of noise she'd been able to tune out in Parker's office increased.

They received a few odd stares, and some downright angry ones, no doubt because most of the police officers knew who Jayce was, and it was a small town, so a lot of people now knew she'd been turned into a shifter. After the way she'd been dragged down to the station, she guessed everyone here knew about her. They might not know the details, but she was still considered different now. And "different" equaled "monster" to some of them. With the killings going on, they probably viewed her as a suspect, even though her DNA had cleared her.

Once they were outside again, her heart rate returned to normal. She glanced at Jayce. "Did you get what you needed?" she asked quietly, even though she already had a good idea what the answer was. She didn't think they'd be leaving if he hadn't.

He nodded, his jaw clenched tight. "Got a name to go with one of the scents."

"That's good, right?" So why did he look so annoyed?

He nodded again.

Placing a hand on his forearm, she stopped him as they neared his motorcycle. "What's wrong?"

Jayce finally turned to face her and she realized nothing was wrong. She could see the gleam in his gray eyes, which had gone startlingly dark, and that wasn't a trick of the light, she was certain. He was incredibly turned on, but she couldn't scent anything, so she guessed he could actually hide his lust when he wanted to. Something he hadn't told her.

"Wh—" Before she could utter a word, his mouth was on hers, claiming and hungry. There was nothing teasing or playful about the way his tongue delved inside her mouth. Heat flooded between her legs, her abdomen clenching as hunger overtook her. Clutching his shoulders, she tried to keep her balance, but the kiss was over almost before it had begun.

Tearing his lips from hers, he stepped back, putting a solid foot of distance between them before he slid onto his bike.

"What was that about?" She quietly got on behind him, wrapping her arms around his waist and pressing her body tight against his.

He didn't answer, but he did put one of his hands over

hers, holding her. With his free hand he pulled out his cell phone and typed in a quick text. She read the message before he sent it. *Check out Derrick Bird, he's w/ the Fontana Sheriff's Dept. Need address.*

"Who'd you send that to?" She didn't say anything about the message. Without asking, she could guess that Jayce had scented Derrick Bird at the house they'd broken into earlier. Nice stroke of luck that he'd been in Parker's office. Of course, Jayce probably would have been able to pick him out even if he'd been surrounded by the entire station.

"Ryan." A curt answer that would normally bother her but she could tell something was going on with Jayce so she didn't push him.

Ryan O'Callaghan was the resident computer genius at the ranch, so it made sense that Jayce would contact him first. Sure enough, Jayce's phone buzzed again moments later, and an address popped up on his screen.

Kat put her helmet on, then repositioned herself so that she was holding on to Jayce again. Wordlessly, he steered out of the parking lot and she had no doubt where they were headed. She wanted to ask him what was going on, but he seemed to be balancing on a tightrope of control. Over what, she had no clue. The only thing she did know was that his kiss had been full of erotic promises he'd better intend on keeping.

Jayce steered past Derrick Bird's house, surveying the surrounding area for any danger. The man's two-story Colonial-style home was right on the border of the next county and far enough from his neighbors that it would be difficult to hear any shouts unless you were a shifter or a vampire. The well-paved road came to a dead end, which meant one exit for his bike.

After Jayce parked and dragged his bike into the trees, he and Kat set off. He hadn't said much to her since they left the police station because he didn't trust himself. Right now all he wanted to do was take her up against a tree and lose himself inside her sweet body. The timing was inappropriate, but after the way she'd spoken to that detective, making it clear she wasn't interested in the guy, Jayce hadn't been able to think straight. The way she'd acted had surprised the hell out of him. She might not have even meant it the way he took it, but she'd been like a mate staking a claim. Every cell in his body hummed with the need to claim her, and the longer he was around her, the worse it got.

Even worse than when they'd been dating. He wasn't sure if it was because he'd marked her as his or if it was because he'd finally admitted to himself what she was to him. The mark had faded, but she now carried his scent. Unless they stopped sleeping with each other, that mating scent wouldn't fade and no other shifter or supernatural male would come near her. That was something he needed to tell her.

As they walked through the thicket of trees that ran behind the quiet, rural neighborhood, Kat held on to his forearm. Not because she needed to, but because she wanted to. It soothed his inner beast in the same way it had when she'd told that detective in so many words to back off. He'd been ready to make it clear she was taken, but she beat him to the punch.

The closer they got to the cop's house Jayce realized there were no animal sounds. Nothing. His nape prickled. Most animals stopped all movement and sound when a predator was nearby. He and Kat were predators here, of course, but the silence stretched much farther than it should have.

He paused and Kat did the same, her grip on his arm tightening. "What is it?"

"You hear that?" he murmured.

She shook her head.

"Exactly."

Before they could take another step, Connor Armstrong moved into view from behind one of the trees. He looked more annoyed than pissed. "Nice of you to tell me where you were going."

Jayce gritted his teeth. He didn't want to be impressed by the appearance of the Alpha. Not many people could sneak up on him. But he knew why Connor was there. Jayce had texted Ryan, but he hadn't told Connor what he'd found out. Jayce worked for the Council, but he should have at least let Connor know what he was doing out of respect. Instead he'd texted one of the Alpha's packmates. Not exactly a smart move on his part, but he'd been feeling edgy. The thought of picking a fight with a worthy opponent held a certain appeal. He shrugged, not willing to apologize just yet. "You knew what the plan was."

Connor growled, taking an aggressive step toward him. "And you were supposed to let me know once you had a name. If you want to use my pack's resources and live on my property, you'll keep me apprised of everything, especially if you plan to stick around my territory for a while." He flicked Kat a glance before looking back at Jayce. "And I'm guessing you plan to."

"You're right." The words scraped his throat like sandpaper.

Connor's eyebrows rose and his stance immediately loosened. It was obvious that he'd expected more of an argument.

Before Jayce could continue, Kat spoke. "Why can't I scent you?" she asked Connor.

Her Alpha gave a little smile. "One of my gifts as Alpha is being able to disguise my scent."

"Oh." She bit her bottom lip, then looked at Jayce with questioning eyes. He could tell she wanted to know if he could do it too, so he nodded. "I *knew* you could hide the scent of your lust!" Her eyes widened as she realized what she'd just said. With pink cheeks she turned to Connor. "Sorry."

Connor just shook his head. "I already checked out the house. There's someone inside. A shifter, definitely a beta. Probably the guy we're looking for."

Jayce wouldn't know for sure until he scented him, but he doubted there was any other beta hanging out with a member of the APL.

Once the trees thinned to the point that they'd be seen if they continued walking, Jayce stopped and turned to Kat, hating what he was going to say but refusing to let her go any farther.

Connor beat him to the punch. "You can't hide your scent and we can. As your Alpha, I'm ordering you to stay put unless you're facing danger. If that happens, I'm ordering you to run as fast as you can away from here."

Kat's blue eyes flashed angrily and her mouth opened once, then snapped shut. She shot Jayce an annoyed look as if she knew he agreed with Connor.

Instead of responding and facing her wrath, he wisely kept his mouth shut.

Connor shook his head as they trekked off. "I figured you should stay out of trouble with your female since you're newly mated. . . . Are you going to bond at the next full moon?"

Jayce's jaw clenched, but he didn't say anything since he wasn't sure if they were out of earshot yet. He had a bad feeling they weren't and that Kat had heard Connor's statement.

After a few beats of silence, Connor asked, "Does Kat know you marked her?"

A quick shake of his head. It was embarrassing to admit what he'd done. As enforcer and someone so old, he should have had more control. Kat wasn't even aware of it, which made him feel worse yet. She didn't understand pack rules and shifter life enough to know what he'd done. Sure, she'd felt him bite her, but he'd never explained mating to her, and as far as he knew, she was aware of only the bonding process. He had no doubt that she scented him on her, but they'd been having a lot of sex so it was only normal that she would.

"Tell her now before someone else congratulates her. I almost did," Connor murmured, the words so low Jayce almost missed them.

He ignored the Alpha. As they reached the clearing near the house, he asked, "How do you want to do this?" Now that he was closer to the house, he had no doubt that Fletcher Monroe was nearby. This beta had been at the last crime scene. Whether he was involved or not, they would find out soon enough. Jayce had a pretty good idea that Monroe was right in the middle of all this.

"I've scoped the place. There's only one person there, the beta. I didn't see trip wires or any other type of trap. I noticed a window on the second floor, east side from our position, partially open. From the size of the window I'm guessing it leads to a bathroom. We can go in that way?" Connor formed it as a question, obviously not caring how they got in as long as they did.

"Sounds good to me. We need this guy alive." Jayce wanted to question him before they turned him over to the cops.

If they even did. Normally human government institutions were more than happy to let shifters mete out justice to their own kind and rarely asked questions, but these killings had been against humans. They would want to parade Fletcher through their system, possibly have a trial. Too much red tape for Jayce's taste, but he had no problem handing him over.

Jayce took off, knowing Connor would follow once he'd reached the window. He couldn't jump as high as vampires could, but he had no problem jumping or even scaling a simple two-story house. As Alpha, Connor would have no issue either. Hell, they'd infiltrated Edward Adler's home—dead APL bastard—with no problem. It was one of the times Jayce had seen the Alpha in action and he'd been impressed. Not to mention he'd heard through the grapevine how Connor had killed his former neighboring Alpha.

Getting in and getting what they wanted should be a simple task. Even if the cop who owned this house had an alarm system, it obviously wasn't rigged to the window that was open. Most people went with the bare minimum with security systems, tagging the doors and a few windows downstairs. But never upstairs. Stupid thinking when there were people like him around.

His legs pumped, straining as he sprinted and vaulted through the air. Using his upper body strength and balance, he latched onto the ledge of the window, extending his claws to get a better grip. Taking a deep breath, he pulled his body up, held tight with one hand, and shoved the window up with the other. Thankfully it didn't squeak; there was just a soft *whoosh* as it moved.

After peeking into the room, which was indeed a small bathroom with black-and-white-checkered tile, he lifted himself up and over the ledge, landing silently on the floor in a roll. Standing back, he waited for Connor to join him.

Moments later, the dark-haired Alpha flew into the room. As Connor stood, he retracted his claws.

Jayce slowly unzipped his jacket and withdrew one of his blades, then pointed to the door. Connor nodded and let his claws out again. They might want this guy alive, but Jayce believed in always being prepared.

Especially since the beta shifter had killed four unsuspecting humans. Even if the humans hadn't been good citizens, he was fucking up the balance between shifters and humans. Something like this could start a full-scale war with countless innocents getting hurt or even killed in the crossfire. At the moment, this was a lot more important than blood trafficking. While he hated having to pick what to focus on, for the time being there was no other choice. Soon, though, Erin would be ready to take a case on her own. He was looking forward to the day that happened.

Easing the door open, he used his senses before stepping into the hall. There were two faint scents upstairs, one human, one shifter. But neither held that strong note that told him someone was directly nearby.

Slowly, he headed down a long, carpeted hallway until he reached a staircase. Paisley-patterned wallpaper lined the stairwell, ending on the first floor in a foyer with cherrywood flooring. Above them hung a chandelier, the sun glinting off it through the high windows above the front door. Too high for anyone to see them from the outside.

He and Connor stilled at the bottom of the stairs, scenting for the beta. At the same time, they both nodded toward the south side of the home. To the east and west open rooms were visible, one living room and a dining room. As they moved south through the house they entered a kitchen, where the scent grew stronger. There was a French door showing the backyard and beyond, where he and Connor had just come from.

As Jayce scanned the kitchen he nodded at a wooden door next to a stainless-steel refrigerator. Connor mouthed the word "basement" and Jayce nodded in agreement. The scent of shifter was so close and so strong now, there was no other place this guy could be. That distinctive fir and spruce blend nearly overwhelmed Jayce because the other shifter knew they were in the house. The guy's fear was spiking his normal scent out of control and his heart was an erratic tattoo. Thanks to Jayce's natural defense mechanisms and his age, he could cloak his own heartbeat, so he knew the beta couldn't hear it. Jayce also had no doubt that Connor could do the same since he couldn't hear the Alpha's heartbeat. Still, the beta knew they were there.

It didn't matter that Jayce and Connor had been deathly silent or that they'd virtually cloaked themselves. It also didn't matter that Fletcher was a beta, physically weaker than they were. He was still a shifter with senses a hell of a lot better than those of humans. He might just sense something different in the air, like danger. Betas always had to be aware of their surroundings in a way alphas and warriors probably took for granted.

Right now, the acrid scent of fear was coming from behind the closed door. Taking a deep breath, Jayce opened it, his blade in one hand, and took a cautious step inside.

He froze as he felt the barrel of a pistol pressing against the side of his skull.

Chapter 17

For one moment Jayce considered telling the beta shifter to drop his weapon, but he didn't want to take the chance that he was trigger-happy. It was unlikely that he could kill Jayce unless the beta took his head off or removed his heart from his chest. Even a silver-injected bullet likely wouldn't kill Jayce, as he was too old, but he didn't want to deal with a mess.

Lightning fast, he brought his right arm up at the same time he stepped forward and twisted his body. Using about fifty percent of his strength, he slammed the shifter into the back of the door. As the gun clattered onto the stairs, Jayce hauled the guy up and threw him down the rest of the stairs.

The basement wasn't dark—not that it would have mattered, given his heightened senses—so as he descended he had a perfect view of the setup beyond the crumpled body of the shifter at the bottom. A pullout couch with rumpled sheets and a quilt thrown haphazardly over it, an older-model television, and a coffee table made up the furnishings. A few pairs of jeans, sweaters, and socks also covered what looked like a wooden bench. At least it was insulated and had wood flooring. Not exactly a dungeon.

Though Connor was silent, Jayce could feel his presence behind him as he descended. Fletcher Monroe pushed up and scooted back, his sock-covered feet sliding on the floor in his attempt to escape. As a lupine shifter he should have been more agile, no matter his ranking in the pack, but fear was an acrid cloak around him.

"I knew you'd find me," he said as Jayce reached the last step. He brought his knees up to his chest and wrapped his arms around them as he slumped against the wall.

"Did you know it was me when you held a gun to my head?" Jayce asked quietly as he crouched in front of him, leaving only inches separating them.

Swallowing hard, the other man shook his head. "I knew it had to be a shifter, though. Almost didn't hear you, but the stairs are above the back of this room." He motioned jerkily with his head.

Though the beta's fear burned Jayce's nostrils, there was none of the almost metallic scent so common with lies. "I'm going to give you a chance to speak since you didn't lie to me just now. I'm assuming you know who I am?"

Fletcher's forest green eyes widened as he nodded. "Jayce Kazan," he said so quietly it couldn't even be called a whisper.

There was nothing but fear in his voice, which was normally a good thing because Jayce didn't like people lying to him. In this instance, however, Jayce was worried the guy might go into shock, so he stood up and motioned to the couch/bed. "Why don't you make that up and have a seat?"

With trembling hands, Fletcher pushed himself up

and began folding his quilt, as Jayce continued. "How long is the cop usually gone?"

The shifter paused in what he was doing, but only for a moment. "Sometimes he comes home for lunch, but not often. He doesn't tell me about his schedule."

"Any video surveillance in this house, inside or out?"

A shake of his head as he shoved the metal frame to fold it back into the couch. "No, and I've thoroughly checked. But I do have this." He lifted his pant leg up to his knee, showing a tracking anklet.

Jayce had seen the kind before. "It doesn't look like there's an explosive attached to it. So why not just cut it and leave?" He had a feeling he knew the answer, but he wanted to hear Fletcher say it.

The beta ran a hand through his dirty blond hair, sending it sticking up everywhere as he sat down on the couch. "They've got my mate. She's pregnant and they only let me talk to her if I obey them."

Jayce planned to get to who exactly "they" were, but first, "How is your mate? Do you have any idea where they're keeping her or what her condition is?" It took a lot to get Jayce's anger truly flowing, but to kidnap a pregnant woman, no matter the species, took a certain kind of monster. One that Jayce was going to rip apart.

"I have no idea where she is, but she's close to her due date. From what I can tell they're taking decent care of her, feeding her and even letting her take prenatal pills, but still, she's due any day now and I should be with her." There was a hint of desperation woven through those words. "How . . . how'd you find me?"

"Doesn't matter. For the record, you're responsible for the four killings in Fontana recently, correct?"

With a miserable expression, Fletcher nodded. "Yeah. I did it for my mate."

Jayce couldn't exactly blame him. If someone took Kat, he'd do anything to get her back. "Why didn't you go to your Alpha or the Council?"

"I'm a beta; your Council wouldn't give a shit about my mate unless we had some political ties. And . . . Luiz is a good Alpha, but if I'd gone to him, they'd have known and they would have killed my mate. He wouldn't have allowed me to go on a killing spree, no matter how good the cause. And he wouldn't have been wrong. I know I'll have to pay for what I did and I'm willing to suffer the consequences. I just want Heather and my unborn child safe."

Before Jayce could respond, he heard light steps on the stairs above them. Turning to face Connor, who stood halfway up the stairs, quiet and ready for anything, he started to speak but then he scented Kat. Sweet, classic roses. He didn't have to say anything because Connor grunted in annoyance and strode up the basement stairs to open the door.

Seconds later Kat came down into the basement with her Alpha, an expression of open defiance on her face. "I got tired of waiting for you two," she snapped before either of them could speak.

Fletcher gasped as he looked between the two of them. "You brought your mate on a mission to kill me?" he asked Jayce, more than a little shock in his voice. "Hell, I didn't even think enforcers got mated," he muttered almost to himself.

"We're not mated," Kat snapped again, the agitation from her seeming to grow with each passing second.

Because they'd left her in the woods or because of the beta's statement, Jayce couldn't be sure. And he didn't have time to dwell on it.

Turning back to Fletcher, Jayce asked, "The cop, Derrick Bird—he lets you keep a weapon?"

A sharp shake of his head. "Hell, no. I lifted this off one of the men I killed the other night. They were both APL members and from the rap sheet the human gave me, not good men."

"What about your first two victims?"

"They both had sheets too. The first not so bad, but the second was a fucking pedophile. The cop seems to have a weird moral code about only killing people with records. His partner, or boss—I'm not sure of the hierarchy—doesn't seem to have that sort of compunction from what I've heard of their phone calls."

"His partner's name?"

"Anthony Mayfield. I think the cop forgets I can hear his phone conversations even when I'm down here and he's outside." Fletcher shrugged, relaxing a fraction for the first time since Jayce and Connor had arrived.

Humans had a tendency to do that, probably because shifters didn't broadcast the scope of their abilities to the world on a regular basis. "What else did he say? I need to know everything you've talked about and everything you've overheard."

Those dark green eyes narrowed slightly. "I know you're going to kill me, but first promise you'll search for my mate. You won't have much time, but—"

"I'm not going to kill you. Not yet anyway. My only concern is bringing down these APL fuckers and stopping the killings in Fontana. I might turn you over to the human government or I might let your Alpha deal with you, so I guarantee you will be punished. But unless you try to kill me again, we're good. And you can be damn sure we're going to search for your mate. Now that we have this cop's name we'll run his phone records and see what we can find." Jayce turned around and gave Connor a questioning look.

The Alpha nodded and went back up the stairs, pulling his phone from his pocket; Jayce assumed he was calling Ryan.

"Wait, did you say unless he tries to kill you *again*?" Kat hissed behind him and he heard the beginnings of a low growl in her throat.

The sound brought a ghost of a smile to his lips. Good to know she cared. Schooling his expression, he focused on Fletcher. "Talk. Now."

The beta swallowed hard but nodded. "Okay. We're going to another bar tonight. Not an APL hangout, just a busy place where he wants to target at least half a dozen criminals. From what I gather, they want to enrage the humans in Fontana and they think a higher body count is the only way to do that. Apparently the men I've killed haven't brought as much of a media shit storm as they originally hoped for."

"Do you know who your targets are?"

He shook his head. "The cop doesn't tell me until right before."

"How much does this cop know about betas and alphas and shifter life?" Kat asked as she stepped forward.

Jayce wondered why she wanted to know, but he didn't interrupt.

The beta looked at him, as if asking for permission to speak, so he nodded. Fletcher cleared his throat nervously. "I don't think he knows that much. Just that we can turn into animals and we have heightened senses. He didn't tell me the two men from the other night were hopped up on vampire blood until the last second. Didn't seem to realize that they were more likely to kill me, as a beta, than the other way around."

"But you did kill them," Jayce said.

Fletcher shrugged. "I have more to lose."

Jayce glanced at Kat, who now stood right next to him. "Why do you want to know what this cop knows about shifters?"

Her eyes had a dangerous glint to them. "Because I have a plan that might bring these APL members out in the open as monsters. They want to start a media war against shifters, right?" she asked Fletcher.

The beta nodded. "They know they can't take us physically, at least not one-on-one. They seem to want the public to ostracize all of us. I'm not sure of their end-game, but I can imagine it's not pretty."

"What are you thinking, Kat?" Jayce asked quietly, not liking the vibe he was getting from her.

"You're not gonna like it, but I was thinking they used his mate against him"—she motioned to Fletcher—"and he's not politically connected to anyone, so imagine what they would do if they got their hands on me again. My previous connection to you was common knowledge and now we're living in the same city again. A lot of people saw us at the police station earlier and—"

"No!" Jayce roared. He didn't know what her plan was and he didn't care. He didn't like the direction she was taking.

"No, what?" Connor asked as he descended the stairs.

"I have a plan to bring the local APL out into the open and expose them as the monsters they are."

"Kat—," Jayce began, his claws protracting against his palms.

Connor completely ignored Jayce. "What kind of plan?"

"We'll need to involve Parker—and probably other law enforcement types," she said, hedging.

Still ignoring Jayce, Connor nodded. "All right. What's the *plan*?"

Kat smiled at her Alpha's words, obviously not expecting them. Hell, Jayce hadn't expected Connor to want to listen after the mention of involving law enforcement.

She crossed her arms over her chest and turned away from Jayce to completely face her Alpha. "It's simple. I'll be the bait."

Kat's grip around Jayce's waist tightened as they flew down the highway at breakneck speed. Yep, he was beyond pissed at her. So much so that she wondered if he would even let her go through with their plan for that night.

Connor was annoyed at her too, but for different reasons. He told her she had to clean out the stables for the next two weeks because she'd disobeyed his orders about staying put and because she'd stolen from a pack member. Liam sure hadn't wasted any time telling his brother about her thievery. Not that she blamed him. The punishment sucked, but it wasn't too bad. At least he hadn't scoffed at her idea for tonight.

Unlike Jayce.

He'd tried to tell her no, but as Connor reminded him, Jayce wasn't her Alpha and they weren't bondmates. There had been a weird look that passed between the two of them in that moment and she hadn't been able to shake the odd feeling she'd been holding on to since Jayce had bitten her. Not that she felt physically different, but his scent seemed stronger somehow, constantly surrounding her. They'd been having quite a bit of sex, though, so she'd chalked it up to that. Now she wondered if there wasn't more to it. Especially since that beta had seemed convinced they were mated. She hated that she didn't understand more about pack life.

As they pulled into the driveway at December's house, Jayce was practically vibrating even after they'd come to a complete stop. Without looking at her, he got off the bike and headed inside the house.

Gritting her teeth, she followed him and slammed the door. "Are you going to sulk?" she called after him as she placed her helmet by the coatrack near the front door. Next she hung up her leather jacket, only to freeze with her hand in midair as Jayce strode out of the kitchen. He sure had that angry walk down.

The look on his face was predatory and vulnerable. An odd combination. One that touched something deep inside her and made her want to reach out and hug him. She didn't like seeing Jayce vulnerable. It threw her world out of order.

"I marked you," he said bluntly, jerking her out of her thoughts.

She blinked once. "What?"

"In the shower, I bit you." Again with the almost monotone voice.

Shrugging, she slid one of her boots off. "Yeah, I know. I was there."

"I marked you as mine. The way I took you," his voice dropped an octave as he walked so close that only a foot separated them, "from behind, biting you as we made love. It makes you my mate, marking you in a way that all other supernatural beings know you're mine and to stay away."

Her other boot fell from her hand, hitting the hardwood floor with a thump. "I thought bondmates—"

He shook his head sharply. "I can't make you my bondmate until the next full moon and unless we both consent."

Her heart pounded erratically as she tried to comprehend what he was telling her. "I don't understand. You bit me, so . . ." So what the heck did it mean?

"There's not a science to it, but since I bit you in that position while I was inside you, it does something to our bodies. At least temporarily. I . . . should have asked you first."

Okay, so his strong scent wasn't her imagination and it wasn't just about sex. She wrapped her arms around herself, unsure how she felt and still a little unsure what he was telling her. "So, we're mates?"

He nodded jerkily, the action so out of character that it stunned her.

"But we can walk away from each other anytime we want?" That thought depressed the hell out of her.

Another nod.

"So this doesn't mean anything, then?" A dark weight settled on her chest, spreading out with burning tendrils to all her nerves. She wondered why he'd even told her.

"It means something." The words were a guttural sound, more animal than human, and his eyes had turned to storm clouds, swirling gray energy.

It does? Some of those tendrils retracted, easing the ache inside her.

Before she could formulate anything that remotely approached coherent words, he continued. "I want to say I'm sorry. Hell, I know I should be, but I'm not. I don't want anyone else to touch you or even think about touching you. I'm *glad* everyone can scent me on you, and if I could go back and ask you first, I don't know that I would."

She swallowed hard. He'd already told her that he loved her, something she was still having a hard time coming to terms with, especially after his lies. "When I was human, why did you lie to me about the bonding process? Why did you tell me there was a one percent chance I'd survive the transition from a shifter's bite?" Technically it was true, but not if he'd taken her as his bondmate instead. There was a hundred percent crossover rate in those instances. Mother Nature was kind that way. But Jayce had withheld that information, letting her believe his lies. When she'd found out the truth, she'd been heartbroken. Hell, part of her still was. It didn't matter that he'd told her he loved her—she still felt like she hadn't been good enough for him then. But now that she was a shifter, he loved her? The knowledge was bittersweet.

Jayce was silent for so long she wondered if he was going to answer. Finally he crossed the rest of the short distance between them and placed both his palms on the door next to her head, caging her in. She didn't mind. His warmth and strength had a soothing effect and she took comfort in it as she braced herself for his answer. He could shred her heart to ribbons in the next few seconds.

"I've made a lot of enemies over the past few centuries, Kat. Enemies who would love to see me suffer. It's damn hard to kill me, but if I'd taken you as a bondmate everyone would have known what you meant to me. How important you were—*are*. By keeping you as a woman I was sleeping with, you weren't a target."

She snorted softly. "Except to the APL."

"I wasn't thinking about them at the time, just my supernatural enemies. No one who was non-human would have messed with you while you were simply a bed partner."

The burning tendrils of pain that had been lapping across her chest completely retreated, to be replaced by a jolt of anger. "So you lied to protect me? You didn't think I could handle making a decision about *my* life?"

Sighing, he pressed his forehead to hers. "This is why I didn't tell you."

"Because you know I'm right. You had no right to make a decision about our future like that. What was the point in staying with me if you never planned to turn me?" She couldn't keep the building anger out of her voice.

He slightly grimaced. "I thought I'd eventually tire of you. I thought maybe if we slept together enough, I'd get you out of my system."

She let out a growl and shoved at his chest.

Jayce was completely immovable, but he did lift his head. "Sorry. I'm being honest. No more lies between us."

"So why'd you mark me now? Is it because I'm a shifter?"

He shook his head. "Are you listening to a word I've said? I marked you because I couldn't *not* do it. My need for you grows every day and I wanted my scent on you for everyone to know you belong to me. My animal side doesn't give a shit about my enemies—it only wants you. There's a full moon in four days and I want to take you as my bondmate then. You'll walk around with a permanent bull's-eye on you once my enemies get wind of it, but it's worth the constant worry. I love and need you more than anyone, Kat. I'm not walking away from you again. I fucking can't do it."

Kat sucked in a jagged breath that made her lungs burn. *Holy shit.* Jayce hadn't lied to her because she hadn't been good enough. However misguided, he'd lied to her out of a need to protect her. He'd given up a chance at his own happiness because he'd wanted to keep her safe. Hot tears stung her eyes and she swallowed past the lump in her throat. "Jayce, I—"

His muscular body pressed up against hers and he laid

a finger over her lips. "Think long and hard about what you plan to say next. Once you cross that line, there's no going back. I'm not walking away from you again. Ever."

She swallowed hard again, understanding what he was saying. If she admitted that she loved him, told him how much she needed him, that was it for them. They'd be bonded and that would be that. She'd be saddled with all his baggage, which translated to countless enemies. Not that she was worried about that. The thought of not being able to spend her life with Jayce was worse than the possible threat of future problems. She opened her mouth again to tell him just that, but he shook his head before covering her mouth with his.

They had a few hours before they would set their plan in motion and she knew exactly how they were going to spend them when he practically ripped her jeans from her body and lifted her up against the front door. As she wrapped her legs around his waist and he entered her in one hard thrust, she couldn't think of a better way to occupy her time.

Kat tried to casually adjust her cleavage against the corset-style top she wore. She'd opted for an intricate leather design because it was easier to secrete the listening device Ryan had picked out to weave into her clothing. The dark color and the cut of the top guaranteed that no one was going to be looking any lower than her breasts anyway.

Jayce might hate this plan, but at least he was nearby, ready to jump into the fray if necessary. She just hoped he didn't act too soon. They needed to show the world what the APL was like, and if Jayce couldn't keep his territorial urges under control, they were screwed. At least they had Parker and some of his Fed contacts that he'd decided to involve all pumped up and ready to bring down this APL group along with them. Involving Parker was the part of her plan that hadn't gone over well *at all*. Even though Connor had listened to her, he'd been pretty unhappy. At least he hadn't been as crazy as Jayce. She tried to understand where they were coming from. They'd lived the majority of their very long lives hiding their identities from humans. To be working with them now must feel incredibly foreign. Luckily it turned out that the Feds were just as concerned with the growing APL movement and wanted to bring these guys down just as badly as the Armstrong-Cordona pack did.

As part of the deal, Connor and Jayce had stipulated that they get their own recording devices, some leeway in their actions, and complete immunity from anything that might transpire short of Kat or Jayce actually killing someone—except in self-defense. The Feds had *not* been happy, but considering they had no inside men in the APL and they couldn't have stopped Kat or the Armstrong pack from doing what they wanted to, they'd gone along with her Alpha's stipulations.

So here she was, about to throw herself into a hornet's nest—with a ton of very capable backup, to be sure, but she was still nervous. Internal pep talks could help only so much. Tango's, the place Fletcher Monroe had told them about, was in full swing tonight. Not a biker bar like the one before, but a bowling alley/bar that had five-dollar pitchers and was open late on weekdays. Kat guessed the reason the cop had chosen this place had to do with the location, which was in the middle of town, and the late hours. The drunker people were, the easier it would be for Fletcher to subdue and kill them. And the location would freak people out once they learned the victims had all been chosen from Tango's.

Unfortunately for the cop, but luckily for the victims, there would be no bloodshed here tonight. Not if things went the way they were supposed to.

She opened the tinted glass door, stepped inside, and inhaled the various scents. Stale cigarettes, beer, greasy food, some nasty chemicals, wax, and of course, body odor. After tonight she was going to take her time soaking in a tub.

Veering to the left, she didn't bother with the bowling alley part of the establishment but headed straight for the door in the corner that was labeled BAR in bright red letters. Before she'd stepped inside she scented Fletcher already there. *Good.*

She spotted him at the bar sitting next to the same cop she'd seen at the station earlier. The two of them might be sitting side by side, but they were pretending they didn't know each other. Scoping out the place.

Somehow she managed to avoid looking at the cop and giving herself away as she sidled up to Fletcher, scooting a seat closer to his. "Buy a shifter a drink?" she murmured, but loud enough for the cop to hear.

Not that she worried he wouldn't recognize her. She just wanted it clear that she was hitting on Fletcher because of what he was.

Fletcher didn't miss a beat. "Beer okay?"

She nodded. "I'll have what you're having."

The green-eyed beta motioned to the bartender for two more beers, then turned to her. "Why are you out without your pack members?" he asked, just like they'd rehearsed.

She flipped her hair over her shoulder in a haughty way. "I'm sick of their rules. I just want to have a good time."

He laughed under his breath before taking a swig of his beer. For the next hour they flirted not so subtly until Fletcher stood and made an excuse about using the restroom. The second he slid off his stool, the cop did the same.

Pretending to be oblivious, she did as Jayce had taught her and focused solely on Fletcher's voice. If she could focus, she'd be able to decipher his voice from the rest of the noise surrounding her.

It sounded as if they were speaking from a tunnel or were surrounded by water, but she could still hear Fletcher's conversation through the fuzziness.

"*What the hell are you doing, flirting with that shifter? We're supposed to be picking out the targets,*" the cop hissed.

"*I'm doing it because of who she is. Everyone knows she was Jayce Kazan's female for a while.*"

"*Tell me something I don't know. Saw them at the station together earlier.*" There was a touch of fear in the cop's voice.

"*His scent is on her, so they're sleeping together but they're not mated.*"

"*Then what the hell are you doing? We can't draw any attention from someone like him. Not yet.*"

"*I know you fuckers want to bring a media shit storm to Fontana and I want my mate back. I can help you do that a hell of a lot faster than you'd planned but only if you promise to bring my mate to me and let us go. Tonight.*"

Unfortunately Ryan hadn't been able to figure out where Fletcher's mate was being held, though he'd tried using the cop's phone records. Kat took a sip of her beer and glanced around the bar while still listening intently.

The cop laughed, the sound harsh. "*How do you plan on doing that?*"

"*Shifters like the enforcer are territorial, especially since he's sleeping with that woman. She's been newly turned so she's not at full strength. She won't be hard to subdue. Do you have silver handcuffs?*"

A snort. "*Of course.*"

"*All you have to do is snap those on her and kidnap her and contact the enforcer. He'll come running. You want the town enraged because of the crimes I'm committing, but what if you get the enforcer to commit a crime and catch him on video? I'm small potatoes, but the enforcer . . .*"

A long beat of silence followed. Then, "*Get the woman to leave the bar with you. You do that, we'll talk about releasing your mate.*"

"*No more talking. You'll do it,*" Fletcher demanded.

"*Fine, fine, you'll see her tonight. Go back to the bar and lure the woman out back.*" The cop's voice was clipped.

"*What are you going to do?*"

"*I need to make a phone call first.*"

"*Fine,*" Fletcher said, and then she heard the sound of a door opening and closing.

Seconds later, Fletcher emerged alone and sat next to her. "You get all that?"

"Yep. I want to hear what he has to say and then we'll leave together," she said, a grin plastered on her face as she pretended to be engrossed in the beta sitting next to her. If anyone was watching, which she doubted, they needed to see her playing her part.

Kat listened as the cop called someone and told them there had been a change of plans. Since he was still in the restroom, she could just barely hear him. He told whomever he was talking to that they needed to knock out or injure some of their members—APL members, she guessed—and lock them up because he had a surprise for tonight. Then he made another call and told someone to get to the warehouse. Well, that was interesting.

Kat hadn't expected that. Looked like there might be a slight change in the original plan. As it was, they wanted a confession from the dirty cop on what he'd been making the beta do, but this could be even better than they'd planned.

"There might be a change in plans. Just go with it," she murmured low enough that only Fletcher and those on the other side of her listening device could hear as she pretended to stumble outside with Fletcher.

Kat had thought that she wanted to bring down the APL more than anything, but the longer she'd talked with Fletcher, the more she realized how depressed the beta was. The scent clung to him like a second skin and all she wanted to do was reunite him with his mate. What he'd done was incredibly wrong, but she couldn't lie and say she didn't understand. If someone took Jayce, there wasn't a lot she wouldn't do to get him back.

As she and Fletcher walked, she said a silent prayer that Jayce didn't lose his temper and do something that could ruin this entire operation.

Chapter 18

Fletcher's body was pressed against the length of Kat's as he nuzzled her neck. She tried to keep her body pliant, to pretend she was enjoying it, but it was hard.

Judging from how tense the beta was, he wasn't having a good time either. "Your mate is so going to kill me," Fletcher murmured.

The statement made her laugh, which slightly eased her body. They were near an SUV behind the bowling alley, just waiting for the cop to arrive.

At the same time she heard footsteps around the side of the building, she scented the cop. "Punch me," she whispered.

Fletcher pulled back, his entire body taut. "Do you *want* the enforcer to kill me?"

She pressed her forehead to his. "Do it and make sure the cop sees you do it." Her words were barely above a whisper, too low for human ears. Anyone watching would have thought they were just two lovers embracing one another.

The footsteps were getting closer.

Her heart rate increased. They had only a few precious moments to pull this off.

Smiling seductively at Fletcher, she said, "So when can we get out of here and go back to your place?"

His fist came from the left, slamming into her jaw, but she knew it wasn't as hard as he could have hit her. With a cry of alarm, she let her arms flail as she fell against the vehicle and then collapsed onto the concrete.

Dirt and wet pavement met her face. Gross.

"I wasn't sure this would work," the cop murmured as he came up on them. "You sure she's out?"

"How can you not know new shifters are so weak?" Fletcher said with an incredulity that even Kat believed. Guy was a damn fine actor. "Slap your cuffs on her."

Kat resisted the urge to wince as the cop yanked her arms behind her back and put on the handcuffs. For one terrifying moment she was back in that barn, being strung up, helpless, with no escape. The world began to spin as their muted voices hummed around her. She couldn't think straight—but then she remembered that Jayce was out there, listening, waiting to help. Keeping her eyes closed, she remained a limp deadweight while the cop patted her down, likely searching for weapons. He was quick and professional before hefting her up and dumping her in the back of the SUV.

"Bitch is a lot heavier than she looks," he said before slamming the door shut.

Kat wanted to growl, but refrained. Hurting this guy would be no problem.

She felt a little bad for Fletcher. He hadn't wanted to punch her. She'd seen the indecision and agony in his eyes, but thankfully he'd done it. As a shifter she'd learned to channel her pain in a way that she would never have been able to do as a human. It wasn't as if she'd enjoyed the punch, but after the past couple of months, there wasn't much that could faze her anymore. Now, she felt only a dull throb as a remnant of the blow Fletcher had inflicted.

Thankfully these bigoted APL members were in the dark about certain shifter practices. That was how she'd come up with this plan in the cop's basement. She'd figured that the general public knew even less than she herself did about shifters. Hell, even now that she *was* a shifter she was still learning things. Granted, that was mostly her fault for not embracing her pack—and pack life—more, but the fact remained that the world at large didn't know much about shifters, and they were going to capitalize on that ignorance tonight.

This cop thought that because she was newly turned she was weak and the perfect bait for Jayce. As they hit a bump in the road, she rolled and her head hit the back of the middle seat. She barely refrained from crying out. Not from pain, but shock. She bit the inside of her lip. She needed to watch her natural reactions.

Talk, talk! she screamed to Fletcher in her mind. They needed to get the cop on tape for the authorities. Sure, she'd heard them talking in the bathroom, but that was thanks to her shifter senses. There was no way the recorder had picked up their conversation.

"When do I get to see my mate?" Fletcher asked, breaking the silence.

"Soon." The cop.

"Not soon. Now that you have Kat Saburova you don't need me anymore. The enforcer will do anything you want."

"That's the plan," the cop muttered.

Kat quietly rolled her body so that she was more on her back than her side. She wanted to make sure the recorder picked up the entire conversation. The hand-cuffs digging into her wrists were an annoyance. Even though she could easily break them, she'd had a moment of panic simply at the feeling of being restrained—until she reminded herself that she wasn't the same woman she'd been a month ago. Never again would anyone restrain or torture her. She'd been training and could defend herself. And if that failed, she knew the cavalry was out there listening to every word. Jayce would never allow her to get hurt. Or he would die trying to stop her pain. Of that she had no doubt. She was actually surprised that he'd allowed her to become bait tonight—though she had an idea why he'd agreed to the plan.

He wanted her to be in control of her life and instrumental in bringing down the APL. He hadn't said the words, but she'd sensed that he understood her need for vengeance.

"What exactly are you going to do with her?" Fletcher asked.

"When did you get so fucking chatty?"

She heard the sound of materials rubbing together. Fletcher probably shrugged against the seat. "If you're going to abuse her, I'm not letting you take her."

A snide laugh. "You really think you can stop us?"

Fletcher growled low in his throat, a reminder that he was an animal.

The cop swallowed hard. They might be holding the guy's mate captive, but he was still stronger than this cop. If he wanted to, Fletcher could rip him apart. Of course, he would never find his mate if he did that, but the cop's primitive side had to recognize that Fletcher was stronger and more dangerous than he himself was.

"Calm down. We're not going to touch her. Just throw

her in a cage and call her boyfriend in. If he does what
we say, we'll let her go," the cop said.

That was a blatant lie. They would never let her go. A
shot of fear surged through her, bitter and fast. What if
she'd damaged the recording device when she landed on
the ground earlier? What if Jayce couldn't hear her,
didn't know where she was being taken?

Her breathing became ragged as blood rushed in her
ears. What if this had been a giant mistake? What if—

"He won't be easy to control," Fletcher said, injecting
fear into his voice and completely cutting off Kat's train
of thought.

The fear was a nice touch, Kat thought, and probably
not all fake.

"He will when I have a gun with silver-injected bullets
pointed at her head."

A new burst of fear bloomed inside her at the mention of the weapon. She might be fast, able to dodge bullets, but she'd never actually put it to the test. Deep down
she worried that she'd crack under pressure, be unable to
react and would get herself killed.

"So when do I get to see my mate?" Fletcher asked.

Kat tensed, knowing what was about to happen. She
and Fletcher had talked outside the bowling alley/bar
before they'd reached the SUV. It wasn't part of the original plan, but Kat wanted Fletcher reunited with his
mate. He'd been a slave for weeks, constantly worrying
about his mate. No one deserved that kind of emotional
pain. Connor and Jayce had to have heard her conversation with Fletcher, so they would know that she'd made
a change. She just hoped all parties—meaning law enforcement—went along with it. Not to mention that this
would make Fletcher's role look more realistic.

The cop had searched her for weapons but not recording devices and she doubted that they would do that. Especially not after what Fletcher was about to do.

"I'm getting sick of your questions," the cop ground out.

"And I'm sick of you," Fletcher snarled.

She heard the sound of a fist connecting with skin, followed by curses, and then the vehicle swerved dangerously, slamming Kat up against the side. Finally the vehicle jerked to a stop, the sound of skidding tires grating on her ears. She didn't make a peep until Fletcher dove over the backseat, yanked her up, and pressed a gun to her temple.

Fear sparked inside her. She might be a shifter now, but she'd been a human a hell of a lot longer. Having a gun to her head sent an icy chill snaking through her.

She opened her eyes and saw the cop staring at the two of them, blood dripping down his nose and from a split lip. "What the fuck are you doing?" he rasped.

"You don't bring my mate here right now, I kill her and you'll never get what you want." As if to prove his intent, he pulled back the slide action to the gun, chambering a round.

Kat swallowed. She might trust Fletcher to an extent, but having a gun pressed against her head was a scary thing.

The cop's features twisted with anger. "You don't get to bargain with me!"

"I'm not stupid. I know you never planned to let my mate go. Now you're going to. It's a win-win situation. You get this bitch and I get my mate. Make the call and have her brought right here in less than twenty minutes. She gets one escort and that's it. If she's not here, I'll kill you." Fletcher's voice was steady as a rock and so damn convincing, Kat didn't have a doubt that he'd kill the cop if pushed.

And she wouldn't blame him. She forced a fake tremble. "Please don't kill me," she begged.

The cop held up his hands in surrender. "No one's going to kill you. I'm reaching into my pocket and pulling out my phone, okay?" he asked Fletcher, a slight tremor to his voice. The thread of fear rolling off him was real too. The scent was rancid, stinging her nostrils.

"Careful. And don't forget I can hear every word you're saying. Try anything and I put a bullet in your brain," Fletcher said.

The cop, or Derrick Bird—it was so much easier to think of him by his profession than to give this monster a name—did as he was ordered.

Then they waited.

Barely ten minutes later, a vehicle pulled up behind them on the side of the deserted highway, high beams shining into the back of the SUV.

"Call your friend and tell him to kill the lights."

Derrick did as ordered and the lights immediately shut off.

"Now send my mate out."

"Not until you let her go," the cop said, nodding at Kat.

Fletcher snorted. "You're not running this show anymore. Send my mate out, let her get in the passenger seat, and I'll let Kat go. There's no other option for you unless you want to die." There was a note in Fletcher's voice that told Kat that sooner or later Derrick Bird was dying. If he didn't die tonight, it would eventually happen at Fletcher's hands.

Indecision flared in the cop's eyes, but finally he stepped out of the SUV and waved his hand at the other vehicle.

"I'm sorry for doing this, Kat. I couldn't take the risk

that they'd kill Heather later. There was no guarantee your pack would have gotten to her in time," he whispered so low she almost didn't hear him.

"I don't blame you," she murmured. And she didn't. They'd had no idea where his mate was being held, and it was the only shitty part of the plan. They'd been hoping the APL would give up her location in return for leniency once they had the bastards locked down.

Moments later a petite, scared, very pregnant blond female slid into the front seat. Fear rolled off her, a bitter, enveloping scent as she turned to look at them. "Fletcher?" There was a question in her scared voice.

"Are you okay, Heather?" Fletcher's voice held a soothing quality reserved only for his mate. Kat was positive of that.

"Me and the baby are fine, but my due date is almost here. I have maybe a couple days," she whispered.

Those words only confirmed Kat's decision that it had been right to help Fletcher in this way.

The cop stood by the open driver's-side door. "Let the woman go."

Fletcher motioned at the cop with his gun. "Keep your hands up, back away from the door. I'll let her out as soon as you're across the street." When the cop hesitated, Fletcher growled. "I'm not risking a high-speed chase with my pregnant mate. I'll let her go as soon as you move!"

"I'll find you," the cop growled.

Behind her, Kat felt Fletcher tense. All he'd have to do was turn the gun on the cop and kill him. It would be so easy. His tormenter would be dead.

But then they wouldn't have what they needed. Bringing down one APL member wasn't newsworthy. Derrick's death would be brushed off and he'd be labeled as a bad seed in the organization. Sensing Fletcher's thoughts, Kat squeezed his thigh tightly. The middle seat of the SUV blocked the lower half of their bodies, and since her arms were still restrained the cop wouldn't be able to see her.

Fletcher relaxed immediately. "You can try, cop. Now move and keep those hands in the air."

Once the cop started backing away, Fletcher helped Kat over the seat and followed her, opening the side door a fraction. Leaning forward so that her lips grazed his ears, she prayed that no one on the other side of her recording device could hear her as she whispered in the beta's ears. "Lose this vehicle as soon as you can and disappear."

Nodding, Fletcher shoved the door open, pushed Kat out and dove for the front seat. Before she'd even hit the pavement, the SUV tore away, tires squealing, dirt and snow flying everywhere.

Playing up her supposed weakness, Kat pretended to try to stand, then stumbled and fell, crying as she did. "I don't want to die," she said.

Hands grabbed her shoulders and lifted her up. "You're not going to die. You're bait," the cop said.

Another male, this one with a slightly crooked nose that looked like it had been broken multiple times, joined them as Derrick started leading her to the waiting car. "Why'd you let them go?"

"We've got bigger fish to fry. Besides, if they ever get his DNA in the system," Derrick said, referring to Fletcher, "they'll bring him down for the men he killed. Any story he tells will just seem like bullshit. I'm a cop and he's a killer. No one will believe we forced him into killing those scum."

Crooked Nose laughed under his breath. "Guess

you're right. Should we put her in the trunk or the back-seat?" he asked as if she wasn't even there.

"Trunk," the cop said.

No! Her inner wolf clawed at her. She didn't want to go in a small, dark enclosure. Didn't want to be captive ever again. It didn't matter that her human side knew this was part of the plan. Her beast wanted freedom.

Struggling and capitalizing on her fear, she twisted and turned, masking her true strength as she lashed out at them with her legs. After she kicked Crooked Nose in the shins, he grunted and wrapped his arms around her legs while the cop got the top of her body.

They threw her into the trunk unceremoniously and Derrick slammed the lid shut with a grunt.

After she'd been left alone, it took her a few long moments to stop thrashing around and get her breathing under control. At least her extrasensory abilities allowed her to see in the dark. Not like when she'd been human, when she'd been blindfolded in that van after those monsters had kidnapped her.

She wasn't sure where they were taking her now, but she knew that wherever it was, it would be to more APL members. Forcing herself to relax, she took deep breaths until her heart rate returned to normal.

Jayce and her pack were out there. They had her back. Nothing bad was going to happen. At least not to her. They were going to bring down these bastards tonight. She kept repeating the words over and over in her head, until calm surged through her.

"I'm okay," she whispered, afraid to say more than that. She just wanted Jayce to know she wasn't harmed. If she was being honest, she knew she was saying the words out loud for herself too, needing to believe them.

Connor had surprised her by pulling her aside earlier

and telling her to give Jayce some leeway when he acted possessive and a little crazy about this operation. She knew it would be hard for him, and that was the only thing that had made her question her decision. But she had to do this. The APL was growing and it wasn't affecting just their part of the world. This group could strengthen if allowed to continue unchecked and she wanted to strike back at them. Maybe she didn't want revenge anymore, but she sure as hell wanted justice.

In the back of an SUV, Jayce sat next to Ryan while Connor and Liam sat in the front seat, with the Alpha driving. Jayce's canines ached and his claws dug into his palms. He didn't even bother trying to retract them. The pain kept him focused on what needed to be done even though it did nothing to dull the fury coursing through him.

Having to listen to Kat get punched, then to her begging for her life had shredded his insides. When he'd heard the strike against her skin, Liam and Connor had both had to physically restrain him until he could get his wolf under control. It didn't matter that she was acting, that the fear in her voice wasn't real—that didn't soothe his inner wolf at all. It only enraged him. She was his to protect in all situations.

Right now he wanted to draw blood, to rake his claws over every single APL member, tear all their bodies to ribbons, and do the same to anyone who got in his way. He also wanted to kill Fletcher for what he'd pulled, but that was the least of his concerns at the moment.

Kat was the only thing that mattered.

"They're taking her inside what looks like a warehouse," Ryan murmured, turning the surveillance screen so that Jayce could see.

In addition to the recording device Ryan had embedded in her clothing, they'd also put two tracking devices on her; one in her boot and one in her watch. Parker's law enforcement friends had wanted to use their own equipment, but Ryan's stuff was far superior and Jayce had been willing to compromise only so much. Ryan had three screens pulled up on his laptop. One showed that the recording device was working perfectly; every single word was being transmitted and downloaded. Another showed Kat's trackers moving, and the third showed an actual map and outline of where the tracker was headed. They were maybe thirty seconds behind her, and if need be he could shift to animal form and race to where she was in ten to fifteen seconds. That had been part of his stipulation in allowing this stupid fucking operation to take place. She would never be separated from him by more than seconds. And as a wolf, he was *damn* fast. Unfortunately for anyone who got in his way, his beast was usually in charge when he allowed himself to shift.

Jayce knew what to expect next. Fletcher had practically hand-fed the cop as to what he needed to do with Kat. Jayce would be receiving a phone call very soon.

"She needs to do this for herself. After what she went through, this is her way of getting control," Connor said quietly from the front.

There were male voices coming through the recorder, then Kat begging them not to lock her up. Hearing her saying that killed Jayce inside. The humans ignored her pleas and he listened as a scuffle took place. It sounded as if Kat was struggling. She screamed "No!" and then the sound of metal clanging against metal vibrated over the airwaves.

He growled, his claws extending even more. His beast was so close to the surface. It would be so easy to give in, to let his wolf take over.

To kill everyone who'd hurt Kat.

The sound of shredding fabric jerked him out of his trance. Looking down, he saw that he'd cut straight through the leather of the seat with one hand and broken off part of the door with his other.

"Let me out!" Kat shouted, her cry falling on deaf ears.

"Are you sure this is a good idea?" a male voice asked.

"Mayfield is on the way, but I want the enforcer en route by the time Mayfield gets here. Have you subdued the others?"

A short pause, and then a sigh. "Yeah. You sure it's necessary to kill them? They're part of the APL."

"And they've all got violent criminal records. We don't need to be associated with people like that. Besides, it's an acceptable loss for our cause. Collateral damage."

"Collateral damage," the unidentified male echoed.

There was a beeping sound, as if someone was making a phone call. When Jayce's phone rang and Kat's number appeared, he realized they'd been scrolling through her contact list.

Ryan plugged earphones into the laptop so the sounds from the recorder wouldn't echo over their call, then nodded at Jayce.

Taking a deep breath, Jayce forced himself to act natural, as if he wasn't expecting a call from a psycho. "Hey, sweetheart."

"We've got your woman," the cop said.

"Who the fuck is this?" Jayce didn't have to act now. The anger in his voice was real.

"Not important. If you ever want to see her alive again, you will do exactly as I say." Jayce was pleased to hear a slight tremor in Derrick's voice.

Even this dumb fucker knew he was messing with the

wrong guy. "How do I know she's even alive? Or how do I know this isn't some prank?"

There was a clanging sound, then Derrick saying, "Speak into the phone. It's your boyfriend."

"Whatever they say, don't do it, Jayce!" Kat's fearful shouts were followed by a sharp clang, as if someone had slammed something against metal, likely the door or cage Kat was being held in.

His free hand flexed and he tore into the seat again, needing to hurt something.

"You can hear she's fine, but she won't be if you don't follow my instructions explicitly." He rattled off an address and told him he had fifteen minutes to get there. When Jayce tried to argue, Derrick snarled, "You'll be burying your woman if you don't make it." Then he ended the call.

Jayce tossed the phone onto the seat next to him so he wouldn't hurl it against the window or crush it in his hands. Right now he was itching to destroy something.

"We can put a recording device on you," Ryan said.

"No." Connor shook his head as he pulled off the highway near the turnoff where they'd taken Kat. He drove until their SUV was hidden behind a cluster of trees.

Jayce nodded in agreement. "They'll search me." He glanced at his watch. He didn't want to show up too early because they might realize he'd been following Kat the whole time.

So he sat with the other three and listened to the APL members bullshit among themselves. They talked about what a stroke of luck it was finding Kat and how they were going to show the world what monsters shifters were. Jayce was going to enjoy hurting them.

The flash of headlights from the opposite direction of

the highway swept through the trees as a truck turned down the road leading to the abandoned warehouse where they were keeping Kat. From the screen that Ryan pulled up, it looked like it had once been a textile plant.

"The cop has already admitted to a lot of shit, but if that's his boss who just drove by and he was involved with Kat's kidnapping or December's attempted kidnapping . . ." Connor trailed off, not needing to finish.

Jayce understood perfectly. From what they'd heard through Kat's wireless bug, it should be Mayfield arriving, a man who had been mentioned more than once by Brianna and Fletcher. From the sound of it, he might be a leader within the organization, and if they could bring him down, so much the better. Jayce just had to keep his wolf in check. If this fucker had been behind Kat's kidnapping and subsequent torture . . . His canines extended fully, earning a sharp intake of breath from Ryan.

"You sure you're up for this?" the other shifter asked.

Ignoring him, Jayce divested himself of his weapons, phone, jacket, and belt, then opened the side door. "I'm going in." If the map was correct he had about half a mile to cover, which would take him no time at all.

He sprinted down the pothole-covered road, reaching the warehouse in time to see a metal roll-up door closing. Whoever had driven up was now inside; the truck was empty. He listened for heartbeats, trying to distinguish how many people were in the warehouse. He counted nine, including Kat's. Eight heartbeats inside and one much closer. Nothing he couldn't handle himself.

Considering the backup he had, he wasn't remotely worried.

"I can smell and hear you," he said to the human doing a piss-poor job of trying to sneak up behind him.

Without giving the human a chance to respond, Jayce

swiveled and struck out with his fist, not bothering to contain his rage. With a crunch, the guy's jaw broke and the human flew through the air. He landed in the dirt with a thud and lay unmoving, his gun landing a few feet away from him.

One down, seven to go.

Pathetic. Jayce had expected more of an army, but maybe since this was a last-minute deal they weren't as prepared as they normally would be. Or maybe most of them had scattered after Jayce, Connor, and the Armstrong pack had thinned their ranks a month ago.

Striding up to the metal door, he banged on it. "I'm here, motherfuckers!" He figured the crass announcement would leave no doubt as to who he was.

Moments later the door opened and he found himself staring down the barrel of a revolver. To his right, Derrick also had a bead on him with what looked like a standard-issue nine-millimeter.

To his left stood a distinguished-looking man in a suit. From what Jayce could tell he didn't have a weapon, although he might have something tucked into the back of his pants or strapped to his ankle. Jayce guessed this was Mayfield. He was the only one who didn't fit in with the rest of the blue-collar-looking people.

Using his peripheral vision, he deduced that they were in what was once a spinning room for the textile factory. Rows of spinning machines and a few combing machines were still scattered around the giant space. He'd had to track down a rogue shifter a few decades ago and the guy had been hiding out under a pseudonym and working in a factory similar to this one. Plenty of places for people to hide. Too bad for them that they couldn't hide from him.

"Where's—"

Jayce cut off Derrick. "Your boy's down. Not dead, but he's got a broken jaw."

Derrick cursed but didn't say anything else, so Jayce looked at the man in the suit. "I'm guessing you're the boss. Want to tell me what the fuck you think you plan to accomplish tonight?"

Instead of responding, the suited man looked over his shoulder at a guy standing near an old spinning machine and made a quick motion with his hand.

Wordlessly the dark-haired man straightened and strode toward him.

"He's going to scan you for electronic devices and check you for weapons. We're more than aware that you can kill him, but if you do, the man holding your female will blow her brains out." His aristocratic voice grated on Jayce's nerves, but hearing him threaten Kat made him see red.

His claws extended as he held his arms out to let the human scan him. Using a wand similar to the kind used by airports and courthouses, the man scanned him from head to toe, then patted him down. It was the reason Jayce had taken off his belt before coming in here. He knew what they'd do and he wanted this over as fast as possible.

Getting Kat out of here was the only important thing. At the moment he didn't care about this entire operation. His inner wolf was howling in pain to get his mate to safety and it didn't give a shit about anything or anyone else. A dangerous position for him to be in, especially considering the type of wolf he was.

Taking a deep, calming breath, he forced his beast down. If he let it out, he would slaughter everyone in this place, and everything he, Kat, and the Armstrong pack had been working toward would be completely fucked. "Satisfied that I'm not wired?"

The suited man nodded. "Yes. Now, you're probably wondering why we called you here."

Jayce obviously knew, but he didn't respond. He just kept his focus on the man in front of him and waited.

The man made another motion with his hand but didn't take his eyes off Jayce. "Bring her out."

A few seconds later the man who'd scanned him with the wand came out from behind a cluster of spinning machines with Kat in tow. He had a gun pressed to her temple.

Jayce growled low in his throat and it wasn't part of the act. Seeing his mate, the woman he wanted to spend the rest of his life with, like this pushed every facet of control he possessed. He gave her a long look, trying to inject all his love into it, trying to tell her nothing would happen to her as long as he was here. Her gaze was unreadable as she stared back at him. It was like a knife pressing into his gut.

Tearing his eyes away from her, he stared at the suited man. "Tell me what you want," he demanded, his voice sounding more animal than human.

"You're going to do exactly what I say when I say until you're no longer useful." Jayce noticed there was no "we" in his statement, just "I."

Yeah, something about his tone was personal. Not toward Jayce specifically—he was almost sure of that—but this was personal against shifters or paranormal beings in general. The men here hated paranormal beings, that much was obvious, but this guy . . . If Jayce had to guess, he hated them because they were physically more powerful and they lived longer. The man just looked like the type. Probably hated that his money couldn't buy him immortality. Jayce knew it was a big assumption, but he'd dealt with rich assholes like this over the years. The type who would sell their souls to be like paranormals. "You think you can blackmail me into working for you?"

"I know I can." There was a bitter bite to the words.

"So what do you want?" Jayce intentionally kept his gaze away from Kat, not trusting himself to look at her when she was being restrained and had a weapon to her head.

"For starters, I want to see what you can do." He snapped his fingers and the man with the revolver jumped into action. Like a trained dog.

Jayce kept his hands loose at his sides. He might look relaxed to these people, but the second he got what he wanted, he was getting Kat to safety. Deep down he understood her need to do this tonight, but he couldn't take it anymore. His beast was clawing at him, furious for his captivity. For a moment his vision hazed over and he had to blink, forcing his beast down again. *Shit.* That had been too close.

The man with the revolver returned with two humans wearing leather APL jackets similar to the ones he'd seen on the bikers from that bar he'd been to with Kat. Obviously these guys weren't hopped up on vamp blood. If they were, the humans here wouldn't have been able to keep them captive.

Jayce glanced back at the suit. "You haven't told me your name." He needed to talk. It helped keep his fury, which was on a very thin leash, at bay.

The man's dark eyes narrowed. "Anthony—"

"So you're basically in charge of everyone in Fontana, huh? You know a man named Adler?" he asked, his tone full of disrespect.

Anthony's eyes turned even darker. "He used to be under my purview, yes." There was a bite to his words.

"So basically you said jump and he asked how high," Jayce spat.

"You're not here to talk about one of my dead subordinates. Now you will kill these two in your human form. I want to see what you're capable of."

"Correct me if I'm wrong, but aren't those guys wearing APL jackets? I thought you guys all banded together."

"Who they are is none of your concern. Kill them or your female dies. Now." The flash of his temper rose through the thin veneer of a man who pretended to be civilized but was nothing more than a monster in Armani.

Jayce looked at Kat and saw not fear in her pale eyes but raw determination. Derrick still had a gun trained on him, but Jayce knew he could take him out with no problem. He could move a hell of a lot faster than the cop could shoot.

That still left Kat unprotected. She'd told him she could handle herself, that she wanted to take these guys down her way, to prove to herself she wasn't a victim anymore. He desperately wanted to give her back that sense of freedom. His wolf said otherwise.

Jayce didn't know if the gun being held to Kat's head had silver-injected bullets, but it was highly likely. A shot to the head wouldn't kill her immediately, but if too much silver got into her bloodstream, it would. As Kat was newly turned, her defenses were still building up.

They'd already gotten everything they needed on tape. Now it was a matter of getting out of this place alive. Giving her an almost imperceptible nod, he lunged. Using all his strength, he let his beast take over as he launched himself through the air. His clothes shredded as his body underwent the change in milliseconds. Unlike others of his kind, thanks to his age and unique breed, his change was always like lightning. Too quick for the human eye.

Everything else around him funneled out. Kat's head slammed back against her captor. She twisted, elbow raised, prepared to strike him again, but Jayce was so much faster. His paws slammed into the guy's chest. The man shouted in pain as Jayce pinned him to the ground. The gun clattered to the floor as Jayce swiped out with his forepaw, slicing the guy across the face with such force that he knocked him out.

It felt like an eternity, but Jayce knew mere seconds had passed. Spinning around, he turned to find Derrick taking aim at them. The two restrained humans dove for cover as the man holding the revolver turned toward him and Kat. Everything moved in slow motion. Kat had snapped off her handcuffs with ease and by the stance of her body he could tell she was ready to go for Mayfield's throat. He could read every tense line in that lean body of hers. She was primed for a fight, regardless of the threat.

He refused to let her go after Mayfield. She would kill him for sure and it would ruin her life. Still in animal form, he threw himself at her, taking her to the floor, using his body as a cushion. Keeping his claws retracted, he encircled her and restrained her.

Bullets flew around them, loud pings ricocheting everywhere. Gunpowder and metallic scents filled the air. He felt the sharp sting of silver entering his body, but he ignored it, keeping Kat down even as she struggled against him, screaming for him to let her go.

Not a chance in hell. The burn of the bullet was nothing compared with the roaring need to protect her. He'd failed her once and he would die before letting that happen again.

Another bullet sliced into his body, and all hell broke loose. Connor, Liam, Ryan, and a bunch of men in uniform stormed through the metal door and the windows. They all carried weapons. Shouts flew from everywhere, but Jayce blocked it all out.

His wolf was in control now. As long as Kat was safe and no one tried to touch her, his beast wouldn't have a problem. God help anyone who came too close to them.

Chapter 19

As men in uniform stormed the place, Kat ceased her struggling underneath Jayce. Blood dripped over her dirty jacket, covering her. *His blood.*

Reaching out, she wrapped her arms around Jayce's neck, pressing her face into his soft fur. The cavalry had arrived, but she'd gone crazy for a moment, consumed with the need to strike out at Anthony Mayfield—the man who likely had ordered Adler to kidnap her, resulting in her subsequent torture and abuse from a total psycho—and kill him. When Mayfield had arrived he'd all but admitted it to her. He'd been talking about how Adler had failed as a subordinate, how the dead man couldn't follow simple orders, but now that he'd taken charge things would be different in Fontana. Then he'd admitted it again to Jayce.

But Jayce had seen what she'd been planning. He'd probably read her body language before she'd even been aware of her actions.

There were so many uniformed men and women running around, slamming the APL members to the ground.

No matter what her packmates or Jayce thought, she was thankful that they had involved law enforcement.

A man in uniform strode toward Kat and Jayce, stretching out a hand as if to help her up, but Jayce snarled and nearly bit his hand off.

Jerking back, the man's eyes widened and he immediately went for his gun.

"No!" Kat tightened her grip around Jayce. "Just step back. He won't hurt you as long as you stay away from me."

Jayce's change to his animal form had been stunningly beautiful. He was a silvery gray, the color of his eyes. All sleek, powerful animal. All hers.

It suddenly registered that everyone was staring at them. Moving underneath Jayce, she changed positions so that she was half-sitting up. Surveying the space, she saw all the APL members in handcuffs. One looked as if he'd been shot. The rest of the Feds and a few local cops were looking at Kat and Jayce, their hands resting uneasily on their weapons.

Kat soon realized why. Jayce hadn't moved off her, but his head was turned toward the others, his lips pulled back, his teeth bared in a blatant show of aggression. He was a huge wolf, probably standing five feet tall on all fours. Maybe taller. He had her caged in and was practically daring anyone to make a move. If she didn't love him and trust him so much, she'd have been scared to see this giant, menacing animal too. But she knew he wasn't dangerous to anyone who kept his distance or didn't pose a threat to her.

He'd told her once that the reason he didn't shift as often as others of his kind was because he wasn't completely in control when he was a wolf. Unlike most shifters. He was aware of his surroundings, but his beast dominated his logical human self. She knew without a doubt that if anyone approached her, Jayce would attack.

Right now she understood on her most primal level that he was protecting her. It didn't matter that these people were here to help them. To him, they were threats. She was his mate and he would kill for her, would die for her.

The knowledge brought hot tears to her eyes. Tightening her grip, she turned his face until he looked at her, surprised that he'd even let her pull his gaze away from the others he viewed as a possible danger. Beautiful gray eyes stared back at her. But the animal was definitely in control now. She could see it clearly.

She stroked a hand over his head tentatively. Not only did he allow the caress, but he immediately lowered his head and pushed into her palm, letting out a soft growl.

"It's okay, Jayce. I'm okay, I'm alive, and these people are here to help us. There is no more threat." She tried to inject all the love she felt for him into her words.

There was a slight movement behind him, someone's feet shifting against the dirty floor. Jayce whipped around, a territorial growl filling the room, which had gone very quiet. Except for the harsh breathing of a few individuals and the rapid sounds of heartbeats, no one, not even the APL members, made a sound.

It was as if everyone knew that a terrifying violence lurked inside the wolf she held in her arms. One wrong move and blood would spill.

"I love you, Jayce," she whispered, continuing to stroke him, needing him to believe it, to protect him from himself. "Please come back to me. I need you right now."

There was a flash of awareness, understanding, in his

gray eyes. After a brief beat of silence, Jayce let out a long, eerie growl and then shifted back to his human form. Gray eyes that still held a bit more animal than human stared at her as he crouched over her in all his naked glory.

His muscles were bunched beneath his smooth skin, a predator ready to attack at the slightest provocation. "I'll kill him for you. I'll kill them all, right here and now," he said quietly. Before she could speak, he continued. "I don't give a damn about the consequences. If you need Mayfield dead for closure or vengeance, I'll give it to you."

It wasn't just his inner wolf talking. He meant it. No matter that it would cost him his freedom, maybe his life. He would do this for her if she asked. The truth was crystal clear in his eyes.

Tears tracked down her cheeks as she shook her head and wrapped her arms around his neck. She wasn't surprised that he would do that for her, only touched. "I just need you. Here, now, forever. Thank you for coming back to me," she whispered, her heart close to bursting.

Jayce growled low in his throat, and she could tell he wanted to kiss her. But something told her that if he did, he wouldn't stop, regardless of their audience. Despite the blood streaking down his torso, he jumped to his feet, scooped her up, and strode to the exit, totally uncaring about his nakedness. She didn't even try to protest. It felt too good to be held in his arms, claimed publicly by this amazing warrior.

"You need a medic." Parker took a step forward, but Connor grabbed his arm and forcibly pulled him back.

"Fuck off, Parker," Jayce growled and gave Connor a questioning look but didn't pause in his stride.

Kat had no idea what the look was for, but her Alpha

seemed to understand. "Keys are in the SUV. I'll be by in the morning."

A man in a blue jacket stepped forward, flashing his badge as if they didn't know whom he worked for. "You can't leave. You have to make a statement, to fill out a report—"

"They'll do it in the morning," Parker snapped. "If it wasn't for them you wouldn't be getting all the credit for this takedown. Leave them alone. You'll have plenty of paperwork to keep you busy tonight anyway."

Kat wasn't sure if it was because of what Parker said or because Jayce snarled at the man, flashing his sharp canines, but the guy immediately backed off, mumbling something about a breach in protocol under his breath.

Outside they were greeted by police cars and SUVs with tinted windows and flashing lights. A lone SUV with no lights sat near the edge of the dirt road leading away from the place.

She figured that one belonged to Connor and she was proved right when Jayce went straight to the passenger side and placed her gently on the seat. Staring down at her, he took a deep breath. "I want to kiss you right now, but I know I won't stop. Soon, though . . . Soon." A soft growl preceded his words, and a delicious thrill coursed through her body.

As soon as he slid into the driver's seat, she reached for his arm, gently holding it. "You're injured. Parker was right about that. You need medical attention and—"

He snorted. "I've already pushed the bullets out of my body."

She drew back. "You can do that?"

He let out another snort, not responding as he started driving. She was concerned for him, for the amount of blood covering his naked, sleek, muscular body, but he didn't seem fazed at all.

Still, all her protective instincts surfaced even as she tried to ignore what the sight of his naked body and sinewy muscles was doing to her. "Please don't shut me out," she whispered.

He shot her a surprised look, those gray eyes darkening. "I'm not. Just want to get you home. To myself."

When he spoke in partial sentences, barely able to get words out, she knew they were going to have a long night. But first, she wanted to talk about what she'd said, to thank him for what he'd offered her. "Jayce, what you did back there . . ."

"Don't want to talk about it," he growled.

"Well, I do," she snapped. "You were willing to give up your life for me. If you'd killed Mayfield with all those Feds around, they'd have either killed you—"

He laughed, the sound sharp and amused.

"Or they'd have locked you up."

"They could have tried."

"Stop being so freaking male about this," she demanded. "What you did . . ." Her voice broke, earning a swift curse from Jayce.

He reached out, stroked the back of his knuckles down her cheek. "Don't cry, honey. We're almost home." His voice was a soothing balm for her frayed emotions.

But it wasn't their home. It was December's. And she didn't know how long he'd be there. He'd said he loved her, but she needed to know exactly what he meant by that. Because she wanted everything from him.

"I want you to live here with me, in Fontana, preferably on the ranch, with the Armstrong pack. I was hoping Connor would let us build a house. Something that's ours. I know you don't have a real home, but I hope you'll consider moving here. If not, I'll go wherever you want. I just want to build a life with you. I want . . ." She wanted everything, but she couldn't figure out all the words she needed to say. "I just want you."

His fingers tightened around the steering wheel, the white knuckles painfully visible. For a moment it seemed as if he'd rip it right off. "You meant what you said? About loving me?" Quiet words.

Batting away runaway tears, she nodded.

"You didn't say it just so I'd return to my human form?" There was such a vulnerable note in his voice, it pulled at her heart.

"Of course not. I love you, Jayce. I have for a long time." It was one of the reasons she'd run from him when she found out he'd lied to her.

He pushed out a harsh breath and then seemed to gather himself before speaking again. "I have so many enemies, Kat. You might not ever be truly safe," he said.

"No one's truly safe, but I have a strong pack to surround me and an even stronger mate. We can't live in fear because of what might happen." That was no way to live, not when she had the man she loved right in front of her, willing to spend the rest of his life with her.

"Will you bond with me, Kat?" The abrupt question had her digging her fingers into her palms.

This was the one thing she'd always wanted from him. She swallowed past the lump of emotion in her throat and whispered, "Yes."

His shoulders relaxed, and it stunned her to realize how afraid he'd been that she would reject him. "I won't be an easy man to live with," he continued, his voice rough with emotion as he kept his gaze on the road.

"I don't want easy." And she didn't. She just wanted Jayce.

He swallowed once. "I might be called away a lot on Council business."

"So? Who says I can't go with you sometimes? And who says I can't work with you?"

His eyes widened. "Ah . . ."

He could make all the choking sounds he wanted. She liked the idea of working with him. "We make a great team." After her attack and her subsequent change into a shifter, she'd quit her job at the ski lodge, and even though she had a degree in education, she had no idea if she would ever want to return to teaching in the classroom. Luckily they didn't have to make a decision right then.

"Well—"

"Well, nothing. You asked, I said yes, and I'm not changing my mind. You're stuck with me." *Forever.* Bonding or not, she could never walk away from Jayce. Never again.

"I'll hold you to that," he said with a slight grin.

Jayce put the vehicle into park as he jerked to a stop in front of December's house, the entire SUV shuddering under the abrupt move. Then he was around the vehicle—still naked!—before she'd blinked, pulled her out of the SUV, and was striding toward the house with such determined steps that her entire body hummed with anticipation.

"I need you, Kat." The words were a guttural growl.

"I need you too." More than she needed revenge. More than anything. Life without Jayce was *unimaginable.*

Before they'd reached the stairs he'd stripped her of her clothes, and by the time they'd made it to the shower, he was already inside her, thrusting, taking, absolutely possessing her.

His claiming was primal and toe-curling, and after her third orgasm she thought they were done for the night. But Jayce was a machine, keeping her awake and pleasuring her until the first hint of daylight trickled through the blinds. He told her he loved her so many times, but she knew she would never tire of hearing those words on his lips.

Kat didn't remember falling asleep. The only thing she was aware of was Jayce's strong arms cradling her against his chest and the feeling of absolute rightness in the world.

Chapter 20

Four days later

Kat tossed her keys onto the kitchen table, shrugged out of her jacket and threw it over one of the chairs. Rolling her shoulders, she went straight for the refrigerator and pulled out an unopened bottle of white wine.

Just what the doctor ordered.

The past four days had been a blur of paperwork and interviews with the FBI, the local cops, and even reporters. She hadn't wanted to talk to the media at all, but since she'd been the kidnap victim of what the media were now calling a crazed hate group, Connor, the North American Council, and even the local police had thought it was a good idea for her to tell her side of the story. They needed public opinion on their side. Of course Jayce hadn't cared what she did as long as she was happy and safe.

Which was one of the many reasons she loved him.

Kidnapping, attempted murder, and a whole mess of other things were being tacked on to the list of crimes of

the men who'd participated in her abduction. The Feds
were still pissed that Fletcher Monroe and his mate had
disappeared. Connor, her pack, and the locals were
pretty angry too, since Fletcher was wanted for four
murders in Fontana. It didn't matter that he'd been
forced into doing it; he'd still committed murder. At least
the locals weren't angry at her pack anymore. There had
been a definite change in the energy toward them.

Kat had no idea where Fletcher was, and she was
thankful for that. She didn't want to know because she
didn't want to knowingly lie to the police. They'd asked
her more than once about his whereabouts, but they
were treading carefully since she'd played a huge part in
their sting operation. Not to mention that she was now
officially known as the enforcer's mate. They might not
admit it, but she'd seen fear and respect in the eyes of
most of the law enforcement guys when they encoun-
tered Jayce.

As she unscrewed the cork, she heard the door open
and immediately scented Jayce. She'd spent most of the
day at the ranch, staying out of the limelight and getting
to know her packmates, including Leila. Kat had come
to adore the teenager and was glad the girl would be
staying on at the ranch. Jayce was still annoyed that Leila
had hacked into the enforcers' forum, but Kat could tell
he was also impressed.

"You better be naked by the time you get in here,"
she called out while pulling down a wineglass from one
of the cabinets. She knew he'd grab a beer.

"That might get a little uncomfortable for everyone,"
a deep, very familiar voice said.

Nearly dropping the glass, she set it down on the
counter, then swirled to find her father standing in the
doorway with Jayce. Without thinking, she launched her-

self at her dad, wrapping her arms around him in a tight hug. They might have had their issues in the past—his criminal enterprises being the biggest one—but he was still her dad. After everything that had happened in the past couple of months, it suddenly hit her how much she'd missed him.

Her incredibly tall and muscular father stumbled back under her assault and she cringed; she'd forgotten that she had to watch her strength now. "What are you doing here?" She sniffled, pulling back and trying to ignore the embarrassment she felt for what she'd just said to Jayce in her father's presence.

"I have to find out my daughter was the kidnap victim of some crazies from the news?" Pale blue eyes so similar to her own stared down at her, more than a touch of hurt in them.

That surprised her, but maybe it shouldn't have. Her father never let his emotions show. But she should have called him.

"Why don't you guys head to the living room? I'll bring our drinks in," Jayce said, already moving to the refrigerator, stopping only to drop a kiss on her forehead.

Moments later Jayce walked in carrying a glass of wine for her and two beers. He smoothly slid onto the couch next to her and pulled her over so that she was sitting on his lap. This was his not-so-subtle way of telling her father what was going on with them. Though she figured he already knew, since she and Jayce were living under the same roof.

Her father lifted a dark eyebrow. "I see you two are back together and evidently serious?"

She nodded. "We're . . . mates."

"Soon to be bondmates," Jayce said, a touch of heat in his voice as his grip on her waist tightened.

Her father smiled. "Good. I want you with someone who can take care of you. And you *will* take care of her." Her father looked at Jayce, a razor-sharp edge to his voice that promised certain death if Jayce ever hurt her. He'd never been good with subtle.

While she loved her father, his overprotectiveness was infuriating even on a good day. "Dad—"

Jayce squeezed her thigh, but kept his gaze steady on her father. "It's fine, Kat. I'll take care of your daughter for as long as I'm alive." No flowery promises or explanations of how he would do that. Just a statement that he would. Anything else wouldn't sound real coming from Jayce.

"Good." Her father surprised her by standing. "I just wanted to stop by on my way to the Armstrong ranch, but I'll let you two have your evening."

Kat turned to look at Jayce in confusion. "He didn't come with you?"

Jayce shook his head while her father answered. "We arrived at the same time. After I saw the news I contacted Connor Armstrong, and he's offered me a place to stay. I'll be in town for a few days, so we'll have plenty of time to catch up."

She started to protest, to tell him to stay for dinner, but Jayce squeezed her leg again and moved so that they both stood. He held out a hand to her father. "We'll be by the ranch early tomorrow morning."

After hugging her father again and saying good-bye, Kat shut the door and swiveled to face Jayce, hands on her hips. "Why didn't you invite him for dinner?"

A slow, sensuous smile curved Jayce's lips, sending heat curling through her body. She recognized that look very well. "Because the only thing I'm eating in the next few minutes is you."

It didn't matter that he'd seen her naked too many times to count and kissed every inch of her body. His words made her cheeks heat up. "He probably thinks we were being rude."

Jayce's grin remained in place as he stalked closer. "I had a talk with him in the driveway before we came inside. Stop worrying."

She wasn't worried about her father; she was worried about what was supposed to happen that night. The sun had already set and it was a full moon. "Oh, well, I'm going to get my wine, then." Trying to brush past him, she found herself caged by his strong embrace, his arms wrapping tight around her waist.

"Are you really thirsty?" he murmured, nipping her ear.

She shook her head and let out a sigh. Might as well be honest. "Just nervous."

Her words made him momentarily freeze. Then he pulled his head back. "About tonight?"

The slight catch in his voice made her fingers clench on his shoulders. "Well . . . yeah. Aren't you?" Bonding was stronger than marriage. Stronger even because they couldn't separate. Not that she wanted to, but still, bonding was forever. Considering their life spans, that was a pretty long time.

"No." He didn't even hesitate.

Which soothed her immediately. "I just don't want you to have any doubts. We can wait until the next full moon. There's no rush."

"I've been waiting forever for you, Kat. I'll wait as long as you want, but I'm ready here and now. When you left me, it ripped my heart out. Like someone literally carved into my chest." He paused, his eyes darkening to storm clouds. "I don't need time. I just need you."

Jayce wasn't big with words, so hearing that confession made her heart beat about a thousand times faster. "I don't need time either." The moment the words were out of her mouth, she knew they were true.

All doubts she'd had disappeared the second he'd told her he lied to her because he was afraid of her becoming a target. And if she'd held on to any tiny remnants, they would have disappeared at that moment in the old textile plant when he'd offered to give up everything for her.

He grabbed her and lifted her so that she had to wrap her legs around his waist. Before she could blink they were at the top of the stairs and Jayce was heading for her room.

Her mate moved so fast that she was flat on her back in a blur of motion that had her gasping for breath. Inhaling the deep, rich scent of his lust, she grinned, knowing what he had in mind as he knelt between her legs.

Keeping his gaze on her, those gray eyes hot enough to burn, he slowly slid her boots off. Her body felt on fire as he carefully, way too slowly, removed each piece of her clothing until finally she was naked and splayed out in front of him.

It was hard not to squirm under that intense gaze, especially when he was still clothed. "Not fair that you still have clothes on," she murmured, propping herself up on her elbows as he stared down at her.

Lifting one of her legs, he pressed his lips to her inner ankle, nipping her skin gently. "If I'm naked, I'm inside you," he murmured against her. But at least he took his shirt off, giving her a perfect view of all those hard muscles.

His simple explanation made her smile. That sounded about right. Falling back against the pillow, she shivered when he raked his teeth against her inner thigh. Quickly he followed up with a teasing swipe of his tongue along her folds.

Fisting the covers beneath her, she arched her back at that first tantalizing feel of his mouth on her most sensitive area. Parting her folds, Jayce dragged his tongue along her heat and she nearly vaulted off the bed. Her hips jerked at that slow, teasing stroke.

"Fuck, you taste good," he growled against her.

Those blunt words lit her on fire. She loved everything about him, especially the rawness of his need for her. No romantic words, just a purity that was all Jayce.

His fingers tightened around her thighs, anchoring her, reminding her that tonight was all about his domination and her surrender. Something that might have scared her at one time. But not now.

Jayce would never hurt her. He would only protect and pleasure her. Not caring that she was abandoning all control, she cupped her breasts, tweaking her nipples while he continued pleasuring her.

"Are you trying to kill me?" he rasped out in between decadent kisses.

"I could ask you the same thing." She arched her back as he inserted one of his fingers and began slowly stroking her.

"No touching yourself," he ordered before circling her clit with his tongue.

Even though it was instinctive to ask him why not, she understood him. He wanted to be the one giving her all the pleasure tonight. Lifting her arms, she grasped the headboard and held on. Considering that she'd had fun teasing him more than once in the past, turnabout was fair play.

They'd made love so many times and in so many positions during the past four days that she should've been tired, sated, but she couldn't get enough. The feel of his finger dragging against her inner walls made her clench with a scorching need that threatened to singe all her nerves.

Heat burned low in her belly, and each time he drew his finger out, he flicked his tongue over her pulsing bud with just the right amount of pressure, guaranteed to drive her insane. If only he would go just a little faster.

"Faster," she demanded, unable to restrain herself.

He chuckled, the feel of his laughter skittering over her clit and making her moan. She thought he might tease her, but instead he pushed another finger into her and began working her body in a rhythm that had her arching off the bed.

Unable to stay still against his delicious torture, Kat threw both legs over his shoulders and dug her heels into his back.

He growled something unintelligible against her wet core as he increased his pressure on her clit. Pleasure shot to all her nerve endings as his tongue worked its magic.

The headboard shook under her trembling. When Jayce so very lightly nipped her clit with his teeth, she lost it. Her orgasm was abrupt, slamming into her with unexpected force as waves of pleasure ripped through her.

She curled her toes against his back as the aftereffects of the climax swept her entire body. Kat wasn't sure if it was a mate thing or a Jayce thing, but the man barely had to stimulate her and she came.

As the orgasm slowly ebbed, she relaxed against the covers, letting her body go completely limp. Keeping her eyes closed, she grinned as she felt Jayce begin to climb her, dropping kisses as he moved. When he sucked one of her nipples into his mouth, she automatically arched into him, giving him better access.

What the man could do with his tongue should be illegal.

When he nipped her ear, her eyes flew open. Propped up on his forearms, he stared down at her, his gray eyes full of desire and love. For the first time since he'd admitted his feelings for her, she could actually see the love in his eyes.

He was finally letting all his guards down with her tonight. That knowledge touched her on a level that reached deep into her soul. She cupped his cheek, brushing her thumb over his scar. "I'm ready," she said, knowing he needed to hear the words.

Before she'd even closed her mouth, his lips covered hers, stroking, teasing, claiming. Raking her fingers down his back, she enjoyed the feel of all that power humming underneath her fingertips.

There was an intangible edginess surrounding him tonight and she understood why. His primal side needed this claiming as much as hers did.

When his hands grasped her hips in a tight hold, she allowed him to guide her until she was on her belly. Pushing up onto her knees, she looked over her shoulder at him, anticipation and hunger washing through her in equal waves.

Her inner walls clenched, her body still not satisfied, despite her recent orgasm. Every inch of her was pulled taut with longing. Only Jayce could fulfill what she needed.

"I don't know if I can be gentle." Jayce's voice was strained, as if saying that much had been a struggle. His gray eyes had darkened to almost midnight black.

"Don't hold back." That wasn't what she wanted. Not tonight. Tonight was about the two of them bonding, about giving up parts of themselves to join with the other.

He'd explained everything about the bonding process, so she knew that after tonight she'd be linked to him in a way she never would be with anyone else.

As she watched, he slid his palm down her spine, stroking her in a completely proprietary manner. His hand slid to her hip, where he clutched her in an almost bruising hold. Not too hard but firmly enough that he was silently staking his claim.

She was his.

And vice versa.

When he thrust his cock into her, she pushed out a long breath, letting her head fall forward at the intrusion. She felt as if she was completely surrendering to him.

It seemed that no matter how often they were together, she always needed a moment to adjust to him. Her sheath stretched and molded around his cock with a familiarity that made her entire body ache. When his hips rolled back, pulling out of her, she immediately felt the loss. Just as quickly he pushed back inside her.

Over and over, he moved inside her, filling her and pushing her over the edge. Even though she couldn't see him, she could feel and scent the lust and love rolling off him. Dark yet sweet, the aroma surrounded her with its intensity.

As Jayce continued thrusting, one of his hands slowly loosened from her hip, as if he didn't want to let go, until he cupped her mound and stroked her clit in that perfect rhythm he'd mastered.

Another orgasm swept through her. Her inner walls clenched, milking his cock as her fingers dug into the covers. Jayce palmed her stomach, bringing her suddenly back up against his chest.

A hard hand fisted in her hair, pulling her head back.

His mouth crushed hers, his tongue tangling with hers for one intense moment before he tore away. Then she felt the sharp sting of his canines sinking into her neck, right where he'd lightly bitten her before in the shower. It prolonged her climax. She trembled as the sting turned into pure liquid pleasure. Jayce's own cries mingled with hers as he released himself inside her.

His orgasm seemed to go on forever as he groaned her name until finally he stilled behind her, nuzzling and kissing her neck where he'd punctured her skin, soothing the small ache. His arm settled around her waist as he held her close, still buried deep inside her. She could feel his heart pounding out of control, the slight tremble that snaked through his body, and his erratic breath on her skin.

"Did I hurt you?" he whispered against her ear.

Shaking her head, she pulled forward, hating to break their contact and the feel of his cock inside her, but she needed to hold him. She twisted around until she faced him. "You could never hurt me," she said, wrapping her arms around his neck.

He teased her lips open with his tongue, kissing her in leisurely strokes that made her tingle. Wrapping her body around his, she sighed in pleasure as her breasts pressed against his chest.

You are so beautiful. Jayce's words sounded in her head as clearly as if he'd said them out loud.

Kat jerked back and her eyes widened. "Did that just happen?"

He grinned, the look on his face almost mischievous. "Did what just happen?" he asked innocently.

She frowned, trying to read his expression. "Did you just project a thought to me?"

You tell me. There was no denying that the deep, utterly masculine voice was Jayce's.

"You did!" *Can I do it too?* She tried it, wondering if there was an art to projecting thoughts.

Guess so. His grin widened and she realized she'd never seen him so relaxed before. Reaching up, Jayce brushed her hair back from her left shoulder. He leaned down and raked his teeth over her skin where he'd bitten her before, growling proprietarily. Her toes curled. Yeah, she could totally get used to this. What they'd had together almost a year ago had been intense, but there had always been a wall between them. Neither had been willing to let it come completely down.

Not so now. After what they'd just shared and how linked they were, there would never be any walls erected again.

Letting her head fall back, she groaned low in her throat as he began to feather kisses along her collarbone. She wrapped her legs around him, plastering herself to him like a second skin. His erection was nestled against her lower abdomen, still pulsing despite his recent orgasm. She shivered, knowing the night wasn't close to being over.

That was when she remembered that he too was supposed to receive a mark after they bonded, something to let the world know he was taken now.

Hers.

Her inner wolf smiled at the thought. Curling her fingers against his shoulders, she lifted herself up, trying to get a better look at the back of his shoulders. On his left side, a tiny red rose bloomed. She ran her fingers over it, feeling the slightly raised mark. It was similar to a tattoo. He'd told her that their bonding would create a symbol on him but seeing it was amazing. The symbol surprised her, though.

"What is it?" he asked quietly.

She bit her bottom lip, hoping he liked it. It wasn't very masculine. "Well, it's a red rose."

"Figures." He laughed under his breath, his grip around her tightening.

"Why do you say that?" Kat continued tracing it, loving that it was there permanently.

"It's what you smell like. All the time we were apart, every time I got a whiff of a rose, I got rock hard. Damn embarrassing," he murmured.

She leaned back to look at him. "You mean that's my natural scent?"

"Mm-hm, and it's also the symbol of love."

She smiled, thinking it was sweet that he knew that, but . . . "You really like it? I assumed you'd want something more . . . kick-ass."

"Sweetheart, I honestly don't care what it is, as long as you're mine." Before she could say another word he kissed her again, this time slow and sensual, as if they had all the time in the world.

And they did.

Chapter 21

Jayce slipped his hand into Kat's as they walked across the main yard toward Ana and Connor's home. This morning Jayce had a feeling it would be empty except for the Alpha and his mate. Normally pack members milled in and out of the main home, but Connor had called Jayce earlier telling them they needed to sit down and talk.

They'd just come from visiting with Kat's father, who was still worried about her safety even though the APL members had all been arrested. He was a guest at the ranch, so they didn't have far to walk.

Even when they'd been dating Jayce had never held her hand. Not so casually, as if they were a normal couple. He'd always held a part of himself back. Well, no more.

Kat owned him, body and soul. Hell, he had her mark on his shoulder and carried her scent. Everyone would know they were bondmates now. While the thought of not always being able to protect her terrified him on a primal level, life without her was a hell of a lot worse.

Kat gently squeezed his hand. "You seem edgy."

I'm not, he projected, flexing his telepathic muscles.

"That is so gonna take some getting used to," she said as they reached the front door of her Alpha's house.

Before they could knock, the door flew open and Vivian jerked to a halt in front of them. "Are you guys in trouble?" she whispered conspiratorially.

"No, why?" Jayce asked just as quietly.

"Because I've been kicked out of the house for a while. Ana told me to go find Lucas and play," she grumbled.

"Which is what you should be doing. I've already called Ryan and told him you're on the way. You've got ten seconds to get over to their cabin," Ana's voice called out.

Vivian's eyes widened and she sprinted past them, diving off the porch, her dark hair flying behind her.

Jayce glanced at Kat to find her fighting a smile. Shaking his head, he entered the house, Kat still holding tight to his hand.

They found Ana and Connor in the living room, sitting side by side on a long couch. Connor held Ana's hand, idly stroking her palm with his thumb.

Jayce nodded at the couple as they entered the room and sat down. He didn't care if this was a formal meeting; he pulled Kat into his lap and kept a protective arm around her anyway.

What are you doing? she asked.

You're mine. It was the only answer she was getting because it was the only one that mattered.

"So, you two are bonded?" Connor asked quietly.

Jayce nodded and Kat said, "Last night."

Ana smiled warmly. "Congrats."

Connor murmured his congratulations as well, then

continued. "We need to discuss your role here for as long as you live at the ranch." His words were directed at Jayce.

Kat stiffened in his arms. *As long as you live here?*

Jayce squeezed her hip, keeping his focus on the Alpha. Kat might not understand what Connor was saying, but he had a pretty good idea. "You're Kat's Alpha and while we're here—which will likely be a semi-permanent situation—I'll respect your land and your rules, but you're not my Alpha." He didn't have one and never would. His father had been his only Alpha, and since he'd died, Jayce had known that another would never rule him. He just wasn't wired that way. Either Connor accepted that or he didn't.

"You've made a lot of enemies over the years," Connor said. It was more a statement than a question.

Jayce nodded. "I have. If you let me live here, it's a risk you'll be taking on."

Connor looked at his mate, then at Kat and Jayce. "As long as you support this pack, it's one we're willing to take. I don't know if you saw the sectioned-off parcel of land next to December and Liam's house, but that's going to be your place. I've already spoken to a local crew about expediting the house. They're going to be starting next week, and with the help of the pack, it shouldn't be more than a month until it's finished."

That was pretty fast, but something told Jayce that Connor had made a nice deal with the contractors. "Just let me know how much—"

Connor shook his head. "Kat's a member of the pack, so by extension you are as well. This is our gift to our newest members."

It was his instinct to argue. Jayce had more than enough money to take care of his mate and he wanted to. With every fiber of his being, he needed to take care of her in every way possible. But this was a gift he couldn't turn down without insulting Connor and Ana. He glanced from Ana to Connor and said, "Thank you."

Next to him, Kat joined in. "Thank you so much. Do you think . . ." She trailed off, the scent of her concern filling the room.

Jayce looked at Kat in confusion, but Ana smiled, kissed her mate, and stood up. "You want to pick out your own tile designs and appliances?"

Kat's cheeks tinged a delicious shade of pink. "Well, yeah."

Ana's smile widened. "I'd be the same way. Come on. They left a book for you to look at."

Jayce waited until Kat and Ana had left. From the murmur of their voices he knew they hadn't gone far, only to the kitchen. The knowledge soothed his wolf. He didn't really want his bondmate out of his sight. Maybe that would change later, but for now the thought of her being too far away made his beast claw angrily at him.

"It doesn't get easier, but you do learn to tame your wolf," Connor said quietly, as if he'd read Jayce's mind.

Jayce grunted, tearing his gaze from the empty doorway and focusing on Connor again. "I can pay for the construction."

"I know you can, but you're not going to." His words held a slight bite.

"Fair enough," Jayce replied, settling back in his seat. "That's not all you want to talk about, is it?"

Connor shook his head. "I need to know what your plans for Erin and Leila are, and I want to talk about the issue of humans trafficking vamp blood."

Jayce had known this was coming. The first two issues were easy. "I plan to continue training Erin and I want to start soon with Leila. However, I have a job I think Erin can handle without my help. It's in New Orleans. She'd need to leave in a few days."

Connor's eyebrows rose. "That's where Noah's old pack lives."

"Yep."

The Alpha gave him a calculating look. "You want him to go with her, don't you?"

"Yep."

Connor was silent for a long moment. "They'll probably come back as bondmates."

Jayce hoped so, but he didn't say that out loud. He wasn't sending Noah with her because he was a fucking matchmaker. Noah seemed to calm Erin in the same way that Kat calmed Jayce. Everyone of their breed needed an anchor, and though Erin wouldn't admit it, Noah anchored her. If he didn't, she wouldn't hang out with him so much. "Are you willing to give up two of your warriors?"

Connor immediately shook his head. "I can't. Not without temporary replacements."

"Done." Jayce had already put out a few feelers. In addition to enemies, he'd made a hell of a lot of contacts over the years and a lot of people owed him favors. He wasn't sure if he would really call any of those contacts friends, but he trusted the men he was thinking of enough that he didn't mind them being around his mate. That said something about their sense of honor.

"How many men?"

"Four males, two of them mated, so six total. Only two of the males are alpha in nature, but no born Alphas. If you're willing, it wouldn't be a temporary arrangement."

Connor was silent for a long moment. "You trust them?"

He answered without hesitation. "With my life.

They're all related. Lost their Alpha a couple years ago and haven't joined another pack since."

"A couple years ago . . . You mean the Gomez pack? I thought they'd all found new packs."

Jayce shook his head. What had happened to the Alpha of the Gomez pack and his second-in-command had been a tragedy. Ambushed by rogue vamps—who'd since been put down by Jayce—they'd been brutally killed, but at least they'd put up a vicious fight. "Not everyone, but now that the females are pregnant they're all looking to put down roots."

Connor's lips curved up slightly. "So technically it'll be eight new additions?"

Jayce couldn't hide his smile. "Nine. One of the females is expecting twins."

Another long silence. Finally Connor scrubbed a hand over his face. "We're already hiring a local crew to build you guys a house—might as well build a few more. It'll put more money back into the local economy. And it'll be nice having more cubs around."

Jayce knew that wasn't the reason Connor was saying yes. He was an Alpha, a protector. It was in his nature to take care of others and he was a better Alpha than most of the ones Jayce had run across.

Before Jayce could say anything, Connor continued. "I'm going to check them out first and interview each of them individually. If for any reason I think they'll be a threat or a bad fit for the pack, no deal."

"I understand." And he did. Once Connor made them part of the pack, there was no going back. He wasn't the type of Alpha to kick anyone out without a damn good reason, and he took his position very seriously. Once in, they were in as long as they wanted to remain members. Jayce had a feeling that would be for life. Sensing that the topic was settled, Jayce moved on. "You wanted to talk about the trafficking of vamp blood?"

Connor nodded and glanced toward the door. "Yeah. Liam should be here in a sec. I want him to be part of this conversation."

Jayce knew the two brothers could communicate telepathically in human and wolf form, a gift that not all related shifters possessed. Moments later, the tall shifter strolled in, a giant smile on his face and the scent of his mate all over him.

Instead of sitting, Liam headed to the fireplace and leaned against the mantel. "You got a plan for finding the fuckers trafficking that shit?" Liam asked, jumping right into the conversation.

Jayce nodded. He'd been waiting until the APL mess was settled in Fontana before moving forward with finding the source of this operation. "If you're willing I want Ryan's help running down some of the financial information from the names we got the other day." He was referring to the drug dealers that he and Connor had practically hand-delivered to the cops.

Connor nodded. "He'll help."

Liam snorted softly. "You could just ask Leila; from what I hear she's pretty skilled."

She was also only sixteen. Jayce didn't want her involved in any of the shit he planned to investigate. Connor shot Liam a sharp look and his brother just shrugged.

"The Council will pay your pack for using Ryan as a resource." Jayce had been very insistent about that when he'd informed them that he would be staying down here on a semi-permanent basis.

Connor nodded. "Fine. They can double Vivian's and Lucas's college funds."

"Fair enough. Unless something's changed in the last

hour, Ryan still hasn't cracked the encryption of that laptop I gave him, but he did have something interesting to tell me earlier today." *Very* interesting.

Connor's mouth was set in a grim line, as if he already knew, which didn't surprise Jayce. "You mean about those dealers?" the Alpha asked.

Jayce nodded. The very same guys who'd turned themselves in were all dead. "I guess you already know they were killed their second day in holding." All of them had been gutted. He was still having Ryan run their financials in addition to the names that the dead guys had given. The fact that they'd all been killed so quickly said a lot about whoever was behind this vampire blood trafficking business. And there was no way in hell Jayce believed the two things weren't connected. His former contact Ned Hartwig had vanished, as if he'd never existed, and now four other people connected to the trafficking were dead. It wasn't a coincidence.

They continued talking about his investigative plans, but Jayce was only half focused, something he had no problem admitting to himself. The majority of his attention was on the woman in the other room.

All he could think about was getting her home, stripping her naked, and losing himself in her for hours. Considering they wouldn't be able to take much of a honeymoon, especially with this vamp blood business, he wanted to take advantage of every second he could spend with her.

Kat set the third dessert plate on the kitchen table, then sat, picking up her glass of wine as she settled across from Leila. Jayce had decided to cook for them—his cooking talent was something she was still trying to come to terms with—and now it was time for dessert.

He had spent most of the day training Erin, then going over some sort of business with Ryan, which he'd promised to fill her in on later. Kat had spent the majority of her day with her dad. It still stunned her that he was in town, but he'd been really worried after seeing her on the news. That made her happy, considering that they hadn't talked in so long. Unfortunately he'd had to leave because of work—she didn't even want to think about what that might mean—but he promised to come back to visit when he could. She'd kept her distance from her father for the past year because of her issues with his illegal activities, but in the end he was her father. She might not agree with what he did, but she could deal with it. After seeing him again, it had hit her how much she'd missed him.

"You think I could have a glass of wine?" Leila asked quietly, as if Jayce couldn't hear them from where he stood by the stove a few feet away.

"Uh, *no*." Kat had begun developing more of a big-sister relationship with the young shifter, but that didn't mean she would let her do whatever she wanted. "So have you decided what you're going to do about school?"

Leila shrugged and absently pulled on one of the blue-highlighted pieces of fake hair she'd clipped in. "I was thinking I might take a few months off until I figure everything out. Maybe I'll apply and sign up for some online classes, but for now, I . . . don't want to leave the ranch."

Kat breathed a silent sigh of relief. She didn't want her to leave either. Even though she already had more college credits than most kids her age, she was still too young to be out on her own. "Good. Speaking of, Jayce and I were thinking, uh . . ." She trailed off, unsure how to continue. She didn't want to overstep her bounds. She worried that maybe Leila was perfectly happy where she was and Kat didn't want to ruin that. Or put her in the awkward position of saying no. Kat glanced at Jayce, who was pulling tiramisu out of the refrigerator. *Freaking tiramisu.*

He set the glass bowl on the table and slid into the seat next to Kat, facing Leila. "Kat and I want you to live with us. We'll be moving back to the ranch in a month, and if you want, you have a place in our home."

"Not that we want to take the place of your parents or anything; we know we won't. We'd just really love it if you wanted to stay with us." Kat forced herself to stop talking, knowing that if she didn't, she would end up just rambling.

A sweet, pure scent rolled off Leila as her eyes widened. "Really? That's awesome. I mean, I love Ana and Connor's place, but Vivian is constantly in my stuff. Not that I mind really. She's a sweet kid, but . . . I'd love to. Unless . . ." Suddenly her shoulders drooped. "What if you have kids?"

Kat shrugged, surprised by the question. She definitely hadn't thought that far ahead. "So what if we do?"

"Well, will you still want me there?"

Kat glanced at Jayce, then back at Leila. "I'm pretty new to pack life, but I can tell you one thing: When Jayce and I open up our home to you, it'll be for life. If we have kids, you'll be their big sister."

Taking her by surprise, Leila jumped up and launched herself at Kat, wrapping her arms around her neck in a tight embrace and then doing the same to Jayce.

Jayce looked more stunned than Kat, and gently patted Leila's back, as if he was afraid he might hurt the young shifter. When she pulled back she smiled almost shyly. "I guess that means I can't tell people you cook tiramisu, huh?"

Jayce's sharp bark of laughter warmed Kat from the inside out. "Not if you want more of it," he said.

For the first time in her life, Kat felt whole in a way she'd never imagined. Yes, she loved her father, but growing up with him had been hard. Add to that the fact that she was also a seer who'd been able to see paranormal beings about a decade before they came out to the world, and it was understandable why she'd always felt like a bit of a freak.

She knew their lives would never be normal as far as human society went, and that was fine with her. Normal was overrated. But their lives would be full. Looking at Jayce as he scooped tiramisu onto Leila's plate, she watched his sinewy muscles flex, and didn't bother trying to control the flush of heat that swept through her. Whatever happened from here on out, she had a pack to stand by her. And she would have the man she loved more than life itself by her side every step of the way.

Acknowledgments

I don't think I'll ever keep this section short, but I'll try! Writing a book is only the beginning stage of publishing it and there are so many wonderful people who have helped in its production. Jill Marsal, agent extraordinaire, you always have such a level head and I'm grateful for how much you do (which is a lot!). Danielle Perez, I'm still awed by your skills as an editor. Your guidance in making this series shine is so appreciated. Erin Galloway, thank you so much for all your help in the publicity department. To the rest of the team at NAL, all your behind-the-scenes work does not go unnoticed. Thanks to Katie Anderson, Christina Brower, Mary Hern, Jan McInroy, and Craig White. Thank you for all you do.

Sarah Romsa, I hope you know how much I love you. Our daily phone calls ensure that I'm not a complete hermit when working on a book. Thank you for all your support. Laura Wright, our weekly phone calls and texts have a way of keeping me sane. You are always a bright spot in my day. Kari Walker and Dara Edmondson, thank you both for all your support with the Moon Shifter series. For my parents, who wonder where the heck I got my love of all things supernatural from, and still support me. I'm so thankful for my husband and son, who put up with me when I'm hibernating in my writing cave. Without your support, my job would be a lot harder. And to my readers, thank you for all the kind, encouraging e-mails about this series. I love hearing from you and appreciate your support so incredibly much. Last, but never least, I'm so thankful to God for keeping me going through the rough patches.

Don't miss the next exciting book
in the Moon Shifter series

AVENGER'S MATE

by Katie Reus

On sale in 2014 from Signet Eclipse.

Erin Flynn shot the tall male shifter next to her a quick glance as yet another female they passed on the street gave him an assessing, purely sexual look. Since they'd arrived in New Orleans an hour ago, it had been the same reaction from practically every woman they'd come across. A few men too. Not that she blamed any of them, even if she did have a sudden urge to claw their eyes out.

Simply put, Noah Campbell was smoking-hot: Tall, broad shoulders, sharp cheekbones, inky black hair a woman could easily imagine running her fingers through, and perfect olive coloring that belied his Greek heritage on his mother's side. Didn't matter that it was an icy January day; he looked like he'd just stepped off a Mediterranean beach, all toned and tan. He definitely evoked thoughts of sex, sin, and sultry summer nights.

They passed a woman dressed in jeans that might as well have been painted on, a bright red coat belted around her tiny waist, and knee-high boots with five-inch heels. When she practically undressed Noah with her eyes, Erin frowned at her friend. "Are you being intentionally oblivious?" No way could he have missed how people were looking at him.

Noah's guarded dark eyes flicked her way once before he continued scanning the nearly deserted cobblestone streets. They'd parked outside the long and narrow shotgun-style house they were staying in with another shifter and a fae warrior, both of whom had decided to hang back while she and Noah scoped out the city. And the tension hadn't left his body since the moment they'd stepped out of that pastel blue and pink house with peeling yellow shutters.

"Not oblivious, just not interested." A curt answer so typical of him when he was annoyed or stressed. Right now she thought he might be a bit of both. He didn't look at her again, but she could practically feel the heat of his dark eyes searing her. Knew what she'd see if he looked her way again. Lust and need.

Some days she wished he'd find a woman. A sweet beta female who would be perfect for him. It would slice up her insides to know that someone else would be touching what she considered hers, waking up every morning to him . . . but at least he'd be happy. Maybe she'd finally be able to move on from this constant state of wanting him but knowing she could never have him.

God, she was so fucked up.

Instinctively she patted the front of her thick coat, needing to feel the two short blades strapped to her chest beneath it. She didn't go anywhere without them. Even slept with one under her pillow. "Did you finally call your father?" she asked.

"Nope."

Resisting the urge to growl at him, she shoved her hands in her jacket pockets.

Just great.

As the newest enforcer-in-training for the North American Council of lupine shifters, Erin was on her first mission by herself. Technically she wasn't in training anymore but she still thought of herself that way. Her mentor, Jayce, had told her that she was ready to go out on her own investigation so here she was. He'd sent Noah with her but it wasn't so Noah could check up on her or look out for her—that would have pissed her off. New Orleans was Noah's father's territory and the situation right now had the potential to be volatile.

Noah's father shared the city with vamps, feline shifters, and fae, and she was pretty sure a few demons made their homes here too. The old city just appealed to them. New Orleans was the one place in the United States paranormal beings had agreed to share. It was either that or endure a bloodbath fighting over it.

Not worth it when they were practically under a microscope by the humans they'd revealed themselves to two decades ago. Erin still thought that was a stupid decision on the Council's part but it was over and done with. Not much anyone could do about it now.

The one thing she'd asked Noah to do was make contact with his father before they'd arrived. It irked her that he hadn't, but in the past year and some odd months since she'd been friends with Noah, he hadn't said more than a handful of sentences about the powerful Alpha and she hadn't pushed. She didn't like talking about her past, so she understood his need for privacy. Still, his father was Alpha of this territory and deserved the respect of a freaking phone call.

"Damn it, Noah," she muttered, but didn't continue as

they rounded another street corner. The difference from the quiet one they'd just come from was vivid.

A variety of scents and noises accosted them. Tobacco, liquor, a mix of cheap and expensive perfumes, raw sex, and some kind of spicy food tickled her nose. Sometimes she cursed her extrasensory abilities. A few bars blasted music, but a steady, low-key stream of tunes flowed out from the Full Moon Bar as they neared it.

Even if she hadn't scented all the paranormal beings inside, the lower level of music was the first giveaway that the place catered to people like her. Paranormal beings had extrasensory everything, something humans usually seemed to forget. And something she was thankful for because it had the potential to make her job as enforcer easier.

"I talked to my mom earlier and she told me my father would be here tonight," Noah said quietly.

Erin knew Noah talked to his mother practically every week, but hadn't talked to his father in years. She might not know everything about his family dynamics, but she knew enough. And this had disaster written all over it. She pulled her cell phone out of her pocket, ready to dial the number of Angus Campbell she'd received from Jayce before she and Noah had left North Carolina.

She should have just taken care of this herself but she'd wanted to let Noah do it. Even if she was on Council business, she was still entering another Alpha's territory and he deserved a heads-up. Noah knew the protocol well. No doubt he was just showing up unannounced to piss his old man off. Not the way she wanted to start this investigation.

As she scrolled to the number as they crossed the street, her head snapped up at a crashing sound. A giant female jaguar tumbled out of the bar they were headed into, fangs and claws extended. Definitely a shifter. The animal let out a loud snarl, then rushed back in through a splintered blue door.

Erin's eyes widened as a shot of adrenaline punched through her.

"Shit," Noah muttered, moving into action.

Unzipping her jacket as she ran, she unsheathed her short blades from their protective casings. They weren't quite two feet long, pure silver, and her best defense in close combat. Which was the type of fighting she preferred.

She respected the hell out of snipers, but this was her game. As a shifter she was unique because she preferred to fight in her human form. Just like the other enforcers across the globe. It wasn't because she was stronger in human form—though she was strong and fast. It was because once she let her beast out, it was difficult to rein her wolf back in. For Erin, keeping the balance between her animal and human sides was a bitch.

After the long drive cooped up in a car with Noah and too much sexual frustration, she needed to let off some steam and this was the way to do it.

To her annoyance Noah rushed into the dimly lit bar first, but she was right behind him. The gorgeous black jaguar with a faint orange background and dark spots was rolling around on the floor with a male vampire. They were slicing each other to ribbons, though Erin knew the big cat was holding back. Jaguars—regular or shifter—had powerful jaws and this one wasn't biting.

There were about two dozen people there, but no one was intervening. What the hell?

A few humans, a handful of tall, ethereal-looking fae, vampires, and lupine and feline shifters in human form all lounged around the bar staring at the two in open amusement. How was this remotely funny?

Screw that. "I'm taking the male down. Stay out of it," she murmured to Noah, hoping he'd listen. Sometimes he was overprotective of her and she had no problem taking care of herself.

Without waiting for a response, she jumped into the fray. She was young for a shifter, but incredibly quick, and knew one day—if she lived long enough—she'd have a better grasp on the strange power she could feel growing inside her every day.

Lightning fast, she sliced at the feline's shoulder, earning a surprised cry. The big cat immediately jumped off the vamp and backed away.

The vamp lunged at Erin, and even though she could sense the power rippling off him in waves, she dodged to the side and sliced her blade across his chest as he sailed past her. Blood spurted everywhere but it wasn't even close to a killing blow. The sweet scent that filled the air was different than the normal coppery scent of human and shifter blood.

The dark-skinned vamp turned with supernatural speed, a look of surprise on his face. She didn't know if it was because of her speed, her sex, or her apparent youth. She also didn't care. His fangs flashed, claws unsheathed as those hostile dark eyes narrowed at her. She heard Noah growl behind her.

"I've got this, Noah!" They'd fought side by side before, and while he might've hated her fighting, he had better at least respect her enough to handle herself.

Out of the corner of her eye she saw the feline shifter crouching, ready to pounce—on her!

What the hell is going on? She'd been trying to help the shifter out. Before Erin could move to defend herself, an eerie growl and the sound of bones breaking ripped through the slight murmur of voices and low music. A flash of dark fur she recognized as Noah flew through the air at the cat.

Annoyed he'd intervened, but having no doubt he could take care of himself, she didn't lose her momentum as she raced at the vamp. Right now all she cared about was subduing this guy as fast as possible. She didn't have time to sing and dance with him. That meant going on the offensive.

Using a bar stool as leverage, she jumped on it then a table before hurtling through the air. Raising a blade with her right hand, she brought it down as if to stab him through the chest. Calculating his attempt to swivel away to the left, she swept up with her left hand, slicing him through the gut.

It wouldn't kill him, but the silver burned vamps and shifters something fierce. His skin sizzled as he cried out under her blow. She didn't stop there. As he instinctively attempted to grapple with the blade, she brought the other one down on his forearm, pinning him to the floor.

Blood pooled everywhere, creating a dark river around them. The sickly sweet scent wafted up. "I'm not going to kill you if you stop struggling," she bit out, flashing her canines in a show of aggression.

Immediately the vampire went limp, but the rage in his eyes didn't diminish. "What the hell is wrong with you?" He wheezed out the words.

Before she could respond she heard a feminine cry behind her. "Don't hurt him! He's my mate!"

Instead of turning around, she quickly glanced at one of the mirrors in front of her displaying a full blue moon and advertising a new beer. In the reflection she saw a naked woman likely of South American descent being restrained by a very naked Noah, since his clothes had shredded during his change. Something sharp and deadly rose up inside Erin at seeing him tangled together with a female, but she forced it back down and focused on the crazy situation in front of her. She narrowed her gaze at the vamp still shooting daggers at her with his eyes. "That's your mate?"

He nodded, his lips pulled into a thin line. "We were just having a bit of an argument. Nothing serious."

It had looked pretty damn serious to her. That's when she scented the feline on him. No, not just on him, but practically *in* him, living under his skin. Yeah, no doubt they were mated. Sure had a weird way of acting like it. Glancing around, Erin noted that everyone had given her and Noah a wide berth and had congregated to the back of the bar.

"Attack me or him," she tilted her head in Noah's direction without taking her gaze off the vamp, "and I'll cut off your head." Without waiting for his response, she withdrew her blades and put a good ten feet between them in a split second. The instant she'd cleared the vamp, Noah let the female go. Erin didn't sheathe her weapons though. She wasn't worried about herself, but the thought of anyone hurting Noah ... it brought out something dark inside her. Some days she hated that feeling because he wasn't hers. It was like this constant battle waging inside her.

Ignoring everyone and uncaring about her nudity, the feline knelt by the vamp, cupping his cheek and stroking a hand down his chest. Blood pooled around him but he was already practically healed. "Are you hurt, baby?"

"For the love of ..." Erin turned toward Noah and, using strength she didn't realize she had, kept her eyes way above his belt line and steady on his face. "What the hell kind of place is this?"

Before he could answer, a booming male voice silenced the room. Even the music shut off. "Martina, Razi, get the hell out of here and don't show your faces on this street for a month."

The vamp and feline—still freaking naked—practically ran from the bar, bleeding all over the place and cursing a blue streak. But not before shooting Erin murderous glares.

Once they were gone her attention was drawn to the back of the bar, where a big male who looked like an older version of Noah, minus the dark hair, was walking through the sudden gap between the onlookers. Definitely Noah's father. Beside her, Noah tensed. It was subtle, something she noticed only because she knew him so well.

And you'd like to know him a whole lot better, wouldn't you?

The big lupine strode right toward them, only stopping a foot away after he'd given them both assessing looks. "You'll have to excuse Martina and Razi. That's just foreplay to them."

"They were fighting like animals," she said, though she had no reason to defend her actions.

"We *are* animals." His dark eyes looked so much like Noah's it rattled her, but she didn't let it show.

Instead Erin shrugged. "I take it you're Angus Campbell."

"And you are Erin Flynn, newest enforcer in North America. Jayce called to let me know you would be here soon, though I *expected* a call from you." His head swiveled to Noah and his dark eyes turned hard.

They were the same height so the two men just glared at each other. She could practically see the flood of testosterone rolling off them. Despite the differences in their appearances, because Noah had certainly been blessed with his mother's features too, the tall broadshouldered Scottish shifter was obviously Noah's father. It was stamped in the harsh, defined facial features.

Angus looked to be about forty by human standards, but Erin knew he was at least three hundred. Very old for a shifter and *very* powerful. He'd have to be to control New Orleans for as long as he had, which had been since the Jazz Age. Almost a century ago and long before most humans had known of paranormal beings' existence.

Clearing her throat and drawing the big shifter's attention back to her, she took a subtle step forward, placing herself in between father and son. One of Noah's hands settled on her shoulder in a way she knew he meant to be proprietary, something his father didn't miss. The feel of Noah touching her like that should have annoyed her. Instead, it soothed her inner wolf in a way she decided to ignore.

Angus's eyes flicked to Noah's hand then back to her face so quickly she would have missed the knowing look if she hadn't been watching him closely. Let the old Alpha make of it what he wanted.

When it was clear that Noah didn't plan to respond to his father's statement, Erin continued. "We need to talk about what's going on. Unless you approve of what's happening in your city." It wasn't a question because no one in their right mind would want things to continue the way they were in New Orleans. But she wanted to gauge his reaction.

Those dark eyes flashed with raw anger and for a moment she saw the wolf lurking beneath the man's surface. "Six pregnant female shifters missing..." His jaw clenched once and she could feel his power radiating for an instant. There was a reason he was an Alpha. "Whoever is responsible will pay." As he spoke, she heard the animal, not the human, talking to her.

And he was right. Someone would pay. But not by his hand. By an enforcer's. *Hers.*

Erin's eyes narrowed. When she got her hands on the culprit or culprits, they'd be judged. And they'd sure as hell suffer for their crimes. Preying on a pregnant female, regardless of species, was the lowest of the low. All the women had been taken while alone. Two from their homes, one from a park, one right outside her real estate office, one from a grocery store parking lot, and one from a restaurant while her mate was in the vicinity. The two homes had been disturbed, but no serious damage. And the others taken had left behind purses and keys at their abduction sites. It was the only reason anyone had any idea of the locations of the kidnappings.

Meli was the last shifter who had been taken and she was the only one linked directly to Angus's pack. The only lupine. It was the main reason the Council had sent Erin here. Angus was a powerful Alpha. The other five missing shifters were all feline with no pack or political pull. Erin had memorized their basic information and was determined to bring them all home, regardless of their species or anything else.

The feline grabbed right before Meli was so *young*. Her name was Ciara. At twenty-five, newly mated for a scant six months, she was two months pregnant and the only redhead in the bunch. Her appearance didn't matter to Erin, but when she'd looked at the girl's picture, it had jarred her straight to her bones. Reminded her of herself, back when she'd been naïve and pretty damn innocent about how truly awful people could be. People she'd trusted.

Something heavy settled on Erin's chest. Hurting a woman in that state when she was weaker, defenseless . . . it was just so wrong on every level. The heaviness seemed to grow inside her, pressing down until it was hard to breathe. The women must have been so terrified.

Noah had been silent, but his hand flexed once on her shoulder and she didn't miss the soft growl he let out. He wanted blood as much as she did. The feel of his fingers clenching around her pulled her from her thoughts and back to reality.

She was going to hunt whoever was behind this like the monsters they were. But first she had to figure out who was behind the disappearances and why. She just hoped Noah would let her handle this investigation her way.